# IVANHOE

John Pettie

THE VIGIL

The Academy Classics

SIR WALTER SCOTT

# IVANHOE

ABRIDGED AND EDITED BY

## J. C. TRESSLER

HEAD OF THE DEPARTMENT OF ENGLISH
RICHMOND HILL HIGH SCHOOL, NEW YORK CITY

1955

ALLYN AND BACON

BOSTON          NEW YORK          CHICAGO
ATLANTA      SAN FRANCISCO          DALLAS

# ACKNOWLEDGMENTS

To the Thompson Publishing Company, Syracuse, New York, I am deeply indebted for the use of twelve of a set of seventy-five *Ivanhoe* pictures. "The Abduction of Rebecca" and the pictures of Penhurst Hall and of armor and weapons are reproduced through the courtesy of the Metropolitan Museum; the Greiffenhagen pictures, by permission of, and special arrangement with, the David McKay Company.

To Miss Lois Dean, Miss Ruth G. Green, Miss Irene R. Haas, Miss A. Elizabeth Lewis, Miss Mary Manchester, Mrs. Dorothea McLaughlin, Miss Mary R. Meagher, Miss Julia A. Plough, and Miss Caroline A. Wolfe, I am grateful for preparing twenty-five of the questions on the text and suggesting five of the chapter headings.

# CONTENTS

# Contents

# Contents

# ILLUSTRATIONS

# Illustrations

# IMPORTANT CHARACTERS

(Webster's diacritical marks are used.)

Isaac of York, a Jewish money lender.
Rebecca, his daughter.

## SAXONS

Cedric of Rotherwood (sĕd′rĭk), a thane.
Wilfred of Ivanhoe, Cedric's son.
Rowena (rô-ē′nà), Cedric's ward.
Athelstane of Coningsburgh (ăth′ĕl-stān), a thane.
Wamba (wŏm′bà), Cedric's jester.
Gurth, Cedric's swineherd.
Ulrica (ōōl-rē′kà), an old woman held captive at Torquilstone.
Robin Hood, chief of a band of outlaws.
Friar Tuck, the Hermit of Copmanhurst.

## NORMANS

Richard Cœur-de-Lion (kûr dē lĕ′ôN′), King of England.
Prince John.
Brian de Bois-Guilbert (brê-äN′dē bwä gēl′bĕr′), a Knight Templar.
Beaumanoir (bō-mà-nwär′), Grand Master of the Knights Templars.
Reginald Front-de-Bœuf (frôN-dē-bûf′), a baron.
Waldemar Fitzurse (fĭts-ērs′), Prince John's adviser.
Maurice de Bracy (brä-sē′), leader of a band of free lances.
Aymer (ā′mēr), prior of Jorvaulx Abbey.

As indicated, the dictionaries give for most of the Norman names the French pronunciation. Many teachers and pupils, however, pronounce all these as if they were English names.

# IVANHOE

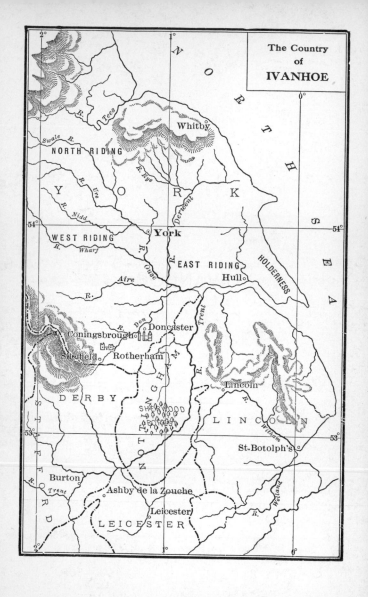

The Country
of
**IVANHOE**

# IVANHOE

## CHAPTER I

### Swineherd and Jester

In that pleasant district of merry England which
is watered by the river Don, there extended in
ancient times a large forest, covering the greater
part of the beautiful hills and valleys which lie
between Sheffield and the pleasant town of Doncas- 5
ter. Here flourished those bands of gallant outlaws
whose deeds have been rendered so popular in
English song.

Such being our chief scene, the date of our story
refers to a period towards the end of the reign of 10
Richard I, when his return from his long captivity
had become an event rather wished than hoped for
by his despairing subjects, who were in the mean
time subjected to every species of subordinate
oppression.                                               15

The situation of the inferior gentry was unusually
precarious. If they placed themselves under the

---

LINE **11**. **Richard I**. See page 615. **17**. **precarious**: uncertain.

I

protection of any of the petty kings in their vicinity,
or bound themselves to support him in his enterprises, they might indeed purchase temporary
repose; but it must be with the sacrifice of that
5 independence which was so dear to every English
bosom, and at the certain hazard of being involved
as a party in whatever rash expedition the ambition
of their protector might lead him to undertake.

A circumstance which greatly tended to enhance
10 the tyranny of the nobility and the sufferings of the
inferior classes arose from the consequences of the
Conquest by Duke William of Normandy. Four
generations had not sufficed to blend the hostile
blood of the Normans and Anglo-Saxons, or to
15 unite, by common language and mutual interests,
two hostile races, one of which still felt the elation of
triumph, while the other groaned under all the consequences of defeat. The power had been completely placed in the hands of the Norman nobility
20 by the event of the battle of Hastings, and it had
been used with no moderate hand. At court, and
in the castles of the great nobles, where the pomp
and state of a court was emulated, Norman-French
was the only language employed; in courts of law,
25 the pleadings and judgments were delivered in the
same tongue. In short, French was the language of

---

LINE 1. **petty kings**: barons. See page 619. **12. William.**
See page 614. **16. elation**: raising of spirits by success or
hope of success. **23. emulated**: rivaled.

2

RICHARD I READY TO SET OUT ON THE THIRD CRUSADE

On his return from this crusade Richard was imprisoned by the Emperor of Germany. (Courtesy of Douglas Fairbanks.)

honor, of chivalry, and even of justice, while the far more manly and expressive Anglo-Saxon was abandoned to the use of rustics and hinds, who knew no other.

The sun was setting upon one of the rich grassy 5 glades of the forest which we have mentioned. Hundreds of broad-headed, short-stemmed, wide-branched oaks flung their gnarled arms over a thick carpet of the most delicious green sward; in some places they were intermingled with beeches, hollies, 10 and copsewood of various descriptions, so closely as totally to intercept the level beams of the sinking sun. Here the red rays of the sun shot a broken and discolored light, that partially hung upon the shattered boughs and mossy trunks of the trees, 15 and there they illuminated in brilliant patches the portions of turf to which they made their way.

The human figures which completed this land-scape were in number two. The eldest of these men had a stern, savage, and wild aspect. His garment 20 was of the simplest form imaginable, being a close jacket with sleeves, composed of the tanned skin of some animal, on which the hair had been originally left, but which had been worn off in so many places that it would have been difficult to distinguish, from 25 the patches that remained, to what creature the fur had belonged. This vestment reached from the

---

LINE **3. hinds**: farm hands. **9. sward**: land thickly covered with grass. **11. copsewood**: low-growing thicket.

throat to the knees, and served at once all the usual
purposes of body-clothing; there was no wider
opening at the collar than was necessary to admit
the passage of the head, from which it may be
5 inferred that it was put on by slipping it over the
head and shoulders, in the manner of a modern
shirt.  Sandals, bound with thongs made of boar's
hide, protected the feet, and a roll of thin leather
was twined round the legs, and, ascending above
10 the calf, left the knees bare, like those of a Scottish
Highlander.  To make the jacket sit yet more
close to the body, it was gathered at the middle by
a broad leathern belt, secured by a brass buckle;
to one side of which was attached a sort of scrip,
15 and to the other a ram's horn, accoutred with a
mouthpiece, for the purpose of blowing.  In the
same belt was stuck a long, broad, sharp-pointed,
and two-edged knife, with a buck's-horn handle.
The man had no covering upon his head, which
20 was only defended by his own thick hair, matted
and twisted together, and scorched by the influence of the sun into a rusty dark-red color, forming a contrast with the overgrown beard upon his
cheeks, which was rather of a yellow or amber hue.
25 One part of his dress only remains, but it is too
remarkable to be suppressed; it was a brass ring,
resembling a dog's collar, but without any opening,

---

LINE **7. thongs**: long, narrow strips of leather.  **14. scrip**:
bag or pouch.

4

and soldered fast round his neck, so loose as to form no impediment to his breathing, yet so tight as to be incapable of being removed, excepting by the use of the file. On this was engraved, in Saxon characters: "Gurth, the son of Beowulph, is the born thrall of Cedric of Rotherwood."

Beside the swineherd, for such was Gurth's occupation, was seated a person about ten years younger in appearance, and whose dress, though resembling his companion's in form, was of better materials, and of a more fantastic description. His jacket had been stained of a bright purple hue, upon which there had been some attempt to paint grotesque ornaments in different colors. To the jacket he added a short cloak, which scarcely reached half-way down his thigh; it was of crimson cloth, though a good deal soiled, lined with bright yellow. He had thin silver bracelets upon his arms, and on his neck a collar of the same metal, bearing the inscription, "Wamba, the son of Witless, is the thrall of Cedric of Rotherwood." This personage had the same sort of sandals with his companion, but instead of the roll of leather thong, his legs were cased in a sort of gaiters, of which one was red and the other yellow. He was provided also with a cap, having around it more than one bell, about the

---

LINE **6. thrall**: serf or slave. **11. fantastic**: of odd appearance. **14. grotesque**: laughably odd or extravagant. **16. thigh**: leg between hip and knee.

size of those attached to hawks, which jingled as
he turned his head to one side or other; and as he
seldom remained a minute in the same posture, the
sound might be considered as incessant. Around
5 the edge of this cap was a stiff bandeau of leather,
cut at the top into open-work, resembling a coronet,
while a prolonged bag arose from within it, and fell
down on one shoulder like an old-fashioned night-
cap, or a jelly-bag. It was to this part of the cap
10 that the bells were attached; which circumstance,
as well as the shape of his head-dress, and his own
half-crazed, half-cunning expression of countenance, sufficiently pointed him out as belonging to
the race of domestic clowns or jesters, maintained
15 in the houses of the wealthy, to help away the
tedium of those lingering hours which they were
obliged to spend within doors. He bore, like his
companion, a scrip attached to his belt, but had
neither horn nor knife, being probably considered
20 as belonging to a class whom it is esteemed dangerous
to entrust with edge-tools. In place of these, he
was equipped with a sword of lath, resembling that
with which harlequin operates his wonders upon
the modern stage.

25 The outward appearance of these two men formed
scarce a stronger contrast than their look and

---

LINE **5. bandeau**: narrow band. **23. harlequin**: character
in comedy or pantomime with shaven head, parti-colored
tights, and sword of lath.

demeanor.   That of the serf, or bondsman, was sad
and sullen; his aspect was bent on the ground with
an air of deep dejection, which might be almost
construed into apathy, had not the fire which
occasionally sparkled in his red eye manifested that 5
there slumbered, under the appearance of sullen
despondency, a sense of oppression, and a disposition to resistance.   The looks of Wamba, on the
other hand, indicated, as usual with his class, a sort
of vacant curiosity, and fidgety impatience of any 10
posture of repose, together with the utmost self-
satisfaction respecting his own situation and the
appearance which he made.

   " The curse of St. Withold upon these infernal
porkers ! " said the swineherd, after blowing his 15
horn obstreperously, to collect together the scattered herd of swine, which, answering his call with
notes equally melodious, made, however, no haste
to remove themselves from the luxurious banquet
of beech-mast and acorns on which they had fat- 20
tened, or to forsake the marshy banks of the rivulet,
where several of them, half plunged in mud, lay
stretched at their ease, altogether regardless of the
voice of their keeper.   " The curse of St. Withold
upon them and upon me ! " said Gurth; " if the 25
two-legged wolf snap not up some of them ere night-

---

LINE **1. demeanor**: behavior.   **4. apathy**: lack of feeling.
**14. St. Withold**: imaginary saint.   **16. obstreperously**:
noisily.   **20. beech-mast**: beechnuts.

fall, I am no true man. Here, Fangs! Fangs!"
he ejaculated at the top of his voice to a ragged,
wolfish-looking dog, half mastiff, half greyhound,
which ran limping about as if with the purpose of
5 seconding his master in collecting the refractory
grunters; but which, in fact, only drove them
hither and thither, and increased the evil which he
seemed to design to remedy. "A devil draw the
teeth of him," said Gurth, "and the mother of
10 mischief confound the ranger of the forest, that
cuts the fore-claws off our dogs, and makes them
unfit for their trade! Wamba, up and help me an
thou beest a man."

"Truly," said Wamba, without stirring from the
15 spot, "I have consulted my legs upon this matter,
and they are altogether of opinion that to carry my
gay garments through these sloughs would be an
act of unfriendship to my sovereign person and royal
wardrobe; wherefore, Gurth, I advise thee to call
20 off Fangs, and leave the herd to their destiny, which,
whether they meet with bands of travelling soldiers,
or of outlaws, or of wandering pilgrims, can be
little else than to be converted into Normans before morning, to thy no small ease and comfort."

---

LINE **3. mastiff**: large, smooth-coated watchdog. **5. refractory**: obstinate. **10. ranger**: officer who enforced forest
laws about hunting. Every third year he cut the claws of
herding dogs in the forest to prevent their hunting deer.
**11. fore-claws**. Three claws were cut off the right foot.
**12. an**: if. **17. sloughs**: muddy places.

"The swine turned Normans to my comfort!"
quoth Gurth; "expound that to me, Wamba, for
my brain is too dull and my mind too vexed to read
riddles."

"Why, how call you those grunting brutes run- 5
ning about on their four legs?" demanded Wamba.

"Swine, fool — swine," said the herd; "every
fool knows that."

"And swine is good Saxon," said the Jester;
"but how call you the sow when she is flayed, and 10
drawn, and quartered, and hung up by the heels,
like a traitor?"

"Pork," answered the swineherd.

"I am very glad every fool knows that too,"
said Wamba, "and pork, I think, is good Norman- 15
French; and so when the brute lives, and is in the
charge of a Saxon slave, she goes by her Saxon
name; but becomes a Norman, and is called pork,
when she is carried to the castle hall to feast among
the nobles. What dost thou think of this, friend 20
Gurth, ha?"

"It is but too true doctrine, friend Wamba, however it got into thy fool's pate."

"Nay, I can tell you more," said Wamba in the
same tone: "there is old Alderman Ox continues 25
to hold his Saxon epithet while he is under the
charge of serfs and bondsmen such as thou, but

---

LINE **10. flayed**: skinned. **11. drawn**. To draw is to remove the intestines. **23. pate**: head.

becomes Beef, a fiery French gallant, when he arrives before the worshipful jaws that are destined to consume him. Mynherr Calf, too, becomes Monsieur de Veau in the like manner: he is Saxon when he requires tendance, and takes a Norman name when he becomes matter of enjoyment."

"By St. Dunstan," answered Gurth, "thou speakest but sad truths; little is left to us but the air we breathe, and that appears to have been reserved with much hesitation, solely for the purpose of enabling us to endure the tasks they lay upon our shoulders. The finest and the fattest is for their board; the loveliest is for their couch; the best and bravest supply their foreign masters with soldiers, and whiten distant lands with their bones, leaving few here who have either will or the power to protect the unfortunate Saxon. God's blessing on our Master Cedric, he hath done the work of a man in standing in the gap; but Reginald Front-de-Bœuf is coming down to this country in person, and we shall soon see how little Cedric's trouble will avail him. Here, here," he exclaimed again, raising his voice, "so ho! so ho! well done, Fangs! thou hast them all before thee now, and bring'st them on bravely, lad."

---

LINE **3. Mynherr**: Dutch word for *mister*. **4. Monsieur**: French word for *mister*. **Veau**: French word for *calf*. *Hog, ox*, and *calf* are from the Anglo-Saxon; *pork, beef*, and *veal*, from the Norman-French. **7. St. Dunstan**: Saxon saint. **20. Front-de-Bœuf**: Bull's Forehead.

"Gurth," said the Jester, "I know thou thinkest me a fool, or thou wouldst not be so rash in putting thy head into my mouth. One word to Reginald Front-de-Bœuf or Philip de Malvoisin, that thou hast spoken treason against the Norman — and thou art but a castaway swineherd; thou wouldst waver on one of these trees as a terror to all evil speakers against dignities."

"Dog, thou wouldst not betray me," said Gurth, "after having led me on to speak so much at disadvantage?"

"Betray thee!" answered the Jester; "no, that were the trick of a wise man; a fool cannot half so well help himself. But soft, whom have we here?" he said, listening to the trampling of several horses.

"Never mind whom," answered Gurth, who had now got his herd before him.

"Nay, but I must see the riders," answered Wamba; "perhaps they are come from Fairyland with a message from King Oberon."

"A murrain take thee!" rejoined the swineherd; "wilt thou talk of such things, while a terrible storm of thunder and lightning is raging within a few miles of us! Hark, how the thunder rumbles! and for summer rain, I never saw such broad downright flat drops fall out of the clouds;

---

LINE **21. King Oberon**: king of the fairies. **22. murrain**: disease of cattle. **27. downright**: straight down.

the oaks, too, notwithstanding the calm weather, sob and creak with their great boughs as if announcing a tempest. Let us home ere the storm begins to rage, for the night will be fearful."

5 Wamba seemed to feel the force of this appeal, and accompanied his companion, who began his journey after catching up a long quarter-staff which lay upon the grass beside him. This second Eumæus strode hastily down the forest glade, 10 driving before him, with the assistance of Fangs, the whole herd of his inharmonious charge.

---

LINE **7. quarter-staff:** staff about six feet long used as weapon. Wielded with one hand in the middle and the other hand between the middle and the end, it was used to ward off blows and to strike. **9. Eumæus:** swineherd of Ulysses, told about in the *Odyssey*.

# CHAPTER II

## Palmer Guides Prior and Warrior

On the road the horsemen soon overtook Wamba and Gurth. Their numbers amounted to ten men, of whom the two who rode foremost seemed to be persons of considerable importance, and the others their attendants. It was not difficult to ascertain 5 the condition and character of one of these personages. He was obviously an ecclesiastic of high rank; his dress was that of a Cistercian monk, but composed of materials much finer than those which the rule of that order admitted. His mantle and 10 hood were of the best Flanders cloth, and fell in ample, and not ungraceful, folds around a handsome though somewhat corpulent person. In defiance of conventual rules and the edicts of popes and councils, the sleeves of this dignitary were 15 lined and turned up with rich furs, his mantle secured at the throat with a golden clasp, and the whole dress proper to his order much refined upon and ornamented.

---

LINE **7. ecclesiastic**: clergyman; priest. **8. Cistercian monk**: monk of a branch of the Benedictine Order. See page 620. **14. conventual**: of convent. **edicts**: orders.

This worthy churchman rode upon a well-fed, ambling mule, whose furniture was highly decorated, and whose bridle, according to the fashion of the day, was ornamented with silver bells. In
5 his seat he had nothing of the awkwardness of the convent, but displayed the easy and habitual grace of a well-trained horseman. Indeed, it seemed that so humble a conveyance as a mule was only used by the gallant monk for travelling on the road.
10 One of those who followed in the train had, for his use on other occasions, one of the most handsome Spanish jennets ever bred in Andalusia. The saddle and housings of this superb palfrey were covered by a long foot-cloth, which reached
15 nearly to the ground, and on which were richly embroidered mitres, crosses, and other ecclesiastical emblems.

The companion of the church dignitary was a man past forty, thin, strong, tall, and muscular;
20 an athletic figure, which long fatigue and constant exercise seemed to have left none of the softer part of the human form, having reduced the whole to brawn, bones, and sinews, which had sustained a thousand toils, and were ready to dare a thousand

---

LINE **2. ambling**: moving at an easy gait by lifting at once both legs on a side. **12. jennets**: small Spanish horses. **13. palfrey**: riding horse for road. On a journey a knight usually rode a palfrey, and his squire led his war-horse. **16. mitres**: two-peaked caps worn by popes, bishops, abbots, etc.

more. His head was covered with a scarlet cap, faced with fur. His countenance was therefore fully displayed, and its expression was calculated to impress a degree of awe, if not of fear, upon strangers. High features, naturally strong and powerfully expressive, had been burnt almost into negro blackness by constant exposure to the tropical sun. His keen, piercing, dark eyes told in every glance a history of difficulties subdued and dangers dared, and seemed to challenge opposition to his wishes; a deep scar on his brow gave additional sternness to his countenance.

The upper dress of this personage resembled that of his companion in shape, being a long monastic mantle; but the color, being scarlet, showed that he did not belong to any of the four regular orders of monks. On the right shoulder of the mantle there was cut, in white cloth, a cross of a peculiar form. This upper robe concealed a shirt of linked mail, with sleeves and gloves of the same, curiously plaited and interwoven, as flexible to the body as those which are now wrought in the stocking-loom out of less obdurate materials. The fore-part of his thighs, where the folds of his mantle permitted them to be seen, were also covered with linked mail;

---

LINE **16. four regular orders**: Dominicans, Franciscans, Augustinians, and Carmelites. **18. cross**: Maltese cross, which has eight points. **20. mail**. See page 623. **23. obdurate**: unbending.

the knees and feet were defended by splints, or
thin plates of steel, ingeniously jointed upon each
other; and mail hose, reaching from the ankle to
the knee, effectually protected the legs, and com-
5 pleted the rider's defensive armor. In his girdle
he wore a long and double-edged dagger, which
was the only offensive weapon about his person.

He rode, not a mule, like his companion, but a
strong hackney for the road, to save his gallant
10 war-horse, which a squire led behind, fully accoutred for battle, with a chamfron or plaited head-
piece upon his head, having a short spike projecting
from the front. On one side of the saddle hung a
short battle-axe; on the other the rider's plumed
15 head-piece and hood of mail, with a long two-
handled sword. A second squire held aloft his
master's lance, from the extremity of which fluttered a small banderole, or streamer, bearing a cross
of the same form with that embroidered upon his
20 cloak. He also carried his small triangular shield,
broad enough at the top to protect the breast, and
from thence diminishing to a point. It was covered with a scarlet cloth, which prevented the
device from being seen.

25 These two squires were followed by two attendants, whose dark visages, white turbans, and the
Oriental form of their garments, showed them to

---

Line 9. **hackney**: horse for ordinary riding. **24. device**:
motto or emblem of a knight. **25. squires**. See page 618.

be natives of some distant Eastern country. The whole appearance of this warrior and his retinue was wild and outlandish; the dress of his squires was gorgeous, and his Eastern attendants wore silver collars round their throats, and bracelets of 5 the same metal upon their swarthy legs and arms, of which the latter were naked from the elbow, and the former from mid-leg to ankle. Silk and embroidery distinguished their dresses, and marked the wealth and importance of their master. 10

The singular appearance of this cavalcade not only attracted the curiosity of Wamba, but excited even that of his companion. The monk he instantly knew to be the Prior of Jorvaulx Abbey, well known for many miles around as a lover of the 15 chase, of the banquet, and of other worldly pleasures.

"My children," said the Prior, "is there in this neighborhood any good man who, for the love of God and devotion to Mother Church, will give two of her humblest servants, with their train, a night's 20 hospitality and refreshment?"

"Two of the humblest servants of Mother Church!" repeated Wamba to himself, but, fool as he was, taking care not to make his observation audible; "I should like to see her seneschals, her 25 chief butlers, and her other principal domestics!"

---

LINE **14**. **Prior**: officer of a religious house next under abbot. In the story Aymer is given both titles. **25**. **seneschals**: stewards; paid managers of house or estate.

After this internal commentary on the Prior's speech, he raised his eyes and replied to the question which had been put.

" If the reverend fathers," he said, " loved good
5 cheer and soft lodging, few miles of riding would carry them to the Priory of Brinxworth, where their quality could not but secure them the most honorable reception; or if they preferred spending a penitential evening, they might turn down yonder
10 wild glade, which would bring them to the hermitage of Copmanhurst, where a pious anchoret would make them sharers for the night of the shelter of his roof and the benefit of his prayers."

The Prior shook his head at both proposals.

15 " Mine honest friend," said he, " if the jangling of thy bells had not dizzied thine understanding, thou mightest know we churchmen do not exhaust each other's hospitality, but rather require that of the laity, giving them thus an opportunity to serve
20 God in honoring and relieving His appointed servants."

" It is true," replied Wamba, " that I, being but an ass, am, nevertheless, honored to bear the bells as well as your reverence's mule; notwithstanding,
25 I did conceive that the charity of Mother Church and her servants might be said, with other charity, to begin at home."

---

LINE **11. anchoret**: hermit.  See page 620.  **19. laity**: the people as distinguished from the clergy.

"A truce to thine insolence, fellow," said the armed rider, breaking in on his prattle with a high and stern voice, "and tell us, if thou canst, the road to ——. How call'd you your franklin, Prior Aymer?" 5

"Cedric," answered the Prior — "Cedric the Saxon. Tell me, good fellow, are we near his dwelling, and can you show us the road?"

"The road will be uneasy to find," answered Gurth, who broke silence for the first time, "and 10 the family of Cedric retire early to rest."

"Tush, tell not me, fellow!" said the military rider; "'tis easy for them to arise and supply the wants of travellers such as we are, who will not stoop to beg the hospitality which we have a right 15 to command."

"I know not," said Gurth, sullenly, "if I should show the way to my master's house to those who demand as a right the shelter which most are fain to ask as a favor." 20

"Do you dispute with me, slave!" said the soldier; and, setting spurs to his horse, he caused him to make a demi-volte across the path, raising at the same time the riding rod which he held in his hand, with a purpose of chastising what he con- 25 sidered as the insolence of the peasant.

Gurth darted at him a savage and revengeful

---

LINE **4. franklin**: landowner of some wealth and dignity.
**23. demi-volte**: half turn with forelegs raised.

scowl, and with a fierce yet hesitating motion laid his hand on the haft of his knife; but the interference of Prior Aymer, who pushed his mule betwixt his companion and the swineherd, prevented 5 the meditated violence.

"Nay, by St. Mary, brother Brian, you must not think you are now in Palestine, predominating over heathen Turks and infidel Saracens; we islanders love not blows. Tell me, good fellow," 10 said he to Wamba, and seconded his speech by a small piece of silver coin, "the way to Cedric the Saxon's; you cannot be ignorant of it, and it is your duty to direct the wanderer even when his character is less sanctified than ours."

15 "In truth, venerable father," answered the Jester, "the Saracen head of your right reverend companion has frightened out of mine the way home: I am not sure I shall get there to-night myself."

20 "Tush," said the Abbot, "thou canst tell us if thou wilt. This reverend brother has been all his life engaged in fighting among the Saracens for the recovery of the Holy Sepulchre; he is of the order of Knights Templars, whom you may have heard 25 of: he is half a monk, half a soldier."

"If he is but half a monk," said the Jester, "he should not be wholly unreasonable with those whom

---

LINE **15**. **venerable**: worthy of respect and honor.
**24**. **Knights Templars**. See page 621.

he meets upon the road, even if they should be in no hurry to answer questions that no way concern them."

"I forgive thy wit," replied the Abbot, "on condition thou wilt show me the way to Cedric's 5 mansion."

"Well, then," answered Wamba, "your reverences must hold on this path till you come to a sunken cross, of which scarce a cubit's length remains above ground; then take the path to the 10 left, for there are four which meet at Sunken Cross, and I trust your reverences will obtain shelter before the storm comes on."

The Abbot thanked his sage adviser; and the cavalcade, setting spurs to their horses, rode on as 15 men do who wish to reach their inn before the bursting of a night-storm.

As their horses' hoofs died away, Gurth said to his companion, "If they follow thy wise direction, the reverend fathers will hardly reach Rotherwood 20 this night."

"No," said the Jester, grinning, "but they may reach Sheffield if they have good luck, and that is as fit a place for them. I am not so bad a woodsman as to show the dog where the deer lies, if I 25 have no mind he should chase him."

"Thou art right," said Gurth; "it were ill that

---

LINE 9. **cubit's length**: originally, length of forearm; about eighteen inches.

Aymer saw the Lady Rowena; and it were worse, it may be, for Cedric to quarrel, as is most likely he would, with this military monk. But, like good servants, let us hear and see, and say nothing."

5 We return to the riders, who had soon left the bondsmen far behind them, and who maintained the following conversation in the Norman-French language, usually employed by the superior classes:

"What mean these fellows by their insolence?" 10 said the Templar, "and why did you prevent me from chastising it?"

"Marry, brother Brian," replied the Prior, "besides that beating this fellow could procure us no information respecting the road to Cedric's 15 house, it would have been sure to have established a quarrel betwixt you and him had we found our way thither. Remember what I told you: this wealthy franklin is proud, fierce, jealous, and irritable, a withstander of the nobility, and even of his 20 neighbors, Reginald Front-de-Bœuf and Philip Malvoisin, who are no babes to strive with. He stands up so sternly for the privileges of his race, and is so proud of his uninterrupted descent from Hereward, a renowned champion of the Heptarchy, 25 that he is universally called Cedric the Saxon."

---

LINE **12. Marry**: indeed. **24. Hereward**: Saxon hero, the last to yield to William the Conqueror. **Heptarchy**: union of the seven Anglo-Saxon kingdoms in England. **25. universally**: by all persons.

" Prior Aymer," said the Templar, " you are a man of gallantry, learned in the study of beauty; but I shall expect much beauty in this celebrated Rowena, to counterbalance the self-denial and forbearance which I must exert if I am to court the 5 favor of such a seditious churl as you have described her father Cedric."

" Cedric is not her father," replied the Prior, " and is but of remote relation: she is descended from higher blood than even he pretends to, and 10 is but distantly connected with him by birth.   Her guardian, however, he is, self-constituted as I believe; but his ward is as dear to him as if she were his own child.   Of her beauty you shall soon be judge; and if the purity of her complexion, and the 15 majestic yet soft expression of a mild blue eye, do not chase from your memory the black-tressed girls of Palestine, I am an infidel and no true son of the church."

" Should your boasted beauty," said the Templar, 20 " be weighed in the balance and found wanting, you know our wager? "

" My gold collar," answered the Prior, " against ten butts of Chian wine: they are mine as securely as if they were already in the convent vaults, under 25 the key of old Dennis, the cellarer."

" And I am myself to be judge," said the Templar, " and I am only to be convicted on my own

---

LINE **6. seditious**: rebellious.   **churl**: rough, surly fellow.

23

admission that I have seen no maiden so beautiful since Pentecost was a twelve month. Ran it not so? Prior, your collar is in danger; I will wear it over my gorget in the lists of Ashby-de-la-5 Zouche."

"Win it fairly," said the Prior, "and wear it as ye will; I will trust your giving true response, on your word as a knight and as a churchman. Yet, brother, take my advice, and file your tongue to a 10 little more courtesy. Cedric the Saxon, if offended — and he is no way slack in taking offence — is a man who, without respect to your knighthood or my high office, would clear his house of us, and send us to lodge with the larks, though the hour 15 were midnight. And be careful how you look on Rowena, whom he cherishes with the most jealous care; an he take the least alarm in that quarter we are but lost men. It is said he banished his only son from his family for lifting his eyes in the way 20 of affection towards this beauty."

"Well, you have said enough," answered the Templar; "I will for a night put on the needful restraint, and deport me as meekly as a maiden; but as for the fear of his expelling us by violence, 25 myself and squires will warrant you against that disgrace."

---

LINE 2. **Pentecost**: church festival now called Whitsunday. 4. **gorget**: armor for throat and upper part of chest. **lists**: space enclosed for tournament.

"We must not let it come so far," answered the Prior. "But here is the clown's sunken cross, and the night is so dark that we can hardly see which of the roads we are to follow. He bid us turn, I think, to the left." 5

"To the right," said Brian, "to the best of my remembrance."

"To the left — certainly the left; I remember his pointing with his wooden sword."

"Ay, but he held his sword in his left hand, and 10 so pointed across his body with it," said the Templar.

Each maintained his opinion with sufficient obstinacy, as is usual in all such cases; the attendants were appealed to, but they had not been near enough to hear Wamba's directions. 15

At length Brian remarked, what had at first escaped him in the twilight: "Here is some one either asleep or lying dead at the foot of this cross. Hugo, stir him with the butt-end of thy lance."

This was no sooner done than the figure arose, 20 exclaiming in good French, "Whosoever thou art, it is discourteous in you to disturb my thoughts."

"We did but wish to ask you," said the Prior, "the road to Rotherwood, the abode of Cedric the Saxon." 25

"I myself am bound thither," replied the stranger; "and if I had a horse I would be your guide, for the way is somewhat intricate, though perfectly well known to me."

"Thou shalt have both thanks and reward, my friend," said the Prior, "if thou wilt bring us to Cedric's in safety."

And he caused one of his attendants to mount
5 his own led horse, and give that upon which he had hitherto ridden to the stranger who was to serve for a guide.

Their conductor pursued an opposite road from that which Wamba had recommended for the pur-
10 pose of misleading them. The path soon led deeper into the woodland, and crossed more than one brook, the approach to which was rendered perilous by the marshes through which it flowed; but the stranger seemed to know, as if by instinct, the
15 soundest ground and the safest points of passage; and, by dint of caution and attention, brought the party safely into a wider avenue than any they had yet seen; and, pointing to a large, low, irregular building at the upper extremity, he said to the
20 Prior, "Yonder is Rotherwood, the dwelling of Cedric the Saxon."

Finding himself now at his ease and near shelter, Prior Aymer demanded of the guide who and what he was.

25 "A palmer, just returned from the Holy Land," was the answer.

"You had better have tarried there to fight for

---

LINE 25. **palmer**: pilgrim to the Holy Land, who brought back a palm branch or a staff of palm wood.

ROTHERWOOD

the recovery of the Holy Sepulchre," said the Templar.

"True, Reverend Sir Knight," answered the Palmer, to whom the appearance of the Templar seemed perfectly familiar; "but when those who 5 are under oath to recover the holy city are found travelling at such a distance from the scene of their duties, can you wonder that a peaceful peasant like me should decline the task which they have abandoned?" 10

The Templar would have made an angry reply, but was interrupted by the Prior, who again expressed his astonishment that their guide, after such long absence, should be so perfectly acquainted with the passes of the forest. 15

"I was born a native of these parts," answered their guide, and as he made the reply they stood before the mansion of Cedric — a low, irregular building, containing several courtyards or inclosures, extending over a considerable space of ground, 20 and which, though its size argued the inhabitant to be a person of wealth, differed entirely from the tall, turreted, and castellated buildings in which the Norman nobility resided, and which had become the universal style of architecture throughout 25 England.

---

LINE **23. turreted**: furnished with small towers. **castellated**: castle-like; having indented low walls at edges of roofs and balconies.

Rotherwood was not, however, without defences;
no habitation, in that disturbed period, could have
been so without the risk of being plundered and
burnt before the next morning. A deep fosse, or
5 ditch, was drawn round the whole building, and
filled with water from a neighboring stream. A
double stockade, or palisade, composed of pointed
beams, which the adjacent forest supplied, defended
the outer and inner bank of the trench. There was
10 an entrance from the west through the outer stockade, which communicated by a drawbridge with a
similar opening in the interior defences.

Before this entrance the Templar wound his
horn loudly; for the rain, which had long threat-
15 ened, began now to descend with great violence.

# CHAPTER III

## Cedric the Saxon

In a hall, the height of which was greatly disproportioned to its extreme length and width, a long oaken table formed of planks rough-hewn from the forest stood ready prepared for the evening meal of Cedric the Saxon. The roof, composed of 5 beams and rafters, had nothing to divide the apartment from the sky excepting the planking and thatch; there was a huge fireplace at either end of the hall, but, as the chimneys were constructed in a very clumsy manner, at least as much of the 10 smoke found its way into the apartment as escaped by the proper vent. The constant vapor which this occasioned had polished the rafters and beams of the low-browed hall, by encrusting them with a black varnish of soot. On the sides of the apart- 15 ment hung implements of war and of the chase, and there were at each corner folding doors, which gave access to other parts of the extensive building.

The other appointments of the mansion partook of the rude simplicity of the Saxon period. The 20 floor was composed of earth mixed with lime, trodden into a hard substance, such as is often employed

in flooring our modern barns. For about one
quarter of the length of the apartment the floor
was raised by a step, and this space, which was
called the dais, was occupied only by the principal
5 members of the family and visitors of distinction.
For this purpose, a table richly covered with scarlet
cloth was placed transversely across the platform,
from the middle of which ran the longer and lower
board, at which the domestics and inferior persons
10 fed, down towards the bottom of the hall. The
whole resembled the form of the letter T. Massive
chairs and settles of carved oak were placed upon
the dais, and over these seats and the more elevated
table was fastened a canopy of cloth, which served in
15 some degree to protect the dignitaries who occupied
that distinguished station from the weather, and
especially from the rain, which in some places
found its way through the ill-constructed roof.

The walls of this upper end of the hall, as far as
20 the dais extended, were covered with hangings or
curtains, and upon the floor there was a carpet,
both of which were adorned with some attempts
at tapestry or embroidery, executed with brilliant,
or rather gaudy, coloring. Over the lower range
25 of table, the roof, as we have noticed, had no covering; the rough plastered walls were left bare, and
the rude earthen floor was uncarpeted; the board

---

LINE 12. settles: seats; benches.

GREAT HALL OF PENHURST CASTLE

This hall of a mansion in 1335, although more modern than Cedric's hall, resembles it in many ways.

was uncovered by a cloth, and rude massive benches supplied the place of chairs.

In the centre of the upper table were placed two chairs more elevated than the rest, for the master and mistress of the family, who presided over the 5 scene of hospitality.

To each of these chairs was added a footstool, curiously carved and inlaid with ivory. One of these seats was at present occupied by Cedric the Saxon, who felt at the delay of his evening meal 10 an irritable impatience.

It appeared, indeed, from the countenance of this proprietor, that he was of a frank, but hasty, temper. He was not above the middle stature, but broad-shouldered, long-armed, and powerfully 15 made, like one accustomed to endure the fatigue of war or of the chase; his face was broad, with large blue eyes, open and frank features, fine teeth, and a well-formed head, altogether expressive of that sort of good humor which often lodges with a sudden 20 and hasty temper. His long yellow hair was equally divided on the top of his head and upon his brow, and combed down on each side to the length of his shoulders: it had but little tendency to grey, although Cedric was approaching to his sixtieth year. 25

His dress was a tunic of forest green, furred at

---

LINE 26. tunic: outer garment, with or without sleeves, reaching about to the knees. It was worn loose or gathered with a belt.

the throat and cuffs with grey squirrel. This
doublet hung unbuttoned over a close dress of scarlet which sate tight to his body; he had breeches
of the same, but they did not reach below the
5 lower part of the thigh, leaving the knee exposed.
His feet had sandals of the same fashion with the
peasants, but of finer materials, and secured in the
front with golden clasps. He had bracelets of gold
upon his arms, and a broad collar of the same pre-
10 cious metal around his neck. About his waist he
wore a richly studded belt, in which was stuck a
short, straight, two-edged sword, with a sharp
point. Behind his seat was hung a scarlet cloth
cloak lined with fur, and a cap of the same materials,
15 richly embroidered. A short boar spear, with a
broad and bright steel head, also reclined against
the back of his chair, which served him, when he
walked abroad, for the purposes of a staff or of a
weapon, as chance might require.
20 Two or three servants of a superior order stood
behind their master upon the dais; the rest occupied the lower part of the hall. Other attendants
there were of a different description: two or three
large and shaggy greyhounds, such as were then
25 employed in hunting the stag and wolf; as many
slow-hounds, of a large bony breed, with thick

---

LINE **2. doublet**: close-fitting outer body-garment for men.
**25. stag**: male of red deer or of other kinds of large deer.
**26. slow-hounds**: hounds that track by scent; bloodhounds.

necks, large heads, and long ears; and one or two
of the smaller dogs, now called terriers, which
waited with impatience the arrival of the supper;
but forbore to intrude upon the moody silence of
their master, apprehensive probably of a small 5
white truncheon which lay by Cedric's trencher,
for the purpose of repelling the advances of his four-
legged dependants. One grisly old wolf-dog alone,
with the liberty of an indulged favorite, had
planted himself close by the chair of state, and 10
occasionally ventured to solicit notice by putting
his large hairy head upon his master's knee, or push-
ing his nose into his hand. Even he was repelled
by the stern command, " Down, Balder — down!
I am not in the humor for foolery." 15

In fact, Cedric, as we have observed, was in no
very placid state of mind. The Lady Rowena,
who had been absent to attend an evening mass at
a distant church, had but just returned, and was
changing her garments, which had been wetted by 20
the storm. There were as yet no tidings of Gurth
and his charge, which should long since have been
driven home from the forest; and such was the inse-
curity of the period as to render it probable that the
delay might be explained by some depredation of the 25
outlaws, with whom the adjacent forest abounded,
or by the violence of some neighboring baron.

---

LINE **5. apprehensive**: fearful.  **6. truncheon**: baton;
staff; club.  **trencher**: wooden plate.

Besides these subjects of anxiety, the Saxon thane was impatient for the presence of his favorite clown, Wamba, whose jests, such as they were, served for a sort of seasoning to his evening meal. 5 Add to all this, Cedric had fasted since noon, and his usual supper hour was long past. His displeasure was expressed in broken sentences, partly muttered to himself, partly addressed to the domestics who stood around — " Why tarries the Lady 10 Rowena ? "

" She is but changing her head-gear," replied a female attendant; " you would not wish her to sit down to the banquet in her hood and kirtle ? "

" I wish her devotion may choose fair weather 15 for the next visit to St. John's Kirk," said the Saxon. "But what, in the name of ten devils," continued he, turning to the cupbearer, and raising his voice — " what, in the name of ten devils, keeps Gurth so long a-field? I suppose we shall 20 have an evil account of the herd."

Oswald, the cupbearer, modestly suggested that it was scarce an hour since the tolling of the curfew — an ill-chosen apology, since it turned upon a topic so harsh to Saxon ears.

---

LINE **2**. **thane**: person ranking between ordinary freeman and noble. **13**. **kirtle**: cloak. **15**. **Kirk**: church. **22**. **curfew**: bell rung in evening as signal for putting out lights and fires. William the Conqueror introduced into England this Norman practice for the protection against fire.

"The foul fiend," exclaimed Cedric, "take the curfew-bell! The curfew! ay, the curfew, which compels true men to extinguish their lights, that thieves and robbers may work their deeds in darkness! Ay, the curfew! Reginald Front-de-Bœuf ₅ and Philip de Malvoisin know the use of the curfew. I shall hear, I guess, that my property has been swept off to save from starving the hungry banditti whom they cannot support but by theft and robbery. My faithful slave is murdered, and my ₁₀ goods are taken for a prey; and Wamba — where is Wamba? Said not some one he had gone forth with Gurth?"

Oswald replied in the affirmative.

"Ay! why, this is better and better! he is car- ₁₅ ried off too, the Saxon fool, to serve the Norman lord. But I will be avenged," he added, starting from his chair in impatience at the supposed injury, and catching hold of his boar spear; "I will go with my complaint to the great council. I have friends, ₂₀ I have followers; man to man will I appeal the Norman to the lists. I have sent such a javelin as this through a stronger fence than three of their war shields! Haply they think me old; but they shall find, alone and childless as I am, the blood of ₂₅ Hereward is in the veins of Cedric. Ah, Wilfred, Wilfred!" he exclaimed in a lower tone, "couldst

---

LINE 21. **appeal**: challenge.

thou have ruled thine unreasonable passion, thy
father had not been left in his age like the solitary
oak that throws out its shattered and unprotected
branches against the full sweep of the tempest!"
5 The reflection seemed to conjure into sadness his
irritated feelings. Replacing his javelin, he resumed his seat, bent his looks downward, and
appeared to be absorbed in melancholy reflection.

From his musing Cedric was suddenly awakened
10 by the blast of a horn, which was replied to by the
clamorous yells and barking of all the dogs in the
hall, and some twenty or thirty which were quartered in other parts of the building.

"To the gate, knaves!" said the Saxon, hastily.
15 "See what tidings that horn tells us of."

Returning in less than three minutes, a warder
announced, "The Prior Aymer of Jorvaulx, and the
good knight Brian de Bois-Guilbert, commander
of the valiant and venerable order of Knights Tem-
20 plars, with a small retinue, request hospitality and
lodging for the night, being on their way to a tournament which was to be held not far from Ashby-
de-la-Zouche on the second day from the present."

"Aymer — the Prior Aymer! Brian de Bois-
25 Guilbert!" muttered Cedric — "Normans both;
but Norman or Saxon, the hospitality of Rotherwood must not be impeached: they are welcome,

---

LINE **8. reflection**: thought.   **21. tournament**: contest
between mounted knights in armor.   **27. impeached**: accused.

since they have chosen to halt; more welcome would they have been to have ridden further on their way. Go, Hundebert," he added, to a sort of major-domo who stood behind him with a white wand; " take six of the attendants and introduce 5 the strangers to the guests' lodging. Look after their horses and mules, and see their train lack nothing. Let them have change of vestments if they require it, and fire, and water to wash, and wine and ale; and bid the cooks add what they hastily 10 can to our evening meal; and let it be put on the board when those strangers are ready to share it. Say to them, Hundebert, that Cedric would himself bid them welcome, but he is under a vow never to step more than three steps from the dais of his own 15 hall to meet any who shares not the blood of Saxon royalty. Begone! see them carefully tended; let them not say in their pride, the Saxon churl has shown at once his poverty and his avarice."

" The Prior Aymer!" repeated Cedric, looking 20 to Oswald. " This Prior is, they say, a free and jovial priest, who loves the wine-cup and the bugle-horn better than bell and book. Good; let him come, he shall be welcome. How named ye the Templar? " 25

" Brian de Bois-Guilbert."

" Bois-Guilbert!" said Cedric. " That name has

---

Line 4. major-domo: steward; manager of household.

been spread wide both for good and evil. They say he is valiant as the bravest of his order; but stained with their usual vices — pride, arrogance, and cruelty — a hard-hearted man, who knows 5 neither fear of earth nor awe of heaven. Well, it is but for one night; he shall be welcome too. Oswald, broach the oldest wine-cask; place the best meat, the mightiest ale upon the board. Elgitha, let thy Lady Rowena know we shall not this 10 night expect her in the hall, unless such be her especial pleasure."

"But it will be her especial pleasure," answered Elgitha, with great readiness, "for she is ever desirous to hear the latest news from Palestine."

15 Cedric darted at the forward damsel a glance of hasty resentment; but Rowena and whatever belonged to her were privileged, and secure from his anger. He only replied, "Silence, maiden; thy tongue outruns thy discretion. Say my mes- 20 sage to thy mistress, and let her do her pleasure. Here, at least, the descendant of Alfred still reigns a princess."

Elgitha left the apartment.

"Palestine!" repeated the Saxon — "Pales- 25 tine! how many ears are turned to the tales from that fatal land! I too might ask — I too might inquire — I too might listen with a beating heart

---

LINE **7. broach**: tap.

to fables which the wily strollers devise to cheat us into hospitality; but no — the son who has disobeyed me is no longer mine; nor will I concern myself for his fate."

He knit his brows, and fixed his eyes for an instant on the ground; as he raised them, the folding doors at the bottom of the hall were cast wide, and preceded by the major-domo with his wand, and four domestics bearing blazing torches, the guests of the evening entered the apartment.

# CHAPTER IV

## Saxon Hospitality

Prior Aymer had taken the opportunity afforded him of changing his riding robe for one of yet more costly materials, over which he wore a cope curiously embroidered. Besides the massive golden
5 signet ring which marked his ecclesiastical dignity, his fingers were loaded with precious gems; his sandals were of the finest leather which was imported from Spain; his beard trimmed to as small dimensions as his order would possibly permit, and
10 his shaven crown concealed by a scarlet cap richly embroidered.

The Knight Templar had exchanged his shirt of mail for an under tunic of dark purple silk, garnished with furs, over which flowed his long robe
15 of spotless white in ample folds. The eight-pointed cross of his order was cut on the shoulder of his mantle in black velvet. The high cap no longer invested his brows, which were only shaded by short and thick curled hair of a raven blackness, corre-
20 sponding to his unusually swart complexion. Nothing could be more gracefully majestic than his

---

LINE **3**. **cope**: long cloak, with hood, worn by priests.
**5**. **signet**: seal.

step and manner, had they not been marked by
haughtiness.

These two dignified persons were followed by
their respective attendants, and at a more humble
distance by their guide, whose figure had nothing 5
more remarkable than it derived from the usual
weeds of a pilgrim. A cloak or mantle of coarse
black serge enveloped his whole body. Coarse
sandals, bound with thongs, on his bare feet; a
broad and shadowy hat, with cockle-shells stitched 10
on its brim, and a long staff shod with iron, to the
upper end of which was attached a branch of palm,
completed the Palmer's attire. He followed modestly the last of the train which entered the hall,
and, observing that the lower table scarce afforded 15
room sufficient for the domestics of Cedric and the
retinue of his guests, he withdrew to a settle placed
beside, and almost under, one of the large chimneys, and seemed to employ himself in drying his
garments, until the retreat of some one should 20
make room at the board, or the hospitality of the
steward should supply him with refreshments in
the place he had chosen apart.

Cedric rose to receive his guests with an air of
dignified hospitality, and, descending from the 25
dais, or elevated part of his hall, made three steps
towards them, and then awaited their approach.

---

LINE **7. weeds**: garment.  **10. cockle-shells**: seashells
worn as sign of a pilgrimage to the Holy Land.

"I grieve," he said, "reverend Prior, that my vow binds me to advance no farther upon this floor of my fathers, even to receive such guests as you and this valiant Knight of the Holy Temple. But 5 my steward has expounded to you the cause of my seeming discourtesy."

Motioning with his hand, Cedric caused his guests to assume two seats a little lower than his own, but placed close beside him, and gave a signal that the 10 evening meal should be placed upon the board.

While the attendants hastened to obey Cedric's commands, his eye distinguished Gurth, the swineherd, who, with his companion Wamba, had just entered the hall. "Send these loitering knaves up 15 hither," said the Saxon, impatiently. And when the culprits came before the dais — "How comes it, villains, that you have loitered abroad so late as this? Hast thou brought home thy charge, sirrah Gurth, or hast thou left them to robbers and ma-20 rauders?"

"The herd is safe, so please ye," said Gurth.

"But it does not please me, thou knave," said Cedric, "that I should be made to suppose otherwise for two hours, and sit here devising vengeance 25 against my neighbors for wrongs they have not done me. I tell thee, shackles and the prison-

---

LINE **17. villains**: formerly meant serfs or slaves. **18. sirrah**: sir or fellow; used in anger, contempt, or jest. **26. shackles**: fetters; something that confines the legs or arms.

house shall punish the next offence of this kind."

Gurth, knowing his master's irritable temper, attempted no exculpation; but the Jester, who could presume upon Cedric's tolerance, by virtue 5 of his privileges as a fool, replied for them both — " In troth, uncle Cedric, you are neither wise nor reasonable to-night."

" How, sir !" said his master; " you shall to the porter's lodge and taste of the discipline there if you 10 give your foolery such license."

" First let your wisdom tell me," said Wamba, " is it just and reasonable to punish one person for the fault of another?"

" Certainly not, fool," answered Cedric.       15

" Then why should you shackle poor Gurth, uncle, for the fault of his dog Fangs? for I dare be sworn we lost not a minute by the way, when we had got our herd together, which Fangs did not manage until we heard the vesper-bell."       20

" Then hang up Fangs," said Cedric, turning hastily towards the swineherd, " if the fault is his, and get thee another dog."

" Under favor, uncle," said the Jester, " it was no fault of Fangs that he was lame and could not 25 gather the herd, but the fault of those that struck off

---

LINE **4. exculpation**: excuse; justification.    **7. uncle**: familiar title used by jester in addressing his master. **10. porter**: keeper of door or gate.

two of his fore-claws, an operation for which, if the poor fellow had been consulted, he would scarce have given his voice."

"And who dared to lame an animal which belonged to my bondsman?" said the Saxon, kindling in wrath.

"Marry, that did old Hubert," said Wamba, "Sir Philip de Malvoisin's keeper of the chase. He caught Fangs strolling in the forest, and said he chased the deer."

"The foul fiend take Malvoisin," answered the Saxon, "and his keeper both! But enough of this. Go to, knave, — go to thy place; and thou, Gurth, get thee another dog, and should the keeper dare to touch it, I will mar his archery; the curse of a coward on my head, if I strike not off the forefinger of his right hand! he shall draw bowstring no more. I crave your pardon, my worthy guests. I am beset here with neighbors that match your infidels, Sir Knight, in Holy Land. But your homely fare is before you; feed, and let welcome make amends for hard fare."

The feast, however, which was spread upon the board needed no apologies from the lord of the mansion. Swine's flesh, dressed in several modes, appeared on the lower part of the board, as also that of fowls, deer, goats, and hares, and various kinds of fish, together with huge loaves and cakes of bread, and sundry confections made of fruits and honey.

# Saxon Hospitality

The smaller sorts of wild-fowl, of which there was abundance, were not served up in platters, but brought in upon small wooden spits or broaches, and offered by the pages and domestics who bore them to each guest in succession, who cut from them such a portion as he pleased. Beside each person of rank was placed a goblet of silver; the lower board was accommodated with large drinking-horns.

When the repast was about to commence, the major-domo, or steward, suddenly raising his wand, said aloud: "Forbear! Place for the Lady Rowena." A side-door at the upper end of the hall now opened behind the banquet table, and Rowena, followed by four female attendants, entered the apartment. Cedric, though surprised, and perhaps not altogether agreeably so, at his ward appearing in public on this occasion, hastened to meet her, and to conduct her, with respectful ceremony, to the elevated seat at his own right hand appropriated to the lady of the mansion. All stood up to receive her; and, replying to their courtesy by a mute gesture of salutation, she moved gracefully forward to assume her place at the board. Ere she had time to do so, the Templar whispered to the Prior: "I shall wear no collar of gold of yours at the tournament. The Chian wine is your own."

"Said I not so?" answered the Prior; "but check your raptures, the franklin observes you."

Unheeding this remonstrance, and accustomed

45

only to act upon the immediate impulse of his own wishes, Brian de Bois-Guilbert kept his eyes riveted on the Saxon beauty, more striking perhaps to his imagination because differing widely from those of
5 the Eastern sultanas.

Rowena was tall in stature, yet not so much so as to attract observation on account of superior height. Her complexion was exquisitely fair, but the noble cast of her head and features prevented the insipid-
10 ity which sometimes attaches to fair beauties. Her clear blue eye seemed capable to kindle as well as melt, to command as well as to beseech. Her profuse hair, of a color betwixt brown and flaxen, was arranged in a fanciful and graceful manner in
15 numerous ringlets, to form which art had probably aided nature. These locks were braided with gems, and being worn at full length, intimated the noble birth and free-born condition of the maiden. A golden chain, to which was attached a small reli-
20 quary of the same metal, hung round her neck. She wore bracelets on her arms, which were bare. Her dress was an under-gown and kirtle of pale sea-green silk, over which hung a long loose robe, which reached to the ground, having very wide sleeves,
25 which came down, however, very little below the

---

LINE **5.** **sultanas**: wives, daughters, or mothers of sultans (rulers of Turks). ⌐**9. insipidity**: lack of flavor or interest. **19. reliquary**: casket for sacred relics. **22. kirtle**: here, close-fitting dress.

elbow. This robe was crimson, and manufactured out of the very finest wool. A veil of silk, interwoven with gold, was attached to the upper part of it, which could be, at the wearer's pleasure, either drawn over the face and bosom after the Spanish 5 fashion, or disposed as a sort of drapery round the shoulders.

When Rowena perceived the Knight Templar's eyes bent on her with ardor, she drew with dignity the veil around her face as an intimation that the 10 determined freedom of his glance was disagreeable.

Cedric saw the motion and its cause. " Sir Templar," said he, " the cheeks of our Saxon maidens have seen too little of the sun to enable them to bear the fixed glance of a crusader." 15

" If I have offended," replied Sir Brian, " I crave your pardon — that is, I crave the Lady Rowena's pardon, for my humility will carry me no lower."

" The Lady Rowena," said the Prior, " has punished us all, in chastising the boldness of my friend. 20 Let me hope she will be less cruel to the splendid train which are to meet at the tournament."

" Our going thither," said Cedric, " is uncertain. I love not these vanities, which were unknown to my fathers when England was free." 25

" Let us hope, nevertheless," said the Prior, " our company may determine you to travel thitherward ; when the roads are so unsafe, the escort of Sir Brian de Bois-Guilbert is not to be despised."

"Sir Prior," answered the Saxon, "wheresoever I have travelled in this land, I have hitherto found myself, with the assistance of my good sword and faithful followers, in no respect needful of other aid.
5 At present, if we indeed journey to Ashby-de-la-Zouche, we do so with my noble neighbor and countryman, Athelstane of Coningsburgh, and with such a train as would set outlaws and feudal enemies at defiance. I drink to you, Sir Prior, in this cup of
10 wine, and I thank you for your courtesy."

"And I," said the Templar, filling his goblet, "drink wassail to the fair Rowena; for since her namesake introduced the word into England, has never been one more worthy of such a tribute."
15 "I will spare your courtesy, Sir Knight," said Rowena with dignity, and without unveiling herself; "or rather I will tax it so far as to require of you the latest news from Palestine, a theme more agreeable to our English ears than the compliments
20 which your French breeding teaches."

"I have little of importance to say, lady," answered Sir Brian de Bois-Guilbert, "excepting the confirmed tidings of a truce with Saladin."

He was interrupted by Wamba, who had taken

---

LINE **12. wassail**: expression of good wishes, meaning, "To your health!" **13. namesake**. Rowena was the name of the daughter of Hengist, a Saxon chief who conquered part of England. **23. Saladin**: sultan of Egypt and Syria against whom Richard fought in the Holy Land.

his appropriated seat upon a chair the back of which was decorated with two ass's ears, and which was placed about two steps behind that of his master, who, from time to time, supplied him with victuals from his own trencher; a favor, however, which the Jester shared with the favorite dogs, of whom, as we have already noticed, there were several in attendance. Here sat Wamba, with a small table before him, his heels tucked up against the bar of the chair, his cheeks sucked up so as to make his jaws resemble a pair of nut-crackers, and his eyes half-shut, yet watching with alertness every opportunity to exercise his licensed foolery.

"These truces with the infidels," he exclaimed, without caring how suddenly he interrupted the stately Templar, "make an old man of me!"

"Go to, knave — how so," said Cedric, his features prepared to receive favorably the expected jest.

"Because," answered Wamba, "I remember three of them in my day, each of which was to endure for the course of fifty years; so that, by computation, I must be at least a hundred and fifty years old."

"I will warrant you against dying of old age, however," said the Templar, who now recognized his friend of the forest; "I will assure you from all deaths but a violent one, if you give such directions to wayfarers as you did this night to the Prior and me."

"How, sirrah!" said Cedric, "misdirect travellers? We must have you whipt; you are at least as much rogue as fool."

"I pray thee, uncle," answered the Jester, "let my folly for once protect my roguery. I did but make a mistake between my right hand and my left; and he might have pardoned a greater who took a fool for his counsellor and guide."

Conversation was here interrupted by the entrance of the porter's page, who announced that there was a stranger at the gate, imploring admittance and hospitality.

"Admit him," said Cedric, "be he who or what he may: a night like that which roars without compels even wild animals to herd with tame, and to seek the protection of man, their mortal foe, rather than perish by the elements. Let his wants be ministered to with all care; look to it, Oswald."

And the steward left the banqueting-hall to see the commands of his patron obeyed.

# CHAPTER V

## " Second to None "

Oswald, returning, whispered into the ear of his master, " It is a Jew, who calls himself Isaac of York ; is it fit I should marshal him into the hall ? "

" Let Gurth do thine office, Oswald," said Wamba, with his usual effrontery : " the swineherd will be a fit usher to the Jew."

" St. Mary," said the Abbot, crossing himself, " an unbelieving Jew, and admitted into this presence !"

" A dog Jew," echoed the Templar, " to approach a defender of the Holy Sepulchre ? "

" By my faith," said Wamba, " it would seem the Templars love the Jews' inheritance better than they do their company."

" Peace, my worthy guests," said Cedric ; " my hospitality must not be bounded by your dislikes. But I constrain no man to converse or to feed with the Jew. Let him have a board and a morsel apart."

Introduced with little ceremony, and advancing with fear and hesitation, and many a bow of deep humility, a tall thin old man, who, however, had

lost by the habit of stooping much of his actual
height, approached the lower end of the board.
His features, keen and regular, with an aquiline
nose, and piercing black eyes; his high and wrinkled
5 forehead, and long grey hair and beard, would have
been considered as handsome, had they not been
the marks of a physiognomy peculiar to a race
which, during those dark ages, was alike detested
by the credulous and prejudiced vulgar, and perse-
10 cuted by the greedy and rapacious nobility.

The Jew's dress, which appeared to have suffered
considerably from the storm, was a plain russet
cloak of many folds, covering a dark purple tunic.
He had large boots lined with fur, and a belt around
15 his waist, which sustained a small knife, together
with a case for writing materials, but no weapon.
He wore a high square yellow cap of a peculiar
fashion, assigned to his nation to distinguish them
from Christians, and which he doffed with great
20 humility at the door of the hall.

The reception of this person in the hall of Cedric
the Saxon was such as might have satisfied the most
prejudiced enemy of the tribes of Israel. Cedric
himself coldly nodded in answer to the Jew's re-
25 peated salutations, and signed to him to take place
at the lower end of the table, where, however, no

---

LINE **3**. **aquiline**: curving.    **7**. **physiognomy**: face, as
revealing character.    **9**. **credulous**: apt to believe on slight
evidence.    **10**. **rapacious**: given to plunder.

one offered to make room for him. On the contrary, as he passed along the file, casting a timid, supplicating glance, and turning towards each of those who occupied the lower end of the board, the Saxon domestics squared their shoulders, and continued 5 to devour their supper with great perseverance, paying not the least attention to the wants of the new guest. The attendants of the Abbot crossed themselves, with looks of pious horror, and the very heathen Saracens, as Isaac drew near them, curled 10 up their whiskers with indignation, and laid their hands on their poniards as if ready to rid themselves by the most desperate means from the apprehended contamination of his nearer approach.

While Isaac thus stood an outcast, looking in 15 vain for welcome or resting-place, the Pilgrim, who sat by the chimney, took compassion upon him, and resigned his seat, saying briefly, " Old man, my garments are dried, my hunger is appeased; thou art both wet and fasting." So saying, he gathered 20 together and brought to a flame the decaying brands which lay scattered on the ample hearth; took from the larger board a mess of pottage and seethed kid, placed it upon the small table at which he had himself supped, and, without waiting the Jew's thanks, 25 went to the other side of the hall, whether from unwillingness to hold more close communication with

---

LINE **12. poniards**: small daggers. **13. apprehended**: feared. **23. pottage**: a thick soup. **seethed**: boiled.

the object of his benevolence, or from a wish to draw near to the upper end of the table, seemed uncertain.

Had there been painters in those days capable to execute such a subject, the Jew, as he bent his withered form and expanded his chilled and trembling hands over the fire, would have formed no bad emblematical personification of the Winter season. Having dispelled the cold, he turned eagerly to the smoking mess which was placed before him, and ate with a haste and an apparent relish that seemed to betoken long abstinence from food.

Meanwhile the Abbot and Cedric continued their discourse upon hunting.

" I marvel, worthy Cedric," said the Abbot, " that, great as your predilection is for your own manly language, you do not receive the Norman-French into your favor, so far at least as the mystery of woodcraft and hunting is concerned.   Surely no tongue is so rich in the various phrases which the field-sports demand, or furnishes means to the experienced woodman so well to express his jovial art."

" Good Father Aymer," said the Saxon, " be it known to you, I care not for those over-sea refinements, without which I can well enough take my pleasure in the woods."

" The French," said the Templar, raising his

LINE **1. benevolence** : act of kindness.   **15. predilection** : preference.

voice with the authoritative tone which he used upon all occasions, " is not only the natural language of the chase, but that of love and of war, in which ladies should be won and enemies defied."

" Pledge me in a cup of wine, Sir Templar," said 5 Cedric, " and fill another to the Abbot, while I look back some thirty years to tell you another tale. As Cedric the Saxon then was, his plain English tale needed no garnish from French troubadours when it was told in the ear of beauty." He went on 10 with increasing warmth : " Ay, the Battle of the Standard was a day of cleaving of shields, when a hundred banners were bent forward over the heads of the valiant, and blood flowed round like water, and death was held better than flight. A Saxon 15 bard had called it a feast of the swords — a gathering of the eagles to the prey — the clashing of bills upon shield and helmet, the shouting of battle more joyful than the clamor of a bridal. But our bards are no more," he said ; " our deeds are lost in those 20 of another race ; our language — our very name — is hastening to decay, and none mourns for it save one solitary old man. Cupbearer ! knave, fill the goblets. To the strong in arms, Sir Templar, be their race or language what it will, who now bear 25

---

LINE **9. troubadours** : originally, poets of the south of France ; later, any wandering musicians. **11. Battle of the Standard.** In this battle, fought in 1138, the English defeated the Scotch invaders. **17. bills** : swords.

55

them best in Palestine among the champions of the
Cross!"

"It becomes not one wearing this badge to answer," said Sir Brian de Bois-Guilbert; "yet to
5 whom, besides the sworn champions of the Holy
Sepulchre, can the palm be assigned among the
champions of the Cross?"

"To the Knights Hospitallers," said the Abbot;
"I have a brother of their order."

10 "I impeach not their fame," said the Templar;
"nevertheless ——"

"I think, friend Cedric," said Wamba, inter-
fering, "that had Richard of the Lion's Heart
been wise enough to have taken a fool's advice,
15 he might have staid at home with his merry
Englishmen, and left the recovery of Jerusalem to
those same Knights who had most to do with the
loss of it."

"Were there, then, none in the English army,"
20 said the Lady Rowena, "whose names are worthy
to be mentioned with the Knights of the Temple and
of St. John?"

"Forgive me, lady," said De Bois-Guilbert;
"the English monarch did indeed bring to Palestine
25 a host of gallant warriors, second only to those

---

LINE 8. **Knights Hospitallers**: like Knights Templars,
military monks. **17. same Knights**. The Knights Templars
and Knights Hospitallers were defeated and driven from
Jerusalem in 1191.

whose breasts have been the unceasing bulwark of that blessed land."

"Second to NONE," said the Pilgrim, who had stood near enough to hear, and had listened to this conversation with marked impatience. All turned towards the spot from whence this unexpected asseveration was heard. "I say," repeated the Pilgrim in a firm and strong voice, "that the English chivalry were second to NONE who ever drew sword in defence of the Holy Land. I say besides, for I saw it, that King Richard himself, and five of his Knights, held a tournament after the taking of St. John-de-Acre, as challengers against all comers. I say that, on that day, each knight ran three courses, and cast to the ground three antagonists. I add, that seven of these assailants were Knights of the Temple; and Sir Brian de Bois-Guilbert well knows the truth of what I tell you."

It is impossible for language to describe the bitter scowl of rage which rendered yet darker the swarthy countenance of the Templar. In the extremity of his resentment and confusion, his quivering fingers griped towards the handle of his sword, and perhaps only withdrew from the consciousness that no act of violence could be safely executed in that place and presence. Cedric, whose feelings were all of a right onward and simple kind, and were seldom

---

LINE **1. bulwark**: fort; defensive wall. **6. asseveration**: emphatic declaration.

occupied by more than one object at once, omitted, in the joyous glee with which he heard of the glory of his countrymen, to remark the angry confusion of his guest. " I would give thee this golden brace-
5 let, Pilgrim," he said, " couldst thou tell me the names of those knights who upheld so gallantly the renown of merry England."

" That will I do blithely," replied the Pilgrim, " and without guerdon ; my oath, for a time, pro-
10 hibits me from touching gold."

" I will wear the bracelet for you, if you will, friend Palmer," said Wamba.

" The first in honor as in arms, in renown as in place," said the Pilgrim, " was the brave Richard,
15 King of England."

" I forgive him," said Cedric — " I forgive him his descent from the tyrant Duke William."

" The Earl of Leicester was the second," con-tinued the Pilgrim. " Sir Thomas Multon of
20 Gilsland was the third."

" Of Saxon descent, he at least," said Cedric, with exultation.

" Sir Foulk Doilly the fourth," proceeded the Pilgrim.

25 " Saxon also, at least by the mother's side," continued Cedric. "And who was the fifth?" he demanded.

---

LINE **9. guerdon** : reward.

"The fifth was Sir Edwin Turneham."

"Genuine Saxon, by the soul of Hengist!" shouted Cedric. "And the sixth?" he continued, with eagerness — "how name you the sixth?"

"The sixth," said the Palmer, after a pause, in 5 which he seemed to recollect himself, "was a young knight of lesser renown and lower rank, assumed into that honorable company less to aid their enterprise than to make up their number; his name dwells not in my memory." 10

"Sir Palmer," said Sir Brian de Bois-Guilbert, scornfully, "this assumed forgetfulness, after so much has been remembered, comes too late to serve your purpose. I will myself tell the name of the knight before whose lance fortune and my 15 horse's fault occasioned my falling: it was the Knight of Ivanhoe; nor was there one of the six that, for his years, had more renown in arms. Yet this will I say, and loudly — that were he in England, and durst repeat, in this week's tournament, 20 the challenge of St. John-de-Acre, I, mounted and armed as I now am, would give him every advantage of weapons, and abide the result."

"Your challenge would be soon answered," replied the Palmer, "were your antagonist near you. 25 As the matter is, disturb not the peaceful hall with vaunts of the issue of a conflict which you well know cannot take place. If Ivanhoe ever returns from Palestine, I will be his surety that he meets you."

" A goodly security ! " said the Knight Templar ;
" and what do you proffer as a pledge ? "

" This reliquary," said the Palmer, taking a small
ivory box from his bosom, and crossing himself,
5 " containing a portion of the true cross, brought
from the monastery of Mount Carmel."

The Templar took from his neck a gold chain,
which he flung on the board, saying, " Let Prior
Aymer hold my pledge and that of this nameless
10 vagrant, in token that, when the Knight of Ivanhoe
comes within the four seas of Britain, he underlies
the challenge of Brian de Bois-Guilbert, which, if he
answer not, I will proclaim him as a coward on the
walls of every Temple court in Europe."

15 " It will not need," said the Lady Rowena, breaking silence : " my voice shall be heard, if no other
in this hall is raised, in behalf of the absent Ivanhoe.
I affirm he will meet fairly every honorable challenge. Could my weak warrant add security to the
20 inestimable pledge of this holy pilgrim, I would
pledge name and fame that Ivanhoe gives this proud
knight the meeting he desires."

A crowd of conflicting emotions seemed to have
occupied Cedric and kept him silent during this
25 discussion. Gratified pride, resentment, embarrassment, chased each other over his broad and open
brow, like the shadow of clouds drifting over a

---

LINE 11. **underlies** : stands liable to answer.

harvest-field; while his attendants, on whom the name of the sixth knight seemed to produce an effect almost electrical, hung in suspense upon their master's looks. But when Rowena spoke, the sound of her voice seemed to startle him from his silence.

"Lady," said Cedric, "were further pledge necessary, I myself, offended, and justly offended, as I am, would yet gage my honor for the honor of Ivanhoe. But the wager of battle is complete, even according to the fantastic fashions of Norman chivalry."

"And now, Sir Cedric," said the Prior, "my ears are chiming vespers with the strength of your good wine: permit us another pledge to the welfare of the Lady Rowena, and indulge us with liberty to pass to our repose."

"By my faith," said Cedric, "a Saxon boy of twelve, in my time, would not so soon have relinquished his goblet."

The Prior had his own reasons for the course of temperance which he had adopted. He was not only a professional peacemaker, but from practice a hater of all feuds and brawls. On the present occasion, he had an instinctive apprehension of the fiery temper of the Saxon, and saw the danger that the reckless spirit of which his companion had

---

LINE **9. gage**: pledge.   **25. instinctive**: natural; depending on natural impulse.

already given so many proofs might at length produce some disagreeable explosion. He therefore
gently insinuated the incapacity of the native of any
other country to engage in the genial conflict of the
5 bowl with the hardy and strong-headed Saxons;
something he mentioned, but slightly, about his
own holy character, and ended by pressing his
proposal to depart to repose.

The grace-cup was accordingly served round, and
10 the guests, after making deep obeisance to their
landlord and to the Lady Rowena, arose and
mingled in the hall, while the heads of the family,
by separate doors, retired with their attendants.

"Unbelieving dog," said the Templar to Isaac the
15 Jew, as he passed him in the throng, "dost thou
bend thy course to the tournament?"

"I do so propose," replied Isaac, bowing in all
humility, "if it please your reverend valor."

"Ay," said the knight, "to gnaw the bowels of
20 our nobles with usury, and to gull women and boys
with gauds and toys: I warrant thee store of shekels
in thy Jewish scrip."

"Not a shekel, not a silver penny," said the Jew,
clasping his hands. "I go but to seek the assist-

---

LINE **3**. **insinuated**: hinted at. **9**. **grace-cup**: cup of wine
passed from guest to guest at close of meal. **10**. **obeisance**:
bow. **20**. **usury**: excessive interest. **21**. **gauds**: trinkets.
**shekels**: silver coins worth about sixty cents. **22**. **scrip**:
small bag.

ance of some brethren of my tribe to aid me to pay
the fine which the Exchequer of the Jews have
imposed upon me. I am an impoverished wretch :
the very gaberdine I wear is borrowed."

The Templar smiled sourly as he replied, " Beshrew thee for a false-hearted liar!" and passing
onward, as if disdaining farther conference, he
communed with his Moslem slaves in a language unknown to the bystanders. The poor Israelite seemed
so staggered by the address of the military monk,
that the Templar had passed on to the extremity of
the hall ere he raised his head from the humble posture which he had assumed, so far as to be sensible
of his departure. And when he did look around, it
was with the astonished air of one at whose feet a
thunderbolt has just burst.

The Templar and Prior were shortly after marshalled to their sleeping apartments by the steward
and the cupbearer, each attended by two torch-
bearers and two servants carrying refreshments,
while servants of inferior condition indicated to
their retinue and to the other guests their respective
places of repose.

---

LINE 2. **Exchequer of the Jews** : court which taxed the
Jews. 4. **gaberdine** : long, loose gown. 5. **Beshrew** : curse.
7. **disdaining** : scorning. 8. **Moslem** : Mohammedan.

# CHAPTER VI

## The Jew Befriended

As the Palmer, lighted by a domestic with a torch, passed through the apartments of this large and irregular mansion, the cupbearer, coming behind him, whispered in his ear, that if he had no objection to 5 a cup of good mead in his apartment, there were many domestics in that family who would gladly hear the news he had brought from the Holy Land, and particularly that which concerned the Knight of Ivanhoe. The Palmer thanked him for his 10 courtesy, but observed that he had included in his religious vow an obligation never to speak in the kitchen on matters which were prohibited in the hall.

The cupbearer shrugged up his shoulders in dis- 15 pleasure. "I thought to have lodged him in the solere chamber," said he; "but since he is so unsocial to Christians, e'en let him take the next stall to Isaac the Jew's. Anwold," said he to the torch bearer, "carry the Pilgrim to the southern cell. J

---

LINE 5. mead: liquor of fermented honey and water.
16. solere chamber: upper, sunlit room.

64

give you good-night," he added, " Sir Palmer, with small thanks for short courtesy."

" Good-night, and Our Lady's benison ! " said the Palmer, with composure; and his guide moved forward.　　　　　　　　　　　　　　　　　5

In a small ante-chamber they met a second interruption from the waiting-maid of Rowena, who, saying in a tone of authority that her mistress desired to speak with the Palmer, took the torch from the hand of Anwold, and, bidding him await 10 her return, made a sign to the Palmer to follow.

A short passage, and an ascent of seven steps, each of which was composed of a solid beam of oak, led him to the apartment of the Lady Rowena. The walls were covered with embroidered hangings, 15 on which different-colored silks, interwoven with gold and silver threads, had been employed to represent the sports of hunting and hawking.　The bed was adorned with the same rich tapestry, and surrounded with curtains dyed with purple.　　20

No fewer than four silver candelabras, holding great waxen torches, served to illuminate this apartment.　Yet let not modern beauty envy the magnificence of a Saxon princess.　The walls of the apartment were so ill-finished and so full of crevices, 25 that the rich hangings shook to the night blast, and the flame of the torches streamed sideways into the

---

LINE **3. benison**: blessing.　**18. hawking**: hunting with trained hawks.　**21. candelabras**: large branched candlesticks.

air, like the unfurled pennon of a chieftain. Magnificence there was, with some rude attempt at taste; but of comfort there was little, and, being unknown, it was unmissed.

5 The Lady Rowena, with three of her attendants standing at her back, and arranging her hair ere she lay down to rest, was seated in a sort of throne, and looked as if born to exact general homage. The Pilgrim acknowledged her claim to it by a low genu-
10 flection.

"Rise, Palmer," said she graciously. "The defender of the absent has a right to favorable reception from all who value truth and honor manhood." She then said to her train, "Retire, ex-
15 cepting only Elgitha; I would speak with this holy Pilgrim."

The maidens, without leaving the apartment, retired to its further extremity, and sat down on a small bench against the wall, where they remained
20 mute as statues.

"Pilgrim," said the lady, after a moment's pause, during which she seemed uncertain how to address him, "you this night mentioned a name — I mean," she said with a degree of effort, "the name of Ivan-
25 hoe — in the halls where by nature and kindred it should have sounded most acceptably; and yet of many whose hearts must have throbbed at the

---

LINE 1. **pennon**: small pointed flag.

sound, I only dare ask you where, and in what condition, you left him of whom you spoke? We
heard that, having remained in Palestine, on
account of his impaired health, after the departure
of the English army, he had experienced the perse- 5
cution of the French faction, to whom the Templars
are known to be attached."

"I know little of the Knight of Ivanhoe,"
answered the Palmer, with a troubled voice. "I
would I knew him better, since you, lady, are inter- 10
ested in his fate. He hath, I believe, surmounted
the persecution of his enemies in Palestine, and is
on the eve of returning to England, where you, lady,
must know better than I what is his chance of happiness." 15

The Lady Rowena sighed deeply, and asked more
particularly when the Knight of Ivanhoe might be
expected in his native country, and whether he
would not be exposed to great dangers by the road.
On the first point, the Palmer professed ignorance; 20
on the second, he said that the voyage might be
safely made by the way of Venice and Genoa, and
from thence through France to England. "Ivanhoe," he said, "was so well acquainted with the
language and manners of the French, that there was 25
no fear of his incurring any hazard during that part
of his travels."

"Would to God," said the Lady Rowena, "he
were here safely arrived, and able to bear arms

in the approaching tourney, in which the chivalry
of this land are expected to display their address
and valor. Should Athelstane of Coningsburgh
obtain the prize, Ivanhoe is like to hear evil tidings when he reaches England. How looked he,
stranger, when you last saw him? Had disease
laid her hand heavy upon his strength and comeli-
ness?"

"He was darker," said the Palmer, "and thinner
than when he came from Cyprus in the train of
Cœur-de-Lion, and care seemed to sit heavy on his
brow; but I approached not his presence, because
he is unknown to me."

"He will," said the lady, "I fear, find little in his
native land to clear those clouds from his
countenance. Thanks, good Pilgrim, for your information concerning the companion of my childhood. Maidens," she said, "draw near, offer the
sleeping-cup to this holy man, whom I will no longer
detain from repose."

One of the maidens presented a silver cup containing a rich mixture of wine and spice, which
Rowena barely put to her lips. It was then offered
to the Palmer, who, after a low obeisance, tasted a
few drops.

"Accept this alms, friend," continued the lady,
offering a piece of gold, "in acknowledgement of thy
painful travail, and of the shrines thou hast visited."

The Palmer received the boon with another low

reverence, and followed Elgitha out of the apartment.

In the ante-room he found his attendant Anwold, who, taking the torch from the hand of the waiting-maid, conducted him to an exterior and ignoble part of the building, where a number of small apartments, or rather cells, served for sleeping-places to the lower order of domestics, and to strangers of mean degree.

"In which of these sleeps the Jew?" said the Pilgrim.

▸ "The unbelieving dog," answered Anwold, "kennels in the cell next your holiness."

"And where sleeps Gurth, the swineherd?" said the stranger.

"Gurth," replied the bondsman, "sleeps in the cell on your right, as the Jew in that to your left. You might have occupied a more honorable place had you accepted of Oswald's invitation."

"It is as well as it is," said the Palmer.

So saying, he entered the cabin allotted to him, and taking the torch from the domestic's hand, thanked him and wished him good-night. Having shut the door of his cell, he placed the torch in a candlestick made of wood, and looked around his sleeping apartment, the furniture of which was of the most simple kind. It consisted of a rude wooden stool, and still ruder hutch or bed-frame, stuffed with clean straw, and accommodated with two or three sheepskins by way of bedclothes.

The Palmer, having extinguished his torch, threw himself, without taking off any part of his clothes, on this rude couch, and slept, or at least retained his recumbent posture, till the earliest sunbeams found 5 their way through the little grated window, which served at once to admit both air and light to his uncomfortable cell. He then started up, and after repeating his matins and adjusting his dress he left it, and entered that of Isaac the Jew, lifting the 10 latch as gently as he could.

The inmate was lying in troubled slumber upon a couch similar to that on which the Palmer himself had passed the night. Such parts of his dress as the Jew had laid aside on the preceding evening were 15 disposed carefully around his person, as if to prevent the hazard of their being carried off during his slumbers. There was a trouble on his brow amounting almost to agony. His hands and arms moved convulsively, as if struggling with the nightmare; and 20 besides several ejaculations in Hebrew, the following were distinctly heard in the Norman-English, or mixed language of the country: "For the sake of the God of Abraham, spare an unhappy old man! I am poor, I am penniless; should your irons 25 wrench my limbs asunder, I could not gratify you!"

The Palmer awaited not the end of the Jew's vision, but stirred him with his pilgrim's staff.

---

LINE **4. recumbent**: reclining; lying. **20. ejaculations**: exclamations.

# The Jew Befriended

The old man started up, his grey hair standing almost erect upon his head, and huddling some part of his garments about him, while he held the detached pieces with the tenacious grasp of a falcon, he fixed upon the Palmer his keen black eyes, 5 expressive of wild surprise and of bodily apprehension.

" Fear nothing from me, Isaac," said the Palmer, " I come as your friend."

" The God of Israel requite you," said the Jew, 10 greatly relieved; " I dreamed — but Father Abraham be praised, it was but a dream!" Then, collecting himself, he added in his usual tone, " And what may it be your pleasure to want at so early an hour with the poor Jew?" 15

" It is to tell you," said the Palmer, " that if you leave not this mansion instantly, and travel not with some haste, your journey may prove a dangerous one."

" Holy father!" said the Jew, " whom could it 20 interest to endanger so poor a wretch as I am?"

" The purpose you can best guess," said the Pilgrim; " but rely on this, that when the Templar crossed the hall yesternight, he spoke to his Mussulman slaves in the Saracen language, which I well 25 understand, and charged them this morning to watch the journey of the Jew, to seize upon him

---

LINE **4. tenacious**: holding fast.  **falcon**: any of various hawks.  **10. requite**: repay.

when at a convenient distance from the mansion, and to conduct him to the castle of Philip de Malvoisin or to that of Reginald Front-de-Bœuf."

5 It is impossible to describe the extremity of terror which seized upon the Jew at this information, and seemed at once to overpower his whole faculties. His arms fell down to his sides, and his head drooped on his breast, his knees bent under his weight, 10 every nerve and muscle of his frame seemed to collapse and lose its energy, and he sunk at the foot of the Palmer.

"Holy God of Abraham!" was his first exclamation, folding and elevating his wrinkled hands, but 15 without raising his grey head from the pavement; "O holy Moses! O blessed Aaron! the dream is not dreamed for nought, and the vision cometh not in vain! I feel their irons already tear my sinews! I feel the rack pass over my body!"

20 "Stand up, Isaac, and hearken to me," said the Palmer; "you have cause for your terror, considering how your brethren have been used, in order to extort from them their hoards, both by princes and nobles; but stand up, I say, and I will point out to 25 you the means of escape. Leave this mansion instantly, while its inmates sleep sound after the last night's revel. I will guide you by the secret paths of the forest, and I will not leave you till you are under safe conduct of some chief or baron going

to the tournament, whose good-will you have probably the means of securing."

As the ears of Isaac received the hopes of escape, he began gradually to raise himself up from the ground, until he fairly rested upon his knees, throwing back his long grey hair and beard, and fixing his keen black eyes upon the Palmer's face. But when he heard the concluding part of the sentence, his original terror appeared to revive in full force, and he dropt once more on his face, exclaiming, " I possess the means of securing good-will! Alas! there is but one road to the favor of a Christian, and how can the poor Jew find it?" Then, as if suspicion had overpowered his other feelings, he suddenly exclaimed, " For the love of God, young man, betray me not; for the sake of the Great Father who made us all, do me no treason! I have not means to secure the good-will of a Christian beggar, were he rating it at a single penny." As he spoke these last words, he raised himself and grasped the Palmer's mantle with a look of the most earnest entreaty. The Pilgrim extricated himself, as if there were contamination in the touch.

" Wert thou loaded with all the wealth of thy tribe," he said, " what interest have I to injure thee? In this dress I am vowed to poverty, nor do I change it for aught save a horse and a coat of mail. Yet think not that I care for thy company, or propose myself advantage by it; remain here if thou wilt — Cedric the Saxon may protect thee."

"Alas!" said the Jew, "he will not let me travel in his train. Saxon or Norman will be equally 5 ashamed of the poor Israelite; and to travel by myself through the domains of Philip de Malvoisin and Reginald Front-de-Bœuf —— Good youth, I will go with you! Let us haste — let us gird up our loins — let us flee! Here is thy staff, why wilt 10 thou tarry?"

"I tarry not," said the Pilgrim, giving way to the urgency of his companion; "but I must secure the means of leaving this place; follow me."

He led the way to the adjoining cell, occupied by 15 Gurth, the swineherd. "Arise, Gurth," said the Pilgrim — "arise quickly. Undo the postern gate, and let out the Jew and me."

Gurth was offended at the familiar and command-ing tone assumed by the Palmer. "The Jew 20 leaving Rotherwood," said he, raising himself on his elbow without quitting his pallet, "and travelling in company with the Palmer to boot ——"

"I should as soon have dreamt," said Wamba, who entered the apartment at the instant, "of his 25 stealing away with a gammon of bacon."

"Nevertheless," said Gurth, again laying down his head on the wooden log which served him for a

---

LINE **16.** postern gate: rear gate. **25.** gammon of bacon: bottom piece of flitch of bacon including hind leg.

pillow, " both Jew and Gentile must be content to abide the opening of the great gate; we suffer no visitors to depart by stealth at these unseasonable hours."

" Nevertheless," said the Pilgrim, in a command- 5 ing tone, "you will not, I think, refuse me that favor."

So saying, he stooped over the bed of the recumbent swineherd, and whispered something in his ear in Saxon. Gurth started up as if electrified. The Pilgrim, raising his finger in an attitude as if to 10 express caution, added, " Gurth, beware; thou art wont to be prudent. I say, undo the postern; thou shalt know more anon."

With hasty alacrity Gurth obeyed him, while Wamba and the Jew followed, both wondering at 15 the sudden change in the swineherd's demeanor.

" My mule — my mule ! " said the Jew, as soon as they stood without the postern.

" Fetch him his mule," said the Pilgrim; " and, hearest thou, let me have another that I may bear 20 him company till he is beyond these parts. I will return it safely to some of Cedric's train at Ashby. And do thou ——" he whispered the rest in Gurth's ear.

" Willingly — most willingly shall it be done," 25 said Gurth, and instantly departed to execute the commission.

---

Line **13. anon:** soon.

In a moment Gurth appeared on the opposite side of the moat with the mules. The travellers crossed the ditch upon a drawbridge of only two planks' breadth, the narrowness of which was 5 matched with the straitness of the postern, and with a little wicket in the exterior palisade, which gave access to the forest. No sooner had they reached the mules, than the Jew, with hasty and trembling hands, secured behind the saddle a small bag of 10 blue buckram, which he took from under his cloak, containing, as he muttered, " a change of raiment — only a change of raiment." Then getting upon the animal with haste, he lost no time in so disposing of the skirts of his gaberdine as to conceal completely 15 from observation the burden.

The Pilgrim mounted with more deliberation, reaching, as he departed, his hand to Gurth, who kissed it with the utmost possible veneration. The swineherd stood gazing after the travellers until 20 they were lost under the boughs of the forest path, when he was disturbed from his reverie by the voice of Wamba.

" Knowest thou," said the Jester, " my good friend Gurth, that thou art strangely courteous and 25 most unwontedly pious on this summer morning?

---

LINE **2. moat**: deep ditch around castle, usually filled with water. **6. wicket**: small door in or near larger gate. **10. buckram**: coarse linen cloth. **21. reverie**: state of being lost in thought.

# The Jew Befriended

I would I were a black prior or a barefoot palmer, to avail myself of thy unwonted zeal and courtesy; certes, I would make more out of it than a kiss of the hand."

"Thou art no fool thus far, Wamba," answered Gurth, "though thou arguest from appearances, and the wisest of us can do no more. But it is time to look after my charge."

So saying, he turned back to the mansion, attended by the Jester.

Meanwhile the travellers continued to press on their journey with a despatch which argued the extremity of the Jew's fears, since persons at his age are seldom fond of rapid motion. The Palmer, to whom every path and outlet in the wood appeared to be familiar, led the way.

When they had pushed on at a rapid rate through many devious paths, the Palmer at length broke silence.

"That large decayed oak," he said, "marks the boundaries over which Front-de-Bœuf claims authority; we are long since far from those of Malvoisin. There is now no fear of pursuit."

"May the wheels of their chariots be taken off," said the Jew, "like those of the host of Pharaoh, that they may drive heavily! But leave me not, good Pilgrim. Think but of that fierce and savage

---

LINE **3. certes:** certainly.

Templar, with his Saracen slaves; they will regard
neither territory nor lordship."

" Our road," said the Palmer, " should here separate; for it beseems not men of my character and
thine to travel together longer than needs must be.
Besides, what succor couldst thou have from me, a
peaceful pilgrim, against two armed heathens?"

" O good youth," answered the Jew, " thou canst
defend me, and I know thou wouldst.  Poor as I
am, I will requite it; not with money, for money,
so help me my Father Abraham!  I have none;
but —— "

" Money and recompense," said the Palmer,
interrupting him, " I have already said I require not
of thee.  Guide thee I can, and, it may be, even in
some sort defend thee.  Therefore, Jew, I will see
thee safe under some fitting escort.  We are now
not far from the town of Sheffield, where thou
mayest easily find many of thy tribe with whom
to take refuge."

" The blessing of Jacob be upon thee, good
youth!" said the Jew; " in Sheffield I can harbor
with my kinsman Zareth, and find some means of
travelling forth with safety."

After a half hour's riding they paused on the top
of a gently rising bank, and the Pilgrim, pointing
to the town of Sheffield, which lay beneath them,
repeated the words, " Here, then, we part."

" Not till you have had the poor Jew's thanks,"

said Isaac; "for I presume not to ask you to
go with me to my kinsman Zareth's, who might
aid me with some means of repaying your good
offices."

"I have already said," answered the Pilgrim, 5
"that I desire no recompense. If, among the huge
list of thy debtors, thou wilt, for my sake, spare the
gyves and the dungeon to some unhappy Christian
who stands in thy danger, I shall hold this morning's
service to thee well bestowed." 10

"Stay — stay," said the Jew, laying hold of his
garment; "something would I do more than this
— something for thyself. God knows the Jew is
poor — yes, Isaac is the beggar of his tribe — but
forgive me should I guess what thou most lackest 15
at this moment."

"If thou wert to guess truly," said the Palmer,
"it is what thou canst not supply, wert thou as
wealthy as thou sayst thou art poor."

"As I say!" echoed the Jew. "Oh! believe it, 20
I say but the truth; I am a plundered, indebted,
distressed man. Hard hands have wrung from me
my goods, my money, my ships, and all that I
possessed. Yet I can tell thee what thou lackest,
and, it may be, supply it too. Thy wish even now 25
is for a horse and armor."

The Palmer started, and turned suddenly towards

---

Line **8. gyves:** fetters; shackles. **9. danger:** power.

79

the Jew. "What fiend prompted that guess?" said he, hastily.

"No matter," said the Jew, smiling, "so that it be a true one; and, as I can guess thy want, so I can supply it."

"But consider," said the Palmer, "my character, my dress, my vow."

"There dropt words from you last night and this morning," said the Jew, "that, like sparks from flint, showed the metal within; and in the bosom of that Palmer's gown is hidden a knight's chain and spurs of gold. They glanced as you stooped over my bed in the morning."

The Pilgrim could not forbear smiling. "Were thy garments searched by as curious an eye, Isaac," said he, "what discoveries might not be made?"

"No more of that," said the Jew, changing color; and drawing forth his writing materials in haste, as if to stop the conversation, he began to write upon a piece of paper which he supported on the top of his yellow cap, without dismounting from his mule. When he had finished, he delivered the scroll, which was in the Hebrew character, to the Pilgrim, saying, "In the town of Leicester all men know the rich Jew, Kirjath Jairam of Lombardy; give him this scroll. He hath on sale six Milan harnesses, the worst would suit a crowned head;

LINE 26. **Milan harnesses.** The armor manufactured in Milan, Italy, was famous.

ten goodly steeds, the worst might mount a king,
were he to do battle for his throne. Of these he will
give thee thy choice, with everything else that can
furnish thee forth for the tournament; when it is
over, thou wilt return them safely — unless thou 5
shouldst have wherewith to pay their value to the
owner."

"But, Isaac," said the Pilgrim, smiling, "dost
thou know that in these sports the arms and steed
of the knight who is unhorsed are forfeit to his 10
victor? Now I may be unfortunate, and so lose
what I cannot replace or repay."

The Jew looked somewhat astounded at this
possibility; but collecting his courage, he replied
hastily, "No — no — no. It is impossible — I 15
will not think so. The blessing of Our Father will
be upon thee. Thy lance will be powerful as the
rod of Moses."

So saying, he was turning his mule's head away,
when the Palmer, in his turn, took hold of his 20
gaberdine. "Nay, but, Isaac, thou knowest not
all the risk. The steed may be slain, the armor
injured; for I will spare neither horse nor man.
Besides, those of thy tribe give nothing for nothing;
something there must be paid for their use." 25

The Jew twisted himself in the saddle, like a man
in a fit of the colic; but his better feelings predomi-
nated over those which were most familiar to him.
"I care not," he said — "I care not; let me go.

If there is damage, it will cost you nothing. Fare thee well! Yet, hark thee, good youth," said he, turning about, " thrust thyself not too forward into this vain hurly-burly: I speak not for endangering 5 the steed and coat of armor, but for the sake of thine own life and limbs."

" Gramercy for thy caution," said the Palmer, again smiling; " I will use thy courtesy frankly, and it will go hard with me but I will requite it."

10 They parted, and took different roads for the town of Sheffield.

---

LINE 7. **Gramercy**: many thanks.

# CHAPTER VII

## Prince John at the Tournament

The condition of the English nation was at this
time sufficiently miserable. King Richard was
absent a prisoner, and in the power of the perfidious
and cruel Duke of Austria. Even the very place of
his captivity was uncertain, and his fate but very 5
imperfectly known to the generality of his subjects,
who were, in the mean time, a prey to every species
of oppression.

Prince John, in league with Philip of France,
Cœur-de-Lion's mortal enemy, was using every 10
species of influence with the Duke of Austria to
prolong the captivity of his brother Richard, to
whom he stood indebted for so many favors. In
the mean time, he was strengthening his own faction in the kingdom. 15

In addition a multitude of outlaws, driven to despair by the oppression of the feudal nobility and
the severe exercise of the forest laws, banded together in large gangs, and, keeping possession of the
forests and the wastes, set at defiance the jus- 20

---

LINE **2. King Richard**. See page 615. **3. perfidious**:
treacherous. **14. faction**: self-interested party.

tice and magistracy of the country. The nobles themselves, each fortified within his own castle, and playing the petty sovereign over his own dominions, were the leaders of bands scarce less lawless and 5 oppressive.

Yet the poor as well as the rich, the vulgar as well as the noble, in the event of a tournament, which was the grand spectacle of that age, felt as much interested as the half-starved citizen of Madrid, who 10 has not a real left to buy provisions for his family, feels in the issue of a bull-feast. Neither duty nor infirmity could keep youth or age from such exhibitions. The passage of arms, as it was called, which was to take place at Ashby, in the county of Leices-15 ter, had attracted universal attention, and an immense confluence of persons of all ranks hastened upon the appointed morning to the place of combat.

The scene was singularly romantic. On the verge of a wood, which approached to within a mile of the 20 town of Ashby, was an extensive meadow of the finest and most beautiful green turf, surrounded on one side by the forest, and fringed on the other by straggling oak-trees, some of which had grown to an immense size. The ground, as if fashioned on 25 purpose for the martial display which was intended, sloped gradually down on all sides to a level bottom,

---

LINE **1. magistracy**: public officers. **10. real**: Spanish silver coin worth about five cents. **16. confluence**: flowing together. **18. romantic**: picturesque.

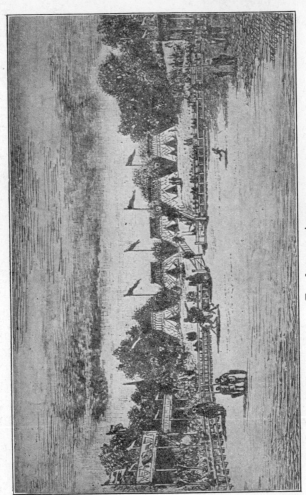

The Lists at Ashby

which was inclosed for the lists with strong palisades, forming a space of a quarter of a mile in
length, and about half as broad.   The form of the inclosure was an oblong square, save that the corners
were considerably rounded off, in order to afford 5
more convenience for the spectators.   The openings
for the entry of the combatants were at the northern
and southern extremities of the lists, accessible by
strong wooden gates, each wide enough to admit two
horsemen riding abreast.   At each of these portals 10
were stationed two heralds, attended by six trumpets, as many pursuivants, and a strong body of
men-at-arms, for maintaining order, and ascertain-
ing the quality of the knights who proposed to engage in this martial game.                                    15

On a platform beyond the southern entrance,
formed by a natural elevation of the ground, were
pitched five magnificent pavilions, adorned with
pennons of russet and black, the chosen colors of
the five knights challengers.   Before each pavilion 20
was suspended the shield of the knight by whom it
was occupied, and beside it stood his squire,
quaintly disguised as a salvage, or in some other
fantastic dress.   The central pavilion, as the place
of honor, had been assigned to Brian de Bois- 25
Guilbert, whose renown in all games of chivalry,

---

LINE **12. pursuivants**: attendants of heralds.   **18. pavilions**: tents.   **23. salvage**: savage; man of the woods.
**26. chivalry**: system of knighthood.   See page 618.

had occasioned him to be eagerly received into the
company of the challengers, and even adopted as
their chief and leader, though he had so recently
joined them. On one side of his tent were pitched
5 those of Reginald Front-de-Bœuf and Richard
[Philip] de Malvoisin, and on the other was the pavilion of Hugh de Grantmesnil, a noble baron in the
vicinity. Ralph de Vipont, a knight of St. John of
Jerusalem, occupied the fifth pavilion. From the
10 entrance into the lists a gently sloping passage, ten
yards in breadth, led up to the platform on which
the tents were pitched. It was strongly secured by
a palisade on each side, as was the esplanade in front
of the pavilions, and the whole was guarded by
15 men-at-arms.

The northern access to the lists terminated in a
similar entrance of thirty feet in breadth, at the
extremity of which was a large inclosed space for
such knights as might be disposed to enter the lists
20 with the challengers, behind which were placed
tents containing refreshments of every kind for
their accommodation, with armorers, farriers, and
other attendants, in readiness to give their services
wherever they might be necessary.

25 The exterior of the lists was in part occupied by
temporary galleries, spread with tapestry and car-

---

LINE **13. esplanade**: level piece of ground. **22. farriers**:
horseshoers. **26. tapestry**: rich woven fabric, usually with
pictorial designs, used for covering walls, etc.

pets, and accommodated with cushions for the convenience of those ladies and nobles who were expected to attend the tournament. A narrow space betwixt these galleries and the lists gave accommodation for yeomanry and spectators of a better degree than the mere vulgar. The promiscuous multitude arranged themselves upon large banks of turf prepared for the purpose, which, aided by the natural elevation of the ground, enabled them to overlook the galleries and obtain a fair view into the lists. Besides the accommodation which these stations afforded, many hundreds had perched themselves on the branches of the trees which surrounded the meadow; and even the steeple of a country church, at some distance, was crowded with spectators.

It only remains to notice that one gallery in the very centre of the eastern side of the lists, and consequently exactly opposite to the spot where the shock of the combat was to take place, was raised higher than the others, more richly decorated, and graced by a sort of throne and canopy, on which the royal arms were emblazoned. Squires, pages, and yeomen in rich liveries waited around this place of honor, which was designed for Prince John and his attendants. Opposite to this gallery was another,

---

LINE **5.** yeomanry: small landowners. **23. emblazoned**: portrayed conspicuously. **pages**. See page 618. **24. yeomen**: here, in the sense of servants.

elevated to the same height, on the western side of
the lists; and more gaily decorated than that destined for the Prince himself. A train of pages and
of young maidens, the most beautiful who could be
5 selected, gaily dressed in green and pink, surrounded
a throne decorated in the same colors. Among
pennons and flags bearing wounded hearts, burning
hearts, bleeding hearts, bows and quivers, and all
the emblems of Cupid, a blazoned inscription in-
10 formed the spectators that this seat of honor was
designed for *La Royne de la Beaulté et des Amours*.
But who was to represent the Queen of Beauty and
of Love on the present occasion no one was prepared
to guess.

15 Meanwhile, spectators of every description
thronged forward to occupy their respective
stations, and not without many quarrels concerning
those which they were entitled to hold. Some of
these were settled by the men-at-arms with brief
20 ceremony; the shafts of their battle-axes and pummels of their swords being readily employed as
arguments to convince the more refractory.
Others, which involved the rival claims of more
elevated persons, were determined by the heralds,
25 or by the two marshals of the field, who, armed at

LINE **8**. quivers: cases for arrows. **9**. Cupid: god of
love. **11**. *La Royne de la Beaulté et des Amours:* the Queen of
Beauty and of Love. **20**. pummels: knobs on hilts of swords.
**22**. refractory: obstinate; unmanageable. **25**. marshals:
officers in charge of tournament.

all points, rode up and down the lists to enforce and preserve good order among the spectators.

Gradually the galleries became filled with knights and nobles, in their robes of peace, whose long and rich-tinted mantles were contrasted with the gayer 5 and more splendid habits of the ladies, who, in a greater proportion than even the men themselves, thronged to witness a sport which one would have thought too bloody and dangerous to afford their sex much pleasure.  The lower and interior space 10 was soon filled by substantial yeomen and burghers, and the lesser gentry.  It was of course amongst these that the most frequent disputes for precedence occurred.

" Dog of an unbeliever," said an old man, whose 15 threadbare tunic bore witness to his poverty, as his sword, and dagger, and golden chain intimated his pretensions to rank — " whelp of a she-wolf ! darest thou press upon a Christian, and a Norman gentleman of the blood of Montdidier ? "  20

This rough expostulation was addressed to no other than our acquaintance Isaac, who, richly and even magnificently dressed in a gaberdine ornamented with lace and lined with fur, was endeavoring to make place in the foremost row beneath the 25 gallery for his daughter, the beautiful Rebecca, who had joined him at Ashby, and who was now

---

LINE **11.** **burghers** : townsmen.

hanging on her father's arm, not a little terrified by
the popular displeasure which seemed generally excited by her parent's presumption. But Isaac,
though we have seen him sufficiently timid on other
5 occasions, knew well that at present he had nothing
to fear. It was not in places of general resort that
any avaricious noble durst offer him injury. At
such meetings the Jews were under the protection
of the general law ; and if that proved a weak assur-
10 ance, it usually happened that there were among the
persons assembled some barons who, for their own
interested motives, were ready to act as their protectors. On the present occasion, Isaac felt more
than usually confident, being aware that Prince
15 John was even then in the very act of negotiating a
large loan from the Jews of York, to be secured
upon certain jewels and lands.

Emboldened by these considerations, the Jew
pursued his point, and jostled the Norman Christian
20 without respect either to his descent, quality, or
religion. The complaints of the old man, however,
excited the indignation of the bystanders. One of
these, a stout well-set yeoman, arrayed in Lincoln
green, having twelve arrows stuck in his belt, with a
25 baldric and badge of silver, and a bow of six feet
length in his hand, turned short round, and while his
countenance, which his constant exposure to

---

LINE **7**. **avaricious** : greedy of gain. **25**. **baldric** : belt
hung from shoulder to opposite hip.

weather had rendered brown as a hazel nut, grew
darker with anger, he advised the Jew to remember
that all the wealth he had acquired by sucking the
blood of his miserable victims had but swelled him
like a bloated spider, which might be overlooked 5
while it kept in a corner, but would be crushed if it
ventured into the light. This intimation, delivered
in Norman-English with a firm voice and a stern
aspect, made the Jew shrink back; and he would
have probably withdrawn himself altogether from a 10
vicinity so dangerous, had not the attention of every
one been called to the sudden entrance of Prince
John, who at that moment entered the lists, attended by a numerous and gay train, consisting
partly of laymen, partly of churchmen, as light in 15
their dress, and as gay in their demeanor, as their
companions. Among the latter was the Prior of
Jorvaulx, in the most gallant trim which a dignitary
of the church could venture to exhibit. Fur and
gold were not spared in his garments; and the point 20
of his boots turned up so very far as to be attached
not to his knees merely, but to his very girdle, and
effectually prevented him from putting his foot
into the stirrup. This, however, was a slight inconvenience to the gallant Abbot, who, perhaps even 25
rejoicing in the opportunity to display his accomplished horsemanship before so many spectators,
dispensed with the use of these supports to a timid
rider.

Attended by this gallant equipage, himself well mounted, and splendidly dressed in crimson and in gold, bearing upon his hand a falcon, and having his head covered by a rich fur bonnet, adorned with 5 a circle of precious stones, from which his long curled hair escaped and overspread his shoulders, Prince John, upon a grey and high-mettled palfrey, caracoled within the lists at the head of his jovial party, laughing loud with his train, and eyeing the 10 beauties who adorned the lofty galleries.

In his joyous caracole round the lists, the attention of the Prince was called by the commotion which had attended the ambitious movement of Isaac towards the higher places of the assembly. 15 The quick eye of Prince John instantly recognized the Jew, but was much more agreeably attracted by the beautiful daughter of Zion, who, terrified by the tumult, clung close to the arm of her aged father.

The figure of Rebecca might indeed have compared with the proudest beauties of England, and 20 was shown to advantage by a sort of Eastern dress. Her turban of yellow silk suited well with the darkness of her complexion. The brilliancy of her eyes, the superb arch of her eyebrows, her well-formed 25 aquiline nose, her teeth as white as pearl, and the profusion of her sable tresses, which, each arranged in its own little spiral of twisted curls, fell down

---

LINE **1. equipage**: body of retainers. **8. caracoled**: wheeled about. **26. sable**: black.

PRINCE JOHN ENTERING THE LISTS

upon as much of a lovely neck and bosom as a simarre of the richest Persian silk, exhibiting flowers in their natural colors embossed upon a purple ground, permitted to be visible — all these constituted a combination of loveliness which yielded 5 not to the most beautiful of the maidens who surrounded her. Of the golden and pearl-studded clasps which closed her vest from the throat to the waist, the three uppermost were left unfastened on account of the heat. A diamond necklace, with 10 pendants of inestimable value, were by this means also made more conspicuous. The feather of an ostrich, fastened in her turban by an agraffe set with brilliants, was another distinction of the beautiful Jewess, scoffed and sneered at by the proud 15 dames who sat above her, but secretly envied by those who affected to deride them.

" By the bald scalp of Abraham," said Prince John, " yonder Jewess must be the very model of that perfection whose charms drove frantic the 20 wisest king that ever lived ! What sayest thou, Prior Aymer ? "

" The Rose of Sharon and the Lily of the Valley, " answered the Prior, in a sort of snuffling tone ; " but your Grace must remember she is still 25 but a Jewess."

---

LINE **2. simarre** : loose robe. **3. embossed** : ornamented with raised work. **13. agraffe** : clasp. **23. Rose of Sharon,** etc. Song of Solomon 2 : 1.

"Ay!" added Prince John, without heeding him, "and there is my Mammon of unrighteousness too, contesting for place with penniless dogs. By the body of St. Mark, my prince of supplies, with his lovely Jewess, shall have a place in the gallery! What is she, Isaac? Thy wife or thy daughter?"

"My daughter Rebecca, so please your Grace," answered Isaac, with a low congee, nothing embarrassed by the Prince's salutation, in which, however, there was at least as much mockery as courtesy.

"The wiser man thou," said John, with a peal of laughter. "But, daughter or wife, she should be preferred according to her beauty and thy merits. Who sits above there?" he continued, bending his eye on the gallery. "Saxon churls, lolling at their lazy length! Out upon them! let them sit close, and make room for my prince of usurers and his lovely daughter."

Those who occupied the gallery, to whom this injurious and unpolite speech was addressed, were the family of Cedric the Saxon, with that of his ally and kinsman, Athelstane of Coningsburgh, a personage who, on account of his descent from the last Saxon monarchs of England, was held in the highest respect by all the Saxon natives of the

---

LINE **2. Mammon**: Syrian god of riches. **9. congee**: bow.

north of England. He was comely in countenance,
bulky and strong in person, and in the flower of his
age; yet dull-eyed, heavy-browed, inactive and
sluggish in all his motions, and so slow in resolution, that he was very generally called Athelstane 5
the Unready.

It was to this person that the Prince addressed
his command to make place for Isaac and Rebecca.
Athelstane, utterly confounded at an order which
the manners and feelings of the times rendered so 10
injuriously insulting, unwilling to obey, yet un-
determined how to resist, without stirring or making
any motion whatever of obedience, opened his
large grey eyes and stared at the Prince with an
astonishment which had in it something extremely 15
ludicrous. But the impatient John regarded it in
no such light.

"The Saxon porker," he said, "is either asleep
or minds me not. Prick him with your lance, De
Bracy," speaking to a knight who rode near him, 20
the leader of a band of Free Companions; that is,
of mercenaries belonging to no particular nation,
but attached for the time to any prince by whom
they were paid. There was a murmur even among
the attendants of Prince John; but De Bracy, 25
whose profession freed him from all scruples, extended his long lance over the space which separated the gallery from the lists, and would have
executed the commands of the Prince before Athel-

stane the Unready had recovered presence of mind
sufficient even to draw back his person from the
weapon, had not Cedric, as prompt as his companion was tardy, unsheathed, with the speed of
5 lightning, the short sword which he wore, and at a
single blow severed the point of the lance from the
handle. The blood rushed into the countenance
of Prince John. He swore one of his deepest oaths,
and was about to utter some threat corresponding
10 in violence, when he was diverted from his purpose,
partly by his own attendants, who gathered around
him conjuring him to be patient, partly by a general
exclamation of the crowd, uttered in loud applause
of the spirited conduct of Cedric. The Prince
15 rolled his eyes in indignation, as if to collect some
safe and easy victim; and chancing to encounter
the firm glance of the same archer whom we have
already noticed, and who seemed to persist in his
gesture of applause, in spite of the frowning aspect
20 which the Prince bent upon him, he demanded his
reason for clamoring thus.

"I always add my hollo," said the yeoman,
"when I see a good shot or a gallant blow."

"Sayst thou?" answered the Prince; "then
25 thou canst hit the white thyself, I'll warrant."

"A woodsman's mark, and at woodsman's distance, I can hit," answered the yeoman.

---

LINE **25**. **white**: inner circle of target.

"By St. Grizzel," said Prince John, "we will try his own skill, who is so ready to give his voice to the feats of others!"

"I shall not fly the trial," said the yeoman, with the composure which marked his whole deport- 5 ment.

"Meanwhile, stand up, ye Saxon churls," said the fiery Prince; "for, by the light of Heaven, since I have said it, the Jew shall have his seat amongst ye!" 10

"By no means, an it please your Grace! It is not fit for such as we to sit with the rulers of the land," said the Jew, whose ambition for precedence, though it had led him to dispute place with the impoverished descendant of the line of Montdidier, 15 by no means stimulated him to an intrusion upon the privileges of the wealthy Saxons.

"Up, infidel dog, when I command you," said Prince John, "or I will have thy swarthy hide stript off and tanned for horse-furniture!" 20

Thus urged, the Jew began to ascend the steep and narrow steps which led up to the gallery.

"Let me see," said the Prince, "who dare stop him!" fixing his eye on Cedric, whose attitude intimated his intention to hurl the Jew down 25 headlong.

The catastrophe was prevented by the clown

LINE 1. **St. Grizzel.** According to the story-tellers Griselda was a model patient wife.

Wamba, who, springing betwixt his master and
Isaac, and exclaiming, in answer to the Prince's
defiance, "Marry, that will I!" opposed to the
beard of the Jew a shield of brawn, which he plucked
5 from beneath his cloak, and with which, doubtless,
he had furnished himself lest the tournament should
have proved longer than his appetite could endure
abstinence. Finding the abomination of his tribe
opposed to his very nose, while the Jester at the
10 same time flourished his wooden sword above his
head, the Jew recoiled, missed his footing, and rolled
down the steps — an excellent jest to the spectators, who set up a loud laughter, in which Prince
John and his attendants heartily joined.

15 " Deal me the prize, cousin Prince," said Wamba ;
" I have vanquished my foe in fair fight with sword
and shield," he added, brandishing the brawn in
one hand and the wooden sword in the other.

" Who and what art thou, noble champion ? "
20 said Prince John, still laughing.

" A fool by right of descent," answered the
Jester ; " I am Wamba, the son of Witless, who was
the son of Weatherbrain, who was the son of an
alderman."

25 " Make room for the Jew in front of the lower
ring," said Prince John, not unwilling, perhaps, to
seize an apology to desist from his original purpose ;

---

LINE **4. brawn**: pork.  **24. alderman**: chieftain; later,
a head magistrate.

" to place the vanquished beside the victor were false heraldry."

" Knave upon fool were worse," answered the Jester, " and Jew upon bacon worst of all."

" Gramercy! good fellow," cried Prince John, [5] " thou pleasest me.  Here, Isaac, lend me a handful of byzants."

As the Jew, stunned by the request, afraid to refuse and unwilling to comply, fumbled in the furred bag which hung by his girdle, and was per- [10] haps endeavoring to ascertain how few coins might pass for a handful, the Prince stooped from his jennet and settled Isaac's doubts by snatching the pouch itself from his side; and flinging to Wamba a couple of the gold pieces which it con- [15] tained, he pursued his career round the lists, leaving the Jew to the derision of those around him, and himself receiving as much applause from the spectators as if he had done some honest and honorable action. [20]

---

LINE **7. byzants**: gold coins of Constantinople, worth from three to five dollars.  **13. jennet**: small Spanish horse.

# CHAPTER VIII

## Disinherited Knight Challenges Templar

In the midst of Prince John's cavalcade, he suddenly stopt, and, appealing to the Prior of Jorvaulx, declared the principal business of the day had been forgotten.

5 "We have neglected, Sir Prior," said he, "to name the fair Sovereign of Love and of Beauty, by whose white hand the palm is to be distributed. For my part, I am liberal in my ideas, and I care not if I give my vote for the black-eyed Rebecca."

10 "Holy Virgin," answered the Prior, turning up his eyes in horror, "a Jewess! We should deserve to be stoned out of the lists. Besides, I swear by my patron saint that she is far inferior to the lovely Saxon, Rowena."

15 "Nay, nay," said De Bracy, "let the fair sovereign's throne remain unoccupied until the conqueror shall be named, and then let him choose the lady by whom it shall be filled. It will add another grace to his triumph, and teach fair ladies to prize
20 the love of valiant knights, who can exalt them to such distinction."

---

LINE 1. **cavalcade**: parade of riders.

"Silence, sirs," said Waldemar Fitzurse, one of the oldest and most important of Prince John's followers, "and let the Prince assume his seat. The knights and spectators are alike impatient, the time advances, and highly fit it is that the sports should commence."

The Prince acquiesced, and, assuming his throne, and being surrounded by his followers, gave signal to the heralds to proclaim the laws of the tournament, which were briefly as follows:

First, the five challengers were to undertake all comers.

Secondly, any knight proposing to combat might, if he pleased, select a special antagonist from among the challengers, by touching his shield. If he did so with the reverse of his lance, the trial of skill was made with what were called the arms of courtesy, that is, with lances at whose extremity a piece of round flat board was fixed, so that no danger was encountered, save from the shock of the horses and riders. But if the shield was touched with the sharp end of the lance, the combat was understood to be at *outrance*, that is, the knights were to fight with sharp weapons, as in actual battle.

Thirdly, when the knights present had accomplished their vow, by each of them breaking five lances, the Prince was to declare the victor in the

---

LINE **23**. *outrance* : to the uttermost; to the death.

first day's tourney, who should receive as prize a war-horse of exquisite beauty and matchless strength; and in addition he should have the peculiar honor of naming the Queen of Love and 5 Beauty, by whom the prize should be given on the ensuing day.

Fourthly, it was announced that, on the second day, there should be a general tournament, in which all the knights present, who were desirous to 10 win praise, might take part; and being divided into two bands, of equal numbers, might fight it out manfully until the signal was given by Prince John to cease the combat. The elected Queen of Love and Beauty was then to crown the knight whom 15 the Prince should adjudge to have borne himself best in this second day, with a coronet composed of thin gold plate, cut into the shape of a laurel crown. On this second day the knightly games ceased. But on that which was to follow, feats of archery, 20 of bull-baiting, and other popular amusements were to be practised, for the more immediate amusement of the populace. In this manner did Prince John endeavor to lay the foundation of a popularity which he was perpetually throwing down by 25 some inconsiderate act of wanton aggression upon the feelings and prejudices of the people.

The lists now presented a most splendid spec-

---

LINE **20. bull-baiting**: tormenting bull with dogs for sport.

tacle. The sloping galleries were crowded with all that was noble, great, wealthy, and beautiful in the northern and midland parts of England; and the contrast of the various dresses of these dignified spectators rendered the view as gay as it was rich, 5 while the interior and lower space, filled with the substantial burgesses and yeomen of merry England, formed, in their more plain attire, a dark fringe, or border, around this circle of brilliant embroidery, relieving, and at the same time setting off, its 10 splendor.

The heralds finished their proclamation with their usual cry of "Largesse, largesse, gallant knights!" and gold and silver pieces were showered on them from the galleries. The bounty of 15 the spectators was acknowledged by the customary shouts of "Love of ladies — Death of champions — Honor to the generous — Glory to the brave!" The more humble spectators added their acclamations, and a numerous band of trumpeters the 20 flourish of their martial instruments. When these sounds had ceased, the heralds withdrew from the lists in gay and glittering procession, and none remained within them save the marshals of the field, who, armed cap-à-pie, sat on horseback, 25 motionless as statues, at the opposite ends of the lists. Meantime, the inclosed space at the north-

---

LINE **13. Largesse:** gift. **21. flourish:** showy musical passage. **25. cap-à-pie:** from head to foot.

ern extremity of the lists, large as it was, was now
completely crowded with knights desirous to prove
their skill against the challengers, and, when viewed
from the galleries, presented the appearance of a
5 sea of waving plumage, intermixed with glistening
helmets and tall lances, to the extremities of which
were, in many cases, attached small pennons of
about a span's breadth, which, fluttering in the air
as the breeze caught them, joined with the restless
10 motion of the feathers to add liveliness to the scene.

At length the barriers were opened, and five
knights, chosen by lot, advanced slowly into the
area; a single champion riding in front, and the
other four following in pairs.

15 With the eyes of an immense concourse of spectators fixed upon them, the five knights advanced
up the platform upon which the tents of the challengers stood, and there separating themselves,
each touched slightly, and with the reverse of his
20 lance, the shield of the antagonist to whom he
wished to oppose himself. The lower order of
spectators in general — nay, many of the higher
class, and it is even said several of the ladies —
were rather disappointed at the champions choosing
25 the arms of courtesy. For the same sort of per-

---

LINE **8.** **span's breadth** : distance from end of thumb to end
of little finger when extended; about nine inches. **11. barriers** : fence or palisade enclosing tournament field. **15. concourse** : throng; assembly.

SEVENTEENTH-CENTURY ARMOR

Twelfth-century armor is explained on page 623, and is pictured in
a number of the illustrations.

sons who, in the present day, applaud most highly
the deepest tragedies were then interested in a
tournament exactly in proportion to the danger
incurred by the champions engaged.

Having intimated their more pacific purpose, the 5
champions retreated to the extremity of the lists,
where they remained drawn up in a line; while
the challengers, sallying each from his pavilion,
mounted their horses, and, headed by Brian de
Bois-Guilbert, descended from the platform and 10
opposed themselves individually to the knights
who had touched their respective shields.

At the flourish of clarions and trumpets, they
started out against each other at full gallop; and
such was the superior dexterity or good fortune of 15
the challengers, that those opposed to Bois-Guilbert,
Malvoisin, and Front-de-Bœuf rolled on the ground.
The antagonist of Grantmesnil, instead of bearing
his lance-point fair against the crest or the shield of
his enemy, swerved so much from the direct line 20
as to break the weapon athwart the person of his
opponent — a circumstance which was accounted
more disgraceful than that of being actually unhorsed, because the latter might happen from accident, whereas the former evinced awkwardness and 25
want of management of the weapon and of the
horse. The fifth knight alone maintained the

LINE **5. pacific**: peaceable.   **13. clarions**: small, shrill
trumpets.   **19. crest**: top of helmet.   **21. athwart**: across.

honor of his party, and parted fairly with the
Knight of St. John, both splintering their lances
without advantage on either side.

The shouts of the multitude, together with the
5 acclamations of the heralds and the clangor of the
trumpets, announced the triumph of the victors
and the defeat of the vanquished. The former
retreated to their pavilions, and the latter, gathering themselves up as they could, withdrew from
10 the lists in disgrace and dejection, to agree with
their victors concerning the redemption of their
arms and their horses, which, according to the laws
of the tournament, they had forfeited. The fifth
of their number alone tarried in the lists long enough
15 to be greeted by the applauses of the spectators.

A second and a third party of knights took the
field; and although they had various success, yet,
upon the whole, the advantage decidedly remained
with the challengers, not one of whom lost his seat
20 or swerved from his charge. Three knights only
appeared on the fourth entry, who, avoiding the
shields of Bois-Guilbert and Front-de-Bœuf, contented themselves with touching those of the three
other knights who had not altogether manifested
25 the same strength and dexterity. This selection
did not alter the fortune of the field: the challengers were still successful. One of their antagonists was overthrown; and both the others failed
in striking the helmet and shield of their antagonist

A Tournament in the Time of *Ivanhoe*
(Courtesy of Douglas Fairbanks.)

firmly and strongly, with the lance held in a direct line, so that the weapon might break unless the champion was overthrown.

After this fourth encounter, there was a considerable pause; nor did it appear that any one was very desirous of renewing the contest. The spectators murmured among themselves; for, among the challengers, Malvoisin and Front-de-Bœuf were unpopular from their characters, and the others, except Grantmesnil, were disliked as strangers and foreigners.

But none shared the general feeling of dissatisfaction so keenly as Cedric the Saxon, who saw, in each advantage gained by the Norman challengers, a repeated triumph over the honor of England. His own education had taught him no skill in the games of chivalry, although, with the arms of his Saxon ancestors, he had manifested himself, on many occasions, a brave and determined soldier. He looked anxiously to Athelstane, who had learned the accomplishments of the age, as if desiring that he should make some personal effort to recover the victory which was passing into the hands of the Templar and his associates. But, though both stout of heart and strong of person, Athelstane had a disposition too inert and unambitious to make the exertions which Cedric seemed to expect from him.

---

LINE **26.** inert: sluggish.

"The day is against England, my lord," said Cedric, in a marked tone; "are you not tempted to take the lance?"

"I shall tilt to-morrow," answered Athelstane, "in the *mêlée;* it is not worth while for me to arm myself to-day."

Two things displeased Cedric in this speech. It contained the Norman word *mêlée* (to express the general conflict), and it evinced some indifference to the honor of the country; but it was spoken by Athelstane, whom he held in profound respect.

The pause in the tournament was still uninterrupted, excepting by the voices of the heralds exclaiming; "Love of ladies, splintering of lances! stand forth, gallant knights, fair eyes look upon your deeds!"

The music also of the challengers breathed from time to time wild bursts expressive of triumph or defiance, while the clowns grudged a holiday which seemed to pass away in inactivity; and old knights and nobles lamented in whispers the decay of martial spirit, spoke of the triumphs of their younger days, but agreed that the land did not now supply dames of such transcendent beauty as had animated the jousts of former times. Prince John began to talk to his attendants about making ready the banquet, and the necessity of adjudging the

---

LINE 24. **transcendent**: surpassing. **25. jousts**: tournaments; tilts.

prize to Brian de Bois-Guilbert, who had, with a single spear, overthrown two knights and foiled a third.

At length, as the Saracenic music of the challengers concluded one of those long and high flourishes with which they had broken the silence of the lists, it was answered by a solitary trumpet, which breathed a note of defiance from the northern extremity. All eyes were turned to see the new champion which these sounds announced, and no sooner were the barriers opened than he paced into the lists. As far as could be judged of a man sheathed in armor, the new adventurer did not greatly exceed the middle size, and seemed to be rather slender than strongly made. His suit of armor was formed of steel, richly inlaid with gold, and the device on his shield was a young oak-tree pulled up by the roots, with the Spanish word *Desdichado*, signifying Disinherited. He was mounted on a gallant black horse, and as he passed through the lists he gracefully saluted the Prince and the ladies by lowering his lance. The dexterity with which he managed his steed, and something of youthful grace which he displayed in his manner, won him the favor of the multitude, which some of the lower classes expressed by calling out, " Touch Ralph de Vipont's shield — touch the Hospitaller's shield; he has the least sure seat, he is your cheapest bargain."

The champion, moving onward amid these well-meant hints, ascended the platform by the sloping alley which led to it from the lists, and, to the astonishment of all present, riding straight up to the central pavilion, struck with the sharp end of his spear the shield of Brian de Bois-Guilbert until it rang again. All stood astonished at his presumption, but none more than the redoubted Knight whom he had thus defied to mortal combat, and who, little expecting so rude a challenge, was standing carelessly at the door of the pavilion.

"Have you confessed yourself, brother," said the Templar, "and have you heard mass this morning, that you peril your life so frankly?"

"I am fitter to meet death than thou art," answered the Disinherited Knight.

"Then take your place in the lists," said Bois-Guilbert, "and look your last upon the sun; for this night thou shalt sleep in paradise."

"Gramercy for thy courtesy," replied the Disinherited Knight, "and to requite it, I advise thee to take a fresh horse and a new lance, for by my honor you will need both."

Having expressed himself thus confidently, he reined his horse backward down the slope which he had ascended, and compelled him to move backward through the lists, till he reached the northern

---

LINE 8. redoubted: formidable; dread.

extremity, where he remained stationary, in expectation of his antagonist. This feat of horsemanship again attracted the applause of the multitude.

However incensed at his adversary for the precautions which he recommended, Brian de Bois- 5 Guilbert did not neglect his advice. He changed his horse for a proved and fresh one of great strength and spirit. He chose a new and tough spear, lest the wood of the former might have been strained in the previous encounters he had sustained. Lastly, 10 he laid aside his shield, which had received some little damage, and received another from his squires. His new shield bore a raven in full flight, holding in its claws a skull, and bearing the motto, *Gare le Corbeau*. 15

When the two champions stood opposed to each other at the two extremities of the lists, the public expectation was strained to the highest pitch. Few augured the possibility that the encounter could terminate well for the Disinherited Knight; 20 yet his courage and gallantry secured the general good wishes of the spectators.

The trumpets had no sooner given the signal, than the champions vanished from their posts with the speed of lightning, and closed in the centre of 25 the lists with the shock of a thunderbolt. The lances burst into shivers up to the very grasp, and

---

LINE **14**. *Gare le Corbeau*. Beware the Raven! **19. augured**: predicted.

it seemed at the moment that both knights had fallen, for the shock had made each horse recoil backwards upon its haunches. The riders recovered their steeds by use of the bridle and spur;
and having glared on each other for an instant with eyes which seemed to flash fire through the bars of their visors, each made a demi-volte, and, retiring to the extremity of the lists, received a fresh lance from the attendants.

A loud shout from the spectators, waving of scarfs and handkerchiefs, and general acclamations, attested the interest taken by the spectators in this encounter — the most equal, as well as the best performed, which had graced the day. But no sooner had the knights resumed their station than the clamor of applause was hushed into a silence so deep and so dead that it seemed the multitude were afraid even to breathe.

A few minutes' pause having been allowed, that the combatants and their horses might recover breath, Prince John with his truncheon signed to the trumpets to sound the onset. The champions a second time sprung from their stations, and closed in the centre of the lists, with the same speed, the same dexterity, the same violence, but not the same equal fortune as before.

---

LINE **7**. **visors** : parts of helmets which protect face and can be lifted or opened. **demi-volte** : half turn with forelegs raised. **21**. **truncheon** : staff of authority or office.

THE COMBAT BETWEEN BOIS-GUILBERT AND THE DISINHERITED KNIGHT

# Disinherited Knight Challenges Templar

In this second encounter, the Templar aimed at the centre of his antagonist's shield, and struck it so fair and forcibly that his spear went to shivers, and the Disinherited Knight reeled in his saddle. On the other hand, that champion had, in the beginning of his career, directed the point of his lance towards Bois-Guilbert's shield, but, changing his aim almost in the moment of encounter, he addressed it to the helmet, a mark more difficult to hit, but which, if attained, rendered the shock more irresistible. Fair and true he hit the Norman on the visor, where his lance's point kept hold of the bars. Yet, even at this disadvantage, the Templar sustained his high reputation; and had not the girths of his saddle burst, he might not have been unhorsed. As it chanced, however, saddle, horse, and man rolled on the ground under a cloud of dust.

To extricate himself from the stirrups and fallen steed was to the Templar scarce the work of a moment; and, stung with madness, both at his disgrace and at the acclamations with which it was hailed by the spectators, he drew his sword and waved it in defiance of his conqueror. The Disinherited Knight sprung from his steed, and also unsheathed his sword. The marshals of the field, however, spurred their horses between them, and reminded them that the laws of the tournament did not, on the present occasion, permit this species of encounter.

" We shall meet again, I trust," said the Templar, casting a resentful glance at his antagonist; " and where there are none to separate us."

" If we do not," said the Disinherited Knight, " the fault shall not be mine. On foot or horseback, with spear, with axe, or with sword, I am alike ready to encounter thee.

More and angrier words would have been exchanged, but the marshals, crossing their lances betwixt them, compelled them to separate. The Disinherited Knight returned to his first station, and Bois-Guilbert to his tent, where he remained for the rest of the day in an agony of despair.

Without alighting from his horse, the conqueror called for a bowl of wine, and opening the beaver, or lower part of his helmet, announced that he quaffed it, " To all true English hearts, and to the confusion of foreign tyrants." He then commanded his trumpet to sound a defiance to the challengers, and desired a herald to announce to them that he should make no election, but was willing to encounter them in the order in which they pleased to advance against him.

The gigantic Front-de-Bœuf, armed in sable armor, was the first who took the field. He bore on a white shield a black bull's head, half defaced by the numerous encounters which he had undergone. Over this champion the Disinherited Knight obtained a slight but decisive advantage. Both

knights broke their lances fairly, but Front-de-
Bœuf, who lost a stirrup in the encounter, was
adjudged to have the disadvantage.

In the stranger's third encounter with Sir Philip
Malvoisin he was equally successful; striking that 5
baron so forcibly on the casque that the laces of the
helmet broke, and Malvoisin, only saved from
falling by being unhelmeted, was declared vanquished like his companions.

In his fourth combat with De Grantmesnil the 10
Disinherited Knight showed as much courtesy as
he had hitherto evinced courage and dexterity.
De Grantmesnil's horse, which was young and
violent, reared and plunged so as to disturb the
rider's aim, and the stranger, declining to take the 15
advantage which this accident afforded him,
raised his lance, and passing his antagonist without
touching him, wheeled his horse and rode back again
to his own end of the lists, offering his antagonist,
by a herald, the chance of a second encounter. 20
This De Grantmesnil declined, avowing himself
vanquished as much by the courtesy as by the
address of his opponent.

Ralph de Vipont summed up the list of the
stranger's triumphs, being hurled to the ground 25
with such force that the blood gushed from his
nose and his mouth, and he was borne senseless
from the lists.

---

Line 6. **casque** : helmet.   **laces** : fastenings.

The acclamations of thousands applauded the unanimous award of the Prince and marshals, announcing that day's honors to the Disinherited Knight.

# CHAPTER IX

## The Queen of Love and Beauty

The marshals of the field were the first to offer their congratulations to the victor, praying him, at the same time, to suffer his helmet to be unlaced, or, at least, that he would raise his visor ere they conducted him to receive the prize of the day's tourney from the hands of Prince John. The Disinherited Knight, with all knightly courtesy, declined their request, alleging, that he could not at this time suffer his face to be seen, for reasons which he had assigned to the heralds when he entered the lists. The marshals were perfectly satisfied by this reply; for amidst the vows by which knights were accustomed to bind themselves in the days of chivalry, there were none more common than those by which they engaged to remain incognito for a certain space, or until some particular adventure was achieved. The marshals, therefore, announcing to Prince John the conqueror's desire to remain unknown, requested permission to bring him before his Grace, in order that he might receive the reward of his valor.

John's curiosity was excited by the mystery

observed by the stranger; and, being already displeased with the issue of the tournament, in which the challengers whom he favored had been successively defeated by one knight, he answered haughtily to the marshals, "By the light of Our Lady's brow, this same knight hath been disinherited as well of his courtesy as of his lands, since he desires to appear before us without uncovering his face. Wot ye, my lords," he said, turning round to his train, "who this gallant can be that bears himself thus proudly?"

"I cannot guess," answered De Bracy, "nor did I think there had been within the four seas that girth Britain a champion that could bear down these five knights in one day's jousting. By my faith, I shall never forget the force with which he shocked De Vipont. The poor Hospitaller was hurled from his saddle like a stone from a sling."

"Boast not of that," said a Knight of St. John who was present; "your Temple champion had no better luck. I saw your brave lance, Bois-Guilbert, roll thrice over, grasping his hands full of sand at every turn."

De Bracy, being attached to the Templars, would have replied, but was prevented by Prince John. "Silence, sirs!" he said; "what unprofitable debate have we here?"

---

LINE 9. Wot: know.

# The Queen of Love and Beauty

"The victor," said a marshal, "still waits the pleasure of your Highness."

"It is our pleasure," answered John, "that he do so wait until we learn whether there is not some one who can at least guess at his name and quality." 5

"Your Grace," said Waldemar Fitzurse, "will do less than due honor to the victor if you compel him to wait till we tell your Highness that which we cannot know; at least I can form no guess — unless he be one of the good lances who accompanied 10 King Richard to Palestine, and who are now straggling homeward from the Holy Land."

"It may be the Earl of Salisbury," said De Bracy; "he is about the same pitch."

A whisper arose among the train, but by whom 15 first suggested could not be ascertained. "It might be the King — it might be Richard Cœur-de-Lion himself!"

"Over God's forbode!" said Prince John, turning at the same time as pale as death, and shrinking 20 as if blighted by a flash of lightning; "Waldemar! De Bracy! brave knights and gentlemen, remember your promises, and stand truly by me!"

"Here is no danger impending," said Waldemar Fitzurse; "are you so little acquainted with the 25 gigantic limbs of your father's son, as to think they can be held within the circumference of yonder

LINE 14. pitch: height. 19. Over God's forbode! God forbid! 24. impending: threatening; hanging over.

suit of armor? Look at him more closely; your Highness will see that he wants three inches of King Richard's height, and twice as much of his shoulder breadth. The very horse he backs could not have 5 carried the ponderous weight of King Richard through a single course."

While he was yet speaking, the marshals brought forward the Disinherited Knight to the foot of a wooden flight of steps, which formed the ascent 10 from the lists to Prince John's throne. Still discomposed with the idea that his brother, so much injured, and to whom he was so much indebted, had suddenly arrived in his native kingdom, even the distinctions pointed out by Fitzurse did not 15 altogether remove the Prince's apprehensions; and while, with a short and embarrassed eulogy upon his valor, he caused to be delivered to him the war-horse assigned as the prize, he trembled lest from the barred visor of the mailed form before him 20 an answer might be returned in the deep and awful accents of Richard the Lion-hearted.

But the Disinherited Knight spoke not a word in reply to the compliment of the Prince, which he only acknowledged with a profound obeisance.

25 The horse was led into the lists by two grooms richly dressed, the animal itself being fully accoutred with the richest war-furniture. Laying one

---

Line **10. discomposed**: disturbed.

hand upon the pommel of the saddle, the Disinherited Knight vaulted at once upon the back of the steed without making use of the stirrup, and, brandishing aloft his lance, rode twice around the lists, exhibiting the points and paces of the horse with the skill of a perfect horseman.

In the meanwhile, the bustling Prior of Jorvaulx had reminded Prince John, in a whisper, that the victor must now display his good judgment, instead of his valor, by selecting from among the beauties who graced the galleries a lady who should fill the throne of the Queen of Beauty and of Love, and deliver the prize of the tourney, upon the ensuing day. The Prince accordingly made a sign with his truncheon as the Knight passed him in his second career around the lists. The Knight turned towards the throne, and, sinking his lance until the point was within a foot of the ground, remained motionless, as if expecting John's commands.

"Sir Disinherited Knight," said Prince John, "since that is the only title by which we can address you, it is now your duty, as well as privilege, to name the fair lady who, as Queen of Honor and of Love, is to preside over next day's festival. If, as a stranger in our land, you should require the aid of other judgment to guide your own, we can only say that Alicia, the daughter of our gallant knight

---

LINE 1. **pommel**: knob at front of saddle.

Waldemar Fitzurse, has at our court been long held the first in beauty as in place. Nevertheless, it is your undoubted prerogative to confer on whom you please this crown, by the delivery of which to the
5 lady of your choice the election of to-morrow's Queen will be formal and complete. Raise your lance."

The Knight obeyed; and Prince John placed upon its point a coronet of green satin, having around its edge a circlet of gold, the upper edge of
10 which was relieved by arrow-points and hearts placed interchangeably.

In the broad hint which he dropped respecting the daughter of Waldemar Fitzurse, John had more than one motive. He wished to banish from the
15 minds of the chivalry around him his jest respecting the Jewess Rebecca; he was desirous of conciliating Alicia's father, Waldemar, of whom he stood in awe, and who had more than once shown himself dissatisfied during the course of the day's proceedings.
20 He had also a wish to establish himself in the good graces of the lady. But besides all these reasons, he was desirous to raise up against the Disinherited Knight, towards whom he already entertained a strong dislike, a powerful enemy in the person of
25 Waldemar Fitzurse, who was likely highly to resent the injury done to his daughter in case, as was not unlikely, the victor should make another choice.

---

LINE **3.** **prerogative**: exclusive right.

And so indeed it proved. For the Disinherited Knight passed the gallery, close to that of the Prince, in which the Lady Alicia was seated in the full pride of triumphant beauty, and pacing forwards slowly around the lists, he seemed to exercise his right of examining the numerous fair faces which adorned that splendid circle.

It was worth while to see the different conduct of the beauties who underwent this examination, during the time it was proceeding. Some blushed; some assumed an air of pride and dignity; some looked straight forward, and essayed to seem utterly unconscious of what was going on; some drew back in alarm, which was perhaps affected; some endeavored to forbear smiling; and there were two or three who laughed outright. There were also some who dropped their veils over their charms; but these were fair ones of ten years' standing, who were willing to withdraw their claim in order to give a fair chance to the rising beauties of the age.

At length the champion paused beneath the balcony in which the Lady Rowena was placed, and the expectation of the spectators was excited to the utmost.

Whether from indecision or some other motive of hesitation, the champion of the day remained stationary for more than a minute, while the eyes of

---

the silent audience were riveted upon his motions; and then, gradually and gracefully sinking the point of his lance, he deposited the coronet which it supported at the feet of the fair Rowena. The trumpets instantly sounded, while the heralds proclaimed the Lady Rowena the Queen of Beauty and of Love for the ensuing day. They then repeated their cry of " Largesse," to which Cedric, in the height of his joy, replied by an ample donative, and to which Athelstane, though less promptly, added one equally large.

There was some murmuring among the damsels of Norman descent, who were as much unused to see the preference given to a Saxon beauty as the Norman nobles were to sustain defeat in the games of chivalry which they themselves had introduced. But these sounds of disaffection were drowned by the popular shout of " Long live the Lady Rowena, the chosen and lawful Queen of Love and of Beauty!" To which many in the lower area added, " Long live the Saxon Princess! long live the race of the immortal Alfred!"

However unacceptable these sounds might be to Prince John and to those around him, he saw himself nevertheless obliged to confirm the nomination of the victor, and accordingly calling to horse, he left his throne, and mounting his jennet, accom-

---

LINE 9. **donative**: gift.

panied by his train, he again entered the lists.
The Prince paused a moment beneath the gallery
of the Lady Alicia, to whom he paid his compliments, observing, at the same time, to those around
him : " By my halidome, sirs ! if the Knight's feats 5
in arms have shown that he hath limbs and sinews,
his choice hath no less proved that his eyes are
none of the clearest."

It was on this occasion, as during his whole life,
John's misfortune not perfectly to understand the 10
characters of those whom he wished to conciliate.
Waldemar Fitzurse was rather offended than
pleased at the Prince stating thus broadly an opinion that his daughter had been slighted.

" I know no right of chivalry," he said, " more 15
precious than that of each free knight to choose his
lady-love by his own judgment. My daughter
courts distinction from no one ; and in her own
character, and in her own sphere, will never fail to
receive the full proportion of that which is her due." 20

Prince John replied not ; but, spurring his horse,
as if to give vent to his vexation, he made the animal bound forward to the gallery where Rowena
was seated, with the crown still at her feet.

" Assume," he said, " fair lady, the mark of your 25
sovereignty, to which none vows homage more sincerely than ourself, John of Anjou ; and if it please

---

LINE **5. halidome** : holy relic.

you to-day, with your noble sire and friends, to grace our banquet in the Castle of Ashby, we shall learn to know the empress to whose service we devote to-morrow."

5 Rowena remained silent, and Cedric answered for her in his native Saxon.

"The Lady Rowena," he said, "possesses not the language in which to reply to your courtesy, or to sustain her part in your festival. I also, and the
10 noble Athelstane of Coningsburgh, speak only the language, and practise only the manners, of our fathers. We therefore decline with thanks your Highness's courteous invitation to the banquet. To-morrow, the Lady Rowena will take upon her
15 the state to which she has been called by the free election of the victor Knight, confirmed by the acclamations of the people."

So saying, he lifted the coronet and placed it upon Rowena's head, in token of her acceptance of
20 the temporary authority assigned to her.

"What says he?" said Prince John, affecting not to understand the Saxon language, in which, however, he was well skilled. The purport of Cedric's speech was repeated to him in French.
25 "It is well," he said; "to-morrow we will ourself conduct this mute sovereign to her seat of dignity. You, at least, Sir Knight," he added, turning to the victor, who had remained near the gallery, "will this day share our banquet?"

# The Queen of Love and Beauty

The Knight, speaking for the first time, in a low and hurried voice, excused himself by pleading fatigue, and the necessity of preparing for to-morrow's encounter.

"It is well," said Prince John, haughtily; "although unused to such refusals, we will endeavor to digest our banquet as we may, though ungraced by the most successful in arms and his elected Queen of Beauty."

So saying, he prepared to leave the lists with his glittering train, and his turning his steed for that purpose was the signal for the breaking up and dispersion of the spectators.

John had hardly proceeded three paces ere again, turning around, he fixed an eye of stern resentment upon the yeoman who had displeased him in the early part of the day, and issued his commands to the men-at-arms who stood near: "On your life, suffer not that fellow to escape."

The yeoman stood the angry glance of the Prince with the same unvaried steadiness which had marked his former deportment, saying, with a smile: "I have no intention to leave Ashby until the day after to-morrow. I must see how Staffordshire and Leicestershire can draw their bows; the forests of Needwood and Charnwood must rear good archers."

"I," said Prince John to his attendants, but not in direct reply — "I will see how he can draw his own; and woe betide him unless his skill should prove some apology for his insolence!"

The Prince resumed his retreat from the lists, and the dispersion of the multitude became general. In various routes the spectators were seen retiring over the plain. By far the most numerous part streamed towards the town of Ashby, where many of the distinguished persons were lodged in the castle, and where others found accommodation in the town itself. Among these were most of the knights who had already appeared in the tournament, or who proposed to fight there the ensuing day, and who, as they rode slowly along, talking over the events of the day, were greeted with loud shouts by the populace. The same acclamations were bestowed upon Prince John, although he was indebted for them rather to the splendor of his appearance and train than to the popularity of his character.

A more sincere and more general, as well as a better-merited acclamation, attended the victor of the day, until, anxious to withdraw himself from popular notice, he accepted the accommodation of one of those pavilions pitched at the extremities of the lists, the use of which was courteously tendered him by the marshals of the field. On his retiring to his tent, many who had lingered in the lists, to look upon and form conjectures concerning him, also dispersed.

# The Queen of Love and Beauty

The signs and sounds of a tumultuous concourse of men lately crowded together in one place, and agitated by the same passing events, were now exchanged for the distant hum of voices of different groups retreating in all directions, and these speed- ily died away in silence.  No other sounds were heard save the voices of the menials who stripped the galleries of their cushions and tapestry, in order to put them in safety for the night, and wrangled among themselves for the half-used bottles of wine and relics of the refreshment which had been served round to the spectators.

Beyond the precincts of the lists more than one forge was erected; and these now began to glimmer through the twilight, announcing the toil of the armorers, which was to continue through the whole night, in order to repair or alter the suits of armor to be used again on the morrow.

A strong guard of men-at-arms, renewed at inter- vals, from two hours to two hours, surrounded the lists, and kept watch during the night.

# CHAPTER X

## Gurth Outwits the Jew

The Disinherited Knight had no sooner reached his pavilion than squires and pages in abundance tendered their services to disarm him, to bring fresh attire, and to offer him the refreshment of the
5 bath. Their zeal on this occasion was perhaps sharpened by curiosity, since every one desired to know who the knight was that had gained so many laurels, yet had refused, even at the command of Prince John, to lift his visor or to name his name.
10 But their officious inquisitiveness was not gratified. The Disinherited Knight refused all other assistance save that of his own squire, or rather yeoman — a clownish-looking man, who, wrapt in a cloak of dark-colored felt, and having his head and face
15 half-buried in a Norman bonnet made of black fur, seemed to affect the incognito as much as his master. All others being excluded from the tent, this attendant relieved his master from the more burdensome parts of his armor, and placed food and wine
20 before him.

The Knight had scarcely finished a hasty meal ere

---

LINE 16. incognito: disguise.

his menial announced to him that five men, each leading a barbed steed, desired to speak with him. The Disinherited Knight had exchanged his armor for a long robe, which, being furnished with a hood, concealed the features, when such was the pleasure 5 of the wearer, almost as completely as the visor of the helmet itself; but the twilight, which was now fast darkening, would of itself have rendered a disguise unnecessary.

The Disinherited Knight, therefore, stept boldly 10 forth to the front of his tent, and found in attendance the squires of the challengers, whom he easily knew by their russet and black dresses, each of whom led his master's charger, loaded with the armor in which he had that day fought.  15

"According to the laws of chivalry," said the foremost of these men, "I, Baldwin de Oyley, squire to the redoubted Knight Brian de Bois-Guilbert, make offer to you, styling yourself for the present the Disinherited Knight, of the horse and 20 armor used by the said Brian de Bois-Guilbert in this day's passage of arms, leaving it with your nobleness to retain or to ransom the same, according to your pleasure; for such is the law of arms."

The other squires repeated nearly the same for-  25 mula, and then stood to await the decision of the Disinherited Knight.

---

LINE 2. **barbed**: covered with armor.

" To you four, sirs," replied the Knight, addressing those who had last spoken, " and to your honorable and valiant masters, I have one common reply. Commend me to the noble knights, your 5 masters, and say, I should do ill to deprive them of steeds and arms which can never be used by braver cavaliers. I would I could here end my message to these gallant knights; but being, as I term myself, in truth and earnest the Disinherited, I must 10 be thus far bound to your masters, that they will, of their courtesy, be pleased to ransom their steeds and armor, since that which I wear I can hardly term mine own."

" We stand commissioned, each of us," answered 15 the squire of Reginald Front-de-Bœuf, " to offer a hundred zecchins in ransom of these horses and suits of armor."

" It is sufficient," said the Disinherited Knight. " Half the sum my present necessities compel me 20 to accept; of the remaining half, distribute one moiety among yourselves, sir squires, and divide the other half betwixt the heralds and minstrels and attendants."

The squires, with cap in hand, and low reverences, expressed their deep sense of a courtesy and generosity not often practised, at least upon a scale so extensive. The Disinherited Knight then ad-

---

LINE **7. cavaliers**: horsemen; knights. **16. zecchins**: gold coins of Venice, worth $2.25. **21. moiety**: half.

dressed his discourse to Baldwin, the squire of Brian
de Bois-Guilbert. " From your master," said he,
" I will accept neither arms nor ransom. Say to
him in my name, that our strife is not ended — no,
not till we have fought as well with swords as with 5
lances, as well on foot as on horseback. To this
mortal quarrel he has himself defied me, and I shall
not forget the challenge. Meantime, let him be
assured that I hold him not as one of his companions, with whom I can with pleasure exchange 10
courtesies; but rather as one with whom I stand
upon terms of mortal defiance."

" My master," answered Baldwin, " knows how
to requite scorn with scorn, and blows with blows,
as well as courtesy with courtesy. Since you dis- 15
dain to accept from him any share of the ransom
at which you have rated the arms of the other
knights, I must leave his armor and his horse here,
being well assured that he will never deign to mount
the one nor wear the other." 20

" You have spoken well, good squire," said the
Disinherited Knight. " Leave not, however, the
horse and armor here. Restore them to thy
master; or, if he scorns to accept them, retain
them, good friend, for thine own use. So far as 25
they are mine, I bestow them upon you freely."

Baldwin made a deep obeisance, and retired with
his companions; and the Disinherited Knight
entered the pavilion.

"Thus far, Gurth," said he, addressing his attendant, "the reputation of English chivalry hath not suffered in my hands."

"And I," said Gurth, "for a Saxon swineherd, have not ill played the personage of a Norman squire-at-arms."

"Yea, but," answered the Disinherited Knight, "thou hast ever kept me in anxiety lest thy clownish bearing should discover thee."

"Tush!" said Gurth, "I fear discovery from none, saving my playfellow, Wamba the Jester, of whom I could never discover whether he were most knave or fool. Yet I could scarce choose but laugh, when my old master passed so near to me, dreaming all the while that Gurth was keeping his porkers many a mile off, in the thickets and swamps of Rotherwood. If I am discovered ——"

"Enough," said the Disinherited Knight, "thou knowest my promise."

"Nay, for that matter," said Gurth, "I will never fail my friend for fear of my skin-cutting. I have a tough hide, that will bear knife or scourge as well as any boar's hide in my herd."

"Trust me, I will requite the risk you run for my love, Gurth," said the Knight. "Meanwhile, I pray you to accept these ten pieces of gold."

"I am richer," said Gurth, putting them into his pouch, "than ever was swineherd or bondsman."

"Take this bag of gold to Ashby," continued his

master, " and find out Isaac the Jew of York, and let him pay himself for the horse and arms with which his credit supplied me."

" Nay, by St. Dunstan," replied Gurth, " that I will not do."  5

" How, knave," replied his master, " wilt thou not obey my commands? "

" So they be honest, reasonable, and Christian commands," replied Gurth; " but this is none of these.  To suffer the Jew to pay himself would be  10 dishonest, for it would be cheating my master; and unreasonable, for it were the part of a fool; and unchristian, since it would be plundering a believer to enrich an infidel."

" See him contented, however, thou stubborn  15 varlet," said the Disinherited Knight.

" I will do so," said Gurth, taking the bag under his cloak and leaving the apartment; " and it will go hard," he muttered, " but I content him with one-half of his own asking."  So saying, he de-  20 parted, and left the Disinherited Knight to his own perplexed ruminations.

We must now change the scene to the village of Ashby, or rather to a country house in its vicinity belonging to a wealthy Israelite, with whom Isaac,  25 his daughter, and retinue had taken up their quarters.

---

LINE **16**. **varlet**: servant or attendant; commonly used as a term of contempt.  **22**. **ruminations**: reflections; thoughts

In an apartment, small indeed, but richly furnished with decorations of an Oriental taste, Rebecca was seated on a heap of embroidered cushions, which, piled along a low platform that surrounded
5 the chamber, served instead of chairs and stools. She was watching the motions of her father with a look of anxious and filial affection, while he paced the apartment with a dejected mien and disordered step, sometimes clasping his hands together, some-
10 times casting his eyes to the roof of the apartment, as one who labored under great mental tribulation. "O Jacob!" he exclaimed — "O all ye twelve Holy Fathers of our tribe! what a losing venture is this for one who hath duly kept every
15 jot and tittle of the law of Moses! Fifty zecchins wrenched from me at one clutch, and by the talons of a tyrant!"

"But, father," said Rebecca, "you seemed to give the gold to Prince John willingly."

20 "Willingly! the blotch of Egypt upon him! Willingly, saidst thou? Ay, as willingly as when, in the Gulf of Lyons, I flung over my merchandise to lighten the ship, while she labored in the tempest. And the goodly steed and the rich armor
25 — there is a dead loss too — ay, a loss which swallows up the gains of a week — and yet it may end better than I now think, for 'tis a good youth."

---

LINE **11. tribulation**: distress. **15. jot and tittle**: smallest trifle. **20. blotch**: eruption of skin.

"Assuredly," said Rebecca, "you shall not repent you of requiting the good deed received of the stranger knight."

"I trust so, daughter," said Isaac, "and I trust too in the rebuilding of Zion; but as well do I hope with my own bodily eyes to see the walls and battlements of the new Temple, as to see a Christian, yea, the very best of Christians, repay a debt to a Jew, unless under the awe of the judge and jailer."

So saying, he resumed his discontented walk through the apartment; and Rebecca, perceiving that her attempts at consolation only served to awaken new subjects of complaint, wisely desisted from her unavailing efforts.

The evening was now becoming dark, when a Jewish servant entered the apartment and placed upon the table two silver lamps, fed with perfumed oil; the richest wines and the most delicate refreshments were at the same time displayed by another Israelitish domestic on a small ebony table, inlaid with silver. At the same time the servant informed Isaac that a Nazarene (so they termed Christians while conversing among themselves) desired to speak with him. Isaac at once replaced on the table the untasted glass of Greek wine which he had just raised to his lips, and say-

---

LINE **21**. ebony: hard, heavy wood, usually black.

ing hastily to his daughter, "Rebecca, veil thy-self," commanded the stranger to be admitted.

Just as Rebecca had dropped over her fine fea-tures a screen of silver gauze which reached to her
5 feet, the door opened, and Gurth entered, wrapt in the ample folds of his Norman mantle. His appearance was rather suspicious than prepossess-ing, especially as, instead of doffing his bonnet, he pulled it still deeper over his rugged brow.

10 "Art thou Isaac the Jew of York?" said Gurth, in Saxon.

"I am," replied Isaac, in the same language, for his traffic had rendered every tongue spoken in Britain familiar to him, "and who art thou?"

15 "That is not to the purpose," answered Gurth.

"As much as my name is to thee," replied Isaac; "for without knowing thine, how can I hold inter-course with thee?"

"Easily," answered Gurth; "I, being to pay
20 money, must know that I deliver it to the right person; thou, who art to receive it, wilt not, I think, care very greatly by whose hands it is de-livered."

"Oh," said the Jew, "you are come to pay
25 monies? Holy Father Abraham! that altereth our relation to each other. And from whom dost thou bring it?"

---

LINE 7. prepossessing: attractive.

"From the Disinherited Knight," said Gurth, "victor in this day's tournament. It is the price of the armor supplied to him by Kirjath Jairam of Leicester, on thy recommendation. The steed is restored to thy stable. I desire to know the amount of the sum which I am to pay for the armor."

"I said he was a good youth!" exclaimed Isaac, with joyful exultation. "A cup of wine will do thee no harm," he added, filling and handing to the swineherd a richer draught than Gurth had ever before tasted. "And how much money," continued Isaac, "hast thou brought with thee?"

"What money have I brought with me?" said the Saxon, "even but a small sum."

"Nay, but," said Isaac, "thy master has won goodly steeds and rich armors with the strength of his lance and of his right hand — but 'tis a good youth; the Jew will take these in present payment, and render him back the surplus."

"My master has disposed of them already," said Gurth.

"Ah! that was wrong," said the Jew — "that was the part of a fool. No Christian here could buy so many horses and armor; no Jew except myself would give him half the values. But thou hast a hundred zecchins with thee in that bag," said Isaac, prying under Gurth's cloak, "it is a heavy one."

"I have heads for crossbow bolts in it," said Gurth, readily.

"Well, then," said Isaac, panting and hesitating between habitual love of gain and a new-born desire 5 to be liberal in the present instance, "if I should say that I would take eighty zecchins for the good steed and the rich armor, which leaves me not a guilder's profit, have you money to pay me?"

"Barely," said Gurth, though the sum de-10 manded was more reasonable than he expected, "and it will leave my master nigh penniless. Nevertheless, if such be your least offer, I must be content."

"Fill thyself another goblet of wine," said the 15 Jew. "Ah! eighty zecchins is too little. It leaveth no profit for the usages of the monies; and, besides, the good horse may have suffered wrong in this day's encounter. Oh, it was a hard and a dangerous meeting! man and steed rushing on each 20 other like wild bulls of Bashan! the horse cannot but have had wrong."

"And I say," replied Gurth, "he is sound, wind and limb; and you may see him now in your stable. And I say, over and above, that seventy zecchins 25 is enough for the armor. If you will not take

---

LINE 1. **bolts**: short, heavy arrows for crossbow. The arrow of the long-bow was called a shaft. **7. guilder**: Dutch silver coin worth forty cents. **20. bulls of Bashan**: Psalms 22 : 12.

seventy, I will carry this bag (and he shook it till
the contents jingled) back to my master."

"Nay, nay!" said Isaac; "lay down the
talents — the shekels — the eighty zecchins; and
thou shalt see I will consider thee liberally." 5

Gurth at length complied; and telling out eighty
zecchins upon the table, the Jew delivered out to
him an acquittance for the horse and suit of armor.    The Jew's hand trembled for joy as he
wrapped up the first seventy pieces of gold.  The 10
last ten he told over with much deliberation, pausing, and saying something as he took each piece
from the table and dropt it into his purse.  His
whole speech ran nearly thus:

"Seventy-one, seventy-two — thy master is a 15
good youth — seventy-three — an excellent youth
— seventy-four — that piece hath been clipt within
the ring — seventy-five — and that looketh light
of weight — seventy-six — when thy master wants
money, let him come to Isaac of York — seventy- 20
seven — that is, with reasonable security."  Here
he made a considerable pause, and Gurth had good
hope that the last three pieces might escape the fate
of their comrades; but the enumeration proceeded;
"Seventy-eight — thou   art   a   good   fellow — 25

---

LINE **4. talents**: an ancient money unit.  **8. acquittance**:
receipt in full.  **17. clipt within the ring**: piece cut off the
edge big enough to come within the circle on the face of the
coin.

seventy-nine — and deservest something for thyself ——"

Here the Jew paused again, and looked at the
last zecchin, intending, doubtless, to bestow it upon
5 Gurth. He weighed it upon the tip of his finger,
and made it ring by dropping it upon the table.
Had it rung too flat, or had it felt a hair's breadth
too light, generosity had carried the day; but, unhappily for Gurth, the chime was full and true, the
10 zecchin plump, newly coined, and a grain above
weight. Isaac could not find in his heart to part
with it, so dropt it into his purse as if in absence of
mind, with the words, " Eighty completes the tale,
and I trust thy master will reward thee handsomely.
15 Surely," he added, looking earnestly at the bag,
" thou hast more coins in that pouch? "

Gurth grinned, which was his nearest approach to
a laugh, as he replied, " About the same quantity
which thou has just told over so carefully." He
20 then folded the quittance, and put it under his cap,
adding, " Peril of thy beard, Jew, see that this be
full and ample!" He filled himself, unbidden, a
third goblet of wine, and left the apartment without
ceremony.

25 Having descended the stair, and, having reached
the dark ante-chamber or hall, Gurth was puzzling
about to discover the entrance, when a figure in

LINE **13**. tale: count. **21**. **beard**. Having one's beard
pulled was a deep disgrace.

white, shown by a small silver lamp which she held in her hand, beckoned him into a side apartment. After a moment's pause, he obeyed the beckoning summons of the apparition, and followed her into the apartment which she indicated, where he found, to his joyful surprise, that his fair guide was the beautiful Jewess whom he had seen at the tournament, and a short time in her father's apartment.

She asked him the particulars of his transaction with Isaac, which he detailed accurately.

" My father did but jest with thee, good fellow," said Rebecca; he owes thy master deeper kindness than these arms and steed could pay, were their value tenfold. What sum didst thou pay my father even now? "

" Eighty zecchins," said Gurth, surprised at the question.

" In this purse," said Rebecca, " thou wilt find a hundred. Restore to thy master that which is his due, and enrich thyself with the remainder. Haste — begone — stay not to render thanks! and beware how you pass through this crowded town, where thou mayst easily lose both thy burden and thy life. Reuben," she added, clapping her hands together, " light forth this stranger, and fail not to draw lock and bar behind him."

Reuben, a dark-browed and black-bearded Israelite, obeyed her summons, with a torch in his hand; undid the outward door of the house, and conducting Gurth across a paved court, let him out through a wicket in the entrance-gate, which he closed behind him with such bolts and chains as would well have become that of a prison.

5 "By St. Dunstan," said Gurth, as he stumbled up the dark avenue, "this is no Jewess, but an angel from heaven! Ten zecchins from my brave young master — twenty from this pearl of Zion! Oh, happy day! Such another, Gurth, will redeem 10 thy bondage, and make thee a brother as free as the best. And then do I lay down my swineherd's horn and staff, and take the freeman's sword and buckler, and follow my young master to the death, without hiding either my face or my name."

---

LINE 12. **buckler**: small round shield.

# CHAPTER XI

## Gurth Wields Quarter-Staff

The nocturnal adventures of Gurth were not yet concluded. After passing one or two straggling houses which stood in the outskirts of the village, he found himself in a deep lane, running between two banks overgrown with hazel and holly, while here and there a dwarf oak hung its arms altogether across the path. It was dark, for the banks and bushes intercepted the light of the harvest moon.

From the village were heard the distant sounds of revelry, mixed occasionally with loud laughter, sometimes broken by screams, and sometimes by wild strains of distant music. All these sounds gave Gurth some uneasiness. "The Jewess was right," he said to himself. "By heaven and St. Dunstan, I would I were safe at my journey's end with all this treasure! Here are such numbers, I will not say of arrant thieves, but of errant knights and errant squires, errant monks and errant minstrels, errant jugglers and errant jesters, that a man

---

LINE **1. nocturnal**: occurring in the night.   **18. arrant**: notoriously bad.   **errant**: wandering.

with a single merk would be in danger, much more
a poor swineherd with a whole bagful of zecchins.
Would I were out of the shade of these infernal
bushes, that I might at least see any of St. Nicholas's clerks before they spring on my shoulders!"

Gurth accordingly hastened his pace, in order to
gain the open common to which the lane led, but
was not so fortunate as to accomplish his object.
Just as he attained the upper end of the lane, where
the underwood was thickest, four men sprung upon
him, two from each side of the road, and seized
him. "Surrender your charge," said one of them;
"we are the deliverers of the commonwealth, who
ease every man of his burden."

"You should not ease me of mine so lightly,"
muttered Gurth, "had I it but in my power to
give three strokes in its defence."

"We shall see that presently," said the robber;
and, speaking to his companions, he added, "bring
along the knave. I see he would have his head
broken as well as his purse cut, and so be let blood
in two veins at once."

Gurth was hurried along, and having been
dragged somewhat roughly over the bank on the left-
hand side of the lane, found himself in a straggling
thicket, which lay betwixt it and the open common.

---

LINE **1. merk**: mark; Anglo-Saxon coin worth $3.23.
**4. St. Nicholas's clerks**: robbers. St. Nicholas (Santa
Claus) was the patron saint of thieves as well as of children.

He was compelled to follow his rough conductors
into the very depth of this cover, where they stopt
unexpectedly in an irregular open space, on which
the beams of the moon fell without much interruption from boughs and leaves. Here his captors 5
were joined by two other persons, apparently belonging to the gang. They had short swords by
their sides, and quarter-staves in their hands, and
Gurth could now observe that all six wore visors.

"What money hast thou, churl?" said one of 10
the thieves.

"Thirty zecchins of my own property," answered Gurth, doggedly.

"A forfeit—a forfeit," shouted the robbers;
"a Saxon hath thirty zecchins, and returns sober 15
from a village!"

"I hoarded it to purchase my freedom," said
Gurth.

"Thou art an ass," replied one of the thieves;
"three quarts of double ale had rendered thee as 20
free as thy master, ay, and freer too, if he be a
Saxon like thyself."

"A sad truth," replied Gurth; "but if these
same thirty zecchins will buy my freedom from you,
unloose my hands and I will pay them to you." 25

"Hold," said one who seemed to exercise some
authority over the others; "this bag which thou

---

LINE 9. **visors**: masks. **20. double**: doubly strong.

bearest, as I can feel through thy cloak, contains more coin than thou hast told us of."

"It is the good knight my master's," answered Gurth, "of which, assuredly, I would not have 5 spoken a word, had you been satisfied with working your will upon mine own property."

"Thou art an honest fellow," replied the robber, "I warrant thee. Thy thirty zecchins may yet escape, if thou deal uprightly with us. Meantime, 10 render up thy trust for the time." So saying, he took from Gurth's breast the large leathern pouch in which the purse given him by Rebecca was inclosed, as well as the rest of the zecchins, and then continued his interrogation; "Who is thy 15 master?"

"The Disinherited Knight," said Gurth.

"Whose good lance," replied the robber, "won the prize in to-day's tourney? What is his name and lineage?"

20 "It is his pleasure," answered Gurth, "that they be concealed; and from me, assuredly, you will learn nought of them."

"What is thine own name and lineage?"

"To tell that," said Gurth, "might reveal my 25 master's."

"Thou art a saucy groom," said the robber; "but of that anon. How comes thy master by this gold?"

---

Line 27. anon: soon; presently.

"By his good lance," answered Gurth. "These bags contain the ransom of four good horses and four good suits of armor."

"How much is there?" demanded the robber.

"Two hundred zecchins." 5

"Only two hundred zecchins!" said the bandit; "your master hath dealt liberally by the vanquished, and put them to a cheap ransom. Name those who paid the gold."

Gurth did so. 10

"The armor and horse of the Templar Brian de Bois-Guilbert — at what ransom were they held? Thou seest thou canst not deceive me."

"My master," replied Gurth, "will take nought from the Templar save his life's-blood. They are 15 on terms of mortal defiance."

"Indeed!" repeated the robber, and paused after he had said the word. "And what wert thou now doing at Ashby with such a charge in thy custody?" 20

"I went thither to render to Isaac the Jew of York," replied Gurth, "the price of a suit of armor with which he fitted my master for this tournament."

"And how much didst thou pay to Isaac? Methinks, to judge by weight, there is still two hundred 25 zecchins in this pouch."

"I paid to Isaac," said the Saxon, "eighty zecchins, and he restored me a hundred in lieu thereof."

"How! what!" exclaimed all the robbers at once; "darest thou trifle with us, that thou tellest such improbable lies?"

"What I tell you," said Gurth, "is as true as the moon is in heaven. You will find the just sum in a silken purse within the leathern pouch, and separate from the rest of the gold."

"Strike a light instantly," said the Captain; "I will examine this said purse."

A light was procured accordingly, and the robber proceeded to examine the purse. The others crowded around him, and even two who had hold of Gurth relaxed their grasp while they stretched their necks to see the issue of the search. Availing himself of their negligence, by a sudden exertion of strength and activity Gurth shook himself free of their hold, and might have escaped, could he have resolved to leave his master's property behind him. But such was no part of his intention. He wrenched a quarter-staff from one of the fellows, struck down the Captain, who was altogether unaware of his purpose, and had well-nigh repossessed himself of the pouch and treasure. The thieves, however, were too nimble for him, and again secured both the bag and the trusty Gurth.

"Knave!" said the Captain, getting up, "thou hast broken my head, and with other men of our sort thou wouldst fare the worse for thy insolence. But thou shalt know thy fate instantly. First let us speak of thy master. Stand thou fast in the mean time; if thou stir again, thou shalt have that will make thee quiet for thy life. Comrades!" he then said, addressing his gang, "this purse is embroidered with Hebrew characters, and I well believe the yeoman's tale is true. The errant knight, his master, must needs pass us toll-free. He is too like ourselves for us to make booty of him, since dogs should not worry dogs where wolves and foxes are to be found in abundance." 10

"Like us!" answered one of the gang; "I should like to hear how that is made good."

"Why, thou fool," answered the Captain, "is he not poor and disinherited as we are? Doth he not win his substance at the sword's point as we do? 15 Hath he not beaten Front-de-Bœuf and Malvoisin, even as we would beat them if we could?"

"And this insolent peasant — he too, I warrant me, is to be dismissed scatheless?" muttered the other fellows. 20

"Not if *thou* canst scathe him," replied the Captain. "Here, fellow," continued he, addressing Gurth, "canst thou use the staff, that thou startst to it so readily?"

"I think," said Gurth, "thou shouldst be best 25 able to reply to that question."

"Nay, by my troth, thou gavest me a round

---

LINE **19. scatheless**: free from harm. **27. troth**: truth; faith.

knock," replied the Captain; "do as much for this fellow, and thou shalt pass scot-free, and if thou dost not — why, by my faith, as thou art such a sturdy knave, I think I must pay thy ransom 5 myself. Take thy staff, Miller," he added, "and keep thy head; and do you others let the fellow go, and give him a staff — there is light enough."

The two champions, being alike armed with quarter-staves, stepped forward into the centre of 10 the open space, in order to have the full benefit of the moonlight; the thieves in the mean time laughing, and crying to their comrade, " Miller! beware thy toll-dish." The Miller, holding his quarterstaff by the middle, and making it flourish round 15 his head, exclaimed boastfully, " Come on, churl, an thou darest: thou shalt feel the strength of a miller's thumb!"

" If thou be'st a miller," answered Gurth, undauntedly, making his weapon play around his 20 head with equal dexterity, " thou art doubly a thief, and I, as a true man, bid thee defiance."

So saying, the two champions closed together,

---

LINE 2. scot-free: unharmed; without paying. 13. toll-dish: head. 17. miller's thumb. As the miller tested his flour between his thumb and finger, his thumb became very skillful. 20. doubly a thief. Millers, because they took as pay a part of the grain they ground, had a good chance to steal and were considered a dishonest class. The man is " doubly a thief " because he is by profession a robber and also a miller.

GURTH'S COMBAT WITH THE MILLER

and for a few minutes they displayed great equality in strength, courage, and skill, intercepting and returning the blows of their adversary with the most rapid dexterity, while, from the continued clatter of their weapons, a person at a distance 5 might have supposed that there were at least six persons engaged on each side.

Long they fought equally, until the Miller began to lose temper at finding himself so stoutly opposed, and at hearing the laughter of his companions. 10 This gave Gurth, whose temper was steady, though surly, the opportunity of acquiring a decided advantage.

The Miller pressed furiously forward, dealing blows with either end of his weapon alternately, 15 and striving to come to half-staff distance, while Gurth defended himself against the attack, keeping his hands about a yard asunder, and covering himself by shifting his weapon with great celerity, so as to protect his head and body. Thus did he 20 maintain the defensive, making his eye, foot, and hand keep true time, until, observing his antagonist to lose wind, he darted the staff at his face with his left hand; and, as the Miller endeavored to parry the thrust, he slid his right hand down to 25 his left, and with the full swing of the weapon struck his opponent on the left side of the head,

---

LINE **19.** celerity : swiftness.

who instantly measured his length upon the green
sward.

"Well and yeomanly done!" shouted the robbers; "fair play and Old England for ever! The
Saxon has saved both his purse and his hide, and
the Miller has met his match."

"Thou mayst go thy ways, my friend," said the
Captain, addressing Gurth, "and I will cause two
of my comrades to guide thee by the best way
to thy master's pavilion, and to guard thee from
night-walkers that might have less tender consciences than ours; for there is many one of them
upon the amble in such a night as this. Take heed,
however," he added sternly; "remember thou
hast refused to tell thy name; ask not after ours,
nor endeavor to discover who or what we are,
for, if thou makest such an attempt, thou wilt
come by worse fortune than has yet befallen
thee."

Gurth thanked the Captain for his courtesy,
and promised to attend to his recommendation.
Two of the outlaws, taking up their quarter-staves,
and desiring Gurth to follow close in the rear,
walked roundly forward along a bye-path. On
the very verge of the thicket two men spoke to his
conductors, and receiving an answer in a whisper,
withdrew into the wood, and suffered them to pass
unmolested. This circumstance induced Gurth to
believe both that the gang was strong in numbers,

and that they kept regular guards around their place
of rendezvous.

When they arrived on the open heath, where
Gurth might have had some trouble in finding his
road, the thieves guided him straight forward to 5
the top of a little eminence, whence he could see,
spread beneath him in the moonlight, the palisades of the lists, the glimmering pavilions pitched
at either end, with the pennons which adorned
them fluttering in the moonbeam, and from which 10
could be heard the hum of the song with which the
sentinels were beguiling their night-watch.

Here the thieves stopt.

"We go with you no farther," said they; "it
were not safe that we should do so. Remember 15
the warning you have received: keep secret what
has this night befallen you, and you will have no
room to repent it; neglect what is now told you,
and the Tower of London shall not protect you
against our revenge." 20

"Good-night to you, kind sirs," said Gurth;
"I shall remember your orders, and trust there is
no offence in wishing you a safer and an honester
trade."

Thus they parted, the outlaws returning in the 25
direction from whence they had come, and Gurth
proceeding to the tent of his master, to whom,

---

Line **2. rendezvous**: place of meeting or common resort.

notwithstanding the injunction he had received, he communicated the whole adventures of the evening.

The Disinherited Knight was filled with astonishment, no less at the generosity of Rebecca, by which, however, he resolved he would not profit, than that of the robbers, to whose profession such a quality seemed totally foreign. His course of reflections upon these singular circumstances was, however, interrupted by the necessity for taking repose.

The knight, therefore, stretched himself upon a rich couch; and the faithful Gurth, extending his hardy limbs upon a bear-skin, laid himself across the opening of the tent, so that no one could enter without awakening him.

# CHAPTER XII

## The General Tournament

Morning arose in unclouded splendor, and ere the sun was much above the horizon the spectators appeared on the common, moving to the lists in order to secure a favorable situation for viewing the expected games. 5

The marshals and their attendants appeared next on the field, together with the heralds, for the purpose of receiving the names of the knights who intended to joust, with the side which each chose to espouse. 10

According to due formality, the Disinherited Knight was to be considered as leader of the one body, while Brian de Bois-Guilbert, who had been rated as having done second-best in the preceding day, was named first champion of the other band. 15 About fifty knights were inscribed as desirous of combating upon each side, when the marshals declared that no more could be admitted.

About ten o'clock the whole plain was crowded with horsemen, horsewomen, and foot-passengers, 20

---

LINE **9. joust**: engage in a combat on horseback between knights in armor. **10. espouse**: support.

hastening to the tournament; and shortly after, a grand flourish of trumpets announced Prince John and his retinue, attended by many knights.

About the same time arrived Cedric the Saxon, with the Lady Rowena, unattended, however, by Athelstane. This Saxon lord had arrayed his tall and strong person in armor, in order to take his place among the combatants; and, considerably to the surprise of Cedric, had chosen to enlist himself on the part of the Knight Templar. The Saxon, indeed, had remonstrated strongly with his friend upon the injudicious choice he had made of his party.

His best, if not his only, reason for adhering to the party of Brian de Bois-Guilbert, Athelstane kept to himself. Though his apathy of disposition prevented his taking any means to recommend himself to the Lady Rowena, he was, nevertheless, by no means insensible to her charms, and considered his union with her as a matter already fixed beyond doubt by the assent of Cedric and her other friends. It had therefore been with smothered displeasure that the proud though indolent Lord of Coningsburgh beheld the victor of the preceding day select Rowena as the object of that honor which it became his privilege to confer. In order to punish him for a preference which

---

LINE **11. remonstrated**: protested. **12. injudicious**: unwise.

seemed to interfere with his own suit, Athelstane, confident of his strength and skill in arms, had determined not only to deprive the Disinherited Knight of his powerful succor, but, if an opportunity should occur, to make him feel the weight of his battle-axe.

De Bracy, and other knights attached to Prince John, in obedience to a hint from him, had joined the party of the challengers. On the other hand, many other knights, both English and Norman, took part against the challengers, the more readily that the opposite band was to be led by so distinguished a champion as the Disinherited Knight had proved himself.

As soon as Prince John observed that the Queen of the day had arrived upon the field, he rode forward to meet her, doffed his bonnet, and, alighting from his horse, assisted the Lady Rowena from her saddle, while his followers uncovered at the same time, and one of the most distinguished dismounted to hold her palfrey.

"It is thus," said Prince John, "that we set the dutiful example of loyalty to the Queen of Love and Beauty, and are ourselves her guide to the throne which she must this day occupy. Ladies," he said, "attend your Queen, as you wish in your turn to be distinguished by like honors."

So saying, the Prince marshalled Rowena to the seat of honor opposite his own, while the fairest and most distinguished ladies present crowded after her to obtain places as near as possible to their temporary sovereign.

No sooner was Rowena seated than a burst of

LADY ROWENA AND PRINCE JOHN

5 music, half drowned by the shouts of the multitude, greeted her new dignity. Meantime, the sun shone fierce and bright upon the polished arms of the

knights of either side, who crowded the opposite extremities of the lists.

The heralds then proclaimed silence until the laws of the tourney should be rehearsed. These were calculated in some degree to abate the dangers of the day — a precaution the more necessary as the conflict was to be maintained with sharp swords and pointed lances.

The champions were therefore prohibited to thrust with the sword, and were confined to striking. A knight, it was announced, might use a mace or battle-axe at pleasure; but the dagger was a prohibited weapon. A knight unhorsed might renew the fight on foot with any other on the opposite side in the same predicament; but mounted horsemen were in that case forbidden to assail him. When any knight could force his antagonist to the extremity of the lists, so as to touch the palisade with his person or arms, such opponent was obliged to yield himself vanquished, and his armor and horse were placed at the disposal of the conqueror. A knight thus overcome was not permitted to take farther share in the combat. If any combatant was struck down, and unable to recover his feet, his squire or page might enter the lists and drag his master out of the press; but in that case the knight was adjudged vanquished,

---

LINE **12.** mace: heavy club with spiked metal head, used for breaking armor. **15. predicament:** trying position.

and his arms and horse declared forfeited. The combat was to cease as soon as Prince John should throw down his leading staff, or truncheon — another precaution usually taken to prevent the unnecessary effusion of blood by the too long endurance of a sport so desperate. Any knight breaking the rules of the tournament, or otherwise transgressing the rules of honorable chivalry, was liable to be stript of his arms, and, having his shield reversed, to be placed in that posture astride upon the bars of the palisade, and exposed to public derision, in punishment of his unknightly conduct.

This proclamation having been made, the heralds withdrew to their stations. The knights, entering at either end of the lists in long procession, arranged themselves in a double file, precisely opposite to each other, the leader of each party being in the centre of the foremost rank.

As yet the knights held their long lances upright, their bright points glancing to the sun, and the streamers with which they were decorated fluttering over the plumage of the helmets. Thus they remained while the marshals of the field surveyed their ranks with the utmost exactness, lest either party had more or fewer than the appointed number. The marshals then withdrew from the lists, and one of them, with a voice of thunder, pro-

---

LINE 5. **effusion**: pouring out.

KNIGHTS IN BATTLE

The tournament prepared for this type of warfare.

nounced the signal words, " *Laissez aller!* " The
trumpets sounded as he spoke; the spears of the
champions were at once lowered and placed in the
rests; the spurs were dashed into the flanks of
the horses; and the two foremost ranks of either 5
party rushed upon each other in full gallop, and
met in the middle of the lists with a shock the
sound of which was heard at a mile's distance.
The rear rank of each party advanced at a slower
pace to sustain the defeated, and follow up the 10
success of the victors.

The consequences of the encounter were not
instantly seen, for the dust raised by the trampling
of so many steeds darkened the air. When the
fight became visible, half the knights on each side 15
were dismounted — some by the dexterity of their
adversary's lance; some by the superior weight
and strength of opponents, which had borne down
both horse and man; some lay stretched on earth
as if never more to rise; some had already gained 20
their feet, and were closing hand to hand with
those of their antagonists who were in the same
predicament; and several on both sides, who had
received wounds by which they were disabled, were
stopping their blood by their scarfs, and endeav- 25
oring to extricate themselves from the tumult.
The mounted knights, whose lances had been al-

---

LINE **1.** *Laissez aller!* Let go! **4. rests:** projections on
armor of knights to support their lances.

most all broken by the fury of the encounter, were now closely engaged with their swords, shouting their war-cries, and exchanging buffets, as if honor and life depended on the issue of the combat.

5 The tumult was presently increased by the advance of the second rank on either side, which, acting as a reserve, now rushed on to aid their companions. The followers of Brian de Bois-Guilbert shouted: " *Ha! Beau-seant! Beau-seant!*
10 For the Temple! For the Temple!" The opposite party shouted in answer; " *Desdichado! Desdichado!* " which watchword they took from the motto upon their leader's shield.

The champions thus encountering each other
15 with the utmost fury, and with alternate success, the tide of battle seemed to flow now toward the southern, now toward the northern, extremity of the lists. Meantime the clang of the blows and the shouts of the combatants mixed fearfully with
20 the sound of the trumpets, and drowned the groans of those who fell, and lay rolling defenceless beneath the feet of the horses. The splendid armor of the combatants was now defaced with dust and blood, and gave way at every stroke of the sword
25 and battle-axe. The gay plumage, shorn from the crests, drifted upon the breeze like snow-flakes. All that was beautiful and graceful in the martial

---

LINE **9.** *Beau-seant!* See page 621. **11.** *Desdichado!* Unfortunate; disinherited.

array had disappeared, and what was now visible was only calculated to awake terror or compassion.

Yet such is the force of habit, that not only the vulgar spectators, who are naturally attracted by sights of horror, but even the ladies of distinction, who crowded the galleries, saw the conflict with a thrilling interest certainly, but without a wish to withdraw their eyes from a sight so terrible. Here and there, indeed, a fair cheek might turn pale, or a faint scream might be heard, as a lover, a brother, or a husband was struck from his horse. But, in general, the ladies around encouraged the combatants, not only by clapping their hands and waving their veils and kerchiefs, but even by exclaiming, "Brave lance! Good sword!" when any successful thrust or blow took place under their observation.

Such being the interest taken by the fair sex in this bloody game, that of the men is the more easily understood. It showed itself in loud acclamations upon every change of fortune, while all eyes were so riveted on the lists that the spectators seemed as if they themselves had dealt and received the blows which were there so freely bestowed. And between every pause was heard the voice of the heralds exclaiming, "Fight on, brave knights! Man dies, but glory lives! Fight on; death is better than defeat! Fight on, brave knights! for bright eyes behold your deeds!"

Amid the varied fortunes of the combat, the eyes of all endeavored to discover the leaders of each band, who, mingling in the thick of the fight, encouraged their companions both by voice and example. Both displayed great feats of gallantry, nor did either Bois-Guilbert or the Disinherited Knight find in the ranks opposed to them a champion who could be termed their unquestioned match. They repeatedly endeavored to single out each other, spurred by mutual animosity, and aware that the fall of either leader might be considered as decisive of victory. Such, however, was the crowd and confusion that, during the earlier part of the conflict, their efforts to meet were unavailing, and they were repeatedly separated by the eagerness of their followers, each of whom was anxious to win honor by measuring his strength against the leader of the opposite party.

But when the field became thin by the numbers on either side who had yielded themselves vanquished, had been compelled to the extremity of the lists, or been otherwise rendered incapable of continuing the strife, the Templar and the Disinherited Knight at length encountered hand to hand, with all the fury that mortal animosity, joined to rivalry of honor, could inspire. Such

LINE 10. **animosity**: violent hatred.

was the address of each in parrying and striking, that the spectators broke forth into a unanimous and involuntary shout of delight and admiration.

But at this moment the party of the Disinherited Knight had the worst; the gigantic arm of Front- 5 de-Bœuf on the one flank, and the ponderous strength of Athelstane on the other, bearing down and dispersing those immediately exposed to them. Finding themselves freed from their immediate antagonists, it seems to have occurred to both these 10 knights at the same instant that they would render the most decisive advantage to their party by aiding the Templar in his contest with his rival. Turning their horses, therefore, at the same moment, the Norman spurred against the Disin- 15 herited Knight on the one side and the Saxon on the other. It was utterly impossible that the object of this unequal and unexpected assault could have sustained it, had he not been warned by a general cry from the spectators. 20

"Beware! beware! Sir Disinherited!" was shouted so universally that the knight became aware of his danger; and striking a full blow at the Templar, he reined back his steed in the same moment, so as to escape the charge of Athelstane 25 and Front-de-Bœuf. These knights, therefore, their aim being thus eluded, rushed from opposite

---

LINE 3. **involuntary**: done without exercise of the will.
**27. eluded**: escaped skillfully from.

sides betwixt the object of their attack and the Templar, almost running their horses against each other ere they could stop their career. Recovering their horses, however, and wheeling them round, the whole three pursued their united purpose of bearing to the earth the Disinherited Knight.

Nothing could have saved him except the remarkable strength and activity of the noble horse which he had won on the preceding day.

This stood him in the more stead, as the horse of Bois-Guilbert was wounded, and those of Front-de-Bœuf and Athelstane were both tired with the weight of their gigantic masters, clad in complete armor, and with the preceding exertions of the day. The masterly horsemanship of the Disinherited Knight, and the activity of the noble animal which he mounted, enabled him for a few minutes to keep at sword's point his three antagonists, turning and wheeling with the agility of a hawk upon the wing, keeping his enemies as far separate as he could, and rushing now against the one, now against the other, dealing sweeping blows with his sword, without waiting to receive those which were aimed at him in return.

But although the lists rang with the applauses of his dexterity, it was evident that he must at last be overpowered; and the nobles around Prince

---

LINE **3.** career: charge; full speed.

John implored him with one voice to throw down his warder, and to save so brave a knight from the disgrace of being overcome by odds.

"Not I, by the light of Heaven!" answered Prince John; "this same springal, who conceals ₅ his name and despises our proffered hospitality, hath already gained one prize, and may now afford to let others have their turn." As he spoke thus, an unexpected incident changed the fortune of the day. ₁₀

There was among the ranks of the Disinherited Knight a champion in black armor, mounted on a black horse, large of size, tall, and to all appearance powerful and strong, like the rider by whom he was mounted. This knight, who bore on his ₁₅ shield no device of any kind, had hitherto evinced very little interest in the event of the fight, beating off with seeming ease those combatants who attacked him, but neither pursuing his advantages nor himself assailing any one. In short, he had ₂₀ hitherto acted the part rather of a spectator than of a party in the tournament, a circumstance which procured him among the spectators the name of the Black Sluggard.

At once this knight seemed to throw aside his ₂₅ apathy, when he discovered the leader of his party

---

LINE **2**. **warder**: staff of office. The casting down of this truncheon or staff was the signal for the fighting to cease. **5**. **springal**: youngster.

so hard bested; for, setting spurs to his horse, which was quite fresh, he came to his assistance like a thunderbolt, exclaiming, in a voice like a trumpet-call, "*Desdichado*, to the rescue!" It was high time; for, while the Disinherited Knight was pressing upon the Templar, Front-de-Bœuf had got nigh to him with his uplifted sword; but ere the blow could descend, the Sable Knight dealt a stroke on his head, which, glancing from the polished helmet, lighted with violence scarcely abated on the chamfron of the steed, and Front-de-Bœuf rolled on the ground, both horse and man equally stunned by the fury of the blow. The Black Sluggard then turned his horse upon Athelstane of Coningsburgh; and his own sword having been broken in his encounter with Front-de-Bœuf, he wrenched from the hand of the bulky Saxon the battle-axe which he wielded, and bestowed him such a blow upon the crest that Athelstane also lay senseless on the field. Having achieved this double feat, the knight seemed to resume the sluggishness of his character, returning calmly to the northern extremity of the lists, leaving his leader to cope as he best could with Brian de Bois-Guilbert. This was no longer matter of so much difficulty. The Templar's horse had bled much, and gave way under the shock of the Disinherited

---

LINE **11. chamfron**: armor for the front of war-horse's head.

Knight's charge. Brian de Bois-Guilbert rolled on the field, encumbered with the stirrup, from which he was unable to draw his foot. His antagonist sprung from horseback, waved his fatal sword over the head of his adversary, and com- 5 manded him to yield himself; when Prince John, more moved by the Templar's dangerous situation than he had been by that of his rival, saved him the mortification of confessing himself vanquished by casting down his warder and putting an end 10 to the conflict.

The squires, who had found it a matter of danger and difficulty to attend their masters during the engagement, now thronged into the lists to pay their dutiful attendance to the wounded, who were 15 removed with the utmost care and attention to the neighboring pavilions, or to the quarters prepared for them in the adjoining village.

Thus ended the memorable field of Ashby-de-la-Zouche, one of the most gallantly contested 20 tournaments of that age; for although only four knights, including one who was smothered by the heat of his armor, had died upon the field, yet upwards of thirty were desperately wounded, four or five of whom never recovered. Several more 25 were disabled for life; and those who escaped best carried the marks of the conflict to the grave with

---

LINE **9. mortification**: humiliation.

them. Hence it is always mentioned in the old records as the " gentle and joyous passage of arms of Ashby."

It being now the duty of Prince John to name the knight who had done best, he determined that the honor of the day remained with the knight whom the popular voice had termed the Black Sluggard. It was pointed out to the Prince that the victory had been in fact won by the Disinherited Knight, who, in the course of the day, had overcome six champions with his own hand, and who had finally unhorsed and struck down the leader of the opposite party. But Prince John adhered to his own opinion, on the ground that the Disinherited Knight and his party had lost the day but for the powerful assistance of the Knight of the Black Armor, to whom, therefore, he persisted in awarding the prize.

To the surprise of all present, however, the knight thus preferred was nowhere to be found. He had left the lists immediately when the conflict ceased, and had been observed by some spectators to move down one of the forest glades with the same slow pace and listless and indifferent manner which had procured him the epithet of the Black Sluggard. After he had been summoned twice by sound of trumpet and proclamation of the heralds, it became necessary to name another to receive the honors which had been assigned to him.

Prince John had now no further excuse for resisting the claim of the Disinherited Knight, whom, therefore, he named the champion of the day.

Through a field slippery with blood and encumbered with broken armor and the bodies of slain 5 and wounded horses, the marshals of the lists again conducted the victor to the foot of Prince John's throne.

"Disinherited Knight," said Prince John, "since by that title only you will consent to be known to 10 us, we a second time award to you the honors of this tournament, and announce to you your right to claim and receive from the hands of the Queen of Love and Beauty the chaplet of honor which your valor has justly deserved." 15

The Knight bowed low and gracefully, but returned no answer.

While the trumpets sounded, while the heralds strained their voices in proclaiming honor to the brave and glory to the victor, while ladies waved 20 their silken kerchiefs and embroidered veils, and while all ranks joined in a clamorous shout of exultation, the marshals conducted the Disinherited Knight across the lists to the foot of that throne of honor which was occupied by the Lady Rowena. 25

On the lower step of this throne the champion was made to kneel down. Indeed, his whole action

---

LINE **14.** **chaplet**: wreath for head.

since the fight had ended seemed rather to have
been upon the impulse of those around him than
from his own free will; and it was observed that he
tottered as they guided him the second time across
5 the lists. Rowena, descending from her station
with a graceful and dignified step, was about to
place the chaplet which she held in her hand upon
the helmet of the champion, when the marshals
exclaimed with one voice, "It must not be thus;
10 his head must be bare." The knight muttered
faintly a few words, which were lost in the hollow
of his helmet; but their purport seemed to be a
desire that his casque might not be removed.

Whether from love of form or from curiosity, the
15 marshals paid no attention to his expressions of
reluctance, but unhelmed him by cutting the laces
of his casque, and undoing the fastening of his
gorget. When the helmet was removed, the well-
formed yet sunburnt features of a young man of
20 twenty-five were seen, amidst a profusion of short
fair hair. His countenance was as pale as death,
and marked in one or two places with streaks of
blood.

Rowena had no sooner beheld him than she
25 uttered a faint shriek; but at once summoning
up the energy of her disposition, and compelling
herself, as it were, to proceed, while her frame yet
trembled with the violence of sudden emotion, she
placed upon the drooping head of the victor the

splendid chaplet which was the destined reward of the day, and pronounced in a clear and distinct tone these words: "I bestow on thee this chaplet, Sir Knight, as the meed of valor assigned to this day's victor." Here she paused a moment, and 5 then firmly added, "And upon brows more worthy could a wreath of chivalry never be placed!"

The knight stooped his head and kissed the hand of the lovely Sovereign by whom his valor had been rewarded; and then, sinking yet farther for- 10 ward, lay prostrate at her feet.

There was a general consternation. Cedric, who had been struck mute by the sudden appearance of his banished son, now rushed forward, as if to separate him from Rowena. But this had been 15 already accomplished by the marshals of the field, who, guessing the cause of Ivanhoe's swoon, had hastened to undo his armor, and found that the head of a lance had penetrated his breastplate and inflicted a wound in his side. 20

LINE 4. meed: reward.

# CHAPTER XIII

## The Archery Contest

The name of Ivanhoe was no sooner pronounced than it flew from mouth to mouth. It was not long ere it reached the circle of the Prince, whose brow darkened as he heard the news. Looking 5 around him, however, with an air of scorn, " My lords," said he, " methinks that I felt the presence of my brother's minion, even when I least guessed whom yonder suit of armor inclosed."

" Front-de-Bœuf must prepare to restore his 10 fief of Ivanhoe," said De Bracy.

" Ay," answered Waldemar Fitzurse, " this gallant is likely to reclaim the castle and manor which Richard assigned to him, and which your Highness's generosity has since given to Front-de-Bœuf."

15 " Front-de-Bœuf," replied John, " is a man more willing to swallow three manors such as Ivanhoe than to disgorge one of them."

Waldemar, whose curiosity had led him towards the place where Ivanhoe had fallen to the ground, 20 now returned. " The gallant," said he, " is likely to give your Highness little disturbance, and to

---

Line 7. **minion**: favorite. **10. fief.** See page 619.

leave Front-de-Bœuf in the quiet possession of his gains; he is severely wounded."

"Whatever becomes of him," said Prince John, "he is victor of the day; and were he tenfold our enemy, or the devoted friend of our brother, which is perhaps the same, his wounds must be looked to; our own physician shall attend him."

A stern smile curled the Prince's lip as he spoke. Waldemar Fitzurse hastened to reply that Ivanhoe was already removed from the lists, and in the custody of his friends.

"I was somewhat afflicted," he said, "to see the grief of the Queen of Love and Beauty, whose sovereignty of a day this event has changed into mourning. I am not a man to be moved by a woman's lament for her lover, but this same Lady Rowena suppressed her sorrow with such dignity of manner that it could only be discovered by her folded hands and her tearless eye, which trembled as it remained fixed on the lifeless form before her."

"Who is this Lady Rowena," said Prince John, "of whom we have heard so much?"

"A Saxon heiress of large possessions," replied the Prior Aymer; "a rose of loveliness, and a jewel of wealth; the fairest among a thousand."

"We shall cheer her sorrows," said Prince John, "and amend her blood, by wedding her to a Norman. She seems a minor, and must therefore be at our royal disposal in marriage. How sayst thou,

De Bracy? What thinkst thou of gaining fair lands and livings, by wedding a Saxon, after the fashion of the followers of the Conqueror?"

"If the lands are to my liking, my lord," answered De Bracy, "it will be hard to displease me with a bride; and deeply will I hold myself bound to your Highness for a good deed."

"We will not forget it," said Prince John; "and that we may instantly go to work, command our seneschal presently to order the attendance of the Lady Rowena and her company — that is, the rude churl her guardian, and the Saxon ox whom the Black Knight struck down in the tournament — upon this evening's banquet. De Bigot," he added to his seneschal, "thou wilt word this our second summons so courteously as to gratify the pride of these Saxons, and make it impossible for them again to refuse; although courtesy to them is casting pearls before swine."

Prince John had proceeded thus far, and was about to give the signal for retiring from the lists, when a small billet was put into his hand.

"From whence?" said Prince John, looking at the person by whom it was delivered.

"From foreign parts, my lord, but from whence I know not," replied his attendant. "A Frenchman brought it hither, who said he had ridden night and day to put it into the hands of your Highness."

The Prince looked narrowly at the superscription,

and then at the seal which bore the impression of three fleurs-de-lis. John then opened the billet with apparent agitation, which visibly and greatly increased when he had perused the contents, which were expressed in these words: 5

*"Take heed to yourself, for the Devil is unchained!"*

The Prince turned as pale as death, looked first on the earth, and then up to heaven, like a man who has received news that sentence of execution has been passed upon him. Recovering from the first 10 effects of his surprise, he took Waldemar Fitzurse and De Bracy aside, and put the billet into their hands successively. "It means," he added, in a faltering voice, "that my brother Richard has obtained his freedom." 15

"This may be a false alarm or a forged letter," said De Bracy.

"It is France's own hand and seal," replied Prince John.

"It is time, then," said Fitzurse, "to draw our 20 party to a head, either at York or some other central place. A few days later, and it will be indeed too late. Your Highness must break short this present mummery."

---

LINE 2. fleurs-de-lis: emblem of French royal family, which resembles in shape the lily. 18. France's own hand and seal. Philip II of France was friendly to Prince John and sent this message in July, 1193, when he heard that Richard had been released from his Austrian prison. 21. centrical: central. 24. mummery: foolish exhibition.

"The yeomen and commons," said De Bracy, "must not be dismissed discontented, for lack of their share in the sports."

"The day," said Waldemar, "is not yet very far spent; let the archers shoot a few rounds at the target, and the prize be adjudged."

"I thank thee, Waldemar," said the Prince; "thou remindest me, too, that I have a debt to pay to that insolent peasant who yesterday insulted our person. Our banquet also shall go forward to-night as we proposed."

The sound of the trumpets soon recalled those spectators who had already begun to leave the field; and proclamation was made that Prince John, suddenly called by high public duties, held himself obliged to discontinue the entertainments of to-morrow's festival; nevertheless, that, unwilling so many good yeomen should depart without a trial of skill, he was pleased to appoint them, before leaving the ground, presently to execute the competition of archery intended for the morrow. To the best archer a prize was to be awarded, being a bugle-horn, mounted with silver, and a silken baldric richly ornamented.

More than thirty yeomen at first presented themselves as competitors. When, however, the archers understood with whom they were to be matched, upwards of twenty withdrew themselves from the contest, unwilling to encounter the dishonor of almost certain defeat.   For in those days the skill of each celebrated marksman was well known for many miles round him.

The diminished list of competitors for silvan fame still amounted to eight.   Prince John stepped from his royal seat to view more nearly the persons of these chosen yeomen, several of whom wore the royal livery.   Having satisfied his curiosity by this investigation, he looked for the object of his resentment, whom he observed standing on the same spot, and with the same composed countenance which he had exhibited upon the preceding day.

" Fellow," said Prince John, " I guessed by thy insolent babble thou wert no true lover of the longbow, and I see thou darest not adventure thy skill among such merry men as stand yonder."

" Under favor, sir," replied the yeoman, " I have another reason for refraining to shoot, besides the fearing discomfiture and disgrace."

" And what is thy other reason ? " said Prince John.

" Because," replied the woodsman, " I know not if these yeomen and I are used to shoot at the same marks ; and because, moreover, I know not how your Grace might relish the winning of a third prize by one who has unwittingly fallen under your displeasure."

---

Line 4. silvan : pertaining to the woods.   8. livery : distinctive clothes worn by servants or retainers.   14. longbow.   See page 624.

Prince John colored as he put the question, "What is thy name, yeoman?"

"Locksley," answered the yeoman.

"Then, Locksley," said Prince John, "thou shalt shoot in thy turn, when these yeomen have displayed their skill. If thou carriest the prize, I will add to it twenty nobles; but if thou losest it, thou shalt be stript of thy Lincoln green and scourged out of the lists with bowstrings, for a wordy and insolent braggart."

"And how if I refuse to shoot on such a wager?" said the yeoman. "Your Grace's power, supported, as it is, by so many men-at-arms, may indeed easily strip and scourge me, but cannot compel me to bend or to draw my bow."

"If thou refusest my fair proffer," said the Prince, "the provost of the lists shall cut thy bowstring, break thy bow and arrows, and expel thee from the presence as a faint-hearted craven."

"This is no fair chance you put on me, proud Prince," said the yeoman, "to compel me to peril myself against the best archers of Leicester and Staffordshire, under the penalty of infamy if they should overshoot me. Nevertheless, I will obey your pleasure."

"Look to him close, men-at-arms," said Prince

---

LINE 7. **nobles**: gold coins worth about $1.60.   17. **provost**: officer inferior in rank to marshal.

John, "his heart is sinking; I am jealous lest he attempt to escape the trial."

A target was placed at the upper end of the southern avenue which led to the lists. The contending archers took their station in turn, at the bottom of 5 the southern access. The archers, having previously determined by lot their order of precedence, were to shoot each three shafts in succession.

One by one the archers, stepping forward, delivered their shafts yeomanlike and bravely. Of 10 twenty-four arrows shot in succession, ten were fixed in the target, and the others ranged so near it that, considering the distance of the mark, it was accounted good archery. Of the ten shafts which hit the target, two within the inner ring were shot 15 by Hubert, a forester in the service of Malvoisin, who was accordingly pronounced victorious.

"Now, Locksley," said Prince John to the bold yeoman, with a bitter smile, "wilt thou try conclusions with Hubert, or wilt thou yield up bow, 20 baldric, and quiver to the provost of the sports?"

"Sith it be no better," said Locksley, "I am content to try my fortune; on condition that when I have shot two shafts at yonder mark of Hubert's, he shall be bound to shoot one at that which I shall 25 propose."

"That is but fair," answered Prince John, "and

LINE 22. Sith: since.

it shall not be refused thee. If thou dost beat this braggart, Hubert, I will fill the bugle with silver pennies for thee."

"A man can but do his best," answered Hubert; "but my grandsire drew a good long-bow at Hastings, and I trust not to dishonor his memory."

The former target was now removed, and a fresh one of the same size placed in its room. Hubert, who, as victor in the first trial of skill, had the right to shoot first, took his aim with great deliberation, long measuring the distance with his eye, while he held in his hand his bended bow, with the arrow placed on the string. At length he made a step forward, and raising the bow at the full stretch of his left arm, till the centre or grasping place was nigh level with his face, he drew his bowstring to his ear. The arrow whistled through the air, and lighted within the inner ring of the target, but not exactly in the centre.

"You have not allowed for the wind, Hubert," said his antagonist, bending his bow, "or that had been a better shot."

So saying, and without showing the least anxiety to pause upon his aim, Locksley stept to the appointed station, and shot his arrow as carelessly in appearance as if he had not even looked at the mark. He was speaking almost at the instant that the shaft

LINE 5. Hastings. See page 614.

left the bowstring, yet it alighted in the target two inches nearer to the white spot which marked the centre than that of Hubert.

" By the light of Heaven !" said Prince John to Hubert, " an thou suffer that runagate knave to overcome thee, thou art worthy of the gallows !" 5

Hubert had but one set speech for all occasions. " An your Highness were to hang me," he said, " a man can but do his best.    Nevertheless, my grandsire drew a good bow ——" 10

" The foul fiend on thy grandsire and all his generation !" interrupted John.  " Shoot, knave, and shoot thy best, or it shall be the worse for thee !"

Thus exhorted, Hubert resumed his place, and not neglecting the caution which he had received 15 from his adversary, he made the necessary allowance for a very light air of wind which had just arisen, and shot so successfully that his arrow alighted in the very centre of the target.

" A Hubert !  a Hubert !" shouted the populace, 20 more interested in a known person than in a stranger.   " In the clout ! in the clout ! a Hubert for ever !"

" Thou canst not mend that shot, Locksley," said the Prince, with an insulting smile. 25

" I will notch his shaft for him, however," replied Locksley.

---

LINE **5. runagate**: renegade ; vagabond.  **22. clout**: centre of target, perhaps marked by a bit of white cloth.

And letting fly his arrow with a little more precaution than before, it lighted right upon that of his
competitor, which it split to shivers. "This must
be the devil, and no man of flesh and blood,"
whispered the yeomen to each other; "such archery was never seen since a bow was first bent in
Britain."

"And now," said Locksley, "I will crave your
Grace's permission to plant such a mark as is used
in the North Country; and welcome every brave
yeoman who shall try a shot at it to win a smile from
the bonny lass he loves best."

He then turned to leave the lists. "Let your
guards attend me," he said, "if you please;
I go but to cut a rod from the next willow-
bush."

Prince John made a signal that some attendants
should follow him in case of his escape; but the
cry of "Shame! shame!" which burst from the
multitude induced him to alter his ungenerous purpose.

Locksley returned almost instantly with a willow
wand about six feet in length, perfectly straight,
and rather thicker than a man's thumb. He began
to peel this with great composure, observing at the
same time that to ask a good woodsman to shoot at a
target so broad as had hitherto been used was to
put shame upon his skill. "For his own part,"
he said, "and in the land where he was bred, men

would as soon take for their mark King Arthur's
round table, which held sixty knights around it.
A child of seven years old," he said, " might hit
yonder target with a headless shaft; but," added
he, walking deliberately to the other end of the lists, 5
and sticking the willow wand upright in the ground,
" he that hits that rod at fivescore yards, I call him
an archer fit to bear both bow and quiver before a
king, an it were the stout King Richard himself."

" My grandsire," said Hubert, " drew a good bow 10
at the battle of Hastings, and never shot at such a
mark in his life — and neither will I. If this
yeoman can cleave that rod, I give him the bucklers;
a man can but do his best, and I will not shoot where
I am sure to miss. I might as well shoot at the 15
edge of our parson's whittle, or at a wheat straw,
or at a sunbeam, as at a twinkling white streak
which I can hardly see."

" Cowardly dog!" said Prince John. " Sirrah
Locksley, do thou shoot; but if thou hittest such a 20
mark, I will say thou art the first man ever did so.
Howe'er it be, thou shalt not crow over us with a
mere show of superior skill."

" I will do my best, as Hubert says," answered
Locksley; " no man can do more." 25

So saying, he again bent his bow, but on the

---

LINE 1. **King Arthur's round table**. The round table of
Arthur, British king of the sixth century, was large enough
to have seats for all his knights. **16. whittle** : knife.

present occasion looked with attention to his weapon, and changed the string, which he thought was no longer truly round, having been a little frayed by the two former shots. He then took his 5 aim with some deliberation, and the multitude awaited the event in breathless silence. The archer vindicated their opinion of his skill: his arrow split the willow rod against which it was aimed. A jubilee of acclamations followed; and even Prince 10 John, in admiration of Locksley's skill, lost for an instant his dislike to his person. "These twenty nobles," he said, "which, with the bugle, thou hast fairly won, are thine own; we will make them fifty if thou wilt take livery and service with us as a 15 yeoman of our body-guard, and be near to our person. For never did so strong a hand bend a bow or so true an eye direct a shaft."

"Pardon me, noble Prince," said Locksley; "but I have vowed that, if ever I take service, it 20 should be with your royal brother King Richard. These twenty nobles I leave to Hubert, who has this day drawn as brave a bow as his grandsire did at Hastings. Had his modesty not refused the trial he would have hit the wand as well as I."

25 Hubert shook his head as he received with reluctance the bounty of the stranger; and Locksley, anxious to escape further observation, mixed with the crowd, and was seen no more.

The victorious archer would not perhaps have

escaped John's attention so easily, had not that
Prince had other more important subjects pressing
upon his mind at that instant.   He called upon his
chamberlain as he gave the signal for retiring from
the lists, and commanded him instantly to gallop to 5
Ashby and seek out Isaac the Jew.   " Tell the dog,"
he said, " to send me, before sundown, two thousand
crowns.   He knows the security; but thou mayst
show him this ring for a token.   The rest of the
money must be paid at York within six days.   If 10
he neglects, I will have the unbelieving villain's
head."

So saying, the Prince resumed his horse, and returned to Ashby, the whole crowd breaking up and
dispersing upon his retreat.                                    15

---

LINE **8.  crowns**: silver coins worth about $1.20.

# CHAPTER XIV

## Prince John Insults Guests

Prince John held his high festival in the Castle of Ashby. Guests were invited in great numbers; and in the necessity in which he then found himself of courting popularity, Prince John had extended 5 his invitation to a few distinguished Saxon and Danish families, as well as to the Norman nobility and gentry of the neighborhood. However despised and degraded on ordinary occasions, the great numbers of the Anglo-Saxons must necessarily 10 render them formidable in the civil commotions which seemed approaching, and it was an obvious point of policy to secure popularity with their leaders. It was accordingly the Prince's intention to treat these unwonted guests with a cour- 15 tesy to which they had been little accustomed.

In execution of the resolution which he had formed during his cooler moments, Prince John received Cedric and Athelstane with distinguished courtesy, and expressed his disappointment, with- 20 out resentment, when the indisposition of Rowena

LINE **14. unwonted:** unusual.

was alleged by the former as a reason for her not attending upon his gracious summons. Cedric and Athelstane were both dressed in the ancient Saxon garb, which, although not unhandsome in itself, and in the present instance composed of costly materials, was so remote in shape and appearance from that of the other guests that Prince John took great credit to himself with Waldemar Fitzurse for refraining from laughter at a sight which the fashion of the day rendered ridiculous. Yet, in the eye of sober judgment, the short close tunic and long mantle of the Saxons was a more graceful, as well as a more convenient, dress than the garb of the Normans, whose undergarment was a long doublet, so loose as to resemble a shirt, covered by a cloak of scanty dimensions, neither fit to defend the wearer from cold or from rain, and the only purpose of which appeared to be to display as much fur, embroidery, and jewellery work as the ingenuity of the tailor could contrive to lay upon it.

The guests were seated at a table which groaned under the quantity of good cheer. With sly gravity, interrupted only by private signs to each other, the Norman knights and nobles beheld the ruder demeanor of Athelstane and Cedric at a banquet to the form and fashion of which they were unaccustomed. And while their manners were thus the subject of sarcastic observation, the

untaught Saxons unwittingly transgressed several
of the arbitrary rules established for the regulation
of society. Thus Cedric, who dried his hands with
a towel, instead of suffering the moisture to exhale
5 by waving them gracefully in the air, incurred more
ridicule than his companion Athelstane, when he
swallowed to his own single share the whole of a
large pasty composed of the most exquisite foreign
delicacies, and termed at that time a " karum pie."
10 When, however, it was discovered, by a serious
cross-examination, that the thane of Coningsburgh
had no idea what he had been devouring, and that
he had taken the contents of the "karum pie"
for larks and pigeons, whereas they were in fact
15 beccaficoes and nightingales, his ignorance brought
him in for an ample share of ridicule.

The long feast had at length its end; and, while
the goblet circulated freely, men talked of the feats
of the preceding tournament — of the unknown
20 victor in the archery games, of the Black Knight,
whose self-denial had induced him to withdraw
from the honors he had won, and of the gallant
Ivanhoe, who had so dearly bought the honors of
the day. The brow of Prince John alone was over-
25 clouded during these discussions; some overpowering care seemed agitating his mind, and it was
only when he received occasional hints from his

---

LINE **2. arbitrary** : absolute ; despot. **15. beccaficoes** :
small birds, probably warblers.

PRINCE JOHN'S BANQUET

(Courtesy of Douglas Fairbanks.)

attendants that he seemed to take interest in what was passing around him. On such occasions he would start up, quaff a cup of wine as if to raise his spirits, and then mingle in the conversation by some observation made abruptly or at random.

"We drink this beaker," said he, "to the health of Wilfred of Ivanhoe, champion of this passage of arms, and grieve that his wound renders him absent from our board. Let all fill to the pledge, and especially Cedric of Rotherwood, the worthy father of a son so promising."

"No, my lord," replied Cedric, standing up, and placing on the table his untasted cup, "I yield not the name of son to the disobedient youth who at once despises my commands and relinquishes the manners and customs of his fathers."

"'Tis impossible," cried Prince John, with well-feigned astonishment, "that so gallant a knight should be an unworthy or disobedient son!"

"Yet, my lord," answered Cedric, "so it is with this Wilfred. He left my homely dwelling to mingle with the gay nobility of your brother's court, where he learned to do those tricks of horsemanship which you prize so highly. He left it contrary to my wish and command; and in the days of Alfred that would have been termed disobedience — ay, and a crime severely punishable."

"I think," said Prince John, after a moment's

pause, " that my brother proposed to confer upon his favorite the rich manor of Ivanhoe."

" He did endow him with it," answered Cedric; " nor is it my least quarrel with my son that he 5 stooped to hold, as a feudal vassal, the very domains which his fathers possessed in free and independent right."

" We shall then have your willing sanction, good Cedric," said Prince John, " to confer this fief upon 10 a person whose dignity will not be diminished by holding land of the British crown. Sir Reginald Front-de-Bœuf," he said, turning towards that baron, " I trust you will so keep the goodly barony of Ivanhoe that Sir Wilfred shall not incur his 15 father's farther displeasure by again entering upon that fief."

" By St. Anthony!" answered the black-browed giant, " I will consent that your Highness shall hold me a Saxon, if either Cedric or Wilfred, or the best 20 that ever bore English blood, shall wrench from me the gift with which your Highness has graced me."

" Whoever shall call thee Saxon, Sir Baron," replied Cedric, " will do thee an honor as great as it is undeserved."

25 Front-de-Bœuf would have replied, but Prince John's petulance and levity got the start.

" Assuredly," said he, " my lords, the noble

---

LINE **2. manor**: landed estate. **5. feudal vassal.** See page 619. **26. levity**: frivolity.

Cedric speaks truth; and his race may claim precedence over us as much in the length of their pedigrees as in the longitude of their cloaks."

" They go before us indeed in the field, as deer before dogs," said Malvoisin.                                             5

" And with good right may they go before us; forget not," said the Prior Aymer, " the superior decency and decorum of their manners."

" Their singular abstemiousness and temperance," said De Bracy, forgetting the plan which 10 promised him a Saxon bride.

" Together with the courage and conduct," said Brian de Bois-Guilbert, " by which they distinguished themselves at Hastings and elsewhere."

While, with smooth and smiling cheek, the cour- 15 tiers, each in turn, followed their Prince's example, and aimed a shaft of ridicule at Cedric, the face of the Saxon became inflamed with passion, and he glanced his eyes fiercely from one to another, as if the quick succession of so many injuries had pre- 20 vented his replying to them in turn; or, like a baited bull, who, surrounded by his tormentors, is at a loss to choose from among them the immediate object of his revenge.    At length he spoke, in a voice half-choked with passion; and, addressing 25 himself to Prince John as the head and front of the offence which he had received, " Whatever," he

---

LINE **8. decorum**: appropriateness; politeness.    **9. abstemiousness**: sparing use of food and drink.

said, " have been the follies and vices of our race, a Saxon would have been held *nidering* (the most emphatic term for worthlessness) who should in his own hall, and while his own wine-cup passed,
5 have treated, or suffered to be treated, an unoffending guest as your Highness has this day beheld me used; and whatever was the misfortune of our fathers on the field of Hastings, those may at least be silent (here he looked at Front-de-Bœuf and the
10 Templar) who have within these few hours once and again lost saddle and stirrup before the lance of a Saxon."

" By my faith, a biting jest!" said Prince John. " How like you it, sirs? Our Saxon subjects rise in
15 spirit and courage, become shrewd in wit and bold in bearing, in these unsettled times. What say ye, my lords? By this good light, I hold it best to take our galleys and return to Normandy in time."

" For fear of the Saxons?" said De Bracy, laugh-
20 ing. " We should need no weapon but our hunting spears to bring these boars to bay."

" A truce with your raillery, Sir Knights," said Fitzurse; " and it were well," he added, addressing the Prince, " that your Highness should assure the
25 worthy Cedric there is no insult intended him by jests which must sound but harshly in the ear of a stranger."

---

LINE **18.** **galleys**: vessels propelled by oars or by oars and sails. **22.** **raillery**: merry jesting.

"Insult!" answered Prince John, resuming his courtesy of demeanor; "I trust it will not be thought that I could mean or permit any to be offered in my presence. Here! I fill my cup to Cedric himself, since he refuses to pledge his son's health." 5

The cup went round amid the well-dissembled applause of the courtiers, which, however, failed to make the impression on the mind of the Saxon that had been designed. He was not naturally acute of perception, but those too much undervalued his 10 understanding who deemed that this flattering compliment would obliterate the sense of the prior insult. He was silent, however, when the royal pledge again passed round, "To Sir Athelstane of Coningsburgh." 15

The knight made his obeisance, and showed his sense of the honor by draining a huge goblet in answer to it.

"And now, sirs," said Prince John, who began to be warmed with the wine which he had drunk, 20 "having done justice to our Saxon guests, we will pray of them some requital to our courtesy. Worthy thane," he continued, addressing Cedric, "may we pray you to name to us some Norman whose mention may least sully your mouth, and to 25 wash down with a goblet of wine all bitterness which the sound may leave behind it?"

---

LINE **6. well-dissembled**: well-pretended. **12. obliterate**: blot out. **25. sully**: defile.

Fitzurse arose while Prince John spoke, and gliding behind the seat of the Saxon, whispered to him not to omit the opportunity of putting an end to unkindness betwixt the two races by naming Prince John. The Saxon replied not, but, rising up, and filling his cup to the brim, he addressed Prince John in these words: " Your Highness has required that I should name a Norman deserving to be remembered at our banquet. This, perchance, is a hard task, since it calls on the slave to sing the praises of the master — upon the vanquished, while pressed by all the evils of conquest, to sing the praises of the conqueror. Yet I *will* name a Norman — the first in arms and in place — the best and the noblest of his race. And the lips that shall refuse to pledge me to his well-earned fame, I term false and dishonored, and will so maintain them with my life. I quaff this goblet to the health of Richard the Lion-hearted!"

Prince John, who had expected that his own name would have closed the Saxon's speech, started when that of his injured brother was so unexpectedly introduced. He raised mechanically the wine-cup to his lips, then instantly set it down, to view the demeanor of the company at this unexpected proposal, which many of them felt it as unsafe to oppose as to comply with. Some of them, ancient and experienced courtiers, closely imitated the example of the Prince himself, raising the goblet to their lips, and again replacing it before them. There were many who, with a more generous feeling, exclaimed, " Long live King Richard! and may he be speedily restored to us!" And some few, among whom were Front-de-Bœuf and the Templar, in sullen disdain suffered their goblets to stand untasted before them. But no man ventured directly to gainsay a pledge filled to the health of the reigning monarch.

Having enjoyed his triumph for about a minute, Cedric said to his companion, " Up, noble Athelstane! we have remained here long enough, since we have requited the hospitable courtesy of Prince John's banquet. Those who wish to know further of our rude Saxon manners must henceforth seek us in the homes of our fathers, since we have seen enough of royal banquets and enough of Norman courtesy."

So saying, he arose and left the banqueting-room, followed by Athelstane, and by several other guests, who, partaking of the Saxon lineage, held themselves insulted by the sarcasms of Prince John and his courtiers.

" By the bones of St. Thomas," said Prince John, as they retreated, " the Saxon churls have borne off the best of the day, and have retreated with triumph!"

" We have drunk and we have shouted," said **Prior Aymer**, " it were time we left our wine flagons.

I must move several miles forward this evening upon my homeward journey."

"They are breaking up," said the Prince in a whisper to Fitzurse; "their fears anticipate the event, and this coward Prior is the first to shrink from me."

"Fear not, my lord," said Waldemar; "I will show him such reasons as shall induce him to join us when we hold our meeting at York. Sir Prior," he said, "I must speak with you in private before you mount your palfrey."

The other guests were now fast dispersing.

"This, then, is the result of your advice," said the Prince, turning an angry countenance upon Fitzurse; "that I should be bearded at my own board by a drunken Saxon churl, and that, on the mere sound of my brother's name, men should fall off from me as if I had the leprosy?"

"Have patience, sir," replied his counsellor; "I might retort your accusation, and blame the inconsiderate levity which foiled my design. But this is no time for recrimination. De Bracy and I will instantly go among these shuffling cowards and convince them they have gone too far to recede."

"It will be in vain," said Prince John, pacing the apartment with disordered steps, and expressing himself with an agitation to which the wine he had

---

LINE **21**. inconsiderate: thoughtless.  **22**. recrimination: accusing in return.

drunk partly contributed — "it will be in vain;
they have seen the handwriting on the wall — they
have marked the paw of the lion in the sand — they
have heard his approaching roar shake the wood;
nothing will reanimate their courage." 5

"Would to God," said Fitzurse to De Bracy,
"that aught could reanimate his own! His
brother's very name is an ague to him. Unhappy
are the counsellors of a prince who wants fortitude
and perseverance alike in good and in evil!" 10

---

LINE **5. reanimate**: revive.  **9. fortitude**: enduring courage.

# CHAPTER XV

## De Bracy Plans to Wed an Heiress

No spider ever took more pains to repair the shattered meshes of his web than did Waldemar Fitzurse to reunite and combine the scattered members of Prince John's cabal. Few of these were attached to him from inclination, and none from personal regard. It was therefore necessary that Fitzurse should open to them new prospects of advantage, and remind them of those which they at present enjoyed. To the young and wild nobles he held out the prospect of uncontrolled revelry, to the ambitious that of power, and to the covetous that of increased wealth and extended domains. The leaders of the mercenaries received a donation in gold. Promises were still more liberally distributed than money by this active agent; and, in fine, nothing was left undone that could determine the wavering or animate the disheartened. The return of King Richard he spoke of as an event

---

LINE **4. cabal**: persons secretly united for private purpose; faction. **13. mercenaries**: soldiers who serve any ruler who pays them.

altogether beyond the reach of probability; yet, when he observed, from the doubtful looks and uncertain answers which he received, that this was the apprehension by which the minds of his accomplices were most haunted, he boldly treated that event, should it really take place, as one which ought not to alter their political calculations.

"If Richard returns," said Fitzurse, "he returns to enrich his needy and impoverished crusaders at the expense of those who did not follow him to the Holy Land. He returns to punish as a rebel every adherent of his brother Prince John. Are ye afraid of his power? We acknowledge him a strong and valiant knight; but these are not the days of King Arthur, when a champion could encounter an army. If Richard indeed comes back, it must be alone, unfollowed, unfriended. The bones of his gallant army have whitened the sands of Palestine. The few of his followers who have returned have straggled hither like this Wilfred of Ivanhoe, beggared and broken men."

These, and many more arguments had the expected weight with the nobles of Prince John's faction. Most of them consented to attend the proposed meeting at York, for the purpose of making general arrangements for placing the crown upon the head of Prince John.

It was late at night when Fitzurse, returning to the Castle of Ashby, met with De Bracy, who had exchanged his banqueting garments for a short green kirtle, with hose of the same cloth and color, a leathern cap or headpiece, a short sword, a horn slung over his shoulder, a long-bow in his hand, 5 and a bundle of arrows stuck in his belt.

"What mummery is this, De Bracy?" said Fitzurse, somewhat angrily; "is this a time for Christmas gambols and quaint maskings, when the fate of our master, Prince John, is on the very verge 10 of decision? Why hast thou not been, like me, among these heartless cravens whom the very name of King Richard terrifies?"

"I have been attending to mine own business," answered De Bracy, calmly, "as you, Fitzurse, have 15 been minding yours."

"I minding mine own business!" echoed Waldemar; "I have been engaged in that of Prince John, our joint patron."

"As if thou hadst any other reason for that, 20 Waldemar," said De Bracy, "than the promotion of thine own individual interest! Come, Fitzurse, we know each other: ambition is thy pursuit, pleasure is mine. Of Prince John thou thinkest as I do — that he is too weak to be a determined 25 monarch, too tyrannical to be an easy monarch, too insolent to be a popular monarch, and too fickle

---

LINE 2. **kirtle**: here, doublet; close-fitting body-garment.
**8. Christmas gambols.** Disguise and masking were common at Christmas time.

and timid to be long a monarch of any kind. But
he is a monarch by whom Fitzurse and De Bracy
hope to rise and thrive; and therefore you aid him
with your policy, and I with the lances of my Free
Companions." 5

"A hopeful auxiliary," said Fitzurse, impatiently,
"playing the fool in the very moment of utter
necessity. What on earth dost thou purpose by
this absurd disguise at a moment so urgent?"

"To get me a wife," answered De Bracy, coolly, 10
"after the manner of the tribe of Benjamin: which
is as much as to say, that in this same equipment I
will fall upon that herd of Saxon bullocks who have
this night left the castle, and carry off from them the
lovely Rowena." 15

"Art thou mad, De Bracy?" said Fitzurse.
"Bethink thee that, though the men be Saxons,
they are rich and powerful."

"I mean no immediate discovery of myself,"
said De Bracy. "Seem I not in this garb as bold 20
a forester as ever blew horn? The blame of the
violence shall rest with the outlaws of the Yorkshire
forests. I have sure spies on the Saxons' motions.
To-morrow's march brings them within our reach,
and, falcon-ways, we swoop on them at once. 25

---

LINE 4. **Free Companions**: military company that served
anywhere for pay. **6. auxiliary**: helper; assistant.
**11. manner of the tribe of Benjamin.** See Judges 21 : 20-23.
**25. falcon-ways**: like a hawk.

Presently after I will appear in mine own shape, play the courteous knight, rescue the unfortunate and afflicted fair one from the hands of the rude ravishers, conduct her to Front-de-Bœuf's castle, 5 or to Normandy, if it should be necessary, and produce her not again to her kindred until she be the bride and dame of Maurice de Bracy."

"A marvellously sage plan," said Fitzurse, "and, as I think, not entirely of thine own device.   Come, 10 be frank, De Bracy, who aided  thee in the invention?  and who is to assist in the execution?  for, as I think, thine own band lies as far off as York."

"Marry, if thou must needs know," said De 15 Bracy, "it was the Templar Brian de Bois-Guilbert that shaped out the enterprise.   He is to aid me in the onslaught, and he and his followers will personate the outlaws, from whom my valorous arm is, after changing my garb, to rescue the lady."

20 "By my halidome," said Fitzurse, "the plan was worthy of your united wisdom!   Thou mayst, I think, succeed in taking her from her Saxon friends, but how thou wilt rescue her afterwards from the clutches of Bois-Guilbert seems considerably more 25 doubtful.   He is a falcon well accustomed to pounce on a partridge and to hold his prey fast."

"He is a Templar," said De Bracy, "and cannot therefore rival me in my plan of wedding this heiress."

"Then, since nought that I can say," said Fitzurse, " will put this folly from thy imagination, for well I know the obstinacy of thy disposition, at least waste as little time as possible; let not thy folly be lasting as well as untimely." 5

"I tell thee," answered De Bracy, "that it will be the work of a few hours, and I shall be at York at the head of my daring and valorous fellows. But I hear my comrades assembling, and the steeds stamping and neighing in the outer court. Fare- 10 well. I go, like a true knight, to win the smiles of beauty."

"Like a true knight!" repeated Fitzurse, looking after him; " like a fool, I should say, or like a child, who will leave the most serious and needful occu- 15 pation to chase the down of the thistle that drives past him. But it is with such tools that I must work — and for whose advantage? For that of a Prince as unwise as he is profligate, and as likely to be an ungrateful master as he has already proved a 20 rebellious son and an unnatural brother. But he — he too is but one of the tools with which I labor; and, proud as he is, should he presume to separate his interest from mine, this is a secret which he shall soon learn." 25

The meditations of the statesman were here interrupted by the voice of the Prince from an

---

LINE 19. **profligate**: abandoned to vice.

interior apartment calling out, " Noble Waldemar Fitzurse! " and, with bonnet doffed, the future Chancellor, for to such high preferment did the wily Norman aspire, hastened to receive the orders of
5 the future sovereign.

---

LINE **3. Chancellor**: chief minister.

# CHAPTER XVI

## Hermit Entertains Knight

The reader cannot have forgotten that the event of the tournament was decided by the exertions of an unknown knight, whom the spectators had entitled the Black Sluggard. This knight had left the field abruptly when the victory was achieved; 5 and when he was called upon to receive the reward of his valor he was nowhere to be found. In the meantime, while summoned by heralds and by trumpets, the knight was holding his course northward, avoiding all frequented paths, and taking 10 the shortest road through the woodlands. He paused for the night at a small hostelry lying out of the ordinary route, where, however, he obtained from a wandering minstrel news of the event of the tourney. 15

On the next morning the knight departed early, with the intention of making a long journey. Yet his purpose was baffled by the devious paths through which he rode, so that when evening closed upon him he only found himself on the frontiers 20 of the West Riding of Yorkshire. By this time both horse and man required refreshment, and it became necessary, moreover, to look out for some place in which they might spend the night, which was now fast approaching.

After having in vain endeavored to select the 5 most beaten path, in hopes it might lead to the cottage of some herdsman or the silvan lodge of a forester, and having repeatedly found himself totally unable to determine on a choice, the knight resolved to trust to the sagacity of his horse.

10 The good steed, grievously fatigued with so long a day's journey under a rider cased in mail, had no sooner found, by the slackened reins, that he was abandoned to his own guidance, than he seemed to assume new strength and spirit; and whereas 15 formerly he had scarce replied to the spur otherwise than by a groan, he now pricked up his ears, and assumed, of his own accord, a more lively motion. The path which the animal adopted rather turned off from the course pursued by the knight during 20 the day; but as the horse seemed confident in his choice, the rider abandoned himself to his discretion.

He was justified by the event, for the footpath soon after appeared a little wider and more worn, 25 and the tinkle of a small bell gave the knight to understand that he was in the vicinity of some chapel or hermitage.

---

LINE 9. **sagacity**: intelligence; judgment.

Accordingly, he soon reached an open plat of
turf, on the opposite side of which a rock rose
abruptly from a gently sloping plain. At the bottom of the rock, and leaning, as it were, against
it, was constructed a rude hut, built chiefly of 5
the trunks of trees felled in the neighboring
forest, and secured against the weather by having
its crevices stuffed with moss mingled with clay.
The stem of a young fir-tree lopped of its branches,
with a piece of wood tied across near the top, was 10
planted upright by the door, as a rude emblem of the
holy cross. At a little distance on the right hand,
a fountain of the purest water trickled out of the
rock, and was received in a hollow stone, which
labor had formed into a rustic basin. 15

Beside this fountain were the ruins of a very small
chapel, of which the roof had partly fallen in. The
entrance to this ancient place of devotion was under
a very low round arch, ornamented by several
courses of that zig-zag moulding, resembling sharks' 20
teeth, which appears so often in the more ancient
Saxon architecture. A belfry rose above the porch
on four small pillars, within which hung the green
and weatherbeaten bell, the feeble sounds of which
had been some time before heard by the Black 25
Knight.

The whole peaceful and quiet scene lay glimmering in twilight before the eyes of the traveller, giving
him good assurance of lodging for the night; since

it was a special duty of those hermits who dwelt in the woods to exercise hospitality towards benighted or bewildered passengers.

Accordingly, the knight leaped from his horse and 5 assailed the door of the hermitage with the butt of his lance, in order to arouse attention and gain admittance.

It was some time before he obtained any answer, and the reply, when made, was unpropitious.

10 " Pass on, whosoever thou art," was the answer given by a deep hoarse voice from within the hut, " and disturb not the servant of God and St. Dunstan in his evening devotions."

" Worthy father," answered the knight, " here 15 is a poor wanderer bewildered in these woods, who gives thee the opportunity of exercising thy charity and hospitality."

" Good brother," replied the inhabitant of the hermitage, " I have no provisions here which even 20 a dog would share with me, and a horse of any tenderness of nurture would despise my couch; pass therefore on thy way, and God speed thee."

" But how," replied the knight, " is it possible for me to find my way through such a wood as this, 25 when darkness is coming on? I pray you, reverend father, as you are a Christian, to undo your door, and at least point out to me my road."

---

LINE **2. benighted**: overtaken by night. **9. unpropitious**: unfavorable.

"And I pray you, good Christian brother," replied the anchorite, "to disturb me no more."

"The road — the road!" vociferated the knight; "give me directions for the road, if I am to expect no more from thee." 5

"The road," replied the hermit, "is easy to hit. The path from the wood leads to a morass, and from thence to a ford, which, as the rains have abated, may now be passable. When thou hast crossed the ford, thou wilt take care of thy footing up the left 10 bank, as it is somewhat precipitous, and the path, which hangs over the river, has lately given way in sundry places. Thou wilt then keep straight forward ——"

"A broken path — a precipice — a ford — and 15 a morass!" said the knight, interrupting him. "Sir Hermit, if you were the holiest that ever wore beard, you shall scarce prevail on me to hold this road to-night. Either open the door quickly, or, by the rood, I will beat it down and make entry for 20 myself."

"Friend wayfarer," replied the hermit, "be not importunate; if thou puttest me to use the carnal weapon in mine own defence, it will be e'en the worse for you." 25

At this moment a distant noise of barking and

---

LINE **2. anchorite:** hermit. **3. vociferated:** cried out loudly. **20. rood:** cross. **23. importunate:** insistent. **carnal:** worldly.

growling became extremely loud and furious, and made the knight suppose that the hermit, alarmed by his threat of making forcible entry, had called the dogs, who made this clamor to aid him in his 5 defence. Incensed at this preparation on the hermit's part for making good his inhospitable purpose, the knight struck the door so furiously with his foot that posts as well as staples shook with violence.

The anchorite, not caring again to expose his 10 door to a similar shock, now called out aloud: " Patience — patience; spare thy strength, good traveller, and I will presently undo the door, though it may be, my doing so will be little to thy pleasure."

The door accordingly was opened; and the her-15 mit, a large, strong-built man, in his sackcloth gown and hood, girt with a rope of rushes, stood before the knight. He had in one hand a lighted torch, and in the other a baton of crab-tree, so thick and heavy that it might well be termed a club. Two 20 large shaggy dogs, half greyhound, half mastiff, stood ready to rush upon the traveller as soon as the door should be opened. But when the torch glanced upon the lofty crest and golden spurs of the knight who stood without, the hermit, altering 25 probably his original intentions, invited the knight to enter his hut, making excuse for his unwillingness to open his lodge after sunset by alleging the

---

LINE 15. **sackcloth**: coarse cloth used for making sacks.

multitude of robbers and outlaws who were abroad.

"The poverty of your cell, good father," said the knight, looking around him, and seeing nothing

THE BLACK KNIGHT AT THE FRIAR'S CELL

but a bed of leaves, a crucifix rudely carved in oak, 5 a missal, with a rough-hewn table and two stools, and one or two clumsy articles of furniture — "the

LINE 6. **missal**: mass-book; book containing the service of the mass.

poverty of your cell should seem a sufficient defence against any risk of thieves, not to mention the aid of two trusty dogs, large and strong enough, I think, to pull down a stag, and, of course, to match with 5 most men."

" The good keeper of the forest," said the hermit, " hath allowed me the use of these animals to protect my solitude until the times shall mend."

Having said this, he fixed his torch in a twisted 10 branch of iron which served for a candlestick; and having refreshed the fire with some dry wood, he placed a stool upon one side of the table, and beckoned to the knight to do the same upon the other.

15 They sat down, and gazed with great gravity at each other, each thinking in his heart that he had seldom seen a stronger or more athletic figure than was placed opposite to him.

" Reverend hermit," said the knight, after look-20 ing long and fixedly at his host, " were it not to interrupt your devout meditations, I would pray to know three things of your holiness; first, where I am to put my horse? secondly, what I can have for supper? thirdly, where I am to take up my couch 25 for the night?"

" I will reply to you," said the hermit, " with my finger, it being against my rule to speak by words where signs can answer the purpose." So saying, he pointed successively to two corners of the hut.

" Your stable," said he, " is there ; your bed there ;
and," reaching down a platter with two handfuls
of parched pease upon it from the neighboring
shelf, and placing it upon the table, he added,
" your supper is here."                                           5

The knight shrugged his shoulders, and leaving
the hut, brought in his horse, unsaddled him with
much attention, and spread upon the steed's weary
back his own mantle.

The hermit was apparently somewhat moved to 10
compassion by the anxiety which the stranger displayed in tending his horse; for he dragged out of
a recess a bundle of forage, which he spread before
the knight's charger, and immediately afterwards
shook down a quantity of dried fern in the corner 15
which he had assigned for the rider's couch. The
knight returned him thanks for his courtesy ; and,
this duty done, both resumed their seats by the
table, whereon stood the trencher of pease placed
between them. The hermit, after a long grace, set 20
example to his guest by modestly putting into a very
large mouth, furnished with teeth which might have
ranked with those of a boar both in sharpness and
whiteness, some three or four dried pease, a miserable grist, as it seemed, for so large and able a mill. 25

The knight, in order to follow so laudable an example, laid aside his helmet, his corselet, and the

---

LINE **27. corselet**: body armor.

greater part of his armor, and showed to the hermit a head thick-curled with yellow hair, high features, blue eyes, remarkably bright and sparkling, a mouth well formed, having an upper lip clothed with mus-
5 tachioes darker than his hair, and bearing altogether the look of a bold, daring, and enterprising man, with which his strong form well corresponded.

The hermit, as if wishing to answer to the confidence of his guest, threw back his cowl, and showed
10 a round bullet-head belonging to a man in the prime of life. It was a bold bluff countenance, with broad black eyebrows, a well-turned forehead, and cheeks as round and vermilion as those of a trumpeter, from which descended a long and curly black beard.
15 Such a visage, joined to the brawny form of the holy man, spoke rather of sirloins and haunches than of pease and pulse. This incongruity did not escape the guest. After he had with great difficulty accomplished the mastication of a mouthful of the
20 dried pease, he found it absolutely necessary to request his pious entertainer to furnish him with some liquor; who replied to his request by placing before him a large can of the purest water from the fountain.
25 "It is from the well of St. Dunstan," said he, "in which, betwixt sun and sun, he baptized five hundred heathen Danes and Britons — blessed be

---

LINE **9. cowl**: hood. **17. pulse**: beans, peas, etc. **incongruity**: disagreement; inconsistency.

his name!" And applying his black beard to the pitcher, he took a draught much more moderate in quantity than his encomium seemed to warrant.

"It seems to me," said the knight, "that the small morsels which you eat, together with this holy but somewhat thin beverage, have thriven with you marvellously. Holy father, permit a sinful layman to crave thy name?"

"Thou mayst call me," answered the hermit, "the Clerk of Copmanhurst, for so I am termed in these parts. They add, it is true, the epithet holy, but I stand not upon that, as being unworthy of such addition. And now, valiant knight, may I pray ye for the name of my honorable guest?"

"Truly," said the knight, "Holy Clerk of Copmanhurst, men call me in these parts the Black Knight; many, sir, add to it the epithet of Sluggard."

The hermit could scarcely forbear from smiling at his guest's reply.

"I see," said he, "Sir Sluggish Knight, that thou art a man of prudence and of counsel; and, moreover, I see that my poor monastic fare likes thee not; and now I bethink me, Sir Sluggard, that when the charitable keeper of this forest-walk left these dogs for my protection, and also those bundles of forage, he left me also some food, which, being unfit

---

LINE **3. encomium**: high praise. **10. Clerk**: priest. **11. epithet**: adjective expressing quality. **23. likes**: pleases.

for my use, the very recollection of it had escaped me
amid my more weighty meditations."

" I dare be sworn he did so," said the knight;
" I was convinced that there was better food in the
5 cell, Holy Clerk, since you first doffed your cowl.
Let us see the keeper's bounty, therefore, without
delay."

The hermit cast a wistful look upon the knight,
in which there was a sort of comic expression of
10 hesitation, as if uncertain how far he should act
prudently in trusting his guest. There was, however, as much of bold frankness in the knight's
countenance as was possible to be expressed by
features.

15 After exchanging a mute glance or two, the hermit
went to the further side of the hut, and opened a
hutch, which was concealed with great care and
some ingenuity. Out of the recesses of a dark
closet, into which this aperture gave admittance, he
20 brought a large pasty, baked in a pewter platter of
unusual dimensions. This mighty dish he placed
before his guest, who, using his poniard to cut it
open, lost no time in making himself acquainted
with its contents.

25 " How long is it since the good keeper has been
here?" said the knight to his host.

"About two months," answered the father, hastily.

---

Line 17. hutch: chest or box.

THE BLACK KNIGHT IN THE HERMIT'S CELL

" By the true Lord," answered the knight, " everything in your hermitage is miraculous, Holy Clerk! for I would have been sworn that the fat buck which furnished this venison had been running on foot within the week." 5

The hermit was somewhat discountenanced by this observation; and, moreover, he made but a poor figure while gazing on the diminution of the pasty on which his guest was making desperate inroads — a warfare in which his previous profession 10 of abstinence left him no pretext for joining.

" I have been in Palestine, Sir Clerk," said the knight, stopping short of a sudden, " and I bethink me it is a custom there that every host who entertains a guest shall assure him of the wholesomeness 15 of his food by partaking of it along with him. Far be it from me to suspect so holy a man of aught inhospitable; nevertheless, I will be highly bound to you would you comply with this Eastern custom." 20

" To ease your unnecessary scruples, Sir Knight, I will for once depart from my rule," replied the hermit. And as there were no forks in those days, his clutches were instantly in the bowels of the pasty. 25

The ice of ceremony being once broken, it seemed matter of rivalry between the guest and the enter-

---

LINE **6. discountenanced**: confused; embarrassed. **13. bethink me**: call to mind.

tainer which should display the best appetite; and although the former had probably fasted longest, yet the hermit fairly surpassed him.

"Holy Clerk," said the knight, when his hunger was appeased, "I would gage my good horse yonder against a zecchin, that that same honest keeper to whom we are obliged for the venison has left thee a stoup of wine, or some such trifle, by way of ally to this noble pasty. I think, were you to search yonder crypt once more, you would find that I am right in my conjecture."

The hermit only replied by a grin; and returning to the hutch, he produced a leathern bottle, which might contain about four quarts. He also brought forth two large drinking cups, made out of the horn of the urus, and hooped with silver. Having made this goodly provision for washing down the supper, he seemed to think no farther ceremonious scruple necessary on his part; but filling both cups, and saying, in the Saxon fashion, "*Waes hael*, Sir Sluggish Knight!" he emptied his own at a draught.

"*Drinc hael*, Holy Clerk of Copmanhurst!" answered the warrior, and did his host reason in a similar brimmer.

"Holy Clerk," said the stranger, after the first cup was thus swallowed, "I cannot but marvel that

---

LINE **8. stoup**: drinking cup. **10. crypt**: vault. **16. urus**: extinct wild ox. **20.** *Waes hael*: your health. **22.** *Drinc hael*: I drink your health.

a man possessed of such thews and sinews as thine should think of abiding by himself in this wilderness. In my judgment, you are fitter to keep a castle or a fort, eating of the fat and drinking of the strong, than to live here upon pulse and water, or even upon 5 the charity of the keeper. At least, were I as thou, I should find myself both disport and plenty out of the king's deer. There is many a goodly herd in these forests, and a buck will never be missed that goes to the use of St. Dunstan's chaplain." 10

"Sir Sluggish Knight," replied the Clerk, "these are dangerous words, and I pray you to forbear them. I am true hermit to the king and law, and were I to spoil my liege's game, I should be sure of the prison, and, an my gown saved me not, were 15 in some peril of hanging."

"Nevertheless, were I as thou," said the knight, "I would take my walk by moonlight, when foresters and keepers were warm in bed, and ever and anon I would let fly a shaft among the herds of dun 20 deer that feed in the glades. Resolve me, Holy Clerk, hast thou never practised such a pastime?"

"Friend Sluggard," answered the hermit, "thou hast seen all that can concern thee of my house-

---

LINE **14.** liege's: sovereign's. **15.** an my gown saved me not. Under old English law the clergy were free from criminal prosecution, and were judged by church courts. Note the phrase "benefit of clergy." **20.** dun: grayish brown. **21. Resolve:** tell.

keeping, and something more than he deserves who takes up his quarters by violence. Credit me, it is better to enjoy the good which God sends thee, than to be impertinently curious how it comes. Fill
5 thy cup, and welcome; and do not, I pray thee, by further impertinent inquiries, put me to show that thou couldst hardly have made good thy lodging had I been earnest to oppose thee."

"By my faith," said the knight, "thou makest
10 me more curious than ever! Thou art the most mysterious hermit I ever met; and I will know more of thee ere we part. As for thy threats, know, holy man, thou speakest to one whose trade it is to find out danger wherever it is to be met with."

15 "Sir Sluggish Knight, I drink to thee," said the hermit, "respecting thy valor much, but deeming wondrous slightly of thy discretion. If thou wilt take equal arms with me, I will give thee, in all friendship and brotherly love, such sufficing penance
20 and complete absolution that thou shalt not for the next twelve months sin the sin of excess of curiosity."

The knight pledged him, and desired him to name his weapons.

25 "There is none," replied the hermit, "from the scissors of Delilah, and the tenpenny nail of Jael

---

LINE **19. sufficing**: sufficient. **20. absolution**: forgiveness. **26. scissors of Delilah**: Judges 16:18–20. **nail of Jael**: Judges 4:18–22.

to the scimitar of Goliath, at which I am not a match for thee. But, if I am to make the election, what sayst thou, good friend, to these trinkets?"

Thus speaking, he opened another hutch, and took out from it a couple of broadswords and bucklers, such as were used by the yeomanry of the period. The knight, who watched his motions, observed that this second place of concealment was furnished with two or three good long-bows, a cross-bow, a bundle of bolts for the latter, and a half a dozen sheaves of arrows for the former. A harp, and other matters of a very uncanonical appearance, were also visible when this dark recess was opened.

"I promise thee, brother Clerk," said he, "I will ask thee no more offensive questions. The contents of that cupboard are an answer to all my inquiries; and I see a weapon there (here he stooped and took out the harp) on which I would more gladly prove my skill with thee than at the sword and buckler."

"I hope, Sir Knight," said the hermit, "thou hast given no good reason for thy surname of the Sluggard. I do promise thee, I suspect thee grievously. Nevertheless, thou art my guest, and I will not put thy manhood to the proof without thine own free will. Sit thee down, then, and fill thy cup; let us drink, sing, and be merry. Come, fill a flagon, for it will crave some time to tune the harp."

---

LINE **1. scimitar of Goliath**: I Samuel 17.  **12. uncanonical**: contrary to rules of church.

## CHAPTER XVII

### Harp and Song

The guest found it no easy matter to bring the harp to harmony.

"Methinks, holy father," said he, "the instrument wants one string, and the rest have been 5 somewhat misused."

"Ay, mark'st thou that?" replied the hermit; "that shows thee a master of the craft. I told Allan-a-Dale, the northern minstrel, that he would damage the harp if he touched it after the seventh 10 cup, but he would not be controlled. Friend, I drink to thy successful performance."

When the knight had brought the strings into some order, after a short prelude he said, "I will assay a ballad composed by a Saxon gleeman, whom 15 I knew in Holy Land."

It speedily appeared that, if the guest was not a complete master of the minstrel art, his taste for it had at least been cultivated under the best instructors. Art had taught him to soften the 20 faults of a voice which had little compass, and was

LINE **8**. **Allan-a-Dale.** See page 617. **14**. **gleeman:** minstrel; entertainer who sang or recited poetry.

naturally rough rather than mellow.  His performance, therefore, might have been termed very
respectable by abler judges than the hermit, especially as the knight threw into the notes now a degree
of spirit, and now of plaintive enthusiasm, which 5
gave force and energy to the verses which he sung.

### THE CRUSADER'S RETURN

#### I

High deeds achieved of knightly fame,
From Palestine the champion came;
The cross upon his shoulders borne                    10
Battle and blast had dimm'd and torn.
Each dint upon his batter'd shield
Was token of a foughten field;
And thus, beneath his lady's bower,
He sung, as fell the twilight hour;                   15

#### 2

" Joy to the fair ! — thy knight behold,
Return'd from yonder land of gold.
No wealth he brings, nor wealth can need
Save his good arms and battle-steed,
His spurs, to dash against a foe,                     20
His lance and sword to lay him low;
Such all the trophies of his toil,
Such — and the hope of Tekla's smile !

#### 3

" Joy to the fair ! whose constant knight
Her favor fired to feats of might;                    25
Unnoted shall she not remain,
Where meet the bright and noble train;

Minstrel shall sing and herald tell :
' Mark yonder maid of beauty well,
'Tis she for whose bright eyes was won
The listed field at Askalon !

### 4

"'Note well her smile ! it edged the blade
Which fifty wives to widows made,
When, vain his strength and Mahound's spell,
Iconium's turban'd Soldan fell.
Seest thou her locks, whose sunny glow
Half shows, half shades, her neck of snow?
Twines not of them one golden thread,
But for its sake a Paynim bled.'

### 5

" Joy to the fair ! — my name unknown,
Each deed and all its praise thine own ;
Then, oh ! unbar this churlish gate,
The night dew falls, the hour is late.
Inured to Syria's glowing breath,
I feel the north breeze chill as death ;
Let grateful love quell maiden shame
And grant him bliss who brings thee fame."

During this performance, the hermit demeaned himself much like a first-rate critic of the present

---

LINE **4. Askalon** : a city about forty miles from Jerusalem.
**7. Mahound's** : Mohammed's.   **8. Iconium's turban'd Soldan** :
sultan of Iconium, a district of Turkey in Asia.   **12. Paynim** :
non-Christian, especially Mohammedan.   **17. Inured** : accustomed.   **21. demeaned** : conducted.

day at a new opera. He reclined back upon his seat with his eyes half shut: now folding his hands and twisting his thumbs, he seemed absorbed in attention, and anon, balancing his expanded palms, he gently flourished them in time to the music. 5 At one or two favorite cadences he threw in a little assistance of his own, where the knight's voice seemed unable to carry the air so high as his worshipful taste approved. When the song was ended, the anchorite emphatically declared it a good one, 10 and well sung.

" And yet," said he, " I think my Saxon countrymen had herded long enough with the Normans to fall into the tone of their melancholy ditties. What took the honest knight from home? or what 15 could he expect but to find his mistress agreeably engaged with a rival on his return, and his serenade, as they call it, as little regarded as the caterwauling of a cat in the gutter? Nevertheless, Sir Knight, I drink this cup to thee, to the success of all true 20 lovers. I fear you are none."

And so saying, he reached the harp and entertained his guest with the following characteristic song, to a sort of derry-down chorus, appropriate to an old English ditty:

25

---

LINE **6. cadences**: closes of musical phrases. **18. caterwauling**: harsh, offensive cry of cats. **24. derry-down**: meaningless refrain in old songs.

## THE BAREFOOTED FRIAR

### 1

I'll give thee, good fellow, a twelvemonth or twain,
To search Europe through, from Byzantium to Spain;
But ne'er shall you find, should you search till you tire,
5 So happy a man as the Barefooted Friar.

### 2

Your knight for his lady pricks forth in career,
And is brought home at evensong prick't through with a spear;
I confess him in haste — for his lady desires
No comfort on earth save the Barefooted Friar's.

### 3

10 Your monarch! Pshaw! many a prince has been known
To barter his robes for our cowl and our gown;
But which of us e'er felt the idle desire
To exchange for a crown the grey hood of a Friar !

### 4

The Friar has walk'd out, and where'er he has gone,
15 The land and its fatness is mark'd for his own;
He can roam where he lists, he can stop when he tires,
For every man's house is the Barefooted Friar's.

### 5

He's expected at noon, and no wight till he comes
May profane the great chair, or the porridge of plums;
20 For the best of the cheer, and the seat by the fire,
Is the undenied right of the Barefooted Friar.

---

LINE **1. FRIAR.** See page 621. **3. Byzantium** : Constantinople. **18. wight** : person.

### 6

He's expected at night, and the pasty's made hot,
They broach the brown ale, and they fill the black pot,
And the goodwife would wish the goodman in the mire
Ere he lack'd a soft pillow, the Barefooted Friar.

### 7

Long flourish the sandal, the cord, and the cope,       5
The dread of the devil and trust of the Pope;
For to gather life's roses, unscathed by the briar
Is granted alone to the Barefooted Friar.


" By my troth," said the knight, " thou hast sung
well and lustily, and in high praise of thine order."  10

Fast and furious grew the mirth of the parties,
and many a song was exchanged betwixt them,
when their revels were interrupted by a loud knock-
ing at the door of the hermitage.

The occasion of this interruption we can only  15
explain by resuming the adventures of another set
of our characters.

---

LINE **2. broach**: tap.    **5. cope**: long hooded cloak.
**7. unscathed**: unhurt.

# CHAPTER XVIII

## Matchmaking on the Homeward Journey

When Cedric the Saxon saw his son drop down senseless in the lists at Ashby, his first impulse was to order him into the custody and care of his own attendants; but the words choked in his throat.
5 He could not bring himself to acknowledge, in presence of such an assembly, the son whom he had renounced and disinherited. He ordered, however, Oswald to keep an eye upon him; and directed that officer, with two of his serfs, to convey Ivan-
10 hoe to Ashby as soon as the crowd had dispersed. Oswald, however, was anticipated in this good office. The crowd dispersed, indeed, but the knight was nowhere to be seen.

It was in vain that Cedric's cupbearer looked
15 around for his young master; it seemed as if the fairies had conveyed him from the spot. Perhaps Oswald — for the Saxons were very superstitious — might have adopted some such hypothesis to account for Ivanhoe's disappearance, had he not
20 suddenly cast his eye upon a person attired like

LINE 7. renounced: refused to acknowledge longer.
18. hypothesis: unproved theory.

232

a squire, in whom he recognized the features of his fellow-servant Gurth. Anxious concerning his master's fate, and in despair at his sudden disappearance, the translated swineherd was searching for him everywhere, and had neglected, in doing so, the concealment on which his own safety depended. Oswald deemed it his duty to secure Gurth, as a fugitive of whose fate his master was to judge.

Renewing his inquiries concerning the fate of Ivanhoe, the only information which the cupbearer could collect from the bystanders was, that the knight had been raised with care by certain well-attired grooms, and placed in a litter belonging to a lady among the spectators, which had immediately transported him out of the press. Oswald, on receiving this intelligence, resolved to return to his master for further instructions, carrying along with him Gurth, whom he considered in some sort as a deserter from the service of Cedric.

The Saxon had been under very intense and agonizing apprehensions concerning his son. But no sooner was he informed that Ivanhoe was in careful, and probably in friendly, hands than the paternal anxiety gave way anew to the feeling of injured pride and resentment at what he termed Wilfred's filial disobedience. " Let him wander

---

LINE **4. translated**: transformed; changed. **13. litter**: couch shut in by curtains and carried on men's shoulders or by horses.

his way," said he; "let those leech his wounds for whose sake he encountered them. He is fitter to do the juggling tricks of the Norman chivalry than to maintain the fame and honor of his 5 English ancestry with the glaive and brown-bill, the good old weapons of his country."

"If to maintain the honor of ancestry," said Rowena, who was present, "it is sufficient to be wise in council and brave in execution, to be boldest 10 among the bold, and gentlest among the gentle, I know no voice, save his father's —— "

"Be silent, Lady Rowena! on this subject only I hear you not. Prepare yourself for the Prince's festival: we have been summoned thither with 15 unwonted circumstance of honor and of courtesy, such as the haughty Normans have rarely used to our race since the fatal day of Hastings. Thither will I go, were it only to show these proud Normans how little the fate of a son who could defeat their 20 bravest can affect a Saxon."

"Thither," said Rowena, "do I NOT go."

"Remain at home then, ungrateful lady," answered Cedric. "I seek the noble Athelstane, and with him attend the banquet of John of An-25 jou."

He went accordingly to the banquet, of which we have already mentioned the principal events. Im-

---

LINE 1. leech: heal. 5. glaive: sword. brown-bill: combined spear and battle-axe.

mediately upon retiring from the castle, the Saxon thanes, with their attendants, took horse; and it was during the bustle which attended their doing so that Cedric for the first time cast his eyes upon the deserter Gurth. The noble Saxon had returned 5 from the banquet, as we have seen, in no very placid humor, and wanted but a pretext for wreaking his anger upon some one. "The gyves!" he said — "the gyves! Oswald — Hundebert! Dogs and villains! why leave ye the knave unfet- 10 tered?"

Without daring to remonstrate, the companions of Gurth bound him with a halter, as the readiest cord which occurred. He submitted to the operation without remonstrance, except that, darting 15 a reproachful look at his master, he said, "This comes of loving your flesh and blood better than mine own."

"To horse, and forward!" said Cedric.

"It is indeed full time," said the noble Athel- 20 stane; "for, if we ride not the faster, the worthy Abbot Waltheoff's preparations for a rere-supper will be altogether spoiled."

The travellers, however, used such speed as to reach the convent of St. Withold's before the appre- 25 hended evil took place. The Abbot, himself of ancient Saxon descent, received the noble Saxons

---

LINE 8. gyves: fetters; shackles. 22. rere-supper: night-meal, sometimes after regular supper.

with the profuse hospitality of their nation, wherein they indulged to a late, or rather an early, hour.

As the cavalcade left the court of the monastery the next morning, an incident happened somewhat alarming the Saxons. The apprehension of impending evil was inspired by no less respectable a prophet than a large lean black dog, which, sitting upright, howled most piteously as the foremost riders left the gate, and presently afterwards, barking wildly, and jumping to and fro, seemed bent upon attaching itself to the party.

"I like not that music, father Cedric," said Athelstane.

"Nor I either, uncle," said Wamba; "I greatly fear we shall have to pay the piper."

"In my mind," said Athelstane, upon whose memory the Abbot's good ale had made a favorable impression — "in my mind we had better turn back and abide with the Abbot until the afternoon. It is unlucky to travel where your path is crossed by a monk, a hare, or a howling dog, until you have eaten your next meal."

"Away!" said Cedric, impatiently; "the day is already too short for our journey. For the dog, I know it to be the cur of the runaway slave Gurth, a useless fugitive like its master."

So saying, and rising at the same time in his stirrups, he launched his javelin at poor Fangs; for Fangs it was, who, having traced his master thus far, had here lost him, and was now rejoicing at his reappearance. The javelin inflicted a wound upon the animal's shoulder, and narrowly missed pinning him to the earth; and Fangs fled howling from the presence of the enraged thane. Gurth's 5 heart swelled within him. Having in vain attempted to raise his hand to his eyes, he said to Wamba, who, seeing his master's ill-humor, had prudently retreated to the rear, "I pray thee, do me the kindness to wipe my eyes with the skirt of 10 thy mantle; the dust offends me, and these bonds will not let me help myself one way or another."

Wamba did him the service he required, and they rode side by side for some time, during which Gurth maintained a moody silence. At length he 15 could repress his feelings no longer.

"Friend Wamba," said he, "of all those who are fools enough to serve Cedric, thou alone hast dexterity enough to make thy folly acceptable to him. Go to him, therefore, and tell him that 20 neither for love nor fear will Gurth serve him longer. He may strike the head from me, he may scourge me, he may load me with irons, but henceforth he shall never compel me either to love or to obey him. Go to him, then, and tell him 25 that Gurth the son of Beowulph renounces his service."

"Assuredly," said Wamba, "fool as I am, I shall not do your fool's errand. Cedric hath another javelin stuck into his girdle, and thou knowest he does not always miss his mark."

"I care not," replied Gurth, "how soon he makes a mark of me. Yesterday he left Wilfred, my young master, in his blood. To-day he has striven to kill before my face the only other living creature that ever showed me kindness. I will never forgive him!"

"To my thinking now," said the Jester, who was frequently wont to act as peacemaker in the family, "our master did not propose to hurt Fangs, but only to affright him. For, if you observed, he rose in his stirrups, as thereby meaning to overcast the mark; and so he would have done, but Fangs happening to bound up at the very moment, received a scratch, which I will be bound to heal with a penny's breadth of tar."

"If I thought so," said Gurth — "if I could but think so; but no, I saw the javelin was well aimed; I heard it whizz through the air, and it quivered after it had pitched in the ground, as if with regret for having missed its mark. By the hog dear to St. Anthony, I renounce him!"

And the indignant swineherd resumed his sullen silence, which no efforts of the Jester could again induce him to break.

Meanwhile Cedric and Athelstane conversed together on the state of the land and on the chance which there was that the oppressed Saxons might

be able to free themselves from the yoke of the
Normans. On this subject Cedric was all animation. The restoration of the independence of his
race was the idol of his heart, to which he had
willingly sacrificed domestic happiness and the 5
interests of his own son. But, in order to achieve
this great revolution in favor of the native English, it was necessary that they should be united
among themselves. The necessity of choosing
their chief from the Saxon blood-royal had been 10
made a solemn condition by those whom Cedric
had entrusted with his secret plans and hopes.
Athelstane had this quality at least; and though
he had few mental accomplishments or talents to
recommend him as a leader, he had still a goodly 15
person, was no coward, had been accustomed to
martial exercises, and was known to be liberal and
hospitable. But whatever pretensions Athelstane
had to be considered as head of the Saxon confed-
eracy, many of that nation were disposed to prefer 20
to his the title of the Lady Rowena, who drew her
descent from Alfred.

It would have been no difficult thing for Cedric
to have placed himself at the head of a third party.
To counterbalance their royal descent, he had 25
courage, activity, energy, and, above all, a devoted
attachment to the cause. Instead, however, of
dividing yet further his weakened nation by forming a faction of his own, it was a leading part of

Cedric's plan to extinguish that which already existed by promoting a marriage betwixt Rowena and Athelstane. An obstacle occurred to this his favorite project in the mutual attachment of his 5 ward and his son; and hence the original cause of the banishment of Wilfred from the house of his father.

This stern measure Cedric had adopted in hopes that, during Wilfred's absence, Rowena might 10 relinquish her preference; but in this hope he was disappointed — a disappointment which might be attributed in part to the mode in which his ward had been educated. Cedric, to whom the name of Alfred was as that of a deity, had treated the sole 15 remaining scion of that great monarch with a degree of observance such as, perhaps, was in those days scarce paid to an acknowledged princess. Rowena's will had been in almost all cases a law to his household; and Cedric himself seemed to take a pride 20 in acting as the first of her subjects.

It was in vain that he attempted to dazzle her with the prospect of a visionary throne. Rowena, who possessed strong sense, neither considered his plan as practicable nor as desirable, so far as she 25 was concerned, could it have been achieved. Without attempting to conceal her preference of Wilfred of Ivanhoe, she declared that, were that fav-

---

LINE **15**. **scion**: descendant.

ored knight out of question, she would rather take refuge in a convent than share a throne with Athelstane, whom, having always despised, she now began, on account of the trouble she received on his account, thoroughly to detest.

Nevertheless, Cedric persisted in using every means in his power to bring about the proposed match, in which he conceived he was rendering an important service to the Saxon cause. The sudden and romantic appearance of his son in the lists at Ashby he had justly regarded as almost a death's blow to his hopes. His paternal affection, it is true, had for an instant gained the victory over pride and patriotism; but both had returned in full force, and under their joint operation he was now bent upon making a determined effort for the union of Athelstane and Rowena, together with expediting those other measures which seemed necessary to forward the restoration of Saxon independence.

On this last subject he was now laboring with Athelstane. If Athelstane had the courage to encounter danger, he at least hated the trouble of going to seek it; and while he agreed in the general principles laid down by Cedric concerning the claim of the Saxons to independence, and was still more easily convinced of his own title to reign over them when that independence should be attained, yet when the means of asserting these rights came to be discussed, he was still Athelstane the Unready — slow, irresolute, procrastinating, and unenterprising. The warm and impassioned exhortations of Cedric had as little effect upon his impassive temper as red-hot balls alighting in the water, which produce a little sound and smoke, and are instantly extinguished.

If, leaving this task, which might be compared to hammering upon cold iron, Cedric fell back to his ward Rowena, he received little more satisfaction from conferring with her. To this sturdy Saxon, therefore, the day's journey was fraught with all manner of displeasure and discomfort.

At noon, upon the motion of Athelstane, the travellers paused in a woodland shade by a fountain, to repose their horses and partake of some provisions. Their repast was a pretty long one; and these several interruptions rendered it impossible for them to hope to reach Rotherwood without travelling all night, a conviction which induced them to proceed on their way at a more hasty pace than they had hitherto used.

---

LINE **2. irresolute**: undecided. **procrastinating**: delaying. **3. impassioned**: stirring. **4. impassive**: lacking feeling.

# CHAPTER XIX

### Prisoners of Masked Bandits

The travellers had now reached the verge of the wooded country, and were about to plunge into its recesses, held dangerous at that time from the number of outlaws who occupied the forests in such large bands as could easily bid defiance to the 5 feeble police of the period. From these rovers, however, notwithstanding the lateness of the hour, Cedric and Athelstane accounted themselves secure, as they had in attendance ten servants, besides Wamba and Gurth, whose aid could not be counted 10 upon, the one being a jester and the other a captive. It may be added, that in travelling thus late through the forest, Cedric and Athelstane relied on their descent and character as well as their courage. The outlaws, whom the severity of the 15 forest laws had reduced to this roving and desperate mode of life, were chiefly peasants and yeomen of Saxon descent, and were generally supposed to respect the persons and property of their countrymen. 20

As the travellers journeyed on their way, they were alarmed by repeated cries for assistance; and when they rode up to the place from whence they came, they were surprised to find a horse-litter placed upon the ground, beside which sat a young woman, richly dressed in the Jewish fashion, while an old man, whose yellow cap proclaimed him to 5 belong to the same nation, walked up and down with gestures expressive of the deepest despair.

To the inquiries of Athelstane and Cedric, Isaac of York (for it was our old friend) explained that he had hired a body-guard of six men at Ashby, 10 together with mules for carrying the litter of a sick friend. This party had undertaken to escort him as far as Doncaster. They had come thus far in safety; but, having received information from a wood-cutter that there was a strong band of out-15 laws lying in wait in the woods before them, Isaac's mercenaries had not only taken flight, but had carried off with them the horses which bore the litter, and left the Jew and his daughter without the means either of defence or of retreat, to be 20 plundered, and probably murdered, by the banditti. " Would it but please your valors," added Isaac, in a tone of deep humiliation, " to permit the poor Jews to travel under your safeguard, I swear that never has favor been conferred which 25 shall be more gratefully acknowledged."

" Dog of a Jew!" said Athelstane, "dost not remember how thou didst beard us in the gallery at the tilt-yard? Ask neither aid nor company from us; and if they rob only such as thee, who rob all the world, I, for mine own share, shall hold them right honest folk."

Cedric did not assent to the severe proposal of his companion. "We shall do better," said he, "to leave them two of our attendants and two horses to convey them back to the next village. It will diminish our strength but little; and with your good sword, noble Athelstane, and the aid of those who remain, it will be light work for us to face twenty of those runagates." 10

Rowena, somewhat alarmed by the mention of outlaws in force, strongly seconded the proposal of her guardian. But Rebecca, suddenly quitting her dejected posture, and making her way through the attendants to the palfrey of the Saxon lady, 15 knelt down, and kissed the hem of Rowena's garment. Then, rising and throwing back her veil, she implored her that she would have compassion upon them, and suffer them to go forward under their safeguard. "It is not for myself that I pray 20 this favor," said Rebecca; "nor is it even for that poor old man. But it is in the name of one dear to many, and dear even to you, that I beseech you to let this sick person be transported with care and tenderness under your protection. For, if 25 evil chance him, the last moment of your life would be embittered with regret for denying that which I ask of you."

---

LINE **10. runagates**: vagabonds.

The noble and solemn air with which Rebecca made this appeal gave it double weight with the fair Saxon.

"The man is old and feeble," she said to her
5 guardian, "the maiden young and beautiful, their friend sick and in peril of his life; we cannot as Christians leave them in this extremity. Let them unload two of the sumpter mules and put the baggage behind two of the serfs. The mules may
10 transport the litter, and we have led horses for the old man and his daughter."

Cedric readily assented to what she proposed, and Athelstane only added the condition that they should travel in the rear of the whole party.

15 The change of baggage was hastily achieved; for the single word "outlaws" rendered every one sufficiently alert, and the approach of twilight made the sound yet more impressive. Amid the bustle, Gurth was taken from horseback, in the course of
20 which removal he prevailed upon the Jester to slack the cord with which his arms were bound. It was so negligently refastened, perhaps intentionally, on the part of Wamba, that Gurth found no difficulty in freeing his arms altogether from
25 bondage, and then, gliding into the thicket, he made his escape from the party.

The bustle had been considerable, and it was

---

LINE 8. **sumpter mules**: mules for carrying baggage.

some time before Gurth was missed. When it began to be whispered among them that Gurth had actually disappeared, they were under such immediate expectation of an attack from the out-laws that it was not held convenient to pay much 5 attention to the circumstance.

The path upon which the party travelled was now so narrow as not to admit above two riders abreast, and began to descend into a dingle, trav-ersed by a brook whose banks were broken, swampy, 10 and overgrown with dwarf willows. Cedric and Athelstane, who were at the head of their retinue, saw the risk of being attacked at this pass; but no better mode of preventing the danger occurred to them than that they should hasten through the 15 defile as fast as possible. Advancing, therefore, with-out much order, they had just crossed the brook with a part of their followers, when they were assailed in front, flank, and rear at once, with an impetuosity to which, in their confused and ill-prepared condi- 20 tion, it was impossible to offer effectual resistance.

Both the Saxon chiefs were made prisoners at the same moment, and each under circumstances expressive of his character. Cedric, the instant that an enemy appeared, launched at him his re- 25 maining javelin, which, taking better effect than that which he had hurled at Fangs, nailed the man

---

LINE **9. dingle** : narrow valley.  **19. impetuosity** : violence.

against an oak-tree that happened to be close
behind him. Thus far successful, Cedric spurred
his horse against a second, drawing his sword at
the same time, and striking with such inconsiderate
5 fury that his weapon encountered a thick branch
which hung over him, and he was disarmed by the
violence of his own blow. He was instantly made
prisoner, and pulled from his horse by two or three
of the banditti who crowded around him. Athel-
10 stane shared his captivity, his bridle having been
seized and he himself forcibly dismounted long before he could draw his weapon. Of all the train
none escaped except Wamba, who showed upon
the occasion much more courage than those who
15 pretended to greater sense. He possessed himself
of a sword belonging to one of the domestics, laid
it about him like a lion, drove back several who
approached him, and made a brave though ineffectual attempt to succor his master. Finding
20 himself overpowered, the Jester at length threw
himself from his horse, plunged into the thicket,
and, favored by the general confusion, escaped
from the scene of action.

Yet the valiant Jester, as soon as he found him-
25 self safe, hesitated more than once whether he
should not turn back and share the captivity of a
master to whom he was sincerely attached.

---

LINE 4. **inconsiderate**: thoughtless; rash.

"I have heard men talk of the blessings of freedom," he said to himself, "but I wish any wise man would teach me what use to make of it now that I have it."

As he pronounced these words aloud, a voice very near him called out in a low and cautious tone, "Wamba!" and at the same time a dog, which he recognized to be Fangs, jumped up and fawned upon him. "Gurth!" answered Wamba with the same caution, and the swineherd immediately stood before him.

"What is the matter?" said he, eagerly; "what mean these cries and that clashing of swords?"

"Only a trick of the times," said Wamba; "they are all prisoners."

"Who are prisoners?" exclaimed Gurth, impatiently.

"My lord, and my lady, and Athelstane, and Hundebert, and Oswald."

"In the name of God!" said Gurth, "how came they prisoners? and to whom?"

"Our master was too ready to fight," said the Jester, "and Athelstane was not ready enough, and no other person was ready at all. And they are prisoners to green cassocks and black visors. And they lie all tumbled about on the green, like the crab-apples that you shake down to your swine. And I would laugh at it," said the honest Jester, "if I could for weeping." And he shed tears of unfeigned sorrow.

Gurth's countenance kindled. "Wamba," he said, "thou hast a weapon, and thy heart was ever stronger than thy brain; we are only two, but a sudden attack from men of resolution will do much; follow me!"

"Whither? and for what purpose?" said the Jester.

"To rescue Cedric."

"But you have renounced his service but now," said Wamba.

"That," said Gurth, "was but while he was fortunate; follow me!"

As the Jester was about to obey, a third person suddenly made his appearance and commanded them both to halt. From his dress and arms, Wamba would have conjectured him to be one of those outlaws who had just assailed his master; but, besides that he wore no mask, the glittering baldric across his shoulder, with the rich bugle-horn which it supported, as well as the calm and commanding expression of his voice and manner, made him, notwithstanding the twilight, recognize Locksley, the yeoman who had been victorious in the contest for the prize of archery.

"What is the meaning of all this," said he, "or who is it that rifle, and ransom, and make prisoners in these forests?"

"You may look at their cassocks close by," said Wamba, "and see whether they be thy children's coats or no; for they are as like thine own as one green pea-cod is to another."

"I will learn that presently," answered Locks- 5 ley; "and I charge ye, on peril of your lives, not to stir from the place where ye stand, until I have returned. Obey me, and it shall be the better for you and your masters. Yet stay, I must render myself as like these men as possible." 10

So saying, he unbuckled his baldric with the bugle, took a feather from his cap, and gave them to Wamba; then drew a vizard from his pouch, and repeating his charges to them to stand fast, went to execute his purposes of reconnoitering. 15

"Shall we stand fast, Gurth?" said Wamba, "or shall we e'en give him leg-bail? In my foolish mind, he had all the equipage of a thief too much in readiness to be himself a true man."

"Let him be the devil," said Gurth, "an he will. 20 We can be no worse of waiting his return. If he belong to that party, he must already have given them the alarm, and it will avail nothing either to fight or fly. Besides, I have late experience that arrant thieves are not the worst men in the world 25 to have to deal with."

---

LINE **1.** **cassocks** : coats or cloaks. **13.** **vizard** : same as *visor;* mask. **17.** **give him leg-bail** : run away.

The yeoman returned in the course of a few minutes.

"Friend Gurth," he said, "I have mingled among yon men, and have learnt to whom they belong, and whither they are bound. There is, I think, no chance that they will proceed to any actual violence against their prisoners. For three men to attempt them at this moment were little else than madness; for they are good men of war, and have, as such, placed sentinels to give the alarm when any one approaches. But I trust soon to gather such a force as may act in defiance of all their precautions. You are both servants, and, as I think, faithful servants, of Cedric the Saxon, the friend of the rights of Englishmen. He shall not want English hands to help him in this extremity. Come, then, with me, until I gather more aid."

So saying, he walked through the wood at a great pace, followed by the jester and the swineherd.

## CHAPTER XX

### Rescuers Assemble

It was after three hours' good walking that the servants of Cedric, with their mysterious guide, arrived at a small opening in the forest, in the centre of which grew an oak-tree of enormous magnitude, throwing its twisted branches in every direction. Beneath this tree four or five yeomen lay stretched on the ground, while another, as sentinel, walked to and fro in the moonlight shade.

Upon hearing the sound of feet approaching, the watch instantly gave the alarm, and the sleepers as suddenly started up and bent their bows. Six arrows placed on the string were pointed towards the quarter from which the travellers approached, when their guide, being recognized, was welcomed with every token of respect and attachment, and all signs and fears of a rough reception at once subsided.

" Where is the Miller? " was his first question.

" On the road towards Rotherham."

" With how many? " demanded the leader, for such he seemed to be.

" With six men, and good hope of booty."

"And where is Allan-a-Dale?" said Locksley.

"Walked up towards the Watling Street to watch for the Prior of Jorvaulx."

"That is well thought on also," replied the Captain; "and where is the Friar?"

"In his cell."

"Thither will I go," said Locksley. "Disperse and seek your companions. Collect what force you can, for there's game afoot that must be hunted hard, and will turn to bay. Meet me here by daybreak. And, stay," he added, "I have forgotten what is most necessary of the whole. Two of you take the road quickly towards Torquilstone, the castle of Front-de-Bœuf. A set of gallants, who have been masquerading in such guise as our own, are carrying a band of prisoners thither. Watch them closely, and despatch one of your comrades, the lightest of foot, to bring the news of the yeomen thereabout."

They promised implicit obedience, and departed with alacrity on their differing errands. In the meanwhile, their leader and his two companions, who now looked upon him with great respect, as well as some fear, pursued their way to the chapel of Copmanhurst.

When they had reached the little moonlight glade, having in front the ruinous chapel and the

---

LINE **2. Watling Street**: a road from Dover to Chester. **10. turn to bay**: turn to fight.

rude hermitage, Wamba whispered to Gurth, " If
this be the habitation of a thief, it makes good the
old proverb, ' The nearer the church the farther
from God.' And by my cockscomb," he added,
" I think it be even so. Harken to the singing in ₅
the hermitage ! "

In fact, the anchorite and his guest were perform-
ing, at the full extent of their very powerful lungs,
an old drinking song, of which this was the burden :

> "Come, trowl the brown bowl to me,          ₁₀
>     Bully boy, bully boy,
>   Come, trowl the brown bowl to me.
>     Ho ! jolly Jenkin, I spy a knave in drinking,
>   Come, trowl the brown bowl to me."

" Now, that is not ill sung," said Wamba, who ₁₅
had thrown in a few of his own flourishes to help
out the chorus. " But who, in the saint's name,
ever expected to have heard such a jolly chant come
from out a hermit's cell at midnight ! "

" Marry, that should I," said Gurth, " for the ₂₀
jolly Clerk of Copmanhurst is a known man, and
kills half the deer that are stolen in this walk."

While they were thus speaking, Locksley's loud
and repeated knocks had at length disturbed the
anchorite and his guest. " By my beads," said the ₂₅
hermit, stopping short in a grand flourish, " here

---

LINE 4. **cockscomb** : jester's cap, which had on it a red
ridge like the comb of a cock or rooster. **9. burden** : chorus
or refrain. **10. trowl** : pass.

come more benighted guests. I would not for my cowl that they found us in this goodly exercise. Get thine iron pot on thy head then, friend Sluggard, while I remove these pewter flagons; and to
5 drown the clatter — for, in faith, I feel somewhat unsteady — strike into the tune which thou hearest me sing. It is no matter for the words; I scarce know them myself."

So saying, he struck up a thundering *De pro-*
10 *fundis clamavi,* under cover of which he removed the apparatus of their banquet; while the knight, laughing heartily, and arming himself all the while, assisted his host with his voice from time to time as his mirth permitted.

15 "What devil's matins are you after at this hour?" said a voice from without.

"Heaven forgive you, Sir Traveller!" said the hermit, whose own voice, and perhaps his nocturnal potations, prevented from recognizing accents
20 which were familiar to him. "Wend on your way, and disturb not the devotions of me and my holy brother."

"Mad priest," answered the voice from without, "open to Locksley!"

25 "All's safe — all's right," said the hermit to his companion.

---

LINE **9.** *De profundis clamavi.* Out of the depths have I cried. **15. matins:** midnight or morning prayers. **19. potations:** drinks.

" But who is he? " said the Black Knight.

" Who is he? " answered the hermit; " I tell thee he is a friend."

" But what friend? " answered the knight; " for he may be friend to thee and none of mine." 5

" What friend! " replied the hermit; " why, he is the very same honest keeper I told thee of a while since."

" Ay, as honest a keeper as thou art a pious hermit," replied the knight, "I doubt it not.  But undo 10 the door to him before he beat it from its hinges."

The dogs, which had made a dreadful baying at the commencement of the disturbance, seemed now to recognize the voice of him who stood without; for, totally changing their manner, they scratched 15 and whined at the door, as if interceding for his admission.  The hermit speedily unbolted his portal, and admitted Locksley, with his two companions.

" Why, hermit," was the yeoman's first question 20 as soon as he beheld the knight, " what boon companion hast thou here? "

" A brother of our order," replied the Friar, shaking his head.

" He is a monk of the church militant, I think," 25 answered Locksley; " and there be more of them abroad.  I tell thee, Friar, thou must take up the

---

LINE **25. militant**: engaged in fighting, especially spiritual warfare.

quarter-staff; we shall need every one of our merry men. But," he added, taking him a step aside, "art thou mad? to give admittance to a knight thou dost not know?"

5 "Not know him!" replied the Friar, boldly, "I know him as well as the beggar knows his dish."

"And what is his name, then?" demanded Locksley.

"His name," said the hermit — "his name is
10 Sir Anthony of Scrablestone; as if I would drink with a man, and did not know his name!"

"Thou hast been drinking more than enough, Friar," said the woodsman, "and I fear, prating more than enough too."

15 "Good yeoman," said the knight, coming forward, "be not wroth with my merry host. He did but afford me the hospitality which I would have compelled from him if he had refused it."

"Thou compel!" said the Friar; "wait but
20 till I have changed this grey gown for a green cassock, and if I make not a quarter-staff ring twelve upon thy pate, I am neither true clerk nor good woodsman."

While he spoke thus, he stript off his gown, and
25 appeared in a close black buckram doublet, over which he speedily did on a cassock of green and hose of the same color. "I pray thee, truss my

---

LINE **27.** **truss my points**: fasten my laces. Buttons were not used.

258

points," said he to Wamba, " and thou shalt have a cup of sack for thy labor."

Wamba accommodated the Friar with his assistance in tying the endless number of points, as the laces which attached the hose to the doublet were 5 then termed.

While they were thus employed, Locksley led the knight a little apart, and addressed him thus : " Deny it not, Sir Knight, you are he who decided the victory to the advantage of the English against 10 the strangers on the second day of the tournament at Ashby."

" And what follows if you guess truly, good yeoman ? " replied the knight.

" I should in that case hold you," replied the yeo- 15 man, " a friend to the weaker party."

" Such is the duty of a true knight at least," replied the Black Champion; " and I would not willingly that there were reason to think otherwise of me." 20

" But for my purpose," said the yeoman, " thou shouldst be as well a good Englishman as a good knight ; for that which I have to speak of concerns, indeed, the duty of every honest man, but is more especially that of a true-born native of 25 England."

" You can speak to no one," replied the knight,

---

LINE 2. sack: a Spanish wine.

" to whom England, and the life of every Englishman, can be dearer than to me."

" I would willingly believe so," said the woodsman, " for never had this country such need to be supported by those who love her. Hear me, and I will tell thee of an enterprise in which, if thou be'st really that which thou seemest, thou mayst take an honorable part. A band of villains, in the disguise of better men than themselves, have made themselves master of the person of a noble Englishman, called Cedric the Saxon, together with his ward and his friend Athelstane of Coningsburgh, and have transported them to a castle in this forest called Torquilstone. I ask of thee, as a good knight and a good Englishman, wilt thou aid in their rescue ? "

" I am bound by my vow to do so," replied the knight ; " but I would willingly know who you are, who request my assistance in their behalf ? "

" I am," said the forester, " a nameless man ; but I am the friend of my country, and of my country's friends. With this account of me you must for the present remain satisfied, the more especially since you yourself desire to continue unknown. Believe, however, that my word, when pledged, is as inviolate as if I wore golden spurs."

" I willingly believe it," said the knight ; " I

---

LINE **26.** golden spurs : badge of a knight.

have been accustomed to study men's countenances, and I can read in thine honesty and resolution. I will, therefore, ask thee no further questions, but aid thee in setting at freedom these oppressed captives; which done, I trust we shall part 5 better acquainted, and well satisfied with each other."

The Friar was now completely accoutred as a yeoman, with sword and buckler, bow and quiver, and a strong partizan over his shoulder. He left 10 his cell at the head of the party, and, having carefully locked the door, deposited the key under the threshold.

"Art thou in condition to do good service, Friar," said Locksley, "or does the brown bowl still 15 run in thy head?"

"Not more than a draught of St. Dunstan's fountain will allay," answered the priest; "something there is of a whizzing in my brain, and of instability in my legs, but you shall presently see 20 both pass away."

So saying, he stepped to the stone basin, in which the waters of the fountain as they fell formed bubbles which danced in the white moonlight, and took so long a draught as if he had meant to exhaust the 25 spring.

Then plunging his hands and head into the fountain, he washed from them all marks of the midnight revel.

Thus refreshed and sobered, the jolly priest twirled his heavy partizan round his head with three fingers, as if he had been balancing a reed, exclaiming at the same time, " Where be those who
5 carry off wenches against their will? May the foul fiend fly off with me, if I am not man enough for a dozen of them."

" Come on, Jack Priest," said Locksley, " and be silent. Come on you, too, my masters, tarry
10 not to talk of it — I say, come on; we must collect all our forces, and few enough we shall have, if we are to storm the castle of Reginald Front-de-Bœuf."

" What! is it Front-de-Bœuf," said the Black Knight, " who has stopt on the king's highway the
15 king's liege subjects? Is he turned thief and oppressor? "

" Oppressor he ever was," said Locksley.

" And for thief," said the priest, " I doubt if ever he were even half so honest a man as many a thief
20 of my acquaintance."

" Move on, priest, and be silent," said the yeoman; " it were better you led the way to the place of rendezvous than say what should be left unsaid."

---

LINE **2. partizan**: combined spear and battle-axe. See page 625. **15. liege**: free; loyal.

# CHAPTER XXI

## Prisoners Reach Torquilstone

While these measures were taking in behalf of Cedric and his companions, the armed men hurried their captives along towards the place of security where they intended to imprison them. But darkness came on fast, and they were compelled to make 5 several long halts. The summer morn had dawned upon them ere they could travel in full assurance that they held the right path. But confidence returned with light, and the cavalcade now moved rapidly forward. Meanwhile, the following dia- 10 logue took place between the two leaders of the banditti:

"It is time thou shouldst leave us, Sir Maurice," said the Templar to De Bracy, "in order to prepare the second part of thy mystery. Thou art next, 15 thou knowest, to act the Knight Deliverer."

"I have thought better of it," said De Bracy; "I will not leave thee till the prize is fairly deposited in Front-de-Bœuf's castle. There will I appear before the Lady Rowena in mine own shape, and 20 trust that she will set down to the vehemence of my passion the violence of which I have been guilty."

"And what has made thee change thy plan, De Bracy?" replied the Knight Templar.

"That concerns thee nothing," answered his companion.

5 "I would hope, however, Sir Knight," said the Templar, "that this alteration of measures arises from no suspicion of my honorable meaning, such as Fitzurse endeavored to instil into thee?"

"My thoughts are my own," answered De 10 Bracy; "suffice it to say, I know the morals of the Temple Order, and I will not give thee the power of cheating me out of the fair prey for which I have run such risks."

"Psha," replied the Templar, "what hast thou 15 to fear? Thou knowest the vows of our order."

"Right well," said De Bracy, "and also how they are kept."

"Hear the truth, then," said the Templar; "I care not for your blue-eyed beauty. There is in that 20 train one who will make me a better mate. I have a prize among the captives as lovely as thine own."

"By the mass, thou meanest the fair Jewess!" said De Bracy.

"And if I do," said Bois-Guilbert, "who shall 25 gainsay me?"

"No one that I know," said De Bracy, "unless it be your vow of celibacy or a check of conscience."

---

LINE 27. celibacy: state of being unmarried.

" For my vow," said the Templar, " our Grand
Master hath granted me a dispensation. And for
my conscience, a man that has slain three hundred
Saracens need not reckon up every little failing."

" Thou knowest best thine own privileges," said 5
De Bracy. " Yet, I would have sworn thy thought
had been more on the old usurer's money-bags than
on the black eyes of the daughter."

" I can admire both," answered the Templar;
" besides, the old Jew is but half-prize. I must 10
share his spoils with Front-de-Bœuf, who will not
lend us the use of his castle for nothing. I must
have something that I can term exclusively my own
by this foray of ours, and I have fixed on the lovely
Jewess as my peculiar prize." 15

While this dialogue was proceeding, Cedric was
endeavoring to wring out of those who guarded
him an avowal of their character and purpose.
" You should be Englishmen," said he; " and yet,
sacred Heaven! you prey upon your countrymen 20
as if you were very Normans. You should be my
neighbors, and, if so, my friends; for which of my
English neighbors have reason to be otherwise?
I tell ye, yeomen, that even those among ye who
have been branded with outlawry have had from 25
me protection; for I have pitied their miseries, and
curst the oppression of their tyrannic nobles.

---

LINE **2**. dispensation : exemption from rule or law.
**18**. avowal : frank acknowledgment.

What, then, would you have of me? or in what
can this violence serve ye? Ye are worse than
brute beasts in your actions, and will you imitate
them in their very dumbness?"

5   It was in vain that Cedric expostulated with his
guards who had too many good reasons for their
silence to be induced to break it. They continued
to hurry him along until, at the end of an avenue of
huge trees, arose Torquilstone, now the hoary and
10 ancient castle of Reginald Front-de-Bœuf. It was
a fortress of no great size, consisting of a donjon,
or large and high square tower, surrounded by
buildings of inferior height, which were encircled
by an inner courtyard. Around the exterior wall
15 was a deep moat, supplied with water from a neighboring rivulet. Front-de-Bœuf, whose character
placed him often at feud with his enemies, had
made considerable additions to the strength of his
castle, by building towers upon the outward wall,
20 so as to flank it at every angle. The access, as usual
in castles of the period, lay through an arched
barbican, or outwork, which was terminated and
defended by a small turret at each corner.

  Cedric no sooner saw the turrets of Front-de-
25 Bœuf's castle raise their grey and moss-grown
battlements, glimmering in the morning sun above
the wood by which they were surrounded, than he

---

LINE **5**. expostulated: reasoned earnestly. **22**. barbican:
outer fortification, usually defending entrance over drawbridge.

instantly augured more truly concerning the cause of his misfortune.

" I did injustice," he said, " to the thieves and outlaws of these woods, when I supposed such banditti to belong to their bands; I might as justly 5 have confounded the foxes of these brakes with the ravening wolves of France. Tell me, dogs, is it my life or my wealth that your master aims at? Is it too much that two Saxons, myself and the noble Athelstane, should hold land in the country 10 which was once the patrimony of our race? Put us, then, to death, and complete your tyranny by taking our lives, as you began with our liberties. If the Saxon Cedric cannot rescue England, he is willing to die for her. Tell your tyrannical master, 15 I do only beseech him to dismiss the Lady Rowena in honor and safety. She is a woman, and he need not dread her; and with us will die all who dare fight in her cause."

The attendants remained as mute to this address 20 as to the former, and they now stood before the gate of the castle. De Bracy winded his horn three times, and the archers and crossbow men, who had manned the wall upon seeing their approach, hastened to lower the drawbridge and 25 admit them. The prisoners were compelled by their guards to alight, and were conducted to an

---

LINE **6. brakes:** thickets. **11. patrimony:** inheritance from father or ancestors.

apartment where a hasty repast was offered them, of which none but Athelstane felt any inclination to partake. The guards gave him and Cedric to understand that they were to be imprisoned in a chamber apart from Rowena. Resistance was vain; and they were compelled to follow to a large room, rising on clumsy Saxon pillars.

The Lady Rowena was next separated from her train, and conducted to a distant apartment. The same alarming distinction was conferred on Rebecca, in spite of her father's entreaties that she might be permitted to abide with him. " Base unbeliever," answered one of his guards, " when thou hast seen thy lair, thou wilt not wish thy daughter to partake it." And, without farther discussion, the old Jew was forcibly dragged off in a different direction from the other prisoners. The domestics, after being carefully searched and disarmed, were confined in another part of the castle; and Rowena was refused even the comfort she might have derived from the attendance of her handmaiden Elgitha.

The apartment in which the Saxon chiefs were confined, although at present used as a sort of guard-room, had formerly been the great hall of the castle. It was now abandoned to meaner purposes, because the present lord, among other additions to the convenience, security, and beauty of his baronial residence, had erected a new and noble hall, whose vaulted roof was supported by lighter and more elegant pillars, and fitted up with that higher degree of ornament which the Normans had already introduced into architecture.

Cedric paced the apartment, filled with indignant reflections on the past and on the present, while [5] the apathy of his companion served to defend him against everything save the inconvenience of the present moment.

" Yes," said Cedric, " it was in this very hall that my [grand-] father feasted with Torquil Wolfganger, [10] when he entertained the valiant and unfortunate Harold, then advancing against the Norwegians, who had united themselves to the rebel Tosti. It was in this hall that Harold returned the magnanimous answer to the ambassador of his rebel brother. [15] The envoy of Tosti was admitted, when this ample room could scarce contain the crowd of noble Saxon leaders who were quaffing the blood-red wine around their monarch."

" I hope," said Athelstane, somewhat moved by [20] this part of his friend's discourse, " they will not forget to send us some wine and refections at noon : we had scarce a breathing-space allowed to break our fast."

Cedric went on with his story without noticing [25] this observation of his friend.

" The envoy of Tosti," he said, " moved up the

LINE **6. apathy** : lack of feeling. **14. Harold.** See page 614. **22. refections** : refreshments.

269

hall, undismayed by the frowning countenances of all around him, until he made his obeisance before the throne of King Harold.

"'What terms,' he said, 'Lord King, hath thy brother Tosti to hope, if he should lay down his arms and crave peace at thy hands?'

"'A brother's love,' cried the generous Harold, 'and the fair earldom of Northumberland.'

"'But should Tosti accept these terms,' continued the envoy, 'what lands shall be assigned to his faithful ally, Hardrada, King of Norway?'

"'Seven feet of English ground,' answered Harold, fiercely, 'or, as Hardrada is said to be a giant, perhaps we may allow him twelve inches more.'

"The hall rung with acclamations, and cup and horn was filled to the Norwegian, who should be speedily in possession of his English territory."

"I could have pledged him with all my soul," said Athelstane, "for my tongue cleaves to my palate."

"Who would have thought that Harold, within a few brief days, would himself possess no more of his kingdom than the share which he allotted in his wrath to the Norwegian invader?  Who would have thought that you, noble Athelstane — that you, descended of Harold's blood, and that I, whose father was not the worst defender of the Saxon crown, should be prisoners to a vile Norman, in the very hall in which our ancestors held such high festival?"

"It is sad enough," replied Athelstane; "but I trust they will hold us to a moderate ransom. At any rate, it cannot be their purpose to starve us 5 outright; and yet, although it is high noon, I see no preparations for serving dinner."

"It is time lost," muttered Cedric apart and impatiently, "to speak to him of aught else but that which concerns his appetite! He hath no 10 pleasure save to fill, to swill, and to call for more. Alas!" said he, looking at Athelstane with compassion, "that so dull a spirit should be lodged in so goodly a form! Alas! that such an enterprise as the regeneration of England should turn on a 15 hinge so imperfect! Wedded to Rowena, indeed, her nobler and more generous soul may yet awake the better nature which is torpid within him. Yet how should this be, while Rowena, Athelstane, and I myself remain the prisoners of this brutal ma- 20 rauder?"

While the Saxon was plunged in these painful reflections, the door of their prison opened and gave entrance to a sewer, holding his white rod of office. This important person advanced into the chamber 25 with a grave pace, followed by four attendants, bearing in a table covered with dishes, the sight

---

LINE **15.** regeneration: giving new life. **24.** sewer: waiter; especially, head waiter.

and smell of which seemed to be an instant compensation to Athelstane for all the inconvenience he had undergone. The persons who attended on the feast were masked and cloaked.

5 "What mummery is this?" said Cedric; "think you that we are ignorant whose prisoners we are, when we are in the castle of your master? Tell your master, Reginald Front-de-Bœuf, that we know no reason he can have for withholding our 10 liberty, excepting his unlawful desire to enrich himself at our expense. Let him name the ransom at which he rates our liberty, and it shall be paid, providing the exaction is suited to our means."

The sewer made no answer, but bowed his head.

15 "And tell Sir Reginald Front-de-Bœuf," said Athelstane, "that I send him my mortal defiance, and challenge him to combat with me, on foot or horseback, at any secure place, within eight days after our liberation; which, if he be a true knight, 20 he will not venture to refuse or to delay."

"I shall deliver to the knight your defiance," answered the sewer; "meanwhile I leave you to your food."

The challenge of Athelstane was delivered with 25 no good grace; for a large mouthful, which required the exercise of both jaws at once, added to a natural hesitation, considerably damped the effect of the bold defiance it contained. Still, however, his speech was hailed by Cedric as a token of reviving

spirit in his companion. He cordially shook hands
with him in token of his approbation, and was
somewhat grieved when Athelstane observed that
he would fight a dozen such men as Front-de-
Bœuf, if by so doing he could hasten his depar- 5
ture from a dungeon where they put so much garlic
into their pottage.

The captives had not long enjoyed their refreshment, however, ere their attention was disturbed
even from this most serious occupation by the blast 10
of a horn winded before the gate. It was repeated
three times with much violence. The Saxons
started from the table and hastened to the window.
But their curiosity was disappointed; for these
outlets only looked upon the court of the castle, and 15
the sound came from beyond its precincts. The
summons, however, seemed of importance, for a
considerable degree of bustle instantly took place
in the castle.

---

LINE 7. **pottage**: a thick soup.

## CHAPTER XXII

### Isaac's Hour of Trial

Leaving the Saxon chiefs to return to their banquet, we have to look in upon the yet more severe imprisonment of Isaac of York. The poor Jew had been hastily thrust into a dungeon-vault of the castle, the floor of which was deep beneath the level of the ground, and very damp, being lower than even the moat itself. The only light was received through one or two loop-holes far above the reach of the captive's hand. These apertures admitted, even at midday, only a dim and uncertain light, which was changed for utter darkness long before the rest of the castle had lost the blessing of day. Chains and shackles hung rusted and empty on the walls of the prison, and in the rings of one of those sets of fetters there remained two mouldering bones, which seemed to have been once those of the human leg, as if some prisoner had been left not only to perish there, but to be consumed to a skeleton.

At one end of this ghastly apartment was a large fire-grate, over the top of which were stretched some iron bars, half-devoured with rust.

The whole appearance of the dungeon might
have appalled a stouter heart than that of Isaac,
who, nevertheless, was more composed under the
imminent pressure of danger than he had seemed to
be while affected by terrors of which the cause was 5
as yet remote.    With his garment collected beneath
him to keep his limbs from the wet pavement,
he sat in a corner of his dungeon, where his folded
hands, his dishevelled hair and beard, his furred
cloak and high cap, seen by the wiry and broken 10
light, would have afforded a study for Rembrandt,
had that celebrated painter existed at the period.
The Jew remained without altering his position for
nearly three hours, at the expiry of which steps were
heard on the dungeon stair.    The bolts screamed 15
as they were withdrawn, the hinges creaked as the
wicket opened, and Reginald Front-de-Bœuf, followed by the two Saracen slaves of the Templar,
entered the prison.

Front-de-Bœuf, a tall and strong man, whose 20
life had been spent in public war or in private feuds
and broils, and who had hesitated at no means of
extending his feudal power, had features which
strongly expressed the fiercer and more malignant
passions of the mind.    The scars with which his 25
visage was seamed added to the ferocity of his
countenance, and to the dread which his presence

---

LINE **4. imminent**: close at hand.    **24. malignant**: showing intense ill-will.

inspired. This formidable baron was clad in a leathern doublet, fitted close to his body, which was frayed and soiled with the stains of his armor. He had no weapon, excepting a poniard at his belt, 5 which served to counterbalance the weight of the bunch of rusty keys that hung at his right side.

The black slaves who attended Front-de-Bœuf were attired in jerkins and trousers of coarse linen, their sleeves being tucked up above the elbow, like 10 those of butchers in the slaughter-house. When they entered the dungeon, they stopt at the door until Front-de-Bœuf himself carefully locked and double-locked it. Having taken this precaution, he advanced slowly up the apartment towards the 15 Jew, upon whom he kept his eye fixed, as if he wished to paralyze him with his glance, as some animals are said to fascinate their prey. The Jew sate with his mouth agape, and his eyes fixed on the savage baron with such earnestness of terror 20 that his frame seemed literally to shrink together, and to diminish in size. The unhappy Isaac was deprived not only of the power of rising to make the obeisance which his terror dictated, but he could not even doff his cap, or utter any word of supplica- 25 tion; so strongly was he agitated by the conviction that tortures and death were impending over him.

On the other hand, the stately form of the Nor-

---

LINE **1. formidable**: worthy of fear.   **8. jerkins**: jackets

man appeared to dilate in magnitude, like that of
the eagle, which ruffles up its plumage when about
to pounce on its defenceless prey. He paused
within three steps of the corner in which the unfortunate Jew had now, as it were, coiled himself up 5
into the smallest possible space, and made a sign
for one of the slaves to approach. The black satellite came forward accordingly, and, producing from
his basket a large pair of scales and several weights,
he laid them at the feet of Front-de-Bœuf, and 10
again retired to the respectful distance at which
his companion had already taken his station.

Front-de-Bœuf himself opened the scene by thus
addressing his ill-fated captive.

"Most accursed dog of an accursed race," he 15
said, awaking with his deep and sullen voice the
sullen echoes of his dungeon-vault, "seest thou
these scales?"

The unhappy Jew returned a feeble affirmative.

"In these very scales shalt thou weigh me out," 20
said the relentless Baron, "a thousand silver
pounds."

"Holy Abraham!" returned the Jew, finding
voice through the very extremity of his danger,
"heard man ever such a demand? Who ever 25
heard, even in a minstrel's tale, of such a sum as a
thousand pounds of silver? Not within the walls

---

LINE 1. dilate: puff out.    7. satellite: attendant of
person in power.

of York, ransack my house and that of all my tribe,
wilt thou find the tithe of that huge sum of silver
that thou speakest of."

"I am reasonable," answered Front-de-Bœuf,
5 " and if silver be scant, I refuse not gold. At the
rate of a mark of gold for each six pounds of silver,
thou shalt free thy unbelieving carcass from such
punishment as thy heart has never even conceived."

10 " Have mercy on me, noble knight ! " exclaimed
Isaac; " I am old, and poor, and helpless. It were
unworthy to triumph over me. It is a poor deed
to crush a worm."

"Old thou mayst be," replied the knight; "feeble
15 thou mayst be; but rich it is well known thou art."

"I swear to you, noble knight," said the Jew,
" by all which I believe, and by all which we believe in common —— "

"Perjure not thyself," said the Norman, inter-
20 rupting him, " and let not thine obstinacy seal thy
doom, until thou hast seen and well considered the
fate that awaits thee. This dungeon is no place
for trifling. Prisoners ten thousand times more
distinguished than thou have died within these
25 walls, and their fate hath never been known ! But
for thee is reserved a long and lingering death, to
which theirs were luxury."

---

LINE 2. tithe : tenth.

He again made a signal for the slaves to approach, and spoke to them apart, in their own language. The Saracens produced from their baskets a quantity of charcoal, a pair of bellows, and a flask of oil. While the one struck a light with a flint and steel, the other disposed the charcoal in the large rusty grate, and exercised the bellows until the fuel came to a red glow.

"Seest thou, Isaac," said Front-de-Bœuf, "the range of iron bars above that glowing charcoal? On that warm couch thou shalt lie, stripped of thy clothes as if thou wert to rest on a bed of down. One of these slaves shall maintain the fire beneath thee, while the other shall anoint thy wretched limbs with oil, lest the roast should burn. Now, choose betwixt such a scorching bed and the payment of a thousand pounds of silver; for, by the head of my father, thou hast no other option."

"It is impossible," exclaimed the miserable Jew — "it is impossible that your purpose can be real! The good God of nature never made a heart capable of exercising such cruelty!"

"Trust not to that, Isaac," said Front-de-Bœuf, "it were a fatal error. Dost thou think that I, who have seen a town sacked, in which thousands of my Christian countrymen perished by sword, by flood, and by fire, will blench from my purpose

---

Line **27. blench**: shrink.

for the outcries or screams of one single wretched
Jew? Or thinkest thou that these swarthy slaves,
who have neither law, country, nor conscience, but
their master's will — who use the poison, or the
5 stake, or the poniard, or the cord, at his slightest
wink — thinkest thou that *they* will have mercy,
who do not even understand the language in which
it is asked? Be wise, old man; tell down thy ransom, I say, and rejoice that at such rate thou canst
10 redeem thee from a dungeon the secrets of which
few have returned to tell. I waste no more words
with thee: choose between thy dross and thy flesh
and blood, and as thou choosest, so shall it be."

"So may Abraham, Jacob, and all the fathers of
15 our people assist me," said Isaac, "I cannot make
the choice, because I have not the means of satisfying your exorbitant demand!"

"Seize him and strip him, slaves," said the
knight, "and let the fathers of his race assist him
20 if they can."

The assistants, taking their directions more from
the Baron's eye and his hand than his tongue, once
more stepped forward, laid hands on the unfortunate Isaac, plucked him up from the ground, and,
25 holding him between them, waited the hard-hearted
Baron's farther signal. The unhappy Jew eyed
their countenances and that of Front-de-Bœuf, in

---

LINE **8. tell**: count. **12. dross**: waste matter· rubbish.

hope of discovering some symptoms of relenting; but that of the Baron exhibited the same cold, half-sullen, half-sarcastic smile which had been the prelude to his cruelty; and the savage eyes of the Saracens, rolling gloomily under their dark brows, evinced rather the secret pleasure which they expected from the approaching scene than any reluctance to be its directors or agents. The Jew then looked at the glowing furnace over which he was presently to be stretched, and seeing no chance of his tormentor's relenting, his resolution gave way.

" I will pay," he said, " the thousand pounds of silver. That is," he added, after a moment's pause, " I will pay it with the help of my brethren; for I must beg as a mendicant at the door of our synagogue ere I make up so unheard-of a sum. When and where must it be delivered? "

" Here," replied Front-de-Bœuf — " here it must be delivered; weighed it must be — weighed and told down on this very dungeon floor. Thinkest thou I will part with thee until thy ransom is secure? "

" And what is to be my surety," said the Jew, " that I shall be at liberty after this ransom is paid? "

" The word of a Norman noble, thou pawnbroking slave," answered Front-de-Bœuf.

---

LINE **15. mendicant**: beggar.

"I crave pardon, noble lord," said Isaac, timidly, "but wherefore should I rely wholly on the word of one who will trust nothing to mine?"

"Because thou canst not help it, Jew," said the knight, sternly. "Wert thou now in thy treasure-chamber at York, and were I craving a loan of thy shekels, it would be thine to dictate the time of payment and the pledge of security. This is *my* treasure-chamber."

The Jew groaned deeply. "Grant me," he said, "at least, with my own liberty, that of the companions with whom I travel."

"If thou meanest yonder Saxon churls," said Front-de-Bœuf, "their ransom will depend upon other terms than thine. Mind thine own concerns, Jew, I warn thee, and meddle not with those of others."

"I am, then," said Isaac, "only to be set at liberty, together with mine wounded friend?"

"Shall I twice recommend it," said Front-de-Bœuf, "to a son of Israel, to meddle with his own concerns, and leave those of others alone? Since thou hast made thy choice, it remains but that thou payest down thy ransom, and that at a short day. When shall I have the shekels, Isaac?"

"Let my daughter Rebecca go forth to York," answered Isaac, "with your safe-conduct, noble knight, and so soon as man and horse can return, the treasure —— " Here he groaned deeply, but added, after the pause of a few seconds — "the treasure shall be told down on this very floor."

"Thy daughter!" said Front-de-Bœuf, as if surprised, "by heavens, Isaac, I would I had known of this. I gave yonder black-browed girl 5 to be a handmaiden to Sir Brian de Bois-Guilbert."

The yell which Isaac raised at this unfeeling communication made the very vault to ring, and astounded the two Saracens so much that they let go their hold of the Jew. He availed himself of 10 his enlargement to throw himself on the pavement and clasp the knees of Front-de-Bœuf.

"Take all that you have asked," said he, "Sir Knight; take ten times more — reduce me to ruin and to beggary, if thou wilt, — nay, pierce me with 15 thy poniard, broil me on that furnace; but spare my daughter. She is the image of my deceased Rachael — she is the last of six pledges of her love. Will you deprive a widowed husband of his sole remaining comfort?" 20

"I would," said the Norman, somewhat relenting, "that I had known of this before. I thought your race had loved nothing save their money-bags."

"Think not so vilely of us," said Isaac, eager 25 to improve the moment of apparent sympathy; "the hunted fox, the tortured wild-cat loves its

---

LINE **11. enlargement**: freedom.

young — the despised and persecuted race of Abraham love their children!"

"Be it so," said Front-de-Bœuf; "I will believe it in future, Isaac, for thy very sake. But it aids us not now; I cannot help what has happened, or what is to follow: my word is passed to my comrade in arms, nor would I break it for ten Jews and Jewesses to boot."

"Robber and villain!" said the Jew, "I will pay thee nothing — not one silver penny will I pay thee — unless my daughter is delivered to me in safety and honor!"

"Art thou in thy senses, Israelite?" said the Norman, sternly; "hast thy flesh and blood a charm against heated iron and scalding oil?"

"I care not!" said the Jew, rendered desperate by paternal affection; "do thy worst. My daughter is my flesh and blood, dearer to me a thousand times than those limbs which thy cruelty threatens. No silver will I give thee, unless I were to pour it molten down thy avaricious throat; no, not a silver penny will I give thee! Take my life if thou wilt, and say the Jew, amidst his tortures, knew how to disappoint the Christian."

"We shall see that," said Front-de-Bœuf; "for thou shalt feel the extremities of fire and steel! Strip him, slaves, and chain him down upon the bars."

In spite of the feeble struggles of the old man,

the Saracens had already torn from him his upper
garment, and were proceeding totally to disrobe
him, when the sound of a bugle penetrated even to
the recesses of the dungeon, and immediately after
loud voices were heard calling for Sir Reginald 5
Front-de-Bœuf. Unwilling to be found engaged
in his hellish occupation, the savage Baron gave
the slaves a signal to restore Isaac's garment, and
quitting the dungeon with his attendants, he left
the Jew to thank God for his own deliverance, or 10
to lament over his daughter's captivity and probable fate, as his personal or parental feelings might
prove strongest.

# CHAPTER XXIII

## Rowena Rejects De Bracy

The apartment to which the Lady Rowena had been introduced was fitted up with some rude attempts at ornament and magnificence, and her being placed there might be considered as a peculiar mark of respect not offered to the other prisoners. But the wife of Front-de-Bœuf, for whom it had been originally furnished, was long dead, and decay and neglect had impaired the few ornaments with which her taste had adorned it. Desolate, however, as it was, this was the apartment of the castle which had been judged most fitting for the accommodation of the Saxon heiress.

It was about the hour of noon when De Bracy, for whose advantage the expedition had been first planned, appeared to prosecute his views upon the hand and possessions of the Lady Rowena.

The interval had not entirely been bestowed in holding council with his confederates, for De Bracy had found leisure to decorate his person with all the foppery of the times. His green cassock and vizard were now flung aside. His long luxuriant hair was trained to flow in quaint tresses down his richly furred cloak. His beard was closely shaved, his doublet reached to the middle of his leg, and the girdle which secured it, and at the same time supported his ponderous sword, was embroidered and embossed with gold work. The points of his shoes were turned up and twisted like the horns of a ram.

He saluted Rowena by doffing his velvet bonnet, garnished with a golden brooch. With this, he gently motioned the lady to a seat and, as she still retained her standing posture, the knight ungloved his right hand, and motioned to conduct her thither. But Rowena declined, by her gesture, the proffered compliment, and replied : " If I be in the presence of my jailer, Sir Knight — nor will circumstances allow me to think otherwise — it best becomes his prisoner to remain standing till she learns her doom."

" Alas ! fair Rowena," returned De Bracy, " you are in presence of your captive, not your jailer ; and it is from your fair eyes that De Bracy must receive that doom which you fondly expect from him."

" I know you not, sir," said the lady, drawing herself up with all the pride of offended rank and beauty — " I know you not ; and the insolent familiarity with which you apply to me the jargon of a troubadour forms no apology for the violence of a robber."

---

Line 25. **jargon** : unintelligible speech.

"That I am unknown to you," said De Bracy, "is indeed my misfortune; yet let me hope that De Bracy's name has not been always unspoken when minstrels or heralds have praised deeds of chivalry, whether in the lists or in the battle-field."

"To heralds and to minstrels, then, leave thy praise, Sir Knight," replied Rowena, "more suiting for their mouths than for thine own; and tell me which of them shall record in song, or in book of tourney, the memorable conquest of this night, a conquest obtained over an old man, followed by a few timid hinds; and its booty, an unfortunate maiden transported against her will to the castle of a robber?"

"You are unjust, Lady Rowena," said the knight, biting his lips in some confusion; "yourself free from passion, you can allow no excuse for the frenzy of another, although caused by your own beauty."

"I pray you, Sir Knight," said Rowena, "to cease a language so commonly used by strolling minstrels that it becomes not the mouth of knights or nobles."

"Proud damsel," said De Bracy, incensed at finding his gallant style procured him nothing but contempt — "proud damsel, thou shalt be as

---

LINE **13.** **hinds**: farm hands.

proudly encountered. Know, then, that I have supported my pretensions to your hand in the way that best suited thy character. It is meeter for thy humor to be wooed with bow and bill than in set terms and in courtly language." 5

"Courtesy of tongue," said Rowena, "when it is used to veil churlishness of deed, is but a knight's girdle around the breast of a base clown. More it were for your honor to have retained the dress and language of an outlaw than to veil the deeds of 10 one under an affectation of gentle language and demeanor."

"You counsel well, lady," said the Norman; "and in the bold language which best justifies bold action, I tell thee, thou shalt never leave this castle, 15 or thou shalt leave it as Maurice de Bracy's wife. I am not wont to be baffled in my enterprises, nor needs a Norman noble scrupulously to vindicate his conduct to the Saxon maiden whom he distinguishes by the offer of his hand. Thou art 20 proud, Rowena, and thou art the fitter to be my wife. By what other means couldst thou be raised to high honor and to princely place, saving by my alliance? How else wouldst thou escape from the mean precincts of a country grange, where 25 Saxons herd with the swine which form their wealth, to take thy seat, honored as thou shouldst be, and

---

LINE **3. meeter**: more suitable. **18. scrupulously**: carefully. **25. grange**: farm with its buildings.

shalt be, amid all in England that is distinguished by beauty or dignified by power?"

"Sir Knight," replied Rowena, "the grange which you contemn hath been my shelter from infancy; and, trust me, when I leave it — should that day ever arrive — it shall be with one who has not learnt to despise the dwelling and manners in which I have been brought up."

"I guess your meaning, lady," said De Bracy. "But dream not that Richard Cœur-de-Lion will ever resume his throne, far less that Wilfred of Ivanhoe, his minion, will ever lead thee to his footstool, to be there welcomed as the bride of a favorite. Know, lady, that this rival is in my power, and that it rests but with me to betray the secret of his being within the castle to Front-de-Bœuf, whose jealousy will be more fatal than mine."

"Wilfred here!" said Rowena, in disdain; "that is as true as that Front-de-Bœuf is his rival."

De Bracy looked at her steadily for an instant. "Wert thou really ignorant of this?" said he; "didst thou not know that Wilfred of Ivanhoe travelled in the litter of the Jew? — a meet conveyance for the crusader whose doughty arm was to reconquer the Holy Sepulchre!" And he laughed scornfully.

---

LINE 25. doughty: strong; brave.

"And if he is here," said Rowena, compelling herself to a tone of indifference, though trembling with an agony of apprehension which she could not suppress, "in what is he the rival of Front-de-Bœuf? or what has he to fear beyond a short imprisonment and an honorable ransom, according to the use of chivalry?"

"Rowena," said De Bracy, "art thou, too, deceived by the common error of thy sex, who think there can be no rivalry but that respecting their own charms? Knowest thou not there is a jealousy of ambition and of wealth, as well as of love; and that this our host, Front-de-Bœuf, will push from his road him who opposes his claim to the fair barony of Ivanhoe? But smile on my suit, lady, and the wounded champion shall have nothing to fear from Front-de-Bœuf, whom else thou mayst mourn for, as in the hands of one who has never shown compassion."

"Save him, for the love of Heaven!" said Rowena, her firmness giving way under terror for her lover's impending fate.

"I can — I will — it is my purpose," said De Bracy; "for, when Rowena consents to be the bride of De Bracy, who is it shall dare to put forth a violent hand upon her kinsman — the son of her guardian — the companion of her youth? But it is thy love must buy his protection. Use thine influence with me in his behalf, and he is safe;

refuse to employ it, Wilfred dies, and thou thyself
art not the nearer to freedom."

"I believe not that thy purpose is so wicked,"
answered Rowena, " or thy power so great."

5 "Flatter thyself, then, with that belief," said De
Bracy, " until time shall prove it false. Thy lover
lies wounded in this castle — thy preferred lover.
He is a bar betwixt Front-de-Bœuf and that which
Front-de-Bœuf loves better than either ambition
10 or beauty. What will it cost beyond the blow of a
poniard, or the thrust of a javelin, to silence his
opposition for ever? Nay, were Front-de-Bœuf
afraid to justify a deed so open, let the leech but
give his patient a wrong draught, let the nurse who
15 tends him, but pluck the pillow from his head, and
Wilfred, in his present condition, is sped without
the effusion of blood. Cedric also —— "

"And Cedric also," said Rowena, repeating his
words — " my noble — my generous guardian!
20 I deserved the evil I have encountered, for forgetting his fate even in that of his son!"

"Cedric's fate also depends upon thy determination," said De Bracy, " and I leave thee to form it."

After casting her eyes around, as if to look for
25 the aid which was nowhere to be found, and after a
few broken interjections, Rowena raised her hands
to heaven, and burst into a passion of uncontrolled

---

LINE **11. poniard**: small dagger. **13. leech**: physician.

vexation and sorrow. It was impossible to see so beautiful a creature in such extremity without feeling for her, and De Bracy was not unmoved, though he was yet more embarrassed than touched. He had, in truth, gone too far to recede; and yet, in Rowena's present condition, she could not be acted on either by argument or threats. He paced the apartment to and fro, now vainly exhorting the terrified maiden to compose herself, now hesitating concerning his own line of conduct.

If, thought he, I should be moved by the tears and sorrow of this disconsolate damsel, what should I reap but the loss of those fair hopes for which I have encountered so much risk, and the ridicule of Prince John and his jovial comrades? "And yet," he said to himself, "I feel myself ill framed for the part which I am playing. I cannot look on so fair a face while it is disturbed with agony, or on those eyes when they are drowned in tears. I would she had retained her original haughtiness of disposition, or that I had a larger share of Front-de-Bœuf's thrice-tempered hardness of heart!"

Agitated by these thoughts, he could only bid the unfortunate Rowena be comforted, and assure her that as yet she had no reason for the excess of despair to which she was now giving way. But in this task of consolation De Bracy was interrupted by the horn, which had at the same time alarmed the other inmates of the castle, and interrupted their several plans. Of them all, perhaps, De Bracy least regretted the interruption; for his conference with the Lady Rowena had arrived at a point where he found it equally difficult to prosecute or to resign his enterprise.

## CHAPTER XXIV

### Rebecca Faces the Templar

While the scenes we have described were passing in other parts of the castle, the Jewess Rebecca awaited her fate in a distant and sequestered turret. She was to expect a doom even more dreadful than that of Rowena; for what probability was there 5 that either softness or ceremony would be used towards one of her oppressed race, whatever shadow of these might be preserved towards a Saxon heiress? Yet had the Jewess this advantage, that she was better prepared by habits of thought, and 10 by natural strength of mind, to encounter the dangers to which she was exposed.

Her first care was to inspect the apartment; but it afforded few hopes either of escape or protection. It contained neither secret passage nor 15 trap-door, and, unless where the door by which she had entered joined the main building, seemed to be circumscribed by the round exterior wall of the turret. The door had no inside bolt or bar. The single window opened upon an embattled space 20

---

LINE **3. sequestered**: secluded. **turret**: small tower connected with main building. **18. circumscribed**: bounded.

surmounting the turret, which gave Rebecca, at first sight, some hopes of escaping; but she soon found it had no communication with any other part of the battlements, being an isolated bartizan, 5 or balcony, secured, as usual, by a parapet, with embrasures, at which a few archers might be stationed for defending the turret, and flanking with their shot the wall of the castle on that side.

The prisoner trembled and changed color, when 10 a step was heard on the stair, and the door of the turret-chamber slowly opened, and a tall man, dressed as one of those banditti to whom they owed their misfortune, slowly entered, and shut the door behind him. His cap, pulled down upon 15 his brows, concealed the upper part of his face, and he held his mantle in such a manner as to muffle the rest. In this guise, as if prepared for the execution of some deed, at the thought of which he was himself ashamed, he stood before the af- 20 frighted prisoner; yet, ruffian as his dress bespoke him, he seemed at a loss to express what purpose had brought him thither, so that Rebecca had time to anticipate his explanation. She had already unclasped two costly bracelets and a collar, which 25 she hastened to proffer to the supposed outlaw.

"Take these," she said, "good friend, and for

---

LINE **4. isolated**: placed by itself.   **5. parapet**: breast-high wall at edge of balcony, roof, etc.   **6. embrasures**: openings in wall for archers to shoot through.

God's sake be merciful to me and my aged father.
These ornaments are of value, yet are they trifling
to what he would bestow to obtain our dismissal
from this castle free and uninjured."

"Fair flower of Palestine," replied the outlaw, 5
"these pearls are orient, but they yield in whiteness to your teeth; the diamonds are brilliant,
but they cannot match your eyes; and ever since
I have taken up this wild trade, I have made a
vow to prefer beauty to wealth." 10

"Do not do yourself such wrong," said Rebecca;
"take ransom, and have mercy! Gold will purchase you pleasure; to misuse us could only bring
thee remorse. My father will willingly satiate thy
utmost wishes." 15

"It is well spoken," replied the outlaw in French,
finding it difficult probably to sustain in Saxon a
conversation which Rebecca had opened in that
language; "but know, bright lily, that thy father
is already in the hands of a powerful alchemist, 20
who knows how to convert into gold and silver
even the rusty bars of a dungeon grate."

"Thou art no outlaw," said Rebecca, in the
same language in which he addressed her; "no
outlaw had refused such offers. No outlaw in this 25
land uses the dialect in which thou hast spoken.

---

LINE **6. orient**: lustrous.   **14. satiate**: gratify to the full.
**20. alchemist**: an early chemist who sought to change base
metals into gold.

Thou art no outlaw, but a Norman — a Norman, noble perhaps in birth. Oh, be so in thy actions, and cast off this fearful mask of outrage and violence!"

5 "And thou, who canst guess so truly," said Brian de Bois-Guilbert, dropping the mantle from his face, "art no true daughter of Israel, but in all save youth and beauty a very witch of Endor. I am not an outlaw then, fair rose of Sharon. And 10 I am one who will be more prompt to hang thy neck and arms with pearls and diamonds, which so well become them, than to deprive thee of these ornaments."

"What wouldst thou have of me," said Rebecca, 15 "if not my wealth? We can have nought in common between us; you are a Christian, I am a Jewess. Our union were contrary to the laws alike of the church and the synagogue."

"It were so, indeed," replied the Templar, 20 laughing. "Wed with a Jewess! Not if she were the Queen of Sheba! And know, besides, sweet daughter of Zion, that were the most Christian king to offer me his most Christian daughter, I could not wed her. I am a Templar. Behold the 25 cross of my holy order."

"Darest thou appeal to it," said Rebecca, "on an occasion like the present?"

---

LINE **8. witch of Endor**: I Samuel 28 : 7–25. **22. most Christian king**: king of France.

"And if I do so," said the Templar, "it concerns not thee, who art no believer in the blessed sign of our salvation."

"I believe as my fathers taught," said Rebecca; "and may God forgive my belief if erroneous! But you, Sir Knight, what is *yours*, when you appeal without scruple to that which you deem most holy, even while you are about to transgress the most solemn of your vows as a knight and as a man of religion?"

"It is gravely and well preached," answered the Templar; "but the protectors of Solomon's temple may claim license by the example of Solomon."

"If thou readest the Scripture," said the Jewess, "and the lives of the saints, only to justify thine own license and profligacy, thy crime is like that of him who extracts poison from the most healthful and necessary herbs."

The eyes of the Templar flashed fire at this reproof. "Hearken," he said, "Rebecca; I have hitherto spoken mildly to thee, but now my language shall be that of a conqueror. Thou art the captive of my bow and spear, subject to my will by the laws of all nations; nor will I abate an inch of my right, or abstain from taking by violence what thou refusest to entreaty or necessity."

"Stand back," said Rebecca — "stand back, and hear me ere thou offerest to commit a sin so deadly! My strength thou mayst indeed overpower, for God made women weak, and trusted their defence to man's generosity. But I will proclaim thy villainy, Templar, from one end of Europe to the other."

5 "Thou art keen-witted, Jewess," replied the Templar; "but loud must be thy voice of complaint if it is heard beyond the iron walls of this castle; within these, murmurs, laments, appeals to justice, and screams for help die alike silent away. 10 One thing only can save thee, Rebecca. Submit to thy fate, embrace our religion, and thou shalt go forth in such state that many a Norman lady shall yield as well in pomp as in beauty to the favorite of the best lance among the defenders of 15 the Temple."

"Submit to my fate!" said Rebecca; "and, sacred Heaven! to what fate? Embrace thy religion! and what religion can it be that harbors such a villain? *Thou* the best lance of the 20 Templars! Craven knight! — forsworn priest! I spit at thee and I defy thee. The God of Abraham's promise hath opened an escape to his daughter — even from this abyss of infamy!"

As she spoke, she threw open the latticed window 25 which led to the bartizan, and in an instant after stood on the very verge of the parapet, with not

---

LINE **20. Craven**: cowardly.   **forsworn**: guilty of breaking an oath.   **25. bartizan**: balcony or small overhanging turret.

REBECCA AND BOIS-GUILBERT

the slightest screen between her and the tremendous depth below. Unprepared for such a desperate effort, for she had hitherto stood perfectly
motionless, Bois-Guilbert had neither time to intercept nor to stop her. As he offered to advance, she 5
exclaimed, " Remain where thou art, proud Templar, or at thy choice advance ! — one foot nearer,
and I plunge myself from the precipice ! "

As she spoke this, she clasped her hands and
extended them towards heaven, as if imploring 10
mercy on her soul before she made the final plunge.
The Templar hesitated, and a resolution which
had never yielded to pity or distress gave way to
his admiration of her fortitude. " Come down,"
he said, " rash girl ! I swear by earth, and sea, 15
and sky, I will offer thee no offence."

" I will not trust thee, Templar," said Rebecca.

" You do me injustice," exclaimed the Templar,
fervently ; " I swear to you by the name which I
bear — by the cross on my bosom — by the sword 20
on my side — by the ancient crest of my fathers
do I swear, I will do thee no injury whatsoever !
If not for thyself, yet for thy father's sake forbear !
I will be his friend, and in this castle he will need a
powerful one." 25

" Alas ! " said Rebecca, " I know it but too well.
Dare I trust thee ? "

---

LINE **21. crest**: device above shield and helmet on coat
of arms.

"May my arms be reversed and my name dishonored," said Brian de Bois-Guilbert, "if thou shalt have reason to complain of me! Many a law, many a commandment have I broken, but 5 my word never."

"I will then trust thee," said Rebecca, "thus far"; and she descended from the verge of the battlement, but remained standing close by one of the embrasures. "Here," she said, "I take 10 my stand. Remain where thou art, and if thou shalt attempt to diminish by one step the distance now between us, thou shalt see that the Jewish maiden will rather trust her soul with God than her honor to the Templar!"

15 While Rebecca spoke thus, her high and firm resolve, which corresponded so well with the expressive beauty of her countenance, gave to her looks, air, and manner a dignity that seemed more than mortal. Her glance quailed not, her cheek 20 blanched not, for the fear of a fate so instant and so horrible; on the contrary, the thought that she had her fate at her command, and could escape at will from infamy to death, gave a yet deeper color of carnation to her complexion, and a yet 25 more brilliant fire to her eye. Bois-Guilbert, proud himself and high-spirited, thought he had never beheld beauty so animated and so commanding.

---

LINE **19. quailed**: gave way. **27. animated**: full of life and spirit.

"Let there be peace between us, Rebecca," he said.

"Peace, if thou wilt," answered Rebecca — "peace; but with this space between."

"Thou needst no longer fear me," said Bois-Guilbert.

"I fear thee not," replied she, "thanks to him that reared this dizzy tower so high that nought could fall from it and live. Thanks to him, and to the God of Israel! I fear thee not."

"Thou dost me injustice," said the Templar; "by earth, sea, and sky, thou dost me injustice! I am not naturally that which you have seen me — hard, selfish, and relentless. It was woman that taught me cruelty, and on woman therefore I have exercised it; but not upon such as thou. Hear me, Rebecca. Never did knight take lance in his hand with a heart more devoted to the lady of his love than Brian de Bois-Guilbert. She, the daughter of a petty baron, who boasted for all his domains but a ruinous tower and an unproductive vineyard, her name was known wherever deeds of arms were done. Yes, my deeds, my danger, my blood made the name of Adelaide de Montemare known from the court of Castile to that of Byzantium. And how was I requited? When I returned with my dear-bought honors purchased by toil and blood,

---

LINE 25. **Castile**: Spain. **Byzantium**: Constantinople.

I found her wedded to a Gascon squire, whose
name was never heard beyond the limits of his own
paltry domain! Truly did I love her, and bitterly
did I revenge me of her broken faith! But my
vengeance has recoiled on myself. Since that day
I have separated myself from life and its ties. My
manhood must know no domestic home, must be
soothed by no affectionate wife. My age must
know no kindly hearth. My grave must be solitary, and no offspring must outlive me, to bear the
ancient name of Bois-Guilbert. At the feet of my
superior I have laid down the right of self-action
— the privilege of independence. The Templar, a
serf in all but the name, can possess neither lands
nor goods, and lives, moves, and breathes but at
the will and pleasure of another."

"Alas!" said Rebecca, "what advantages
could compensate for such an absolute sacrifice?"

"The power of vengeance, Rebecca," replied the
Templar, "and the prospects of ambition."

"An evil recompense," said Rebecca, "for the
surrender of the rights which are dearest to human-
ity."

"Say not so, maiden," answered the Templar;
"revenge is a feast for the gods! And ambition!
it is a temptation which could disturb even the
bliss of Heaven itself." He paused a moment, and

Line **5. recoiled**: rebounded.

then added, " Rebecca! she who could prefer
death to dishonor must have a proud and a powerful soul. Mine thou must be! Nay, start not,"
he added, " it must be with thine own consent, and
on thine own terms. Thou must consent to share 5
with me hopes more extended than can be viewed
from the throne of a monarch! Hear me ere you
answer, and judge ere you refuse. The Templar
loses his social rights, his power of free agency, but
he becomes a member and a limb of a mighty body, 10
before which thrones already tremble. Of this
mighty order I am no mean member, but already
one of the chief commanders, and may well aspire
one day to hold the batoon of Grand Master. The
poor soldiers of the Temple will not alone place 15
their foot upon the necks of kings. Our mailed
step shall ascend their throne, our gauntlet shall
wrench the sceptre from their gripe. I have sought
but a kindred spirit to share my ambition, and I
have found such in thee." 20

" Sayst thou this to one of my people? "
answered Rebecca. " Bethink thee —— "

" Answer me not," said the Templar, " by urging
the difference of our creeds; within our secret conclaves we hold these nursery tales in derision. 25
That bugle-sound announces something which may
require my presence. Think on what I have said.

---

LINE 14. batoon: staff of office. 24. conclaves: private
meetings.

Farewell! I do not say forgive me the violence 1 have threatened, for it was necessary to the display of thy character. Gold can be only known by the application of the touchstone. I will soon return, 5 and hold further conference with thee."

He re-entered the turret-chamber, and descended the stair, leaving Rebecca scarcely more terrified at the prospect of the death to which she had been so lately exposed, than at the furious ambition of 10 the bold bad man in whose power she found herself so unhappily placed. When she entered the turret-chamber, her first duty was to return thanks to the God of Jacob for the protection which He had afforded her, and to implore its continuance for 15 her and for her father. Another name glided into her petition; it was that of the wounded Christian, whom fate had placed in the hands of bloodthirsty men, his avowed enemies.

# CHAPTER XXV

## A Challenge and a Reply

When the Templar reached the hall of the castle, he found De Bracy already there. " Your love-suit," said De Bracy, " hath, I suppose, been disturbed, like mine, by this obstreperous summons. But you have come later and more reluctantly, and therefore I presume your interview has proved more agreeable than mine."

" Has your suit, then, been unsuccessfully paid to the Saxon heiress? " said the Templar.

" By the bones of Thomas à Becket," answered De Bracy, " the Lady Rowena must have heard that I cannot endure the sight of women's tears."

"Away!" said the Templar; " thou a leader of a Free Company, and regard a woman's tears! A few drops sprinkled on the torch of love make the flame blaze the brighter."

" Gramercy for the few drops of thy sprinkling," replied De Bracy; " but this damsel hath wept enough to extinguish a beacon-light. Never was such wringing of hands and such overflowing of

---

LINE **17. Gramercy**: many thanks.  **19. beacon-light**: signal on high point near shore to guide mariners.

eyes, since the days of St. Niobe. A water-fiend hath possessed the fair Saxon."

"A legion of fiends have occupied the bosom of the Jewess," replied the Templar; "for I think no 5 single one could have inspired such indomitable pride and resolution. But where is Front-de-Bœuf? That horn is sounded more and more clamorously."

"He is negotiating with the Jew, I suppose," 10 replied De Bracy, coolly; "probably the howls of Isaac have drowned the blast of the bugle. Thou mayst know, by experience, Sir Brian, that a Jew parting with his treasures on such terms as our friend Front-de-Bœuf is like to offer will raise a 15 clamor loud enough to be heard over twenty horns and trumpets to boot."

They were soon joined by Front-de-Bœuf, who had been disturbed in his tyrannic cruelty in the manner with which the reader is acquainted. "Let 20 us see the cause of this cursed clamor," said Front-de-Bœuf; "here is a letter, and, if I mistake not, it is in Saxon."

He looked at it, turning it round and round as if he had had really some hopes of coming at the 25 meaning by inverting the position of the paper, and then handed it to De Bracy.

---

LINE 1. **Niobe**: in mythology, a mother who boasted of her fourteen children. Apollo and Artemis, jealous and angry, had all the children slain. **5. indomitable**: unconquerable.

# A Challenge and a Reply

" It may be magic spells for aught I know," said
De Bracy, who possessed his full proportion of the
ignorance which characterized the chivalry of the
period. " Our chaplain attempted to teach me to
write," he said, " but all my letters were formed like 5
spear-heads and sword-blades."

" Give it me," said the Templar. " We have
that of the priestly character, that we have some
knowledge to enlighten our valor."

" Let us profit by your most reverend knowledge, 10
then," said De Bracy; " what says the scroll?"

" It is a formal letter of defiance," answered the
Templar; " but if it be not a foolish jest, it is the
most extraordinary cartel that ever was sent across
the drawbridge of a baronial castle." 15

" Jest!" said Front-de-Bœuf, " I would gladly
know who dares jest with me in such a matter.
Read it, Sir Brian."

The Templar accordingly read it as follows:

" I, Wamba, the son of Witless, jester to a noble 20
and freeborn man, Cedric of Rotherwood, called
the Saxon: and I, Gurth, the son of Beowulph,
the swineherd —— "

" Thou art mad," said Front-de-Bœuf, interrupting the reader. 25

" By St. Luke, it is so set down," answered the
Templar. Then resuming his task, he went on —

---

LINE 14. **cartel**: formal challenge.

'I, Gurth, the son of Beowulph, swineherd unto
the said Cedric, with the assistance of our allies
and confederates; namely, the good knight, called
for the present the Black Sluggard and the stout
5 yeoman, Robert Locksley, called Cleave-the-Wand,
to you, Reginald Front-de-Bœuf, and your allies
and accomplices whomsoever, to wit, that whereas
you have, without cause given or feud declared,
wrongfully and by mastery seized upon the person
10 of our lord and master the said Cedric; also upon
the person of a noble and freeborn damsel, the Lady
Rowena of Hargottstandstede; also upon the
person of a noble and freeborn man, Athelstane of
Coningsburgh; also upon the persons of certain
15 freeborn men, their *cnichts;* also upon certain serfs,
their born bondsmen; also upon a certain Jew,
named Isaac of York, together with his daughter,
a Jewess, and certain horses and mules: which
noble persons, with their *cnichts* and slaves, and
20 also with the horses and mules, Jew and Jewess
beforesaid, were all in peace with his Majesty, and
travelling as liege subjects upon the king's highway;
therefore we require and demand that the said noble
persons, namely, Cedric of Rotherwood, Rowena
25 of Hargottstandstede, Athelstane of Coningsburgh,
with their servants, *cnichts*, and followers, also the
horses and mules, Jew and Jewess aforesaid, to-

LINE **15.** *cnichts:* attendants. **22. liege:** free; loyal.

gether with all goods and chattels to them pertaining, be, within an hour after the delivery hereof,
delivered to us, or to those whom we shall appoint
to receive the same, and that untouched and unharmed in body and goods.   Failing of which, we do 5
pronounce to you, that we hold ye as robbers and
traitors, and will wager our bodies against ye in
battle, siege, or otherwise, and do our utmost to
your annoyance and destruction.   Wherefore may
God have you in His keeping.   Signed by us upon 10
the eve of St. Withold's day, under the great trysting oak in the Harthill Walk, the above being
written by a holy man, clerk to God, our Lady, and
St. Dunstan, in the chapel of Copmanhurst.''

At the bottom of this document was scrawled, in 15
the first place, a rude sketch of a cock's head and
comb, with a legend expressing this hieroglyphic
to be the sign-manual of Wamba, son of Witless.
Under this respectable emblem stood a cross, stated
to be the mark of Gurth, the son of Beowulph. 20
Then was written, in rough bold characters, *The
Black Sluggard*.   And, to conclude the whole, an
arrow, neatly enough drawn, was described as the
mark of the yeoman Locksley.

The knights heard this uncommon document read 25
from end to end, and then gazed upon each other in

---

LINE **1. chattels** : movable property.   **11. trysting** : chosen
for place of meeting.   **17. hieroglyphic** : character in picture writing of ancients.

silent amazement. De Bracy was the first to break silence by an uncontrollable fit of laughter, wherein he was joined, though with more moderation, by the Templar. Front-de-Bœuf, on the contrary, 5 seemed impatient of their ill-timed jocularity.

"I give you plain warning," he said, "fair sirs, that you had better consult how to bear yourselves under these circumstances than give way to such misplaced merriment."

10 "Front-de-Bœuf has not recovered his temper since his late overthrow," said De Bracy to the Templar; "he is cowed at the very idea of a cartel, though it come but from a fool and a swineherd."

"By St. Michael," answered Front-de-Bœuf, 15 "I would thou couldst stand the whole brunt of this adventure thyself, De Bracy. These fellows dared not have acted with such inconceivable impudence, had they not been supported by some strong bands. There are enough of outlaws in this forest to resent 20 my protecting the deer. I did but tie one fellow, who was taken red-handed and in the fact, to the horns of a wild stag, which gored him to death in five minutes, and I had as many arrows shot at me as there were launched against yonder target at 25 Ashby. Here, fellow," he added, to one of his attendants, "hast thou sent out to see by what force this precious challenge is to be supported?"

---

LINE **21. fact**: act.

# A Challenge and a Reply

"There are at least two hundred men assembled in the woods," answered the squire who was in attendance.

"Here is a proper matter!" said Front-de-Bœuf; "this comes of lending you the use of my castle, that cannot manage your undertaking quietly, but you must bring this nest of hornets about my ears!"

"Of hornets!" said De Bracy; "of stingless drones rather; a band of lazy knaves, who take to the wood and destroy the venison rather than labor for their maintenance."

"Stingless!" replied Front-de-Bœuf; "fork-headed shafts of a cloth-yard in length, and these shot within the breadth of a French crown, are sting enough."

"For shame, Sir Knight!" said the Templar. "Let us summon our people and sally forth upon them. One knight — ay, one man-at-arms, were enough for twenty such peasants."

"Enough, and too much," said De Bracy; "I should only be ashamed to couch lance against them."

"True," answered Front-de-Bœuf; "were they black Turks or Moors, Sir Templar, or the craven peasants of France, most valiant De Bracy; but these are English yeomen, over whom we shall have no advantage, save what we may derive from

---

LINE 4. **proper matter**: fine state of things.   14. **crown**: small gold coin.   17. **sally**: rush out suddenly.

our arms and horses, which will avail us little in the
glades of the forest.   Sally, saidst thou?   We have
scarce men enough to defend the castle.   The best
of mine are at York; so is all your band, De Bracy;
5 and we have scarcely twenty, besides the handful
that were engaged in this mad business."

"Thou dost not fear," said the Templar, "that
they can assemble in force sufficient to attempt the
castle?"

10   "Not so, Sir Brian," answered Front-de-Bœuf.
"These outlaws have indeed a daring captain; but
without machines, scaling ladders, and experienced
leaders, my castle may defy them."

"Send to thy neighbors," said the Templar;
15 "let them assemble their people and come to the
rescue of three knights, besieged by a jester and a
swineherd in the baronial castle of Reginald Front-
de-Bœuf."

"You jest, Sir Knight," answered the baron;
20 "but to whom should I send?   Malvoisin is by this
time at York with his retainers, and so are my other
allies; and so should I have been, but for this infernal enterprise."

"Then send to York and recall our people," said
25 De Bracy.   "If they abide the shaking of my
standard, or the sight of my Free Companions,
I will give them credit for the boldest outlaws ever
bent bow in greenwood."

"And who shall bear such a message?" said

Front-de-Bœuf; "they will beset every path, and rip the errand out of his bosom. I have it," he added, after pausing for a moment. "Sir Templar, thou canst write as well as read, and if we can but find the writing materials of my chaplain, who died a twelvemonth since —— "

"So please ye," said the squire, who was still in attendance, "I think old Urfried has them somewhere in keeping, for love of the confessor."

"Go, search them out, Engelred," said Front-de-Bœuf; "and then, Sir Templar, thou shalt return an answer to this bold challenge."

"I would rather do it at the sword's point than at that of the pen," said Bois-Guilbert; "but be it as you will."

He sat down accordingly, and indited, in the French language, an epistle of the following tenor:

"Sir Reginald Front-de-Bœuf, with his noble and knightly allies and confederates, receive no defiances at the hands of slaves, bondsmen, or fugitives. If the person calling himself the Black Knight have indeed a claim to the honors of chivalry, he ought to know that he stands degraded by his present association, and has no right to ask reckoning at the hands of good men of noble blood. Touching the prisoners we have made, we do in Christian charity require you to send a man of religion to receive their confession and reconcile them with God; since it is our fixed intention to

315

execute them this morning before noon, so that their heads, being placed on the battlements, shall show to all men how lightly we esteem those who have bestirred themselves in their rescue. Wherefore, as above, we require you to send a priest to reconcile them to God, in doing which you shall render them the last earthly service."

This letter, being folded, was delivered to the squire, and by him to the messenger who waited without, as the answer to that which he had brought.

The yeoman, having thus accomplished his mission, returned to the headquarters of the allies, which were for the present established under a venerable oak-tree, about three arrow-flights distant from the castle. Here Wamba and Gurth, with their allies the Black Knight and Locksley, and the jovial hermit, awaited with impatience an answer to their summons. Around, and at a distance from them, were seen many a bold yeoman, whose silvan dress and weatherbeaten countenances showed the ordinary nature of their occupation. More than two hundred had already assembled, and others were fast coming in. Those whom they obeyed as leaders were only distinguished from the others by a feather in the cap, their dress, arms, and equipments being in all other respects the same.

---

LINE 20. silvan: pertaining to woods.

LOCKSLEY'S BAND

(Courtesy of Douglas Fairbanks.)

# A Challenge and a Reply

Besides these bands, a less orderly and a worse armed force, consisting of the Saxon inhabitants of the neighboring township, as well as many bondsmen and servants from Cedric's extensive estate, had already arrived, for the purpose of 5 assisting in his rescue. Few of these were armed otherwise than with such rustic weapons as necessity sometimes converts to military purposes. Boar-spears, scythes, flails, and the like, were their chief arms; for the Normans, with the usual policy 10 of conquerors, were jealous of permitting to the vanquished Saxons the possession or the use of swords and spears. It was to the leaders of this motley army that the letter of the Templar was now delivered. 15

Reference was at first made to the chaplain for an exposition of its contents.

" By St. Dunstan," said that worthy ecclesiastic, " I swear that I cannot expound unto you this jargon, which, whether it be French or Arabic, is 20 beyond my guess."

He then gave the letter to Gurth, who shook his head gruffly, and passed it to Wamba. The Jester looked at each of the four corners of the paper with such a grin of affected intelligence as a monkey is 25 apt to assume upon similar occasions, then cut a caper, and gave the letter to Locksley.

---

LINE **18. ecclesiastic** : clergyman; priest.

317

"If the long letters were bows, and the short letters broad arrows, I might know something of the matter," said the brave yeoman.

"I must be clerk, then," said the Black Knight; 5 and taking the letter from Locksley, he first read it over to himself, and then explained the meaning in Saxon to his confederates.

"Execute the noble Cedric!" exclaimed Wamba; "by the rood, thou must be mistaken, Sir Knight."

10 "Not I, my worthy friend," replied the knight, "I have explained the words as they are here set down."

"Then," replied Gurth, "we will have the castle, should we tear it down with our hands!"

15 "'Tis but a contrivance to gain time," said Locksley; "they dare not do a deed for which I could exact a fearful penalty."

"I would," said the Black Knight, "there were some one among us who could obtain admission into 20 the castle, and discover how the case stands with the besieged. Methinks, as they require a confessor to be sent, this holy hermit might at once exercise his pious vocation and procure us the information we desire."

25 "A plague on thee and thy advice!" said the pious hermit; "I tell thee, Sir Slothful Knight, that when I doff my friar's frock, my priesthood,

---

LINE **9. rood**: cross.

my sanctity, my very Latin, are put off along with it."

"I fear," said the Black Knight—"I fear greatly there is no one here that is qualified to take upon him this character of father confessor?" 5

All looked on each other, and were silent.

"I see," said Wamba, after a short pause, "that the fool must be still the fool, and put his neck in the venture which wise men shrink from. You must know, my dear cousins and countrymen, that I 10 was bred to be a friar, until a brain-fever came upon me and left me just wit enough to be a fool. I trust, with the assistance of the good hermit's frock, I shall be found qualified to administer both worldly and ghostly comfort to our worthy master Cedric 15 and his companions in adversity."

"Hath he sense enough, thinkst thou?" said the Black Knight, addressing Gurth.

"I know not," said Gurth; "but if he hath not, it will be the first time he hath wanted wit to turn 20 his folly to account."

"On with the frock, then, good fellow," quoth the Knight, "and let thy master send us an account of their situation within the castle. Their numbers must be few, and it is five to one they may be acces- 25 sible by a sudden and bold attack. Time wears — away with thee."

---

LINE 15. ghostly: spiritual.

"And, in the meantime," said Locksley, "we will beset the place so closely that not so much as a fly shall carry news from thence. So that, my good friend," he continued, addressing Wamba, "thou mayst assure these tyrants that whatever violence they exercise on the persons of their prisoners shall be most severely repaid upon their own."

"*Pax vobiscum,*" said Wamba, who was now muffled in his religious disguise.

And so saying, he imitated the solemn and stately deportment of a friar, and departed to execute his mission.

---

LINE 8. *Pax vobiscum.* Peace be with you.

# CHAPTER XXVI

## Wamba in a Friar's Frock

When the Jester, arrayed in the cowl and frock of
the hermit, and having his knotted cord twisted
round his middle, stood before the portal of the
castle of Front-de-Bœuf, the warder demanded of
him his name and errand.                                   5

"*Pax vobiscum*," answered the Jester, "I am a
poor brother of the Order of St. Francis, who come
hither to do my office to certain unhappy prisoners
now secured within this castle. I pray thee, do
mine errand to the lord of the castle; trust me, it 10
will find good acceptance with him."

"Gramercy," said the warder; "but if I come
to shame for leaving my post upon thine errand,
I will try whether a friar's grey gown be proof
against a grey-goose shaft."                               15

With this threat he left his turret, and carried to
the hall of the castle his unwonted intelligence, that
a holy friar stood before the gate and demanded
instant admission. With no small wonder he received his master's commands to admit the holy 20

---

LINE 7. **Order of St. Francis**: Franciscans. See page 621.
**15. grey-goose shaft**: arrow. **17. unwonted**: unusual.

321

man immediately; and, having previously manned the entrance to guard against surprise, he obeyed the commands which he had received. The hare-brained self-conceit which had emboldened Wamba
5 to undertake this dangerous office was scarce sufficient to support him when he found himself in the presence of a man so dreadful, and so much dreaded, as Reginald Front-de-Bœuf, and he brought out his " *Pax vobiscum*," to which he, in a good measure,
10 trusted for supporting his character, with more anxiety and hesitation than had hitherto accompanied it. But Front-de-Bœuf was accustomed to see men of all ranks tremble in his presence, so that the timidity of the supposed father did not
15 give him any cause of suspicion. "Who and whence art thou, priest?" said he.

" *Pax vobiscum*," reiterated the Jester; "I am a poor servant of St. Francis, who, travelling through this wilderness, have fallen among thieves, which
20 thieves have sent me unto this castle in order to do my ghostly office on two persons condemned by your honorable justice."

"Ay, right," answered Front-de-Bœuf; "and canst thou tell me, holy father, the number of those
25 banditti?"

"Gallant sir," answered the Jester, "their name is legion."

---

LINE 3. hare-brained: foolish; rash.

"Tell me in plain terms what numbers there are, or, priest, thy cloak and cord will ill protect thee."

"I conceive," said the supposed friar, "they may be, what of yeomen, what of commons, at least five hundred men." 5

"What!" said the Templar, who came into the hall that moment, "muster the wasps so thick here? It is time to stifle such a mischievous brood." Then taking Front-de-Bœuf aside, "Knowest thou the priest?" 10

"He is a stranger from a distant convent," said Front-de-Bœuf; "I know him not."

"Then trust him not with thy purpose in words," answered the Templar. "Let him carry a written order to De Bracy's company of Free Companions, 15 to repair instantly to their master's aid. In the meantime, and that the shaveling may suspect nothing, permit him to go freely about his task of preparing these Saxon hogs for the slaughter-house." 20

"It shall be so," said Front-de-Bœuf. And he forthwith appointed a domestic to conduct Wamba to the apartment where Cedric and Athelstane were confined.

The impatience of Cedric had been enhanced by 25 his confinement. He walked from one end of the hall to the other, sometimes ejaculating to himself,

---

LINE 17. shaveling: monk or friar.

sometimes addressing Athelstane, who was not greatly interesting himself about the duration of his captivity, which he concluded would, like all earthly evils, find an end in Heaven's good time.

5 " *Pax vobiscum*," said the Jester, entering the apartment; "the blessing of St. Dunstan, St. Denis, St. Duthoc, and all other saints whatsoever, be upon ye and about ye."

" Enter freely," answered Cedric to the supposed 10 friar; "with what intent art thou come hither?"

" To bid you prepare yourselves for death," answered the Jester.

" Hearest thou this, Athelstane?" said Cedric. " We must rouse up our hearts to this last action, 15 since better it is we should die like men than live like slaves."

" I am ready," answered Athelstane, " to stand the worst of their malice, and shall walk to my death with as much composure as ever I did to my 20 dinner."

" Let us then unto our holy gear, father," said Cedric.

" Wait yet a moment, good uncle," said the Jester, in his natural tone; " better look long before 25 you leap in the dark."

" By my faith," said Cedric, " I should know that voice!"

---

LINE 21. gear: business.

"It is that of your trusty slave and jester," answered Wamba, throwing back his cowl. "Had you taken a fool's advice formerly, you would not have been here at all. Take a fool's advice now, and you will not be here long." 5

"How mean'st thou, knave?" answered the Saxon.

"Even thus," replied Wamba; "take thou this frock and cord, and march quietly out of the castle, leaving me your cloak and girdle to take the long 10 leap in thy stead."

"Leave thee in my stead!" said Cedric, astonished at the proposal; "why, they would hang thee, my poor knave."

"E'en let them do as they are permitted," said 15 Wamba; "I trust — no disparagement to your birth — that the son of Witless may hang in a chain with as much gravity as the chain hung upon his ancestor the alderman."

"Well, Wamba," answered Cedric, "for one 20 thing will I grant thy request. And that is, if thou wilt make the exchange of garments with Lord Athelstane instead of me."

"No, by St. Dunstan," answered Wamba; "there were little reason in that. Good right there 25 is that the son of Witless should suffer to save the son of Hereward; but little wisdom there were in

---

LINE **2. cowl**: hood. **17. chain**: his badge of office.

his dying for the benefit of one whose fathers were strangers to his."

"Villain," said Cedric, "the fathers of Athelstane were monarchs of England!"

5 "They might be whomsoever they pleased," replied Wamba; "but my neck stands too straight upon my shoulders to have it twisted for their sake. Wherefore, good my master, either take my proffer yourself or suffer me to leave this dungeon as free as 10 I entered."

"Let the old tree wither," continued Cedric, "so the stately hope of the forest be preserved. Save the noble Athelstane, my trusty Wamba! it is the duty of each who has Saxon blood in his 15 veins."

"Not so, father Cedric," said Athelstane, grasping his hand, for, when roused to think or act, his deeds and sentiments were not unbecoming his high race — "not so," he continued; "I would rather 20 remain in this hall a week without food save the prisoner's stinted loaf, or drink save the prisoner's measure of water, than embrace the opportunity to escape which the slave's untaught kindness has purveyed for his master."

25 "You are called wise men, sirs," said the Jester, "and I a crazed fool; but, uncle Cedric and cousin Athelstane, the fool shall decide this controversy

---

LINE **21. stinted**: scant. **24. purveyed**: provided.

for ye. I am like John-a-Duck's mare, that will let no man mount her but John-a-Duck. I'll hang for no man but my own born master."

"Go, then, noble Cedric," said Athelstane, "neglect not this opportunity. Your presence without may encourage friends to our rescue; your remaining here would ruin us all."

"And is there any prospect, then, of rescue from without?" said Cedric, looking to the Jester.

"Prospect, indeed!" echoed Wamba; "let me tell you, when you fill my cloak, you are wrapped in a general's cassock. Five hundred men are there without, and I was this morning one of their chief leaders. My fool's cap was a casque, and my bauble a truncheon. Well, we shall see what good they will make by exchanging a fool for a wise man. Truly, I fear they will lose in valor what they may gain in discretion. And so farewell, master, and be kind to poor Gurth and his dog Fangs; and let my cockscomb hang in the hall at Rotherwood, in memory that I flung away my life for my master, like a faithful — fool." The last word came out with a sort of double expression, betwixt jest and earnest.

The tears stood in Cedric's eyes. "Thy memory

---

LINE **12. cassock**: coat or cloak. **14. casque**: helmet. **15. bauble**: stick with ass-eared head carved on it. **truncheon**: staff of authority or office. **20. cockscomb**: jester's cap, which had on it a red ridge like the comb of a cock.

shall be preserved," he said, " while fidelity and affection have honor upon earth! But that I trust I shall find the means of saving Rowena, and thee, Athelstane, and thee also, my poor Wamba, thou shouldst not overbear me in this matter."

The exchange of dress was now accomplished, when a sudden doubt struck Cedric.

" I know no language," he said, " but my own, and a few words of their mincing Norman. How shall I bear myself like a reverend brother?"

" The spell lies in two words," replied Wamba. " *Pax vobiscum* will answer all queries. Speak it but thus, in a deep grave tone — *Pax vobiscum* — it is irresistible. Watch and ward, knight and squire, foot and horse, it acts as a charm upon them all. I think, if they bring me out to be hanged to-morrow, as is much to be doubted they may, I will try its weight upon the finisher of the sentence."

" If such prove the case," said his master, " my religious orders are soon taken — *Pax vobiscum.* I trust I shall remember the password. Noble Athelstane, farewell; and farewell, my poor boy, whose heart might make amends for a weaker head; I will save you, or return and die with you. The royal blood of our Saxon kings shall not be spilt while mine beats in my veins; nor shall one hair

---

LINE **5**. **overbear**: overcome. **9**. **mincing**: affected. **17**. **doubted**: feared. **20**. **orders**: admittance into the ministry or priesthood.

fall from the head of the kind knave who risked himself for his master, if Cedric's peril can prevent it. Farewell."

"Farewell, noble Cedric," said Athelstane; "remember, it is the true part of a friar to accept refreshment, if you are offered any."

"Farewell, uncle," added Wamba; "and remember *Pax vobiscum.*"

Thus exhorted, Cedric sallied forth upon his expedition; and it was not long ere he had occasion to try the force of that spell which his Jester had recommended as omnipotent. In a low-arched and dusky passage, by which he endeavored to work his way to the hall of the castle, he was interrupted by a female form.

"*Pax vobiscum!*" said the pseudo friar, and was endeavoring to hurry past, when a soft voice replied, "*Et vobis; quæso, domine reverendissime, pro misericordia vestra.*"

"I am somewhat deaf," replied Cedric, in good Saxon, and at the same time muttered to himself, "A curse on the fool and his *Pax vobiscum!* I have lost my javelin at the first cast."

It was, however, no unusual thing for a priest of those days to be deaf of his Latin ear, and this the person who now addressed Cedric knew full well.

"I pray you of dear love, reverend father," she

---

LINE **16.** pseudo: pretended. **18.** *Et vobis*, etc. And with you. I pray, most reverend father, for your pity.

replied in his own language, " that you will deign
to visit with your ghostly comfort a wounded
prisoner of this castle, and have such compassion
upon him and us as thy holy office teaches."

5    " Daughter," answered Cedric, much embarrassed, " my time in this castle will not permit
me to exercise the duties of mine office.  I must
presently forth : there is life and death upon my
speed."

10    " Yet, father, let me entreat you by the vow you
have taken on you," replied the suppliant, " not to
leave the oppressed and endangered without counsel
or succor."

The colloquy was interrupted by the harsh voice
15 of Urfried, the old crone of the turret.

" Come this way, father," said the old hag, " thou
art a stranger in this castle, and canst not leave it
without a guide.  Come thither, for I would speak
with thee.  And you, Jewess, go to the sick man's
20 chamber, and tend him until my return ; and woe
betide you if you again quit it without my permission ! "

Rebecca retreated.  Her importunities had prevailed upon Urfried to suffer her to quit the turret,
25 and Urfried had employed her services where she
herself would most gladly have paid them, by the
bedside of the wounded Ivanhoe.  Prompt to avail

---

LINE **14. colloquy** : conversation. **15. crone** : withered
old woman. **23. importunities** : troubling insistence.

herself of each means of safety which occurred, Rebecca had hoped something from the presence of a man of religion, who, she learned from Urfried, had penetrated into this godless castle. She watched the return of the supposed ecclesiastic, s with the purpose of addressing him, and interesting him in favor of the prisoners; with what imperfect success the reader has been just acquainted.

# CHAPTER XXVII

## Cedric's Escape

Urfried proceeded to conduct the unwilling Cedric into a small apartment, the door of which she heedfully secured. Then fetching from a cupboard a stoup of wine and two flagons, she placed them on 5 the table, and said, " Thou art Saxon, father. Deny it not; the sounds of my native language are sweet to mine ears, though seldom heard save from the tongues of the wretched and degraded serfs on whom the proud Normans impose the meanest 10 drudgery of this dwelling. Thou art a Saxon — a Saxon priest, and I have one question to ask of thee."

" I am Saxon," answered Cedric, " but unworthy, surely, of the name of priest. Let me begone on my 15 way. I swear I will return, or send one of our fathers more worthy to hear your confession."

" Stay yet a while," said Urfried; " the voice which thou hearest now will soon be choked with the cold earth, and I would not descend to it like the 20 beast I have lived. But wine must give me strength to tell the horrors of my tale." She poured

out a cup, and drank it with a frightful avidity.
"It stupefies," she said, looking upwards as she
finished her draught, "but it cannot cheer. Partake it, father, if you would hear my tale without
sinking down upon the pavement." He complied 5
with her request, and answered her challenge in a
large wine-cup; she then proceeded with her
story.

"I was not born," she said, "father, the wretch
that thou now seest me. I was free, was happy, 10
was honored, loved, and was beloved. I am now a
slave, miserable and degraded. Dost thou wonder,
father, that I should hate mankind, and, above all,
the race that has wrought this change in me? Can
the wrinkled decrepit hag before thee, whose wrath 15
must vent itself in impotent curses, forget she was
once the daughter of the noble thane of Torquilstone, before whose frown a thousand vassals
trembled?"

"Thou the daughter of Torquil Wolfganger!" 20
said Cedric, receding as he spoke; "thou — thou
— the daughter of that noble Saxon, my father's
friend and companion in arms!"

"Thy father's friend!" echoed Urfried; "then
Cedric called the Saxon stands before me, for the 25
noble Hereward of Rotherwood had but one son,
whose name is well known among his countrymen.

---

But if thou art Cedric of Rotherwood, why this religious dress?"

"It matters not who I am," said Cedric; "proceed, unhappy woman, with thy tale!"

5 "There is — there is," answered the wretched woman, "deep, black, damning guilt — guilt that lies like a load at my breast. Yes, in these halls, stained with the noble and pure blood of my father and my brethren — in these very halls, to have lived 10 the paramour of their murderer, the slave at once and the partaker of his pleasures, was to render every breath which I drew of air a crime and a curse."

"Wretched woman!" exclaimed Cedric. "And while the friends of thy father — while each true 15 Saxon heart, as it breathed a requiem for his soul, and those of his valiant sons, forgot not in their prayers the murdered Ulrica — while all mourned and honored the dead, thou hast lived to merit our hate and execration — lived to unite thyself 20 with the vile tyrant who murdered thy nearest and dearest. Had I but dreamed of the daughter of Torquil living with the murderer of her father, the sword of a true Saxon had found thee out."

"Wouldst thou indeed have done this justice to 25 the name of Torquil?" said Ulrica, for we may now lay aside her assumed name of Urfried; "thou art then the true Saxon report speaks thee! for even

---

LINE **15. requiem**: mass for repose of souls of dead.

within these accursed walls has the name of **Cedric** been sounded; and I, wretched and degraded, have rejoiced to think that there yet breathed an avenger of our unhappy nation. I also have had my hours of vengeance. I have fomented the quarrels of our foes, and heated drunken revelry into murderous broil. I have seen their blood flow — I have heard their dying groans! I was able to set at variance the elder Front-de-Bœuf and his son Reginald! Long had the smouldering fire of discord glowed between the tyrant father and his savage son; long had I nursed, in secret, the unnatural hatred; it blazed forth in an hour of drunken wassail, and at his own board fell my oppressor by the hand of his own son."

"And thou, creature of guilt and misery," said Cedric, "what became thy lot on his death?"

"Guess it, but ask it not. Here — here I dwelt, till age, premature age, has stamped its ghastly features on my countenance — scorned and insulted where I was once obeyed, and condemned to hear from my lonely turret the sounds of revelry in which I once partook, or the shrieks and groans of new victims. Tell me, if thou canst, what fate is prepared beyond the grave for her to whom God has assigned on earth a lot of such unspeakable wretchedness."

---

LINE **13. wassail**: carouse.   **19. premature**: occurring before usual time.

"I am no priest," said Cedric, turning with disgust from this miserable picture of guilt, wretchedness, and despair — "I am no priest, though I wear a priest's garment."

5  "Priest or layman," answered Ulrica, "thou art the first I have seen for twenty years by whom God was feared or man regarded; and dost thou bid me despair?"

"I bid thee repent," said Cedric. "Seek to 10 prayer and penance, and mayest thou find acceptance! But I cannot, I will not, longer abide with thee."

"Stay yet a moment!" said Ulrica; "leave me not now, son of my father's friend, lest the demon 15 who has governed my life should tempt me to avenge myself of thy hard-hearted scorn. Thinkest thou, if Front-de-Bœuf found Cedric the Saxon in his castle, in such a disguise, that thy life would be a long one? Already his eye has been upon thee like 20 a falcon on his prey."

"And be it so," said Cedric; "and let him tear me with beak and talons, ere my tongue say one word which my heart doth not warrant. I will die a Saxon — true in word, open in deed. I bid thee 25 avaunt! touch me not, stay me not!"

"Be it so," said Ulrica; "go thy way, and forget that the wretch before thee is the daughter of thy

---

Line 25. **avaunt**: begone.

father's friend. Go thy way; if I am separated from mankind by my sufferings, not less will I be separated from them in my revenge! No man shall aid me, but the ears of all men shall tingle to hear of the deed which I shall do! All is possible for those who dare to die! Thou thyself shalt say that, whatever was the life of Ulrica, her death well became the daughter of the noble Torquil. There is a force without beleaguering this accursed castle; hasten to lead them to the attack, and when thou shalt see a red flag wave from the turret on the eastern angle of the donjon, press the Normans hard: they will then have enough to dc within, and you may win the wall in spite both of bow and mangonel. Begone, I pray thee; follow thine own fate, and leave me to mine."

Cedric would have inquired farther into the purpose which she thus darkly announced, but the stern voice of Front-de-Bœuf was heard exclaiming, "Where tarries this loitering priest? I will make a martyr of him, if he loiters here to hatch treason among my domestics!"

Ulrica vanished through a private door, and Reginald Front-de-Bœuf entered the apartment. Cedric, with some difficulty, compelled himself to make obeisance to the haughty Baron, who returned his courtesy with a slight inclination of the head.

---

LINE **12. donjon**: keep, or great tower, of castle. **15. man- gonel**: machine for hurling stones.

"Thy penitents, father, have made a long shrift: it is the better for them, since it is the last they shall ever make. Hast thou prepared them for death?"

"I found them," said Cedric, in such French as as he could command, "expecting the worst."

"How now, Sir Friar," replied Front-de-Bœuf, "thy speech, methinks, smacks of a Saxon tongue?"

"I was bred in the convent of St. Withold of Burton," answered Cedric.

"Ay?" said the Baron; "it had been better for thee to have been a Norman, and better for my purpose too; but need has no choice of messengers. The day will soon come that the frock shall protect the Saxon as little as the mail-coat."

"God's will be done," said Cedric, in a voice tremulous with passion, which Front-de-Bœuf imputed to fear.

"But do me one cast of thy holy office," said he, "and, come what list of others, thou shalt sleep as safe in thy cell as a snail within his shell of proof."

"Speak your commands," said Cedric, with suppressed emotion.

"Follow me through this passage, then, that I may dismiss thee by the postern."

And as he strode on his way before the supposed friar, Front-de-Bœuf thus schooled him in the part which he desired he should act.

---

LINE **1. shrift**: confession to priest. **18. cast**: service; stroke. **20. proof**: tried strength. **24. postern**: rear gate.

"Thou seest, Sir Friar, yon herd of Saxon swine, who have dared to environ this castle of Torquilstone. Tell them whatever thou hast a mind of the weakness of this fortalice, or aught else that can detain them before it for twenty-four hours. Meantime bear thou this scroll. But soft — canst read, Sir Priest?"

"Not a jot I," answered Cedric, "save on my breviary; and then I know the characters, because I have the holy service by heart."

"The fitter messenger for my purpose. Carry thou this scroll to the castle of Philip de Malvoisin; say it cometh from me, and is written by the Templar Brian de Bois-Guilbert, and that I pray him to send it to York with all the speed man and horse can make. Meanwhile, tell him he shall find us whole and sound behind our battlement. I say to thee, priest, contrive some cast of thine art to keep the knaves where they are, until our friends bring up their lances."

"By my patron saint," said Cedric, with deeper energy than became his character, "and by every saint who has lived and died in England, your commands shall be obeyed! Not a Saxon shall stir from before these walls, if I have art and influence to detain them there."

"Ha!" said Front-de-Bœuf, "thou changest thy

---

LINE **4. fortalice**: small fort.  **9. breviary**: book containing daily prayers of Roman Catholic Church.

tone, Sir Priest, and speakest brief and bold, as if thy heart were in the slaughter of the Saxon herd; and yet thou art thyself of kindred to the swine?"

Cedric was no ready practiser of the art of dissimulation, and would at this moment have been much the better of a hint from Wamba's more fertile brain. But necessity, according to the ancient proverb, sharpens invention, and he muttered something under his cowl concerning the men in question being excommunicated outlaws both to church and to kingdom.

Front-de-Bœuf, in the meanwhile, led the way to a postern, where, passing the moat on a single plank, they reached a small barbican, or exterior defence, which communicated with the open field by a well-fortified sallyport.

"Begone, then; and if thou wilt do mine errand, and if thou return hither when it is done, thou shalt see Saxon flesh cheap as ever was hog's in the shambles of Sheffield."

"Assuredly we shall meet again," answered Cedric.

"Something in hand the whilst," continued the Norman; and, as they parted at the postern door, he thrust into Cedric's reluctant hand a gold byzant,

---

LINE **4**. dissimulation: false pretense.   **10**. excommunicated: cut off from church-membership.   **16**. sallyport: gate through which besieged might suddenly launch an attack. **20**. shambles: slaughter-house.

adding, "Remember, I will flay off both cowl and skin if thou failest in thy purpose."

"And full leave will I give thee to do both," answered Cedric, leaving the postern, and striding forth over the free field with a joyful step, "if, when we meet next, I deserve not better at thine hand." Turning then back towards the castle, he threw the piece of gold towards the donor, exclaiming at the same time, "False Norman, thy money perish with thee!"

Front-de-Bœuf heard the words imperfectly, but the action was suspicious. "Archers," he called to the warders on the outward battlements, "send me an arrow through yon monk's frock! Yet stay," he said, as his retainers were bending their bows, "it avails not; we must thus far trust him since we have no better shift. I think he dares not betray me; at the worst I can but treat with these Saxon dogs whom I have safe in kennel. Ho! Giles jailer, let them bring Cedric of Rotherwood before me, and the other churl, his companion, Athelstane there. Give me a stoup of wine; place it in the armory, and thither lead the prisoners."

His commands were obeyed; and, upon entering that Gothic apartment, hung with many spoils won by his own valor and that of his father, he found a flagon of wine on the massive oaken table, and the two Saxon captives under the guard of four of his dependants. Front-de-Bœuf took a long

draught of wine, and then addressed his prisoners;
for the manner in which Wamba drew the cap over
his face, the change of dress, the gloomy and broken
light, and the Baron's imperfect acquaintance with
5 the features of Cedric prevented him from discovering that the most important of his captives had
made his escape.

"Gallants of England," said Front-de-Bœuf,
"how relish ye your entertainment at Torquil-
10 stone? By God and St. Denis, an ye pay not the
richer ransom, I will hang ye up by the feet from the
iron bars of these windows, till the kites and hooded
crows have made skeletons of you! Speak out, ye
Saxon dogs — what bid ye for your worthless lives?
15 How say you, you of Rotherwood?"

"Not a doit I," answered poor Wamba; "and
for hanging up by the feet, my brain has been topsy-
turvy, they say, ever since the biggin was bound
first round my head; so turning me upside down
20 may peradventure restore it again."

"St. Genevieve!" said Front-de-Bœuf, "what
have we got here?"

And with the back of his hand he struck Cedric's
cap from the head of the Jester, and throwing open
25 his collar, discovered the fatal badge of servitude,
the silver collar round his neck

---

LINE **12. kites**: hawk-like birds. **16. doit**: Dutch coin
worth quarter of cent; any small sum. **18. biggin**: child's
cap.

"Giles — Clement — dogs and varlets!" exclaimed the furious Norman, "what have you brought me here?"

"I think I can tell you," said De Bracy, who just entered the apartment. "This is Cedric's clown, who fought so manful a skirmish with Isaac of York about a question of precedence."

"I shall settle it for them both," replied Front-de-Bœuf; "they shall hang on the same gallows, unless his master and this boar of Coningsburgh will pay well for their lives. They must also carry off with them the swarms that are besetting the castle, and live under us as serfs and vassals. Go," said he to two of his attendants, "fetch me the right Cedric hither, and I pardon your error for once; the rather that you but mistook a fool for a Saxon franklin."

"Ay, but," said Wamba, "your chivalrous excellency will find there are more fools than franklins among us."

"What means the knave?" said Front-de-Bœuf, looking towards his followers, who faltered forth their belief that, if this were not Cedric who was there in presence, they knew not what was become of him.

"Saints of Heaven!" exclaimed De Bracy, "he must have escaped in the monk's garments!"

"Fiends of hell!" echoed Front-de-Bœuf, "it

---

LINE 1. **varlets**: rascals.

was then the boar of Rotherwood whom I ushered
to the postern, and dismissed with my own hands!
And thou," he said to Wamba, " I will give thee
holy orders — I will shave thy crown for thee!
5 Here, let them tear the scalp from his head, and
then pitch him headlong from the battlements.
Thy trade is to jest, canst thou jest now?"

" You deal with me better than your word, noble
knight," whimpered forth poor Wamba; " if you
10 give me the red cap you propose, out of a simple
monk you will make a cardinal."

" The poor wretch," said De Bracy, " is resolved
to die in his vocation. Front-de-Bœuf, you shall
not slay him. Give him to me to make sport for
15 my Free Companions. How sayst thou, knave?
Wilt thou take heart of grace, and go to the wars
with me?"

" Ay, with my master's leave," said Wamba;
" for, look you, I must not slip collar (and he
20 touched that which he wore) without his
permission."

" Oh, a Norman saw will soon cut a Saxon
collar," said De Bracy.

" Ay, noble sir," said Wamba, " and thence goes
25 the proverb:

> Norman saw an English oak,
> On English neck a Norman yoke;

---

LINE 11. cardinal: church dignitary next in rank to the
Pope. His badge of office is a red cap or hat.

Norman spoon in English dish,
And England ruled as Normans wish;
Blythe world to England never will be more,
Till England's rid of all the four."

"Thou dost well, De Bracy," said Front-de- 5
Bœuf, " to stand there listening to a fool's jargon,
when destruction is gaping for us!"

"To the battlements then," said De Bracy;
" when didst thou ever see me the graver for the
thoughts of battle? Call the Templar yonder, 10
and let him fight but half so well for his life as he has
done for his order. Make thou to the walls thyself
with thy huge body. Let me do my poor endeavor
in my own way, and I tell thee the Saxon outlaws
may as well attempt to scale the clouds as the castle 15
of Torquilstone. Here, Saxon," he continued, addressing Athelstane, and handing the cup to him,
" rinse thy throat with that noble liquor, and rouse
up thy soul to say what thou wilt do for thy
liberty." 20

"What a man of mould may," answered Athelstane, " providing it be what a man of manhood
ought. Dismiss me free, with my companions, and
I will pay a ransom of a thousand marks."

"And wilt moreover assure us the retreat of that 25
scum of mankind who are swarming around the
castle?" said Front-de-Bœuf.

---

LINE 21. man of mould : mortal man.

"In so far as I can," answered Athelstane, "I will withdraw them."

"We are agreed then," said Front-de-Bœuf; "thou and they are to be set at freedom, and peace
5 is to be on both sides, for payment of a thousand marks. But this extends not to the Jew Isaac."

"Nor to the Jew Isaac's daughter," said the Templar, who had now joined them.

"Neither," said Front-de-Bœuf, "belong to this
10 Saxon's company."

"Neither does the ransom include the Lady Rowena," said De Bracy.

"Neither," said Front-de-Bœuf, "does our treaty refer to this wretched Jester, whom I retain,
15 that I may make him an example to every knave who turns jest into earnest."

"The Lady Rowena," answered Athelstane, with the most steady countenance, "is my affianced bride. I will be drawn by wild horses before I
20 consent to part with her. The slave Wamba has this day saved the life of my father Cedric. I will lose mine ere a hair of his head be injured."

"Thy affianced bride! The Lady Rowena the
25 affianced bride of a vassal like thee!" said De Bracy. "Saxon, thou dreamest that the days of thy seven kingdoms are returned again. I tell thee,

---

LINE 18. affianced: promised in marriage.

the princes of the house of Anjou confer not their wards on men of such lineage as thine."

"My lineage, proud Norman," replied Athelstane, "is drawn from a source more pure and ancient than that of a beggarly Frenchman, whose living is won by selling the blood of the thieves whom he assembles under his paltry standard. Kings were my ancestors, strong in war, and wise in council, who every day feasted in their hall more hundreds than thou canst number individual followers; whose names have been sung by minstrels, and whose bones were interred amid the prayers of saints."

The conversation was interrupted by the arrival of a menial, who announced that a monk demanded admittance at the postern gate.

"In the name of St. Bennet," said Front-de-Bœuf, "have we a real monk this time, or another impostor? Search him, slaves; for an ye suffer a second impostor to be palmed upon you, I will have your eyes torn out, and hot coals put into the sockets."

"Let me endure the extremity of your anger, my lord," said Giles, "if this be not Brother Ambrose, a monk in attendance upon the Prior of Jorvaulx."

"Admit him," said Front-de-Bœuf; "most likely he brings us news from his jovial master. Remove these prisoners; and, Saxon, think on what thou hast heard."

"I claim," said Athelstane, "an honorable imprisonment, as becomes my rank. Moreover, I hold him that deems himself the best of you bound to answer to me with his body for this aggression on my freedom. There lies my glove."

5 "I answer not the challenge of my prisoner," said Front-de-Bœuf, "nor shalt thou, Maurice de Bracy. Giles," he continued, "hang the franklin's glove upon the tine of yonder branched antlers; there shall it remain until he is a free man. Should 10 he then presume to demand it, or to affirm he was unlawfully made my prisoner, he will speak to one who hath never refused to meet a foe on foot or on horseback!"

The Saxon prisoners were accordingly removed, 15 just as they introduced the monk Ambrose, who appeared to be in great perturbation.

"So please you," said Ambrose, "violent hands having been imposed on my reverend superior, and the infesters of these woods having rifled his mails 20 and budgets, and stripped him of two hundred marks of pure refined gold, they do yet demand of him a large sum beside, ere they will suffer him to depart. Wherefore the reverend father in God prays you, as his dear friends, to rescue him either 25 by paying down the ransom at which they hold him, or by force of arms."

"Here is a new argument for our swords, sirs,"

---

LINE 8. **tine**: point; prong. **19. mails**: bags; saddle bags. **20. budgets**: wallets.

said Front-de-Bœuf, turning to his companions; " and so, instead of reaching us any assistance, the Prior of Jorvaulx requests aid at our hands? When did thy master hear of a Norman baron unbuckling his purse to relieve a churchman? And how can 5 we do aught by valor to free him, that are cooped up here by ten times our number, and expect an assault every moment?"

" To the battlements!" cried De Bracy, " and let us mark what these knaves do without; " and 10 so saying, he opened a latticed window which led to a sort of bartizan or projecting balcony, and immediately called from thence to those in the apartment, " They bring forward mantelets and pavisses, and the archers muster on the skirts of the wood 15 like a dark cloud before a hail-storm."

Reginald Front-de-Bœuf also looked out upon the field, and immediately snatched his bugle; and after winding a long and loud blast, commanded his men to their posts on the walls. 20

" De Bracy, look to the eastern side where the walls are lowest. Noble Bois-Guilbert, thy trade hath well taught thee how to attack and defend, look thou to the western side. I myself will take post at the barbican. Yet, do not confine your 25

---

LINE **14. mantelets**: movable defenses made of planks. **pavisses**: shields large enough to cover whole body. **25. barbican**: outer fortification, usually defending entrance over a drawbridge.

exertions to any one spot, noble friends! We must this day be everywhere, and multiply ourselves, were it possible, so as to carry by our presence succor and relief wherever the attack is hottest. Our numbers are few, but activity and courage may supply that defect."

"But, noble knights," exclaimed Father Ambrose, amidst the bustle and confusion occasioned by the preparations for defence, "will none of ye hear the message of the reverend father in God, Aymer, Prior of Jorvaulx? I beseech thee to hear me, noble Sir Reginald!"

"Go patter thy petitions to Heaven," said the fierce Norman, "for we on earth have no time to listen to them. Ho! there, Anselm! see that seething pitch and oil are ready to pour on the heads of these audacious traitors. Look that the crossbowmen lack not bolts. Fling abroad my banner with the old bull's head; the knaves shall soon find with whom they have to do this day!"

The Templar had been looking out on the proceedings of the besiegers, with rather more attention than the brutal Front-de-Bœuf or his giddy companion.

"By the faith of mine order," he said, "these men approach with more touch of discipline than could have been judged, however they come by it. See ye how dexterously they avail themselves of every cover which a tree or bush affords, and shun

exposing themselves to the shot of our crossbows?
I spy neither banner nor pennon among them, and
yet will I gage my golden chain that they are led on
by some noble knight or gentleman, skilful in the
practice of wars." 5

"I espy him," said De Bracy; "I see the waving
of a knight's crest, and the gleam of his armor.
See yon tall man in the black mail, who is busied
marshalling the farther troop of yeomen; by St.
Denis, I hold him to be the same whom we called the 10
Black Sluggard, who overthrew thee, Front-de-
Bœuf, in the lists at Ashby."

"So much the better," said Front-de-Bœuf,
" that he comes here to give me my revenge. Some
hilding fellow he must be, who dared not stay to 15
assert his claim to the tourney prize which chance
had assigned him. I should in vain have sought
for him where knights and nobles seek their foes,
and right glad am I he hath here shown himself
among yon villain yeomanry." 20

The demonstrations of the enemy's immediate
approach cut off all farther discourse. Each knight
repaired to his post, and at the head of the few
followers whom they were able to muster, they
awaited with calm determination the threatened 25
assault.

---

LINE 15. hilding: cowardly.

# CHAPTER XXVIII

## Rebecca Nurses Ivanhoe

Our history must needs retrograde to inform the reader that, when Ivanhoe sunk down, and seemed abandoned by all the world, it was the importunity of Rebecca which prevailed on her father to have 5 the gallant young warrior transported from the lists to the house which, for the time, the Jews inhabited in the suburbs of Ashby.

Rebecca's knowledge of medicine and of the heal-ing art had been acquired under an aged Jewess, 10 the daughter of one of their most celebrated doctors, who loved Rebecca as her own child, and was believed to have communicated to her secrets which had been left to herself by her sage father. The fate of Miriam had indeed been to fall a sacrifice 15 to the fanaticism of the times; but her secrets had survived in her apt pupil. Rebecca, thus endowed with knowledge as with beauty, was universally revered and admired by her own tribe, who almost regarded her as one of those gifted women mentioned 20 in the sacred history.

When Ivanhoe reached the habitation of Isaac,

LINE 15. **fanaticism**: unreasoning enthusiasm.

he was still in a state of unconsciousness, owing to the profuse loss of blood which had taken place during his exertions in the lists.   Rebecca examined the wound, and having applied to it such remedies as her art prescribed, informed her father that if 5 fever could be averted, and if the healing balsam of Miriam retained its virtue, there was nothing to fear for his guest's life, and that he might with safety travel to York with them on the ensuing day. Isaac looked a little blank at this annunciation. 10 His charity would willingly have stopped short at Ashby, or at most would have left the wounded Christian to be tended in the house where he was residing at present, with an assurance to the Hebrew to whom it belonged that all expenses should be 15 duly discharged.   To this, however, Rebecca opposed many reasons, of which we shall only mention two that had peculiar weight with Isaac.   The one was, that she would on no account put the phial of precious balsam into the hands of another physi- 20 cian even of her own tribe, lest that valuable mystery should be discovered; the other, that this wounded knight, Wilfred of Ivanhoe, was an intimate favorite of Richard Cœur-de-Lion, and that, in case the monarch should return, Isaac, who had 25 supplied his brother John with treasure to prosecute his rebellious purposes, would stand in no small

---

LINE 10. **annunciation** : announcement.

need of a powerful protector who enjoyed Richard's
favor.

"Thou art speaking but sooth, Rebecca," said
Isaac, giving way to these weighty arguments:
"it were an offending of Heaven to betray the
secrets of the blessed Miriam. And him whom
the Nazarenes of England call the Lion's Heart
assuredly it were better for me to fall into the hands
of a strong lion than into his, if he shall have got
assurance of my dealing with his brother. Wherefore I will lend ear to thy counsel, and this youth
shall journey with us unto York, and our house
shall be as a home to him until his wounds shall be
healed. And if he of the Lion Heart shall return
to the land, as is now noised abroad, then shall this
Wilfred of Ivanhoe be unto me as a wall of defence,
when the king's displeasure shall burn high against
thy father."

It was not until evening was nearly closed that
Ivanhoe was restored to consciousness of his situation. He awoke from a broken slumber, under the
confused impressions which are naturally attendant
on the recovery from a state of insensibility. He
was unable for some time to recall exactly to
memory the circumstances which had preceded his
fall in the lists, or to make out any connected chain
of the events in which he had been engaged upon

---

LINE **3. sooth**: truth.

the yesterday. A sense of wounds and injury, joined to great weakness and exhaustion, was mingled with the recollection of blows dealt and received, of steeds rushing upon each other, over-throwing and overthrown, of shouts and clashing 5 of arms, and all the heavy tumult of a confused fight. An effort to draw aside the curtain of his couch was in some degree successful, although rendered difficult by the pain of his wound.

To his great surprise, he found himself in a room 10 magnificently furnished, but having cushions in-stead of chairs to rest upon, and in other respects partaking so much of Oriental costume that he began to doubt whether he had not, during his sleep, been transported back again to the land of 15 Palestine. The impression was increased when, the tapestry being drawn aside, a female form, dressed in a rich habit, which partook more of the Eastern taste than that of Europe, glided through the door which it concealed, and was followed by a 20 swarthy domestic.

As the wounded knight was about to address this fair apparition, she imposed silence by placing her slender finger upon her ruby lips, while the attend-ant, approaching him, proceeded to uncover Ivan- 25 hoe's side, and the lovely Jewess satisfied herself that the bandage was in its place, and the wound doing well. Rebecca performed her task with a graceful and dignified simplicity and modesty.

Her few and brief directions were given in the Hebrew language to the old domestic; and he obeyed them without reply.

Without making an attempt at further question, Ivanhoe suffered them in silence to take the measures they thought most proper for his recovery; and it was not until those were completed, and this kind physician about to retire, that his curiosity could no longer be suppressed. "Gentle maiden," he began in the Arabian tongue, with which his Eastern travels had rendered him familiar, and which he thought most likely to be understood by the turbaned damsel who stood before him, "I pray you, gentle maiden, of your courtesy —— "

But here he was interrupted by his fair physician, a smile which she could scarce suppress dimpling for an instant a face whose general expression was that of contemplative melancholy. "I am of England, Sir Knight, and speak the English tongue, although my dress and my lineage belong to another climate."

"Noble damsel —— " again the Knight of Ivanhoe began, and again Rebecca hastened to interrupt him.

"Bestow not on me, Sir Knight," she said, "the epithet of noble. It is well you should speedily know that your hand-maiden is a poor Jewess, the

---

LINE **18**. **contemplative**: thoughtful.

daughter of that Isaac of York to whom you were so lately a good and kind lord. It well becomes him and those of his household to render to you such careful tendance as your present state necessarily demands." 5

I know not whether the fair Rowena would have been altogether satisfied with the species of emotion with which her devoted knight had hitherto gazed on the beautiful features, and fair form, and lustrous eyes of the lovely Rebecca — eyes whose brilliancy 10 was shaded, and, as it were, mellowed, by the fringe of her long silken eyelashes. But now the glance of respectful admiration, not altogether unmixed with tenderness, with which Ivanhoe had hitherto regarded his unknown benefactress, was exchanged 15 at once for a manner cold, composed, and collected, and fraught with no deeper feeling than that which expressed a grateful sense of courtesy received from an unexpected quarter, and from one of an inferior race. 20

The fair Jewess, though sensible her patient now regarded her as one of a race of reprobation, with whom it was disgraceful to hold any beyond the most necessary intercourse, ceased not to pay the same patient and devoted attention to his safety 25 and convalescence. She informed him of the necessity they were under of removing to York, and of

---

LINE **22. reprobation**: strong disapproval.

her father's resolution to transport him thither,
and tend him in his own house until his health
should be restored. Ivanhoe expressed great
repugnance to this plan, which he grounded on
5 unwillingness to give farther trouble to his benefactors.

" Was there not," he said, " in Ashby, or near it,
some Saxon franklin, or even some wealthy peasant,
who would endure the burden of a wounded coun-
10 tryman's residence with him until he should be
again able to bear his armor? Was there no convent of Saxon endowment, where he could be
received? Or could he not be transported as far
as Burton, where he was sure to find hospitality
15 with the Abbot of St. Withold's, to whom he was
related? "

" Any, the worst of these harborages," said
Rebecca, with a melancholy smile, " would unques-
tionably be more fitting for your residence than the
20 abode of a despised Jew; yet, Sir Knight, unless
you would dismiss your physician, you cannot
change your lodging. Our nation, as you well
know, can cure wounds, though we deal not in
inflicting them; and in our own family, in par-
25 ticular, are secrets which have been handed down
since the days of Solomon, and of which you have
already experienced the advantages. No Christian

---

LINE **4. repugnance**: dislike. **5. benefactors**: friendly
helpers.

leech, within the four seas of Britain, could enable you to bear your corselet within a month."

"And how soon wilt *thou* enable me to brook it?" said Ivanhoe, impatiently.

"Within eight days, if thou wilt be patient and 5 conformable to my directions," replied Rebecca.

"By Our Blessed Lady," said Wilfred, "if it be not a sin to name her here, it is no time for me or any true knight to be bedridden; and if thou accomplish thy promise, maiden, I will pay thee with 10 my casque full of crowns, come by them as I may."

"I will accomplish my promise," said Rebecca, "and thou shalt bear thine armor on the eighth day from hence, if thou wilt grant me but one boon in the stead of the silver thou dost promise me." 15

"If it be within my power, and such as a true Christian knight may yield to one of thy people," replied Ivanhoe, "I will grant thy boon blythely and thankfully."

"Nay," answered Rebecca, "I will but pray of 20 thee to believe henceforward that a Jew may do good service to a Christian, without desiring other guerdon than the blessing of the Great Father who made both Jew and Gentile."

"It were sin to doubt it, maiden," replied Ivan- 25 hoe; "and I repose myself on thy skill without further question, well trusting you will enable me

---

LINE **2. corselet**: body armor.   **3. brook**: bear; endure.
**23. guerdon**: reward.

to bear my corselet on the eighth day. And now,
my kind leech, let me inquire of the news abroad.
What of the noble Saxon Cedric and his household?
what of the lovely Lady —— " He stopt, as if
5 unwilling to speak Rowena's name in the house of
a Jew; "Of her, I mean, who was named Queen of
the tournament?"

"And who was selected by you, Sir Knight, to
hold that dignity, with judgment which was
10 admired as much as your valor," replied Rebecca.

The blood which Ivanhoe had lost did not prevent a flush from crossing his cheek, feeling that he
had incautiously betrayed his deep interest in
Rowena by the awkward attempt he had made
15 to conceal it.

"It was less of her I would speak," said he,
"than of Prince John; and I would fain know
somewhat of a faithful squire, and why he now
attends me not?"

20 "Let me use my authority as a leech," answered
Rebecca, "and enjoin you to keep silence. Prince
John hath broken off the tournament, and set forward in all haste towards York, with the nobles,
knights, and churchmen of his party, after collect-
25 ing such sums as they could wring, by fair means or
foul, from those who are esteemed the wealthy of
the land. It is said he designs to assume his
brother's crown."

"Not without a blow struck in its defence," said

Ivanhoe, raising himself upon the couch, " if there were but one true subject in England. I will fight for Richard's title with the best of them — ay, one to two, in his just quarrel ! "

" But that you may be able to do so," said Re-5 becca, touching his shoulder with her hand, " you must now observe my directions, and remain quiet."

" True, maiden," said Ivanhoe, " as quiet as these disquieted times will permit. And of Cedric and his household ? " 10

" Cedric and Athelstane of Coningsburgh," said the Jewess, " left Prince John's lodging in high displeasure, and set forth on their return homeward."

" Went any lady with them to the banquet ? " said Wilfred. 15

" The Lady Rowena," said Rebecca, " went not to the Prince's feast, and she is now on her journey back to Rotherwood with her guardian Cedric. And touching your faithful squire Gurth —— "

" Ha ! " exclaimed the knight, " knowest thou 20 his name ? But thou dost," he immediately added, " and well thou mayst, for it was from thy hand, and from thine own generosity of spirit, that he received but yesterday a hundred zecchins."

" Speak not of that," said Rebecca, blushing 25 deeply.

" But this sum of gold," said Ivanhoe, gravely, " my honor is concerned in repaying it to your father."

"Let it be as thou wilt," said Rebecca, "when eight days have passed away; but think not, and speak not, now of aught that may retard thy recovery."

5 "Be it so, kind maiden," said Ivanhoe; "I were most ungrateful to dispute thy commands. But one word of the fate of poor Gurth, and I have done with questioning thee."

"I grieve to tell thee, Sir Knight," answered the 10 Jewess, "that he is in custody by the order of Cedric." And then observing the distress which her communication gave to Wilfred, she instantly added: "But the steward Oswald said, that if nothing occurred to renew his master's displeasure 15 against him, he was sure that Cedric would pardon Gurth, a faithful serf, and one who stood high in favor, and who had but committed this error out of the love which he bore to Cedric's son. And he said, moreover, that he and his comrades, and 20 especially Wamba, the Jester, were resolved to warn Gurth to make his escape by the way, in case Cedric's ire against him could not be mitigated."

"Would to God they may keep their purpose!" said Ivanhoe; "but it seems as if I were destined 25 to bring ruin on whomsoever hath shown kindness to me. My king, by whom I was honored and distinguished — thou seest that the brother most

---

LINE 22. **mitigated**: lessened.

indebted to him is raising his arms to grasp his crown; my regard hath brought restraint and trouble on the fairest of her sex; and now my father in his mood may slay this poor bondsman, but for his love and loyal service to me! Thou 5 seest, maiden, what an ill-fated wretch thou dost labor to assist; be wise, and let me go, ere the misfortunes which track my footsteps like slot-hounds shall involve thee also in their pursuit."

"Nay," said Rebecca, "thy weakness and thy 10 grief, Sir Knight, make thee miscalculate the purposes of Heaven. Thou hast been restored to thy country when it most needed the assistance of a strong hand and a true heart. Therefore, be of good courage, and trust that thou art preserved for some 15 marvel which thine arm shall work before this people. Adieu; and having taken the medicine which I shall send thee by the hand of Reuben, compose thyself again to rest, that thou mayst be the more able to endure the journey on the succeeding day." 20

Ivanhoe was convinced by the reasoning, and obeyed the directions, of Rebecca. The draught which Reuben administered secured the patient sound and undisturbed slumbers. In the morning his kind physician found him entirely free from 25 feverish symptoms, and fit to undergo the fatigue of a journey.

---

LINE 8. slot-hounds: hounds that track by scent; bloodhounds.

He was deposited in the horse-litter which had brought him from the lists, and every precaution taken for his travelling with ease. In one circumstance only even the entreaties of Rebecca were unable to secure sufficient attention to the accommodation of the wounded knight. Isaac had ever the fear of robbery before his eyes, conscious that he would be alike accounted fair game by the marauding Norman noble and by the Saxon outlaw. He therefore journeyed at a great rate, and made short halts and shorter repasts, so that he passed by Cedric and Athelstane. Yet such was the virtue of Miriam's balsam, or such the strength of Ivanhoe's constitution, that he did not sustain from the hurried journey that inconvenience which his kind physician had apprehended.

In another point of view, however, the Jew's haste proved somewhat more than good speed. The rapidity with which he insisted on travelling bred several disputes between him and the party whom he had hired to attend him as a guard. These men were Saxons, and not free by any means from the national love of ease and good living. They remonstrated upon the risk of damage to their horses by these forced marches. Finally, there arose a deadly feud concerning the quantity of wine and ale to be allowed for consumption at each meal. And thus it happened, that when the alarm of danger approached, and that which Isaac feared was likely to come upon him, he was deserted by the discontented mercenaries, on whose protection he had relied.

In this deplorable condition, the Jew, with his daughter and her wounded patient, were found by Cedric, and soon afterwards fell into the power of De Bracy and his confederates. Little notice was at first taken of the horse-litter, and it might have remained behind but for the curiosity of De Bracy, who looked into it under the impression that it might contain the object of his enterprise, for Rowena had not unveiled herself. But De Bracy's astonishment was considerable when he discovered that the litter contained a wounded man, who, conceiving himself to have fallen into the power of Saxon outlaws, with whom his name might be a protection for himself and his friends, frankly avowed himself to be Wilfred of Ivanhoe.

The ideas of chivalrous honor, which never utterly abandoned De Bracy, prohibited him from doing the knight any injury in his defenceless condition, and equally interdicted his betraying him to Front-de-Bœuf, who would have had no scruples to put to death, under any circumstances, the rival claimant of the fief of Ivanhoe. On the other hand, to liberate a suitor preferred by the Lady Rowena was a pitch far above the flight of De Bracy's gen-

---

LINE **22.** **interdicted**: forbade. **27. pitch**: height.

erosity. A middle course betwixt good and evil was all which he found himself capable of adopting, and he commanded two of his own squires to keep close by the litter, and to suffer no one to approach it. If questioned, they were directed by their master to say that the empty litter of the Lady Rowena was employed to transport one of their comrades who had been wounded in the scuffle. On arriving at Torquilstone, De Bracy's squires conveyed Ivanhoe, still under the name of a wounded comrade, to a distant apartment. This explanation was returned by these men to Front-de-Bœuf, when he questioned them why they did not make for the battlements upon the alarm.

"A wounded companion!" he replied in great wrath and astonishment. "No wonder that clowns and swineherds send defiances to nobles, since men-at-arms have turned sick men's nurses. To the battlements, ye loitering villains!" he exclaimed, raising his stentorian voice till the arches around rung again — "to the battlements, or I will splinter your bones with this truncheon!"

The men sulkily replied that they desired nothing better than to go to the battlements, providing Front-de-Bœuf would bear them out with their master, who had commanded them to tend the dying man.

---

LINE **20.** stentorian: uncommonly powerful.

"The dying man, knaves!" rejoined the baron; "I promise thee, we shall all be dying men an we stand not to it the more stoutly. But I will relieve the guard upon this caitiff companion of yours. Here, Urfried — hag — fiend of a Saxon witch — hearest me not? Tend me this bedridden fellow, since he must needs be tended, whilst these knaves use their weapons. Here be two arblasts, comrades, with windlaces and quarrells — to the barbican with you, and see you drive each bolt through a Saxon brain."

The men, who were fond of enterprise and detested inaction, went joyfully to the scene of danger as they were commanded, and thus the charge of Ivanhoe was transferred to Urfried, or Ulrica. But she, whose brain was burning with remembrance of injuries and with hopes of vengeance, was readily induced to devolve upon Rebecca the care of her patient.

---

LINE **4. caitiff**: base. **8. arblasts**, etc. The arblast was a crossbow, the windlace the machine used in bending that weapon, and the quarrell, so called from its square or diamond-shaped head, was the bolt adapted to it. — Scott

# CHAPTER XXIX

## Rebecca Describes the Battle

In finding herself once more by the side of Ivanhoe, Rebecca was astonished at the keen sensation of pleasure which she experienced, even at a time when all around them both was danger, if not despair. As she felt his pulse, and inquired after his health, there was a softness in her touch and in her accents, implying a kinder interest than she would herself have been pleased to have voluntarily expressed. Her voice faltered and her hand trembled, and it was only the cold question of Ivanhoe, " Is it you, gentle maiden? " which recalled her to herself, and reminded her the sensations which she felt were not and could not be mutual. A sigh escaped, but it was scarce audible; and the questions which she asked the knight concerning his state of health were put in the tone of calm friendship. Ivanhoe answered her hastily that he was, in point of health, as well, and better, than he could have expected. " Thanks," he said, " dear Rebecca, to thy helpful skill."

" He calls me *dear* Rebecca," said the maiden to herself, " but it is in the cold and careless tone which ill suits the word. His war-horse, his hunting hound, are dearer to him than the despised Jewess!"

The noise within the castle, occasioned by the defensive preparations, which had been considerable for some time, now increased into tenfold 5 bustle and clamor. The heavy yet hasty step of the men-at-arms traversed the battlements, or resounded on the narrow and winding passages and stairs. The voices of the knights were heard, animating their followers, or directing means of 10 defence, while their commands were often drowned in the clashing of armor, or the clamorous shouts of those whom they addressed. Rebecca's eye kindled, although the blood fled from her cheeks; and there was a strong mixture of fear, and of a 15 thrilling sense of the sublime, as she repeated, half-whispering to herself, half-speaking to her companion, the sacred text — " The quiver rattleth — the glittering spear and the shield — the noise of the captains and the shouting!" 20

But Ivanhoe was like the war-horse of that sublime passage, glowing with impatience at his inactivity, and with his ardent desire to mingle in the affray. " If I could but drag myself," he said, " to yonder window, that I might see how this brave 25 game is like to go! If I had but bow to shoot a shaft, or battle-axe to strike were it but a single

LINE **18.** sacred text: Job 39 : 19–25.

blow for our deliverance! It is in vain — it is in vain — I am alike nerveless and weaponless!"

"Fret not thyself, noble knight," answered Rebecca, "the sounds have ceased of a sudden; it 5 may be they join not battle."

"Thou knowest nought of it," said Wilfred, impatiently; "this dead pause only shows that the men are at their posts on the walls, and expecting an instant attack; what we have heard was but the 10 distant muttering of the storm: it will burst anon in all its fury. Could I but reach yonder window!"

"Thou wilt but injure thyself by the attempt, noble knight," replied his attendant. "I myself will stand at the lattice, and describe to you as I 15 can what passes without."

"You must not — you shall not!" exclaimed Ivanhoe. "Each lattice, each aperture, will be soon a mark for the archers; some random shaft —— "

20 "It shall be welcome!" murmured Rebecca, as with firm pace she ascended two or three steps, which led to the window of which they spoke.

"Rebecca — dear Rebecca!" exclaimed Ivanhoe, "this is no maiden's pastime; do not expose 25 thyself to wounds and death, and render me for ever miserable for having given the occasion; at least, cover thyself with yonder ancient buckler,

---

LINE 17. aperture: opening.

and show as little of your person at the lattice as may be."

Availing herself of the protection of the large ancient shield, which she placed against the lower part of the window, Rebecca, with tolerable security to herself, could witness part of what was passing without the castle, and report to Ivanhoe the preparations which the assailants were making for the storm. Being placed on an angle of the main building, Rebecca could not only see what passed beyond the precincts of the castle, but also commanded a view of the outwork likely to be the first object of the meditated assault. It was an exterior fortification of no great height or strength, intended to protect the postern-gate, through which Cedric had been recently dismissed by Front-de-Bœuf. The castle moat divided this species of barbican from the rest of the fortress, so that, in case of its being taken, it was easy to cut off the communication with the main building, by withdrawing the temporary bridge. In the outwork was a sallyport corresponding to the postern of the castle, and the whole was surrounded by a strong palisade. Rebecca could observe, from the number of men placed for the defence of this post, that the besieged entertained apprehensions for its safety; and from the mustering of the assailants nearly opposite to the outwork, it seemed no less plain that it had been selected as a vulnerable point of attack.

These appearances she hastily communicated to Ivanhoe, and added, " The skirts of the wood seem lined with archers, although only a few are advanced from its dark shadow."

5 " Under what banner? " asked Ivanhoe.

" Under no ensign of war which I can observe," answered Rebecca.

" A singular novelty," muttered the knight, " to advance to storm such a castle without pennon or 10 banner displayed! Seest thou who they be that act as leaders? "

" A knight, clad in sable armor, is the most conspicuous," said the Jewess; " he alone is armed from head to heel, and seems to assume the direc-15 tion of all around him."

" What device does he bear on his shield? " replied Ivanhoe.

" Something resembling a bar of iron, and a padlock painted blue on the black shield."

20 " A fetterlock and shacklebolt azure," said Ivanhoe; " I know not who may bear the device, but well I ween it might now be mine own. Canst thou not see the motto? "

" Scarce the device itself at this distance," replied 25 Rebecca; " but when the sun glances fair upon his shield it shows as I tell you."

---

LINE **20**. **fetterlock**: attachment put on leg of horse to prevent his running away. **shacklebolt**: curved bar of padlock; bolt. **azure**: blue.

" Seem there no other leaders? " exclaimed the anxious inquirer.

" None of mark and distinction that I can behold from this station," said Rebecca; " but doubtless the other side of the castle is also assailed. They ⁵ appear even now preparing to advance — God of

THE ATTACK OF THE YEOMEN
(Courtesy of Douglas Fairbanks.)

Zion protect us! What a dreadful sight! Those who advance first bear huge shields and defences made of plank; the others follow, bending their bows as they come on. They raise their bows! ¹⁰ God of Moses, forgive the creatures Thou hast made! "

Her description was here suddenly interrupted by the signal for assault, which was given by the blast of a shrill bugle, and at once answered by a flourish of the Norman trumpets from the battlements, 5 mingled with the deep and hollow clang of the nakers (a species of kettle-drum). The shouts of both parties augmented the fearful din, the assailants crying, "St. George for merry England!" and the Normans answering them with loud cries 10 of "*En avant De Bracy! Beau-seant! Beau-seant! Front-de-Bœuf à la rescousse!*"

It was not, however, by clamor that the contest was to be decided, and the desperate efforts of the assailants were met by an equally vigorous defence 15 on the part of the besieged. The archers, trained by their woodland pastimes to the most effective use of the long-bow, shot so "wholly together," that no point at which a defender could show the least part of his person escaped their cloth-yard 20 shafts. By this heavy discharge, which continued as thick and sharp as hail, while, notwithstanding, every arrow had its individual aim, and flew by scores together against each embrasure and opening in the parapets, as well as at every window where a 25 defender either occasionally had post, or might be suspected to be stationed — by this sustained dis-

---

LINE **10.** *En avant:* forward. **11.** *à la rescousse:* to the rescue. **19. cloth-yard shafts:** arrows a yard long. **23. embrasure:** opening in wall for archers to shoot through.

charge, two or three of the garrison were slain and several others wounded. But, confident in their armor of proof, and in the cover which their situation afforded, the followers of Front-de-Bœuf and his allies showed an obstinacy in defence proportioned to the fury of the attack, and replied with the discharge of their large crossbows, as well as with their long-bows, slings, and other missile weapons, to the close and continued shower of arrows; and, as the assailants were necessarily but indifferently protected, did considerably more damage than they received at their hand. The whizzing of shafts and of missiles on both sides was only interrupted by the shouts which arose when either side inflicted or sustained some notable loss.

"And I must lie here like a bedridden monk," exclaimed Ivanhoe, "while the game that gives me freedom or death is played out by the hand of others! Look from the window once again, kind maiden, but beware that you are not marked by the archers beneath. Look out once more, and tell me if they yet advance to the storm."

With patient courage Rebecca again took post at the lattice, sheltering herself, however, so as not to be visible from beneath.

"What dost thou see, Rebecca?" again demanded the wounded knight.

---

LINE 10. indifferently: neither very well nor very badly.

"Nothing but the cloud of arrows flying so thick as to dazzle mine eyes, and to hide the bowmen who shoot them."

"That cannot endure," said Ivanhoe; "if they 5 press not right on to carry the castle by pure force of arms, the archery may avail but little against stone walls. Look for the Knight of the Fetterlock, fair Rebecca, and see how he bears himself; for as the leader is, so will his follow- 10 ers be."

"I see him not," said Rebecca.

"Foul craven!" exclaimed Ivanhoe; "does he blench from the helm when the wind blows highest?"

15 "He blenches not!—he blenches not!" said Rebecca, "I see him now; he leads a body of men close under the outer barrier of the barbican. They pull down the palisades; they hew down the barriers with axes. His high black plume floats abroad 20 over the throng, like a raven over the field of the slain. They have made a breach in the barriers — they rush in — they are thrust back! Front-de-Bœuf heads the defenders; I see his gigantic form above the press. They throng again to the breach,

---

LINE 17. **barbican.** Every Gothic castle and city had, beyond the outer walls, a fortification composed of palisades, called the barriers, which were often the scene of severe skirmishes, as these must necessarily be carried before the walls themselves could be approached. — Scott. **18. palisades:** fence made of strong stakes, pointed at top.

and the pass is disputed hand to hand, and man to man. God of Jacob! it is the meeting of two fierce tides — the conflict of two oceans moved by adverse winds!"

She turned her head from the lattice, as if unable longer to endure a sight so terrible.

"Look forth again, Rebecca," said Ivanhoe, mistaking the cause of her retiring; "the archery must in some degree have ceased, since they are now fighting hand to hand. Look again, there is now less danger."

Rebecca again looked forth, and almost immediately exclaimed, "Front-de-Bœuf and the Black Knight fight hand to hand on the breach, amid the roar of their followers, who watch the progress of the strife. Heaven strike with the cause of the oppressed and of the captive!" She then uttered a loud shriek, and exclaimed, "He is down! — he is down!"

"Who is down?" cried Ivanhoe; "for our dear Lady's sake, tell me which has fallen?"

"The Black Knight," answered Rebecca, faintly; then instantly again shouted with joyful eagerness: "But no — but no! the name of the Lord of Hosts be blessed! he is on foot again, and fights as if there were twenty men's strength in his single arm. His sword is broken — he snatches an axe from a yeoman — he presses Front-de-Bœuf with blow on blow. The giant stoops and totters like an oak under the steel of the woodman — he falls — he falls!"

"Front-de-Bœuf?" exclaimed Ivanhoe.

"Front-de-Bœuf," answered the Jewess. "His men rush to the rescue, headed by the haughty Templar; their united force compels the champion to pause. They drag Front-de-Bœuf within the walls."

"The assailants have won the barriers, have they not?" said Ivanhoe.

"They have — they have!" exclaimed Rebecca; "and they press the besieged hard upon the outer wall; some plant ladders, some swarm like bees, and endeavor to ascend upon the shoulders of each other; down go stones, beams, and trunks of trees upon their heads, and as fast as they bear the wounded to the rear, fresh men supply their places in the assault. Great God! hast Thou given men Thine own image that it should be thus cruelly defaced by the hands of their brethren!"

"Think not of that," said Ivanhoe; "this is no time for such thoughts. Who yield? who push their way?"

"The ladders are thrown down," replied Rebecca, shuddering; "the soldiers lie grovelling under them like crushed reptiles. The besieged have the better."

"St. George strike for us!" exclaimed the knight; "do the false yeomen give way?"

378

THE BLACK KNIGHT'S ENCOUNTER WITH FRONT-DE-BŒUF

"No!" exclaimed Rebecca, "they bear themselves right yeomanly. The Black Knight approaches the postern with his huge axe; the thundering blows which he deals, you may hear them above all the din and shouts of the battle. Stones and beams are hailed down on the bold champion: he regards them no more than if they were thistle-down or feathers!"

"By St. John of Acre," said Ivanhoe, raising himself joyfully on his couch, "methought there was but one man in England that might do such a deed!"

"The postern gate shakes," continued Rebecca — "it crashes — it is splintered by his blows — they rush in — the outwork is won. O God! they hurl the defenders from the battlements — they throw them into the moat. O men, if ye be indeed men, spare them that can resist no longer!"

"The bridge — the bridge which communicates with the castle — have they won that pass?" exclaimed Ivanhoe.

"No," replied Rebecca; "the Templar has destroyed the plank on which they crossed; few of the defenders escaped with him into the castle — the shrieks and cries which you hear tell the fate of the others. Alas! I see it is still more difficult to look upon victory than upon battle."

"What do they now, maiden?" said Ivanhoe;

"look forth yet again — this is no time to faint at bloodshed."

"It is over for the time," answered Rebecca; "our friends strengthen themselves within the out-work which they have mastered, and it affords them so good a shelter from the foeman's shot that the garrison only bestow a few bolts on it from interval to interval, as if rather to disquiet than effectually to injure them."

"Our friends," said Wilfred, "will surely not abandon an enterprise so gloriously begun and so happily attained. Oh, no! I will put my faith in the good knight whose axe hath rent heart-of-oak and bars of iron. Singular," he again muttered to himself, "if there be two who can do a deed of such *derring-do!* A fetterlock, and a shacklebolt on a field sable — what may that mean? Seest thou nought else, Rebecca, by which the Black Knight may be distinguished?"

"Nothing," said the Jewess; "all about him is black as the wing of the night raven. Nothing can I spy that can mark him further; but having once seen him put forth his strength in battle, methinks I could know him again among a thousand war-riors. He rushes to the fray as if he were sum-moned to a banquet. There is more than mere strength — there seems as if the whole soul and

---

LINE 16. *derring-do:* desperate courage.

spirit of the champion were given to every blow
which he deals upon his enemies."

"Rebecca," said Ivanhoe, "thou hast painted
a hero; surely they rest but to refresh their force,
or to provide the means of crossing the moat. 5
Under such a leader as thou hast spoken this knight
to be, there are no craven fears, no cold-blooded
delays. I swear by the honor of my house — I
vow by the name of my bright lady-love, I would
endure ten years' captivity to fight one day by that 10
good knight's side in such a quarrel as this!"

"Alas!" said Rebecca, leaving her station at the
window, and approaching the couch of the wounded
knight, "this impatient yearning after action
will not fail to injure your returning health. How 15
couldst thou hope to inflict wounds on others, ere
that be healed which thou thyself hast received?"

"Rebecca," he replied, "thou knowest not how
impossible it is for one trained to actions of chivalry
to remain passive as a priest, or a woman, when 20
they are acting deeds of honor around him. The
love of battle is the food upon which we live — the
dust of the *mêlée* is the breath of our nostrils! We
live not — we wish not to live — longer than while
we are victorious and renowned. Such, maiden, 25
are the laws of chivalry to which we are sworn, and
to which we offer all that we hold dear."

---

LINE **23**. *mêlée:* hand-to-hand fight among a number of
people.

"Alas!" said the fair Jewess, "and what remains to you as the prize of all the blood you have spilled, of all the pain you have endured, of all the tears which your deeds have caused, when death hath broken the strong man's spear, and overtaken the speed of his war-horse?"

"What remains?" cried Ivanhoe. "Glory, maiden — glory! which gilds our sepulchre and embalms our name."

"Glory!" continued Rebecca; "alas! is the rusted mail which hangs over the champion's dim and mouldering tomb, is the defaced sculpture of the inscription which the ignorant monk can hardly read to the inquiring pilgrim — are these sufficient rewards for the sacrifice of every kindly affection, for a life spent miserably that ye may make others miserable?"

"By the soul of Hereward!" replied the knight, impatiently, "thou speakest, maiden, of thou knowest not what. Thou wouldst quench the pure light of chivalry, which alone distinguishes the noble from the base, the gentle knight from the churl and the savage; which rates our life far, far beneath the pitch of our honor, raises us victorious over pain, toil, and suffering, and teaches us to fear no evil but disgrace. Chivalry! Why, maiden, she is the nurse of pure and high affection, the stay of the oppressed, the redresser of grievances, the curb of the power of the tyrant. Nobility were but an empty name without her, and liberty finds the best protection in her lance and her sword."

"I am indeed," said Rebecca, "sprung from a race whose courage was distinguished in the defence of their own land, but who warred not, even while yet a nation, save at the command of the Deity, or in defending their country from oppression. The sound of the trumpet wakes Judah no longer, and her despised children are now but the unresisting victims of hostile and military oppression."

The high-minded maiden concluded the argument in a tone of sorrow, embittered perhaps by the idea that Ivanhoe considered her incapable of entertaining or expressing sentiments of honor and generosity.

"How little he knows this bosom," she said, "to imagine that cowardice or meanness of soul must needs be its guests! Would to Heaven that the shedding of mine own blood, drop by drop, could redeem the captivity of Judah! Nay, would to God it could avail to set free my father, and this his benefactor, from the chains of the oppressor!"

She then looked towards the couch of the wounded knight.

"He sleeps," she said; "nature exhausted, his wearied frame embraces the first moment of temporary relaxation to sink into slumber. Alas! is it a crime that I should look upon him, when it may be for the last time? When yet but a short space, and those fair features will be no longer animated

by the bold and buoyant spirit which forsakes them
not even in sleep! And my father! — oh, my
father! evil is it with his daughter, when his grey
hairs are not remembered because of the golden
5 locks of youth! But I will tear this folly from my
heart, though every fibre bleed as I rend it away!"

She wrapped herself closely in her veil, and sat
down at a distance from the couch of the wounded
knight, with her back turned towards it, fortify-
10 ing, or endeavoring to fortify, her mind not only
against the impending evils from without, but also
against those treacherous feelings which assailed
her from within.

## CHAPTER XXX

### Front-de-Bœuf's Last Fight

During the interval of quiet which followed the first success of the besiegers, while the one party was preparing to pursue their advantage and the other to strengthen their means of defence, the Templar and De Bracy held brief counsel together 5 in the hall of the castle.

"Where is Front-de-Bœuf?" said the latter, who had superintended the defence of the fortress on the other side; "men say he hath been slain."

"He lives," said the Templar, coolly — "lives 10 as yet; but had he worn the bull's head of which he bears the name, and ten plates of iron to fence it withal, he must have gone down before yonder fatal axe. Yet a few hours, and Front-de-Bœuf is with his fathers — a powerful limb lopped off Prince 15 John's enterprise."

"And a brave addition to the kingdom of Satan," said De Bracy; "this comes of reviling saints and angels."

"Go to, thou art a fool," said the Templar; 20 "thy superstition is upon a level with Front-de-

---

LINE 13. withal: with.

Bœuf's want of faith. But let us think of making
good the castle. How fought these villain yeomen
on thy side?"

"Like fiends incarnate," said De Bracy. "They
5 swarmed close up to the walls, headed, as I think,
by the knave who won the prize at the archery, for
I knew his horn and baldric. Had I not been
armed in proof, the villain had marked me down
seven times with as little remorse as if I had been a
10 buck in season. He told every rivet on my armor
with a cloth-yard shaft. But that I wore a shirt
of Spanish mail under my plate-coat, I had been
fairly sped."

"But you maintained your post?" said the
15 Templar. "We lost the outwork on our part."

"That is a shrewd loss," said De Bracy; "the
knaves will find cover there to assault the castle
more closely, and may, if not well watched, gain
some unguarded corner of a tower, or some for-
20 gotten window, and so break in upon us. Our
numbers are too few for the defence of every point,
and the men complain that they can nowhere show
themselves, but they are the mark for as many
arrows as a parish-butt on a holyday even. Front-
25 de-Bœuf is dying too, so we shall receive no more aid
from his bull's head and brutal strength. How

---

LINE **4. incarnate**: embodied in flesh. **12. plate-coat**. See
page 623. **24. butt**: target for use in archery. "The butt
of jokes" is the target or mark at which the jokes are aimed.

think you, Sir Brian, were we not better make a virtue of necessity, and compound with the rogues by delivering up our prisoners?"

"How!" exclaimed the Templar; "deliver up our prisoners, and stand an object of ridicule, as 5 the doughty warriors who dared by a night-attack to possess themselves of the persons of a party of defenceless travellers, yet could not make good a strong castle against a vagabond troop of outlaws, led by swineherds, jesters, and the very refuse of 10 mankind? Shame on thy counsel, Maurice de Bracy! The ruins of this castle shall bury both my body and my shame, ere I consent to such base and dishonorable composition."

"Let us to the walls, then," said De Bracy, care- 15 lessly; "that man never breathed, be he Turk or Templar, who held life at lighter rate than I do. Let us up and be doing; and, live or die, thou shalt see Maurice de Bracy bear himself this day as a gentleman of blood and lineage." 20

"To the walls!" answered the Templar; and they both ascended the battlements to do all that skill could dictate, and manhood accomplish, in defence of the place. They readily agreed that the point of greatest danger was that opposite to the 25 outwork of which the assailants had possessed themselves. The castle, indeed, was divided from

---

LINE 6. **doughty**: strong; brave.  **14. composition**: agreement; settlement.

that barbican by the moat, and it was impossible that the besiegers could assail the postern door, with which the outwork corresponded, without surmounting that obstacle; but it was the opinion
5 both of the Templar and De Bracy that the besiegers would endeavor, by a formidable assault, to draw the chief part of the defenders' observation to this point, and take measures to avail themselves of every negligence which might take place
10 in the defence elsewhere. They agreed that De Bracy should command the defence at the postern, and the Templar should keep with him a score of men or thereabouts as a body of reserve, ready to hasten to any other point which might be suddenly
15 threatened. The loss of the barbican had also this unfortunate effect, that, notwithstanding the superior height of the castle walls, the besieged could not see from them, with the same precision as before, the operations of the enemy; for some straggling
20 underwood approached so near the sallyport of the outwork that the assailants might introduce into it whatever force they thought proper, not only under cover, but even without the knowledge of the defenders. Utterly uncertain, therefore, upon what
25 point the storm was to burst, De Bracy and his companion were under the necessity of providing against every possible contingency.

---

LINE **27. contingency**: chance occurrence.

Meanwhile, the lord of the beleaguered and endangered castle lay upon a bed of bodily pain and mental agony. The moment had now arrived when earth and all his treasures were gliding from before his eyes, and when the savage baron's heart, though hard as a nether millstone, became appalled as he gazed forward into the waste darkness of futurity.

"Where be these dog-priests now?" growled the baron. "Me they suffer to die like the houseless dog on yonder common! Tell the Templar to come hither; he is a priest, and may do something. But no! as well confess myself to the devil as to Brian de Bois-Guilbert, who recks neither of Heaven nor of Hell. I have heard old men talk of prayer — prayer by their own voice. But I — I dare not!"

"Lives Reginald Front-de-Bœuf," said a broken and shrill voice close by his bedside, "to say there is that which he dares not?"

The evil conscience and the shaken nerves of Front-de-Bœuf heard, in this strange interruption, the voice of one of those demons who, as the superstition of the times believed, beset the beds of dying men. He shuddered and drew himself together; but, instantly summoning up his wonted resolution, he exclaimed, "Who is there? what art thou, that

---

LINE **6. nether**: lower.

darest to echo my words in a tone like that of the night raven? Come before my couch that I may see thee."

"I am thine evil angel, Reginald Front-de-Bœuf," replied the voice.

"Let me behold thee then in thy bodily shape, if thou be'st indeed a fiend," replied the dying knight; "think not that I will blench from thee."

"Think on thy sins, Reginald Front-de-Bœuf," said the almost unearthly voice — "on rebellion, on rapine, on murder! Who stirred up John to war against his grey-headed father — against his generous brother?"

"Be thou fiend, priest, or devil," replied Front-de-Bœuf, "thou liest in thy throat! Not I stirred John to rebellion — not I alone; there were fifty knights and barons. And must I answer for the fault done by fifty? False fiend, I defy thee! Depart, and haunt my couch no more. Let me die in peace."

"In peace thou shalt NOT die," repeated the voice; "even in death shalt thou think on thy murders — on the groans which this castle has echoed — on the blood that is engrained in its floors!"

"Thou canst not shake me by thy petty malice," answered Front-de-Bœuf, with a ghastly and con-

---

LINE 8. **blench**: shrink.

strained laugh. " The Saxon porkers whom I have slain — they were the foes of my country, and of my lineage, and of my liege lord. Art thou fled? art thou silenced? "

" No, foul parricide ! " replied the voice ; " think of thy father ! — think of his death ! — think of his banquet-room flooded with his gore, and that poured forth by the hand of a son ! "

" Ha ! " answered the Baron, after a long pause, " an thou knowest that, thou art indeed the Author of Evil, and as omniscient as the monks call thee ! That secret I deemed locked in my own breast, and in that of one besides — the temptress, the partaker of my guilt. Go, leave me, fiend ! and seek the Saxon witch Ulrica, who alone could tell thee what she and I alone witnessed. Go to her ; she was my temptress ; let her, as well as I, taste of the tortures which anticipate Hell ! "

" She already tastes them," said Ulrica, stepping before the couch of Front-de-Bœuf ; " she hath long drunken of this cup, and its bitterness is now sweetened to see that thou dost partake it. Grind not thy teeth, Front-de-Bœuf — roll not thine eyes — clench not thy hand, nor shake it at me with that gesture of menace ! The hand which, like that of thy renowned ancestor who gained thy name, could have broken with one stroke the skull

---

LINE 5. parricide : murderer of a parent.

of a mountain-bull, is now unnerved and powerless as mine own!"

"Vile, murderous hag!" replied Front-de-Bœuf — "detestable screech-owl! it is then thou who art to come to exult over the ruins thou hast assisted to lay low?"

"Ay, Reginald Front-de-Bœuf," answered she, "it is Ulrica! — it is the daughter of the murdered Torquil Wolfganger! — it is the sister of his slaughtered sons! Thou hast been my evil angel, and I will be thine!"

"Ho! Giles, Clement, and Eustace!" exclaimed Front-de-Bœuf, "St. Maur and Stephen! seize this damned witch, and hurl her from the battlements headlong; she has betrayed us to the Saxon! Ho! St. Maur! Clement! false-hearted knaves, where tarry ye?"

"Call on them again, valiant baron," said the hag, with a smile of grisly mockery; "but know, mighty chief, thou shalt have neither answer, nor aid, nor obedience at their hands. Listen to these horrid sounds! The Saxon, Reginald! — the scorned Saxon assails thy walls! Why liest thou here, like a worn-out hind, when the Saxon storms thy place of strength?"

"Gods and fiends!" exclaimed the wounded knight. "Oh, for one moment's strength, to drag myself to the *mêlée*, and perish as becomes my name!"

" Think not of it, valiant warrior ! " replied she;
" thou shalt die no soldier's death, but perish like
the fox in his den, when the peasants have set fire
to the cover around it. Markest thou the smouldering and suffocating vapor which already eddies
in sable folds through the chamber? Didst thou
think it was but the darkening of thy bursting
eyes, the difficulty of thy cumbered breathing?
No! Front-de-Bœuf, there is another cause.
Rememberest thou the magazine of fuel that is
stored beneath these apartments? "

" Woman ! " he exclaimed with fury, " thou hast
not set fire to it? By Heaven, thou hast, and the
castle is in flames ! "

" They are fast rising at least," said Ulrica, with
frightful composure; " and a signal shall soon
wave to warn the besiegers to press hard upon those
who would extinguish them. Farewell, Front-de-
Bœuf ! Parricide, farewell forever ! May each
stone of this vaulted roof find a tongue to echo
that title into thine ear ! "

So saying, she left the apartment; and Front-
de-Bœuf could hear the crash of the ponderous key
as she locked and double-locked the door behind
her, thus cutting off the most slender chance of
escape. In the extremity of agony, he shouted
upon his servants and allies: " Stephen and St.
Maur ! Clement and Giles ! I burn here unaided !
To the rescue — to the rescue, brave Bois-Guilbert,

valiant De Bracy! It is Front-de-Bœuf who calls!
It is your master, ye traitor squires! Your ally —
your brother in arms, ye perjured and faithless
knights! They hear me not — they cannot hear
5 me — my voice is lost in the din of battle. The
smoke rolls thicker and thicker, the fire has caught
upon the floor below. Oh, for one draught of the
air of heaven, were it to be purchased by instant
annihilation!" And in the mad frenzy of despair,
10 the wretch now shouted with the shouts of the
fighters, now muttered curses on himself, on mankind, and on Heaven itself.

# CHAPTER XXXI

## Victory

Cedric, although not greatly confident in Ulrica's message, omitted not to communicate her promise to the Black Knight and Locksley. They were well pleased to find they had a friend within the place, and readily agreed with the Saxon that a storm ought to be attempted, as the only means of liberating the prisoners now in the hands of the cruel Front-de-Bœuf.

"The royal blood of Alfred is endangered," said Cedric.

"The honor of a noble lady is in peril," said the Black Knight.

"And, by the St. Christopher at my baldric," said the good yeoman, "were there no other cause than the safety of that poor faithful knave, Wamba, I would jeopard a joint ere a hair of his head were hurt."

"And now, Locksley," said the Black Knight, "were it not well that noble Cedric should assume the direction of this assault?"

---

LINE 13. baldric : belt hung from shoulder to opposite hip.

"Not a jot I," returned Cedric; "I have never been wont to study either how to take or how to hold out those abodes of tyrannic power which the Normans have erected in this groaning land. I will fight among the foremost; but my honest neighbors well know I am not a trained soldier in the discipline of wars or the attack of strongholds."

"Since it stands thus with noble Cedric," said Locksley, "I am most willing to take on me the direction of the archery."

"And if I be thought worthy to have a charge in these matters," answered the Black Knight, "and can find among these men as many as are willing to follow a true English knight, I am ready to lead them to the attack of these walls."

The parts being thus distributed to the leaders, they commenced the first assault, of which the reader has already heard the issue.

When the barbican was carried, the Sable Knight sent notice of the happy event to Locksley, requesting him at the same time to keep such a strict observation on the castle as might prevent the defenders from combining their force for a sudden sally, and recovering the outwork which they had lost.

The knight employed the interval in causing to be constructed a sort of floating bridge, or long raft, by means of which he hoped to cross the moat in despite of the resistance of the enemy. This was the work of some time, which the leaders the less regretted, as it gave Ulrica leisure to execute her plan of diversion in their favor, whatever that might be.

When the raft was completed, the Black Knight addressed the besiegers: "It avails not waiting here longer, my friends; the sun is descending to the west, and I have that upon my hands which will not permit me to tarry with you another day. Besides, it will be a marvel if the horsemen come not upon us from York, unless we speedily accomplish our purpose. Wherefore, one of ye go to Locksley, and bid him commence a discharge of arrows on the opposite side of the castle, and move forward as if about to assault it; and you, true English hearts, stand by me, and be ready to thrust the raft endlong over the moat whenever the postern on our side is thrown open. Follow me boldly across, and aid me to burst yon sallyport in the main wall of the castle. As many of you as like not this service, or are but ill armed to meet it, do you man the top of the outwork, draw your bowstrings to your ears, and mind you quell with your shot whatever shall appear to man the rampart. Noble Cedric, wilt thou take the direction of those which remain?"

"Not so, by the soul of Hereward!" said the Saxon; "lead I cannot; but may posterity curse me in my grave, if I follow not with the foremost

wherever thou shalt point the way. The quarrel
is mine, and well it becomes me to be in the van of
the battle."

"Yet, bethink thee, noble Saxon," said the
5 knight, "thou hast neither hauberk, nor corselet,
nor aught but that light helmet, target, and sword."

"The better!" answered Cedric; "I shall be
the lighter to climb these walls. And — forgive
the boast, Sir Knight — thou shalt this day see the
10 naked breast of a Saxon as boldly presented to the
battle as ever ye beheld the steel corselet of a
Norman."

"In the name of God, then," said the knight,
"fling open the door, and launch the floating
15 bridge."

The portal, which led from the inner wall of the
barbican to the moat, and which corresponded with
a sallyport in the main wall of the castle, was now
suddenly opened; the temporary bridge was then
20 thrust forward, and soon flashed in the waters,
extending its length between the castle and outwork, and forming a slippery and precarious passage
for two men abreast to cross the moat. Well aware
of the importance of taking the foe by surprise, the
25 Black Knight, closely followed by Cedric, threw
himself upon the bridge, and reached the opposite

---

LINE **5**. **hauberk**: sleeveless coat of mail made of interwoven steel rings and coming below the knees. **6**. **target**:
targe; small shield.

side. Here he began to thunder with his axe upon
the gate of the castle, protected in part from the
shot and stones cast by the defenders by the ruins
of the former drawbridge, which the Templar had
demolished in his retreat from the barbican. The 5
followers of the knight had no such shelter; two

THE BLACK KNIGHT AT THE CASTLE GATE

were instantly shot with crossbow bolts, and two
more fell into the moat; the others retreated back
into the barbican.

The situation of Cedric and of the Black Knight 10
was now truly dangerous, and would have been still
more so but for the constancy of the archers in the

barbican, who ceased not to shower their arrows upon the battlements, distracting the attention of those by whom they were manned, and thus affording a respite to their two chiefs from the storm of 5 missiles which must otherwise have overwhelmed them. But their situation was eminently perilous and was becoming more so with every moment.

"Shame on ye all!" cried De Bracy to the soldiers around him; "do ye call yourselves cross-10 bowmen, and let these two dogs keep their station under the walls of the castle? Heave over the coping stones from the battlement, an better may not be. Get pickaxe and levers, and down with that huge pinnacle!" pointing to a heavy piece 15 of stone carved-work that projected from the parapet.

At this moment the besiegers caught sight of the red flag upon the angle of the tower which Ulrica had described to Cedric. The stout yeoman Locks-20 ley was the first who was aware of it, as he was hasting to the outwork, impatient to see the progress of the assault.

"St. George!" he cried — "Merry St. George for England! To the charge, bold yeomen! why 25 leave ye the good knight and noble Cedric to storm the pass alone? Make in, mad priest; make in,

---

LINE 12. **coping stones**: flat, heavy stones on top of wall. **battlement**: breast-high wall at edge of balcony or roof with alternate solid and open spaces.

brave yeomen! — the castle is ours, we have friends
within.  See yonder flag, it is the appointed signal
— Torquilstone is ours!  Think of honor — think
of spoil!  One effort, and the place is ours!"

With that he bent his good bow, and sent a shaft 5
right through the breast of one of the men-at-arms,
who, under De Bracy's direction, was loosening a
fragment from one of the battlements to precipitate
on the heads of Cedric and the Black Knight!  A
second soldier caught from the hands of the dying 10
man the iron crow with which he heaved at and had
loosened the stone pinnacle, when, receiving an
arrow through his head-piece, he dropped from the
battlements into the moat a dead man.  The men-
at-arms were daunted, for no armor seemed proof 15
against the shot of this tremendous archer.

"Do you give ground, base knaves!" said De
Bracy.  "Give me the lever!"

And, snatching it up, he again assailed the
loosened pinnacle, which was of weight enough, if 20
thrown down, not only to have destroyed the remnant of the drawbridge which sheltered the two
foremost assailants, but also to have sunk the rude
float of planks over which they had crossed.  All
saw the danger, and the boldest, even the stout 25
Friar himself, avoided setting foot on the raft.
Thrice did Locksley bend his shaft against De

LINE 11. **crow**: crowbar; straight bar flattened at one
end.  15. **daunted**: frightened.

Bracy, and thrice did his arrow bound back from the knight's armor of proof.

"Curse on thy Spanish steel-coat!" said Locksley; "had English smith forged it, these arrows had gone through, an as if it had been silk." He then began to call out, "Comrades! friends! noble Cedric! bear back and let the ruin fall."

His warning voice was unheard, for the din which the knight himself occasioned by his strokes upon the postern would have drowned twenty wartrumpets. The faithful Gurth indeed sprung forward on the planked bridge, to warn Cedric of his impending fate, or to share it with him. But his warning would have come too late; the massive pinnacle already tottered, and De Bracy, who still heaved at his task, would have accomplished it, had not the voice of the Templar sounded close in his ear:

"All is lost, De Bracy; the castle burns."

"Thou art mad to say so!" replied the knight.

"It is all in a light flame on the western side. I have striven in vain to extinguish it."

With the stern coolness which formed the basis of his character, Brian de Bois-Guilbert communicated this hideous intelligence, which was not so calmly received by his astonished comrade.

"Saints of Paradise!" said De Bracy; "what is to be done?"

"Lead thy men down," said the Templar, "as if

to a sally; throw the postern gate open. There are but two men who occupy the float, fling them into the moat, and push across for the barbican. I will charge from the main gate, and attack the barbican on the outside; and if we can regain that post, be 5 assured we shall defend ourselves until we are relieved, or at least till they grant us fair quarter."

"It is well thought upon," said De Bracy; "I will play my part. Templar, thou wilt not fail me?" 10

"Hand and glove, I will not!" said Bois-Guilbert. "But haste thee, in the name of God!"

De Bracy hastily drew his men together, and rushed down to the postern gate, which he caused instantly to be thrown open. But scarce was this 15 done ere the portentous strength of the Black Knight forced his way inward in despite of De Bracy and his followers. Two of the foremost instantly fell, and the rest gave way notwithstanding all their leader's efforts to stop them. 20

"Dogs!" said De Bracy, "will ye let *two* men win our only pass for safety?"

"He is the devil!" said a veteran man-at-arms, bearing back from the blows of their sable antagonist. 25

"And if he be the devil," replied De Bracy, "would you fly from him into the mouth of hell?

---

LINE **16. portentous**: marvelous.

The castle burns behind us, villains! — let despair give you courage, or let me forward! I will cope with this champion myself."

And well and chivalrous did De Bracy that day maintain the fame he had acquired in the civil wars of that dreadful period. The vaulted passage to which the postern gave entrance, and in which these two redoubted champions were now fighting hand to hand, rung with the furious blows which they dealt each other, De Bracy with his sword, the Black Knight with his ponderous axe. At length the Norman received a blow which, though its force was partly parried by his shield, descended yet with such violence on his crest that he measured his length on the paved floor.

"Yield thee, De Bracy," said the Black Champion, stooping over him, and holding against the bars of his helmet the fatal poniard — "yield thee, Maurice de Bracy, rescue or no rescue, or thou art but a dead man."

"I will not yield," replied De Bracy, faintly, "to an unknown conqueror. Tell me thy name, or work thy pleasure on me; it shall never be said that Maurice de Bracy was prisoner to a nameless churl."

The Black Knight whispered something into the ear of the vanquished.

"I yield me to be true prisoner, rescue or no

---

LINE 8. redoubted: formidable; dread.

rescue," answered the Norman, exchanging his tone of stern and determined obstinacy for one of deep though sullen submission.

" Go to the barbican," said the victor, in a tone of authority, " and there wait my further orders."5

" Yet first let me say," said De Bracy, " what it imports thee to know. Wilfred of Ivanhoe is wounded and a prisoner, and will perish in the burning castle without present help."

" Wilfred of Ivanhoe!" exclaimed the Black 10 Knight — " prisoner, and perish! The life of every man in the castle shall answer it if a hair of his head be singed. Show me his chamber!"

" Ascend yonder winding stair," said De Bracy; " it leads to his apartment. Wilt thou not accept 15 my guidance?" he added, in a submissive voice.

" No. To the barbican, and there wait my orders. I trust thee not, De Bracy."

During this combat and the brief conversation which ensued, Cedric, at the head of a body of men, 20 among whom the Friar was conspicuous, had pushed across the bridge as soon as they saw the postern open, and drove back the dispirited and despairing followers of De Bracy, of whom some asked quarter, some offered vain resistance, and the 25 greater part fled towards the courtyard. De Bracy himself arose from the ground, and cast a sorrowful glance after his conqueror. " He trusts me not!" he repeated; " but have I deserved his trust?"

He then lifted his sword from the floor, took off his helmet in token of submission, and, going to the barbican, gave up his sword to Locksley, whom he met by the way.

5 As the fire augmented, symptoms of it became soon apparent in the chamber where Ivanhoe was watched and tended by the Jewess Rebecca. He had been awakened from his brief slumber by the noise of the battle; and his attendant, who had, at 10 his anxious desire, again placed herself at the window to watch and report to him the fate of the attack, was for some time prevented from observing either by the increase of the smouldering and stifling vapor. At length the volumes of smoke 15 which rolled into the apartment, the cries for water, which were heard even above the din of the battle, made them sensible of the progress of this new danger.

"The castle burns," said Rebecca — "it burns! 20 What can we do to save ourselves?"

"Fly, Rebecca, and save thine own life," said Ivanhoe, "for no human aid can avail me."

"I will not fly," answered Rebecca; "we will be saved or perish together. And yet, great God! 25 my father — my father, what will be his fate?"

At this moment the door of the apartment flew open, and the Templar presented himself — a ghastly figure, for his gilded armor was broken and bloody, and the plume was partly shorn away, partly burnt from his casque. "I have found thee," said he to Rebecca; " thou shalt prove I will keep my word to share weal and woe with thee. There is but one path to safety: I have cut my way through fifty dangers to point it to thee; up, and instantly follow me!"

"Alone," answered Rebecca, "I will not follow thee. If thou hast but a touch of human charity in thee — if thy heart be not hard as thy breast-plate — save my aged father — save this wounded knight!"

"A knight," answered the Templar, with his characteristic calmness — "a knight, Rebecca, must encounter his fate, whether it meet him in the shape of sword or flame; and who recks how or where a Jew meets with his?"

"Savage warrior," said Rebecca, "rather will I perish in the flames than accept safety from thee!"

"Thou shalt not choose, Rebecca; once didst thou foil me, but never mortal did so twice."

So saying, he seized on the terrified maiden, who filled the air with her shrieks, and bore her out of the room in his arms, in spite of her cries, and without regarding the menaces and defiance which Ivanhoe thundered against him. "Hound of the Temple — stain to thine order — set free the damsel! Traitor of Bois-Guilbert, it is Ivanhoe com-

---

LINE 15. **recks**: cares.

mands thee! Villain, I will have thy heart's blood!"

"I had not found thee, Wilfred," said the Black Knight, who at that instant entered the apartment, "but for thy shouts."

"If thou be'st true knight," said Wilfred, "think not of me — pursue yon ravisher — save the Lady Rowena — look to the noble Cedric!"

"In their turn," answered he of the Fetterlock, "but thine is first."

And seizing upon Ivanhoe, he bore him off with as much ease as the Templar had carried off Rebecca, rushed with him to the postern, and having there delivered his burden to the care of two yeomen, he again entered the castle to assist in the rescue of the other prisoners.

One turret was now in bright flames, which flashed out furiously from window and shot-hole. But in other parts the great thickness of the walls and the vaulted roofs of the apartments resisted the progress of the flames, and there the rage of man still triumphed, as the scarce more dreadful element held mastery elsewhere; for the besiegers pursued the defenders of the castle from chamber to chamber. Most of the garrison resisted to the uttermost; few of them asked quarter; none received it. The air was filled with groans and

LINE **26. quarter :** mercy shown in sparing the life of an enemy.

LOCKSLEY
(Courtesy of Douglas Fairbanks.)

clashing of arms; the floors were slippery with the blood of despairing and expiring wretches.

Through this scene of confusion, Cedric rushed in quest of Rowena, while the faithful Gurth, following him closely, neglected his own safety while he strove to avert the blows that were aimed at his master. The noble Saxon was so fortunate as to reach his ward's apartment just as she had abandoned all hope of safety, and, with a crucifix clasped in agony to her bosom, sat in expectation of instant death. He committed her to the charge of Gurth, to be conducted in safety to the barbican, the road to which was now cleared of the enemy, and not yet interrupted by the flames. This accomplished, the loyal Cedric hastened in quest of his friend Athelstane. But ere Cedric penetrated as far as the old hall in which he had himself been a prisoner, the inventive genius of Wamba had procured liberation for himself and his companion in adversity.

When the noise of the conflict announced that it was at the hottest, the Jester began to shout, with the utmost power of his lungs, " St. George and the dragon! Bonny St. George for merry England! The castle is won!" And these sounds he rendered yet more fearful by banging against each other two or three pieces of rusty armor which lay scattered around the hall.

A guard, stationed in the outer room, took fright

at Wamba's clamor, and, leaving the door open
behind them, ran to tell the Templar that foemen
had entered the old hall. Meantime the prisoners
found no difficulty in making their escape into the
5 court of the castle, which was now the last scene of
contest. Here sat the fierce Templar, mounted on
horseback, surrounded by several of the garrison
both on horse and foot. The drawbridge had been
lowered by his orders, but the passage was beset;
10 for the archers, who had hitherto only annoyed the
castle on that side by their missiles, no sooner saw
the flames breaking out, and the bridge lowered,
than they thronged to the entrance, as well to prevent the escape of the garrison as to secure their
15 own share of booty ere the castle should be burnt
down. On the other hand, a party of the besiegers,
who had entered by the postern, were now issuing
out into the courtyard, and attacking with fury
the remnant of the defenders, who were thus
20 assaulted on both sides at once.

Animated, however, by despair, and supported
by the example of their indomitable leader, the
remaining soldiers of the castle fought with the
utmost valor; and, being well armed, succeeded
25 more than once in driving back the assailants,
though much inferior in numbers. Rebecca, placed
on horseback before one of the Templar's Saracen

---

LINE 22. indomitable: unconquerable.

slaves, was in the midst of the little party; and
Bois-Guilbert showed every attention to her safety.
Repeatedly he was by her side, and, neglecting his
own defence, held before her the fence of his triangular steel-plated shield; and anon starting from 5
his position by her, he cried his war-cry, dashed
forward, struck to earth the most forward of the
assailants, and was on the same instant once more
at her bridle rein.

Athelstane beheld the female form whom the 10
Templar protected, and doubted not that it was
Rowena whom the knight was carrying off, in de-
spite of all resistance which could be offered.

"By the soul of St. Edward," he said, "I will
rescue her from yonder over-proud knight, and he 15
shall die by my hand!"

"Think what you do!" cried Wamba; "hasty
hand catches frog for fish; by my bauble, yonder is
none of my Lady Rowena, see but her long dark
locks! Nay, an ye will not know black from white, 20
ye may be leader, but I will be no follower; no
bones of mine shall be broken unless I know for
whom. And you without armor too! Bethink
you, silk bonnet never kept out steel blade."

To snatch a mace from the pavement, on which 25
it lay beside one whose dying grasp had just relin-

---

LINE **18. bauble**: stick with ass-eared head carved on it.
**25. mace**: heavy club with spiked metal head, used for
breaking armor.

quished it, to rush on the Templar's band, and to
strike in quick succession to the right and left,
levelling a warrior at each blow, was, for Athelstane's great strength, now animated with unusual
5 fury, but the work of a single moment; he was soon
within two yards of Bois-Guilbert, whom he defied
in his loudest tone.

"Turn, false-hearted Templar! let go her whom
thou art unworthy to touch!"

10 "Dog!" said the Templar, and half-wheeling
his steed, he made a demi-courbette towards the
Saxon, and rising in the stirrups, so as to take full
advantage of the descent of the horse, he discharged
a fearful blow upon the head of Athelstane.

15 Well said Wamba, that silken bonnet keeps out
no steel blade! So trenchant was the Templar's
weapon, that it shore asunder, as it had been a
willow twig, the tough handle of the mace, which
the ill-fated Saxon reared to parry the blow, and,
20 descending on his head, levelled him with the earth.

Taking advantage of the dismay which was
spread by the fall of Athelstane, and calling aloud,
"Those who would save themselves, follow me!"
he pushed across the drawbridge, dispersing the
25 archers who would have intercepted them. He
was followed by his Saracens, and some five or six
men-at-arms, who had mounted their horses. The

---

LINE **11. made a demi-courbette**: caused the horse to
rise on its hind legs.

ATHELSTANE AND BOIS-GUILBERT

" Turn, false-hearted Templar! let go her whom thou art unworthy
to touch! "

*Delacroix*

THE ABDUCTION OF REBECCA

Templar's retreat was rendered perilous by the
numbers of arrows shot off at him and his party;
but this did not prevent him from galloping round
to the barbican, of which, according to his previous
plan, he supposed it possible De Bracy might have 5
been in possession.

"De Bracy! De Bracy!" he shouted, "art
thou there?"

"I am here," replied De Bracy, "but I am a
prisoner." 10

"Can I rescue thee?" cried Bois-Guilbert.

"No," replied De Bracy; "I have rendered me,
rescue or no rescue. I will be true prisoner. Save
thyself; there are hawks abroad. Put the seas
betwixt you and England; I dare not say more." 15

"Well," answered the Templar, "an thou wilt
tarry there, remember I have redeemed word and
glove. Be the hawks where they will, methinks
the walls of the preceptory of Templestowe will be
cover sufficient, and thither will I." 20

Having thus spoken, he galloped off with his
followers.

Those of the castle who had not gotten to horse
still continued to fight desperately with the besiegers, after the departure of the Templar, but 25
rather in despair of quarter than that they entertained any hope of escape. The fire was spreading
rapidly through all parts of the castle, when Ulrica,
who had first kindled it, appeared on a turret, in

the guise of one of the ancient furies, yelling forth a war-song, such as was of yore raised on the field of battle by the scalds of the yet heathen Saxons. Her long dishevelled grey hair flew back from her 5 uncovered head; the delight of gratified vengeance contended in her eyes with the fire of insanity; and she brandished the distaff which she held in her hand. Tradition has preserved a wild strophe of the barbarous hymn which she chanted wildly amid 10 that scene of fire and of slaughter:

> All must perish!
> The sword cleaveth the helmet;
> The strong armor is pierced by the lance;
> Fire devoureth the dwelling of princes;
> 15   Engines break down the fences of the battle.
> All must perish!
> The race of Hengist is gone —
> The name of Horsa is no more!
> Shrink not then from your doom, sons of the sword!
> 20   Let your blades drink blood like wine;
> Feast ye in the banquet of slaughter,
> By the light of the blazing halls!
> Strong be your swords while your blood is warm,
> And spare neither for pity nor fear,
> 25   For vengeance hath but an hour;
> Strong hath itself shall expire!
> I also must perish!

---

LINE 1. **furies**; snake-haired goddesses sent to punish crimes. 3. **scalds**: poets. 4. **dishevelled**: loose; flung about. 7. **distaff**: staff about three feet long, on which wool or flax was wound for spinning by hand. 8. **strophe**: stanza; division.

# Victory

The towering flames had now surmounted every obstruction, and rose to the evening skies one huge and burning beacon, seen far and wide. Tower after tower crashed down, with blazing roof and rafter. The victors, assembling in large bands, gazed with wonder, not unmixed with fear, upon the flames, in which their own ranks and arms glanced dusky red. The maniac figure of the Saxon Ulrica was for a long time visible on the lofty stand she had chosen, tossing her arms abroad with wild exultation, as if she reigned empress of the conflagration which she had raised. At length, with a terrific crash, the whole turret gave way, and she perished in the flames which had consumed her tyrant. An awful pause of horror silenced each murmur of the armed spectators, who, for the space of several minutes, stirred not a finger, save to sign the cross. The voice of Locksley was then heard: "Shout, yeomen! the den of tyrants is no more! Let each bring his spoil to our chosen place of rendezvous at the trysting-tree in the Harthill Walk; for there at break of day will we make just partition among our own bands, together with our worthy allies in this great deed of vengeance."

# CHAPTER XXXII

## Spoils Divided

The daylight had dawned upon the glades of the oak forest. The green boughs glittered with all their pearls of dew. The hind led her fawn from the covert of high fern to the more open walks of 5 the greenwood, and no huntsman was there to watch or intercept the stately hart, as he paced at the head of the antlered herd.

The outlaws were all assembled around the trysting-tree in the Harthill Walk, where they had 10 spent the night in refreshing themselves after the fatigues of the siege — some with wine, some with slumber, many with hearing and recounting the events of the day, and computing the heaps of plunder which their success had placed at the dis- 15 posal of their chief.

The spoils were indeed very large; for, notwith-standing that much was consumed, a great deal of plate, rich armor, and splendid clothing had been secured by the exertions of the dauntless outlaws, 20 who could be appalled by no danger when such

---

LINE **9. trysting-tree**: tree chosen as place of meeting. **18. plate**: vessels and utensils of gold and silver.

rewards were in view.   Yet so strict were the laws
of their society, that no one ventured to appropriate
any part of the booty, which was brought into one
common mass, to be at the disposal of their leader.

The place of rendezvous was an aged oak within 5
half a mile of the demolished castle of Torquilstone.
Here Locksley assumed his seat — a throne of turf
erected under the twisted branches of the huge oak,
and the silvan followers were gathered around him.
He assigned to the Black Knight a seat at his right 10
hand, and to Cedric a place upon his left.

"Pardon my freedom, noble sirs," he said,
"but in these glades I am monarch: they are my
kingdom; and these my wild subjects would reck
but little of my power, were I, within my own 15
dominions, to yield place to mortal man.   Now,
sirs, who hath seen our chaplain? where is our
curtal friar?"   No one had seen the clerk of Copmanhurst.

"I," quoth the Miller, "marked him busy about 20
the door of a cellar, swearing by each saint in the
calendar he would taste the smack of Front-de-
Bœuf's Gascoigne wine."

"Now, the saints, as many as there be of them,"
said the captain, "forefend, lest he has drunk too 25
deep of the wine-butts, and perished by the fall of

---

LINE **14. reck**: pay heed to.    **18. curtal friar**: friar
attendant at the gate of a monastery.    **25. forefend**: ward
off.

the castle! Away, Miller! take with you enow of
men, seek the place where you last saw him, throw
water from the moat on the scorching ruins; I will
have them removed stone by stone ere I lose my
5 curtal friar."

The numbers who hastened to execute this duty,
considering that an interesting division of spoil
was about to take place, showed how much the
troop had at heart the safety of their spiritual
10 father.

"Meanwhile, let us proceed," said Locksley;
"for when this bold deed shall be sounded abroad,
the bands of De Bracy, of Malvoisin, and other
allies of Front-de-Bœuf, will be in motion against
15 us, and it were well for our safety that we retreat
from the vicinity. Noble Cedric," he said, turning
to the Saxon, "that spoil is divided into two portions; do thou make choice of that which best suits
thee, to recompense thy people who were partakers
20 with us in this adventure."

"Good yeoman," said Cedric, "my heart is
oppressed with sadness. The noble Athelstane of
Coningsburgh is no more! Hopes have perished
with him which can never return! My people do
25 but tarry my presence to transport his honored
remains to their last mansion. The Lady Rowena
is desirous to return to Rotherwood, and must be

---

Line 1. **enow**: enough.

escorted by a sufficient force. I should, therefore, ere now have left this place; and I waited, not to share the booty, for neither I nor any of mine will touch the value of a liard — I waited but to render my thanks to thee and to thy bold yeomen, for the life and honor ye have saved."

"Nay, but," said the chief outlaw, "we did but half the work at most; take of the spoil what may reward your own neighbors and followers."

"I am rich enough to reward them from mine own wealth," answered Cedric.

"And some," said Wamba, "have been wise enough to reward themselves; they do not march off empty-handed altogether. We do not all wear motley."

"They are welcome," said Locksley; "our laws bind none but ourselves."

"But thou, my poor knave," said Cedric, turning about and embracing his Jester, "how shall I reward thee, who feared not to give thy body to chains and death instead of mine? All forsook me, when the poor fool was faithful!"

A tear stood in the eye of the rough thane as he spoke.

"Nay," said the Jester, extricating himself from his master's caress, "if you pay my service with the water of your eye, the Jester must weep for com-

---

LINE 4. liard: French coin of small value. 15. motley: fool's parti-colored clothes.

pany, and then what becomes of his vocation? But, uncle, if you would indeed pleasure me, I pray you to pardon my playfellow Gurth, who stole a week from your service to bestow it on your son."

5 "Pardon him!" exclaimed Cedric; "I will both pardon and reward him. Kneel down, Gurth." The swineherd was in an instant at his master's feet. "*Theow and Esne* art thou no longer," said Cedric, touching him with a wand;
10 *Folkfree and Sacless* art thou in town and from town, in the forest as in the field. A hide of land I give to thee in my steads of Walbrugham, from me and mine to thee and thine aye and for ever."

15 No longer a serf but a freeman and a landholder, Gurth sprung upon his feet, and twice bounded aloft to almost his own height from the ground.

"A smith and a file," he cried, "to do away the collar from the neck of a freeman! Noble master!
20 doubled is my strength by your gift, and doubly will I fight for you! There is a free spirit in my breast. Ha, Fangs!" he continued, for that faithful cur, seeing his master thus transported, began to jump upon him to express his sympathy,
25 "knowest thou thy master still?"

---

LINE **8.** *Theow and Esne:* thrall and bondman. **10.** *Folkfree and Sacless:* lawful freeman. **11. hide:** portion of land, varying from sixty to a hundred twenty acres. **12. steads:** estates. **13. aye:** ever.

"Ay," said Wamba, "Fangs and I still know thee, Gurth. though we must needs abide by the collar; it is only thou art likely to forget both us and thyself."

"I shall forget myself indeed ere I forget thee, true comrade," said Gurth; "and were freedom fit for thee, Wamba, the master would not let thee want it."

"Nay," said Wamba, "never think I envy thee, brother Gurth; the serf sits by the hall fire when the freeman must forth to the field of battle. And what saith Aldhelm of Malmsbury — 'Better a fool at a feast than a wise man at a fray.'"

The tramp of horses was now heard, and the Lady Rowena appeared, surrounded by several riders, and a much stronger party of footmen. As she bent her steed towards Locksley's seat, that bold yeoman, with all his followers, rose to receive her, as if by a general instinct of courtesy. The blood rose to her cheeks as, courteously waving her hand, and bending so low that her beautiful and loose tresses were for an instant mixed with the flowing mane of her palfrey, she expressed in few but apt words her gratitude to Locksley and her other deliverers. "God bless you, brave men," she concluded — "God and Our Lady bless you and requite you for gallantly perilling yourselves

---

LINE **23**. palfrey: riding horse for the road.

in the cause of the oppressed! If any of you should hunger, remember Rowena has food; if you should thirst, she has many a butt of wine and brown ale; and if the Normans drive ye from these walks, Rowena has forests of her own, where her gallant deliverers may range at full freedom, and never ranger ask whose arrow hath struck down the deer."

"Thanks, gentle lady," said Locksley — "thanks from my company and myself. But to have saved you requites itself. We who walk the greenwood do many a wild deed, and the Lady Rowena's deliverance may be received as an atonement."

Cedric, ere they departed, expressed his peculiar gratitude to the Black Champion, and earnestly entreated him to accompany him to Rotherwood.

"I know," he said, "that ye errant knights desire to carry your fortunes on the point of your lance, and reck not of land or goods; but war is a changeful mistress, and a home is sometimes desirable even to the champion whose trade is wandering. Thou hast earned one in the halls of Rotherwood, noble knight. Cedric has wealth enough to repair the injuries of fortune, and all he has is his deliverer's. Come, therefore, to Rotherwood, not as a guest, but as a son or brother."

"Cedric has already made me rich," said the Knight; "he has taught me the value of Saxon

---

LINE **7. ranger**: officer who enforced forest laws about hunting. **16. errant**: wandering.

virtue. To Rotherwood will I come, brave Saxon, and that speedily; but, as now, pressing matters of moment detain me from your halls. Peradventure, when I come hither, I will ask such a boon as will put even thy generosity to the test." 5

"It is granted ere spoken out," said Cedric, striking his ready hand into the gauntleted palm of the Black Knight — "it is granted already, were it to affect half my fortune."

"Gage not thy promise so lightly," said the 10 Knight of the Fetterlock; "yet well I hope to gain the boon I shall ask. Meanwhile, adieu."

"I have but to say," added the Saxon, "that, during the funeral rites of the noble Athelstane, I shall be an inhabitant of the halls of his castle of 15 Coningsburgh. They will be open to all who choose to partake of the funeral banqueting; and — I speak in name of the noble Edith, mother of the fallen prince — they will never be shut against him who labored so bravely, though unsuccessfully, to save 20 Athelstane from Norman chains and Norman steel."

"Ay, ay," said Wamba, who had resumed his attendance on his master, "rare feeding there will be; pity that the noble Athelstane cannot banquet at his own funeral. But he," continued the Jester, 25 lifting up his eyes gravely, "is supping in Paradise, and doubtless does honor to the cheer."

---

LINE 10. Gage: pledge.

"Peace, and move on," said Cedric, his anger at this untimely jest being checked by the recollection of Wamba's recent services. Rowena waved a graceful adieu to him of the Fetterlock, the Saxon bade God speed him, and on they moved through a wide glade of the forest.

"Valiant knight," said Locksley to the Black Champion, "without whose good heart and mighty arm our enterprise must altogether have failed, will it please you to take from that mass of spoil whatever may best serve to pleasure you, and to remind you of this my trysting-tree?"

"I accept the offer," said the Knight, "as frankly as it is given; and I ask permission to dispose of Sir Maurice de Bracy at my own pleasure."

"He is thine already," said Locksley, "and well for him! else the tyrant had graced the highest bough of this oak."

"De Bracy," said the Knight, "thou art free — depart. He whose prisoner thou art scorns to take mean revenge for what is past. But beware of the future, lest a worse thing befall thee. Maurice de Bracy, I say BEWARE!"

De Bracy bowed low and in silence, and was about to withdraw, when the yeomen burst at once into a shout of derision. The proud knight instantly stopped, turned back, folded his arms, drew up his form to its full height, and exclaimed, "Peace, ye yelping curs! De Bracy scorns your censure as he would disdain your applause. To your brakes and caves, ye outlawed thieves!"

This ill-timed defiance might have procured for De Bracy a volley of arrows, but for the hasty and imperative interference of the outlaw chief. Meanwhile, the knight caught a horse by the rein, for several which had been taken in the stables of Front-de-Bœuf stood around, and were a valuable part of the booty. He threw himself upon the saddle, and galloped off through the wood.

When the bustle occasioned by this incident was somewhat composed, the chief outlaw took from his neck the rich horn and baldric which he had recently gained at the strife of archery near Ashby.

"Noble knight," he said to him of the Fetterlock, "if you disdain not to grace by your acceptance a bugle which an English yeoman has once worn, this I will pray you to keep as a memorial of your gallant bearing; and if ye chance to be hard bested in any forest between Trent and Tees, wind three mots upon the horn thus, *Wa-sa-hoa!* and it may well chance ye shall find helpers and rescue."

He then gave breath to the bugle, and winded once and again the call which he described, until the Knight had caught the notes.

"Gramercy for the gift, bold yeoman," said the Knight; "and better help than thine and thy

---

LINE 21. mots: notes upon bugle.

rangers would I never seek, were it at my utmost need." And then in his turn he winded the call till all the greenwood rang.

"Well blown and clearly," said the yeoman. "Comrades, mark these three mots, it is the call of the Knight of the Fetterlock; and he who hears it, and hastens not to serve him at his need, I will have him scourged out of our band with his own bowstring."

"Long live our leader!" shouted the yeoman, "and long live the Black Knight of the Fetterlock! May he soon use our service to prove how readily it will be paid."

Locksley now proceeded to the distribution of the spoil, which he performed with the most laudable impartiality. A tenth part of the whole was set apart for the church; a portion was next allotted to a sort of public treasury; a part was assigned to the widows and children of those who had fallen. The rest was divided amongst the outlaws, according to their rank and merit; and the judgment of the chief, on all such doubtful questions as occurred, was delivered with great shrewdness, and received with absolute submission. The Black Knight was not a little surprised to find that men in a state so lawless were nevertheless among themselves so regularly and equitably governed.

---

LINE 27. **equitably**: justly.

# Spoils Divided

When each had taken his own proportion of the booty, the portion devoted to the church still remained unappropriated.

" I would," said the leader, " we could hear tidings of our joyous chaplain; he was never wont to be absent when meat was to be blessed, or spoil to be parted; and it is his duty to take care of these the tithes of our successful enterprise. I greatly misdoubt the safety of the bluff priest."

" I were right sorry for that," said the Knight of the Fetterlock, " for I stand indebted to him for the joyous hospitality of a merry night in his cell."

While they thus spoke, a loud shout among the yeomen announced the arrival of him for whom they feared, as they learned from the stentorian voice of the Friar himself, long before they saw his burly person.

" Make room, my merry men ! " he exclaimed — " room for your godly father and his prisoner. Cry welcome once more. I come, noble leader, like an eagle with my prey in my clutch." And making his way through the ring, amidst the laughter of all around, he appeared in majestic triumph, his huge partizan in one hand, and in the other a halter, one end of which was fastened to the neck of the unfortunate Isaac of York, who, bent down by sorrow and terror, was dragged on bv the victorious priest.

"Curtal priest," said the captain, "whom hast thou got here?"

"A captive to my sword and to my lance, noble captain," replied the Clerk of Copmanhurst —"to my bow and to my halberd, I should rather say. By St. Dunstan! I found him where I sought for better ware! I did step into the cellarage to see what might be rescued there, and had caught up one runlet of sack, and was coming to call more aid among these lazy knaves, who are ever to seek when a good deed is to be done, when I was avised of a strong door. 'Aha!' thought I, 'here is the choicest juice of all in this secret crypt; and the knave butler hath left the key in the door.' In therefore I went, and found just nought besides a commodity of rusted chains and this dog of a Jew. I did but refresh myself after the fatigue of the action with one cup of sack, and was proceeding to lead forth my captive, when, crash after crash, down toppled the masonry of an outer tower and blocked up the passage. The roar of one falling tower followed another. I gave up thought of life, and took up my spiritual weapon for the conversion of the Jew. And truly, by the blessing of St. Dunstan, the seed has been sown in good soil; only that, with speaking to him of mysteries through the

---

LINE **5**. **halberd**: broad, sharp blade on long handle. **11**. **was avised of**: noticed. **13**. **crypt**: vault. **16**. **commodity**: quantity.

whole night, and being in a manner fasting — for the few draughts of sack which I sharpened my wits with were not worth marking — my head is well-nigh dizzied, I trow. But I was clean exhausted. Gilbert and Wibbald know in what state 5 they found me — quite and clean exhausted."

"We can bear witness," said Gilbert; "for when we had cleared away the ruin, and by St. Dunstan's help lighted upon the dungeon stair, we found the runlet of sack half-empty, the Jew half-dead, and 10 the Friar more than half — exhausted, as he calls it."

"Ye be knaves! ye lie!" retorted the offended Friar; "it was you and your gormandizing companions that drank up the sack, and called it your 15 morning draught. But what recks it? The Jew is converted, and understands all I have told him, very nearly, if not altogether, as well as myself."

"Jew," said the captain, "is this true? Hast thou renounced thine unbelief?" 20

"May I so find mercy in your eyes," said the Jew, "as I know not one word which the reverend prelate spake to me all this fearful night."

"Thou liest, Jew, and thou knowest thou dost," said the Friar; "I will remind thee but of one word 25 of our conference: thou didst promise to give all thy substance to our holy order."

---

LINE 4. **trow**: think; believe. **14. gormandizing**: eating greedily. **16. recks**: matters.

"So help me the promise, fair sirs," said Isaac, even more alarmed than before, "as no such sounds ever crossed my lips! Alas! I am an aged beggar'd man — I fear me a childless; have ruth on me, 5 and let me go!"

"Nay," said the Friar, "if thou dost retract vows made in favor of holy church, thou must do penance."

Accordingly, he raised his halberd, and would 10 have laid the staff of it lustily on the Jew's shoulders, had not the Black Knight stopped the blow, and thereby transferred the holy clerk's resentment to himself.

"By St. Thomas of Kent," said he, "I will teach 15 thee, sir lazy lover, to mell with thine own matters, maugre thine iron case there!"

"Nay, be not wroth with me," said the Knight; "thou knowest I am thy sworn friend and comrade."

20 "I know no such thing," answered the Friar; "and defy thee for a meddling coxcomb!"

"Nay, but," said the Knight, "hast thou forgotten how, that for my sake — for I say nothing of the temptation of the flagon and the pasty — 25 thou didst break thy vow of fast and vigil?"

"Truly, friend," said the Friar, clenching his huge fist, "I will bestow a buffet on thee."

---

LINE 4. ruth: pity. 15. mell: meddle. 16. maugre: in spite of. 21. coxcomb: conceited, showy person.

"I accept of no such presents," said the Knight; "I am content to take thy cuff as a loan, but I will repay thee with usury."

"I will prove that presently," said the Friar.

"Hola!" cried the captain, "what art thou after, mad Friar — brawling beneath our trysting-tree?"

"No brawling," said the Knight; "it is but a friendly interchange of courtesy. Friar, strike an thou darest; I will stand thy blow, if thou wilt stand mine."

"Thou hast the advantage with that iron pot on thy head," said the churchman; "but have at thee. Down thou goest, an thou wert Goliath of Gath in his brazen helmet."

The Friar bared his brawny arm up to the elbow, and putting his full strength to the blow, gave the Knight a buffet that might have felled an ox. But his adversary stood firm as a rock. A loud shout was uttered by all the yeomen around; for the clerk's cuff was proverbial amongst them, and there were few who, in jest or earnest, had not had occasion to know its vigor. "Now, priest," said the Knight, pulling off his gauntlet, "if I had vantage on my head, I will have none on my hand; stand fast as a true man."

"I have given my cheek to the smiter," said the priest; "an thou canst stir me from the spot, fellow, I will freely bestow on thee the Jew's ransom."

So spoke the burly priest, assuming, on his part, high defiance. But who may resist his fate? The buffet of the Knight was given with such strength and good-will that the Friar rolled head over heels 5 upon the plain, to the great amazement of all the spectators. But he arose neither angry nor crestfallen.

"Brother," said he to the Knight, "thou shouldst have used thy strength with more discre- 10 tion. I had mumbled but a lame mass an thou hadst broken my jaw. Nevertheless, there is my hand, in friendly witness that I will exchange no more cuffs with thee, having been a loser by the barter."

15 "And thou, Jew," said the captain, "think of thy ransom while I examine a prisoner of another cast."

"Were many of Front-de-Bœuf's men taken?" demanded the Black Knight.

20 "None of note enough to be put to ransom," answered the captain; "a set of hilding fellows there were, whom we dismissed to find them a new master. The prisoner I speak of is better booty — a jolly monk. Here cometh the worthy prelate, as 25 pert as a pyet." And between two yeomen was brought before the silvan throne of the outlaw chief our old friend, Prior Aymer of Jorvaulx.

---

LINE 6. **crestfallen**: dejected. **25. pyet**: magpie.

## CHAPTER XXXIII

### Ransoms Fixed

The captive Abbot's features and manners exhibited a whimsical mixture of offended pride and bodily terror. "Why, how now, my masters?" said he. "What order is this among ye? Be ye Turks or Christians, that handle a churchman? Ye have plundered my mails, torn my cope of curious cut lace, which might have served a cardinal. Another in my place would have been at his *excommunicabo vos*, but I am placable, and if ye order forth my palfreys, release my brethren, and restore my mails, tell down with all speed an hundred crowns to be expended in masses at the high altar of Jorvaulx Abbey, and make your vow to eat no venison until next Pentecost, it may be you shall hear little more of this mad frolic."

"Holy Father," said the chief outlaw, " it grieves me to think that you have met with such usage from any of my followers."

"Usage!" echoed the priest, encouraged by the mild tone of the silvan leader; " it were usage fit

---

LINE **6. mails**: bags; saddle bags. **8.** *excommunicabo vos*. I will excommunicate you. **9. placable**: forgiving.

for no hound of good race, much less for a Christian, far less for a priest, and least of all for the prior of the holy community of Jorvaulx. Here is a profane and drunken minstrel, called Allan-a-Dale, who has menaced me with corporal punishment — nay, with death itself, an I pay not down four hundred crowns of ransom, to the boot of all the treasure he hath already robbed me of — gold chains and rings to an unknown value."

"It is impossible that Allan-a-Dale can have thus treated a man of your reverend bearing," replied the captain.

"It is true as gospel," said the Prior; "he swore that he would hang me up on the highest tree in the greenwood."

"Did he so in very deed? Nay, then, reverend father, I think you had better comply with his demands, for Allan-a-Dale is the very man to abide by his word when he has so pledged it."

"You do but jest with me," said the astounded Prior, with a forced laugh; "and I love a good jest with all my heart. But, ha! ha! ha! when the mirth has lasted the livelong night, it is time to be grave in the morning."

"And I am as grave as a father confessor," replied the outlaw; "you must pay a round ransom, Sir Prior, or your convent is likely to be called to a new election; for your place will know you no more."

"Are ye Christians," said the Prior, "and hold this language to a churchman?"

"Were it not well," said the lieutenant of the gang apart to the captain, "that the Prior should name the Jew's ransom, and the Jew name the Prior's?"

"Thou art a mad knave," said the captain, "but thy plan transcends! Here, Jew, step forth. Look at that holy Father Aymer, Prior of the rich Abbey of Jorvaulx, and tell us at what ransom we should hold him? Thou knowest the income of his convent, I warrant thee."

"Oh, assuredly," said Isaac. "I have trafficked with the good fathers, and bought wheat and barley, and fruits of the earth, and also much wool. Oh, it is a rich abbey-stede. Ah, if an outcast like me had such a home to go to, and such incomings by the year and by the month, I would pay much gold and silver to redeem my captivity."

"Pronounce what he may pay," said the leader, "without flaying both hide and hair."

"An six hundred crowns," said Isaac, "the good Prior might well pay to your honored valors, and never sit less soft in his stall."

"Six hundred crowns," said the leader, gravely; "I am contented — thou hast well spoken, Isaac — six hundred crowns. It is a sentence, Sir Prior."

---

LINE 16. **abbey-stede**: abbey with its lands. **21. flaying**: stripping off.

"A sentence!—a sentence!" exclaimed the band; "Solomon had not done it better."

"Thou hearest thy doom, Prior," said the leader.

"Ye are mad, my masters," said the Prior; 5 "where am I to find such a sum? If I sell the very pyx and candlesticks on the altar at Jorvaulx, I shall scarce raise the half; and it will be necessary for that purpose that I go to Jorvaulx myself; ye may retain as borrows my two priests."

10 "That will be but blind trust," said the outlaw; "we will retain thee, Prior, and send them to fetch thy ransom."

"Or, if so please you," said Isaac, willing to curry favor with the outlaws, "I can send to York for 15 the six hundred crowns, out of certain monies in my hands, if so be that the most reverend Prior present will grant me a quittance."

"He shall grant thee whatever thou dost list, Isaac," said the captain; "and thou shalt lay down 20 the redemption money for Prior Aymer as well as for thyself."

"For myself! ah, courageous sirs," said the Jew, "I am a broken and impoverished man; a beggar's staff must be my portion through life, supposing I 25 were to pay you fifty crowns."

---

LINE **6. pyx:** vessel holding the wafer consecrated for the communion. **9. borrows:** pledges. **13. curry favor:** seek favor by flattery and attention. **17. quittance:** receipt. **25. crowns:** silver coins worth about $1.20.

"The Prior shall judge of that matter," replied the captain. "How say you, Father Aymer? Can the Jew afford a good ransom?"

"*Can* he afford a ransom?" answered the Prior. "Is he not Isaac of York, rich enough to redeem the captivity of the ten tribes of Israel who were led into Assyrian bondage? I have seen but little of him myself, but our cellarer and treasurer have dealt largely with him, and report says that his house at York is so full of gold and silver as is a shame in any Christian land."

"Prior," said the captain, "do thou name his ransom, as he named thine."

"Since ye require me to put a price upon this caitiff," said the Prior, "I tell you openly that ye will wrong yourselves if you take from him a penny under a thousand crowns."

"A sentence! — a sentence!" exclaimed the chief outlaw.

"A sentence! — a sentence!" shouted his assessors; "the Christian has shown his good nurture, and dealt with us more generously than the Jew."

"The God of my fathers help me!" said the Jew; "will ye bear to the ground an impoverished creature? I am this day childless, and will ye deprive me of the means of livelihood?"

"Thou wilt have the less to provide for, Jew, if thou art childless," said Aymer.

"Alas! my lord," said Isaac, "your law permits
you not to know how the child of our bosom is
entwined with the strings of our heart. O Rebecca!
daughter of my beloved Rachael! were each leaf
5 on that tree a zecchin, and each zecchin mine own,
all that mass of wealth would I give to know
whether thou art alive, and escaped the hands of
the Nazarene!"

"Was not thy daughter dark-haired?" said
10 one of the outlaws; "and wore she not a veil of
twisted sendal, broidered with silver?"

"She did! — she did!" said the old man, trembling with eagerness, as formerly with fear. "The
blessing of Jacob be upon thee! canst thou tell me
15 aught of her safety?"

"It was she, then," said the yeoman, "who was
carried off by the proud Templar, when he broke
through our ranks on yestereven. I had drawn my
bow to send a shaft after him, but spared him even
20 for the sake of the damsel, who I feared might take
harm from the arrow."

"Oh," answered the Jew, "I would to God thou
hadst shot, though the arrow had pierced her
bosom! Ichabod! Ichabod! the glory hath de-
25 parted from my house!"

"Friends," said the chief, looking round, "the

---

LINE **5**. **zecchin**: gold coin of Venice, worth $2.25.
**11. sendal**: thin silken material. **24. Ichabod**: Hebrew
word meaning the glory has departed.

old man's grief touches me. Deal uprightly with us, Isaac: will paying this ransom of a thousand crowns leave thee altogether penniless? "

Isaac could not deny there might be some small surplus. 5

" Well, go to, what though there be," said the outlaw, " we will not reckon with thee too closely. Without treasure thou mayst as well hope to redeem thy child from the clutches of Sir Brian de Bois-Guilbert as to shoot a stag-royal with a headless 10 shaft. We will take thee at the same ransom with Prior Aymer, or rather at one hundred crowns lower, which hundred crowns shall be mine own peculiar loss, and not light upon this worshipful community; and thou wilt have six [five] hundred 15 crowns remaining to treat for thy daughter's ransom. Templars love the glitter of silver shekels as well as the sparkle of black eyes. Hasten to make thy crowns chink in the ear of De Bois-Guilbert, ere worse comes of it. Thou wilt find 20 him, as our scouts have brought notice, at the next preceptory house of his order. Said I well, my merry mates? "

The yeomen expressed their wonted acquiescence in their leader's opinion; and Isaac, relieved of one- 25 half of his apprehensions, by learning that his

---

LINE **10.** **stag-royal**: stag with antlers of twelve or more points. **22.** **preceptory.** See page 621. **24.** **acquiescence**: consent.

daughter lived, and might possibly be ransomed, threw himself at the feet of the generous outlaw, and, rubbing his beard against his buskins, sought to kiss the hem of his green cassock. The captain 5 drew himself back, and extricated himself from the Jew's grasp, not without some marks of contempt.

"Nay, beshrew thee, man, up with thee! I am English born, and love no such Eastern prostrations. Kneel to God, and not to a poor sinner 10 like me."

"Ay, Jew," said Prior Aymer, "kneel to God, and who knows, with thy sincere repentance and due gifts to the shrine of St. Robert, what grace thou mayst acquire for thyself and thy daughter 15 Rebecca? I grieve for the maiden, for she is of fair and comely countenance: I beheld her in the lists of Ashby. Also Brian de Bois-Guilbert is one with whom I may do much: bethink thee how thou mayst deserve my good word with him."

20 Isaac groaned deeply, and began to wring his hands, and to relapse into his state of desolation and despair. But the leader of the yeomen led him aside.

"Advise thee well, Isaac," said Locksley, "what 25 thou wilt do in this matter; my counsel to thee is to make a friend of this churchman. He is vain, Isaac, and he needs money to supply his profusion.

---

LINE 3. **buskins**: laced half-boots.

Thou canst easily gratify his greed; for think not
that I am blinded by thy pretexts of poverty. I
am intimately acquainted, Isaac, with the very iron
chest in which thou dost keep thy money-bags.
What! know I not the great stone beneath the
apple tree, that leads into the vaulted chamber
under thy garden at York?" The Jew grew as
pale as death. "But fear nothing from me," continued the yeoman, "for we are of old acquainted.
Dost thou not remember the sick yeoman whom thy
fair daughter Rebecca redeemed from the gyves at
York, and kept him in thy house till his health was
restored, when thou didst dismiss him recovered,
and with a piece of money? Usurer as thou art,
thou didst never place coin at better interest than
that poor silver mark, for it has this day saved thee
five hundred crowns."

"And thou art he whom we called Diccon Bend-
the-Bow?" said Isaac; "I thought ever I knew
the accent of thy voice."

"I am Bend-the-Bow," said the captain, "and
Locksley, and have a good name besides all these."

"But thou art mistaken, good Bend-the-Bow,
concerning that same vaulted apartment. So help
me Heaven, as there is nought in it but some merchandises which I will gladly part with to you —
these will I send thee for thy good will, honest Diccon, an thou wilt keep silence about the vault, my
good Diccon."

"Silent as a dormouse," said the outlaw; "and never trust me but I am grieved for thy daughter. But I may not help it. The Templar's lances are too strong for my archery in the open field; they
5 would scatter us like dust. Had I but known it was Rebecca when she was borne off, something might have been done; but now thou must needs proceed by policy. Come, shall I treat for thee with the Prior?"

10 "In God's name, Diccon, an thou canst, aid me to recover the child of my bosom!"

"Do not thou interrupt me with thine ill-timed avarice," said the outlaw, "and I will deal with him in thy behalf."

15 He then turned from the Jew, who followed him, however, as closely as his shadow.

"Prior Aymer," said the captain, "come apart with me under this tree. Here is Isaac willing to give thee the means of pleasure and pastime in a
20 bag containing one hundred marks of silver, if thy intercession with thine ally the Templar shall avail to procure the freedom of his daughter."

"In safety and honor, as when taken from me," said the Jew, "otherwise it is no bargain."

25 "Peace, Isaac," said the outlaw, "or I give up thine interest. What say you to this my purpose, Prior Aymer?"

"If the Israelite will advantage the church by giving me somewhat over to the building of our dortour," quoth the Prior, " I will take it on my conscience to aid him in the matter of his daughter."

" For a score of marks to the dortour," said the outlaw — " Be still, I say, Isaac! — or for a brace of silver candlesticks to the altar, we will not stand ₅ with you."

" Nay, but, good Diccon Bend-the-Bow," said Isaac, endeavoring to interpose.

" Good Jew — good beast — good earthworm! " said the yeoman, losing patience; " an thou dost ₁₀ go on to put thy filthy lucre in the balance with thy daughter's life and honor, by Heaven, I will strip thee of every maravedi thou hast in the world before three days are out! "

Isaac shrunk together, and was silent.          ₁₅

" And what pledge am I to have for all this? " said the Prior.

" When Isaac returns successful through your mediation," said the outlaw, " I swear by St. Hubert, I will see that he pays thee the money in ₂₀ good silver, or I will reckon with him for it in such sort, he had better have paid twenty such sums."

" Well then, Jew," said Aymer, " since I must needs meddle in this matter, let me have the use of thy writing-tablets — though, hold — rather than ₂₅ use thy pen, I would fast for twenty-four hours, and where shall I find one? "

---

LINE 1. **dortour**: dormitory; sleeping rooms.    **13. mara-vedi**: Spanish coin worth less than a cent.

"If your holy scruples can dispense with using the Jew's tablets, for the pen I can find a remedy," said the yeoman; and, bending his bow, he aimed his shaft at a wild goose which was soaring over 5 their heads. The bird came fluttering down, transfixed with the arrow.

"There, Prior," said the captain, "are quills enow to supply all the monks of Jorvaulx for the next hundred years, an they take not to writing chronicles."

10 The Prior sat down, and at great leisure indited an epistle to Brian de Bois-Guilbert, and having carefully sealed up the tablets, delivered them to the Jew, saying: "This will be thy safe-conduct to the preceptory of Templestowe, and, as I think, is 15 most likely to accomplish the delivery of thy daughter, if it be well backed with proffers of advantage and commodity at thine own hand."

"Well, Prior," said the outlaw, "I will detain thee no longer here than to give the Jew a quittance 20 for the six hundred crowns at which thy ransom is fixed — I accept of him for my paymaster."

With a much worse grace than that wherewith he had penned the letter to Bois-Guilbert, the Prior wrote an acquittance, discharging Isaac of York 25 of six hundred crowns, advanced to him in his need for acquittal of his ransom, and faithfully promising to hold true compt with him for that sum.

---

LINE 27. compt: account.

" And now," said Prior Aymer, " I will pray you
of restitution of my mules and palfreys, and the
freedom of the reverend brethren attending upon
me, and also of the rings, jewels, and fair vestures
of which I have been despoiled, having now satisfied 5
you for my ransom as a true prisoner."

" Touching your brethren, Sir Prior," said Locksley, " they shall have present freedom ; touching
ur horses and mules, they shall also be restored,
such spending money as may enable you to 10
York. But as concerning rings, jewels,
s, and what else, you must understand that
e men of tender consciences, and will not yield
venerable man like yourself, who should be
to the vanities of this life, the strong tempta- 15
to break the rule of his foundation, by wearing
, chains, or other vain gauds."

e Prior, at length being joined by his attend-
, rode off with considerably less pomp than he
exhibited before this rencounter. 20

remained that the Jew should produce some
rity for the ransom which he was to pay on the
r's account, as well as upon his own. He gave,
rdingly, an order sealed with his signet, to a
ther of his tribe at York, requiring him to pay to 25
the bearer the sum of a thousand [eleven hundred]
crowns, and to deliver certain merchandises speci-
fied in the note.

Ere Isaac departed, the outlaw chief bestowed

445

on him this parting advice: " Be liberal of thine offers, Isaac, and spare not thy purse for thy daughter's safety. Credit me, that the gold thou shalt spare in her cause will hereafter give thee as 5 much agony as if it were poured molten down thy throat."

Isaac acquiesced with a deep groan, and set forth on his journey, accompanied by two tall foresters, who were to be his guides, and at the same time h 10 guards, through the wood.

The Black Knight, who had seen with no interest these various procecdings, now took leave of the outlaw in turn; nor could he a expressing his surprise at having witnessed so 15 of civil policy amongst persons cast out from al ordinary protection and influence of the laws.

" Good fruit, Sir Knight," said the yeor " will sometimes grow on a sorry tree; and times are not always productive of evil alone 20 unmixed. Amongst those who are drawn into lawless state, there are, doubtless, numbers wish to exercise its license with some moderat and some who regret, it may be, that they obliged to follow such a trade at all."

25 " And to one of those," said the Knight, " I a now, I presume, speaking?"

" Sir Knight," said the outlaw, " we have each our secret. You are welcome to form your judg-ment of me, and I may use my conjectures touching you, though neither of our shafts may hit the mark they are shot at. But as I do not pray to be admitted into your mystery, be not offended that I preserve my own."

" I crave pardon, brave outlaw," said the Knight, " your reproof is just. But it may be we shall meet hereafter with less of concealment on either side. Meanwhile we part friends, do we not? "

" There is my hand upon it," said Locksley; " and I will call it the hand of a true Englishman, though an outlaw for the present."

" And there is mine in return," said the Knight, " and I hold it honored by being clasped with yours. For he that does good, having the unlimited power to do evil, deserves praise not only for the good which he performs, but for the evil which he forbears. Fare thee well, gallant outlaw! "

Thus parted that fair fellowship; and he of the Fetterlock, mounting upon his strong war-horse, rode off through the forest.

### CHAPTER XXXIV

## Plot against the King

There was brav[e] [fe]asting in the Castle of York,
to which Princ[e] [Jo]hn had invited those nobles,
prelates, and *us* [leader]s by whose assistance he hoped
to carry th[e] *small* [hi]s ambitious projects upon his
5 brother's *small* [...] Waldemar Fitzurse, his able
and politic *his* was at secret work among them,
tempering *void* [t]hat pitch of courage which was
necessary *such* [...]ing an open declaration of their
purpose. *the* [th]eir enterprise was delayed by the
10 absence *nan,* than one main limb of the con-
federacy *nan,* [...]tubborn and daring, though brutal,
courage *evil* [Fro]nt-de-Bœuf; the buoyant spirits
and bol[d] *and* [...]g of De Bracy; the sagacity, martial
experie[nce] *this* [...]l renowned valor of Brian de Bois-
15 Guilbe[rt] *who* [...]e important to the success of their
conspi[racy] *ion,* and, while cursing in secret their
absen[ce] *are* [...]her John nor his adviser dared to
procee[d] *m* [...]out them. Isaac the Jew also seemed
to have *m* [...]shed, and with him the hope of certain
20 sums of [m]oney. This deficiency was likely to
prove perilous in an emergency so critical.

It was on the morning after the fall of Torquilstone, that a confused report began to spread abroad in the city of York that De Bracy and Bois-Guilbert, with their confederate Front-de-Bœuf, had been taken or slain. Waldemar brought the rumor to Prince John.

"Your Grace is well aware," said Fitzurse coolly, "it will be dangerous to stir without Front-de-Bœuf, De Bracy, and the Templar; and yet we have gone too far to recede with safety."

Prince John struck his forehead with impatience, and then began to stride up and down the apartment.

"The villains," he said —"the base, treacherous villains, to desert me at this pinch! But whom have we here? De Bracy himself, by the rood! and in strange guise doth he come before us."

It was indeed De Bracy, "bloody with spurring, fiery red with speed." His armor bore all the marks of the late obstinate fray, being broken, defaced, and stained with blood in many places, and covered with clay and dust from the crest to the spur. Undoing his helmet, he placed it on the table, and stood a moment as if to collect himself before he told his news.

"De Bracy," said Prince John, "what means this? Speak, I charge thee! Are the Saxons in rebellion?"

"Speak, De Bracy," said Fitzurse, almost in the same moment with his master, "thou wert wont to be a man. Where is the Templar? where Front-de-Bœuf?"

"The Templar is fled," said De Bracy; "Front-de-Bœuf you will never see more. He has found a red grave among the blazing rafters of his own castle, and I alone am escaped to tell you."

"Cold news," said Waldemar, " to us, though you speak of fire and conflagration."

"The worst news is not yet said," answered De Bracy; and, coming up to Prince John, he uttered in a low and emphatic tone: "Richard is in England; I have seen and spoken with him."

Prince John turned pale, tottered, and caught at the back of an oaken bench to support himself, much like to a man who receives an arrow in his bosom.

"Thou ravest, De Bracy," said Fitzurse, "it cannot be."

"It is as true as truth itself," said De Bracy; "I was his prisoner, and spoke with him."

"With Richard Plantagenet, sayest thou?" continued Fitzurse.

"With Richard Plantagenet," replied De Bracy — "with Richard Cœur-de-Lion — with Richard of England."

"And thou wert his prisoner?" said Waldemar; "he is then at the head of a power?"

"No; only a few outlawed yeomen were around him, and to these his person is unknown. I heard him say he was about to depart from them. He joined them only to assist at the storming of Torquilstone."

"Ay," said Fitzurse, " such is indeed the fashion of Richard — a true knight-errant he, and will wander in wild adventure, trusting the prowess of his single arm, while the weighty affairs of his kingdom slumber, and his own safety is endangered. What dost thou propose to do, De Bracy?"

"I? I offered Richard the service of my Free Lances, and he refused them. I will lead them to Hull, seize on shipping, and embark for Flanders; thanks to the bustling times, a man of action will always find employment. And thou, Waldemar, wilt thou take lance and shield, and lay down thy policies, and wend along with me, and share the fate which God sends us?"

"I am too old, Maurice, and I have a daughter," answered Waldemar.

"Give her to me, Fitzurse, and I will maintain her as fits her rank, with the help of lance and stirrup," said De Bracy.

"Not so," answered Fitzurse; " I will take sanctuary in this church of St. Peter; the Archbishop is my sworn brother."

---

LINE 23. **sanctuary.** Some churches had the right to grant freedom from arrest to criminals who took refuge within them. **25. sworn brother.** According to the law of chivalry, sworn brothers were companions in arms who vowed to share dangers and successes.

During this discourse, Prince John had gradually awakened from the stupor into which he had been thrown by the unexpected intelligence, and had been attentive to the conversation which passed
5 betwixt his followers. " They fall off from me," he said to himself : " they hold no more by me than a withered leaf by the bough when a breeze blows on it ! Hell and fiends ! can I shape no means for myself when I am deserted by these cravens ? "
10 He paused, and there was an expression of diabolical passion in the constrained laugh with which he at length broke in on their conversation.

" Ha, ha, ha ! my good lords, by the light of Our Lady's brow, I held ye sage men, bold men,
15 ready-witted men, loving things which are costly to come by ; yet ye throw down wealth, honor, pleasure, all that our noble game promised you, at the moment it might be won by one bold cast ! "

" I understand you not," said De Bracy. " As
20 soon as Richard's return is blown abroad, he will be at the head of an army, and all is then over with us. I would counsel you, my lord, either to fly to France or take the protection of the Queen Mother."

25 " I seek no safety for myself," said Prince John, haughtily ; " that I could secure by a word spoken to my brother. But although you, De Bracy, and

---

LINE **10. diabolical** : devilish. **23. Queen Mother** : Eleanor, the widow of Henry II.

you, Waldemar Fitzurse, are so ready to abandon
me, I should not greatly delight to see your heads
blackening on Clifford's gate yonder.  Thinkest
thou, Waldemar, that the wily Archbishop will not
suffer thee to be taken from the very horns of the 5
altar, would it make his peace with King Richard?
And forgettest thou, De Bracy, that Robert Estoteville lies betwixt thee and Hull with all his forces,
and that the Earl of Essex is gathering his
followers?"  Waldemar Fitzurse and De Bracy 10
looked in each other's faces with blank dismay.
"There is but one road to safety," continued the
Prince, and his brow grew black as midnight: "this
object of our terror journeys alone; he must be
met withal."                                         15

"Not by me," said De Bracy, hastily; "I was
his prisoner, and he took me to mercy.  I will not
harm a feather in his crest."

"Who spoke of harming him?" said Prince
John, with a hardened laugh; "the knave will say 20
next that I meant he should slay him!  No — a
prison were better."

"Ay, but," said Waldemar, "I say the best
prison is that which is made by the sexton: no
dungeon like a church-vault!  I have said my say." 25

"Prison or tomb," said De Bracy, "I wash my
hands of the whole matter."

---

LINE 7. **Robert Estoteville** and **Earl of Essex**: leaders
loyal to King Richard.

"Villain!" said Prince John, "thou wouldst not bewray our counsel?"

"Counsel was never bewrayed by me," said De Bracy, haughtily, "nor must the name of villain 5 be coupled with mine!"

"Peace, Sir Knight!" said Waldemar; "and you, good my lord, forgive the scruples of valiant De Bracy; I trust I shall soon remove them."

"That passes your eloquence, Fitzurse," replied 10 the knight.

"Why, good Sir Maurice," rejoined the wily politician, "but a day since, and it would have been thy dearest wish to have met this Richard hand to hand in the ranks of battle; a hundred times I have 15 heard thee wish it."

"Ay," said De Bracy, "but that was, as thou sayest, hand to hand, and in the ranks of battle! Thou never heardest me breathe a thought of assaulting him alone, and in a forest. I will abide 20 by you in aught that becomes a knight, whether in the lists or in the camp; but this highway practice comes not within my vow."

"I will take on me the conduct of this perilous enterprise," said Fitzurse. "Page, hie to my lodg- 25 ings, and tell my armorer to be there in readiness; and bid Stephen Wetheral, Broad Thoresby, and the Three Spears of Spyinghow come to me in-

---

LINE 2. bewray: betray.

stantly; and let the scout-master, Hugh Bardon, attend me also. Adieu, my Prince, till better times." Thus speaking, he left the apartment.

"He goes to make my brother prisoner," said Prince John to De Bracy. "I trust he will observe 5 our orders, and use our dear Richard's person with all due respect."

De Bracy only answered by a smile.

"By the light of Our Lady's brow," said Prince John, "most clear and positive was our charge that 10 Richard's safety should be cared for, and woe to Waldemar's head if he transgress it!"

"I had better pass to his lodgings," said De Bracy, "and make him fully aware of your Grace's pleasure; for, as it quite escaped my ear, it may not 15 perchance have reached that of Waldemar."

"Nay, nay," said Prince John, impatiently, "I promise thee he heard me; and, besides, I have farther occupation for thee. Maurice, come hither; let me lean on thy shoulder."                                                   20

They walked a turn through the hall in this familiar posture, and Prince John, with an air of the most confidential intimacy, proceeded to say: "What thinkest thou of this Waldemar Fitzurse, my De Bracy? He trusts to be our Chancellor. 25 Surely we will pause ere we give an office so high to one who shows evidently how little he reverences

---

LINE 25. **Chancellor**: chief minister.

our blood, by his so readily undertaking this enterprise against Richard. Thou dost think, I warrant,
that thou hast lost somewhat of our regard by thy
boldly declining this unpleasing task. But no,
5 Maurice! I rather honor thee for thy virtuous
constancy. The arrest of my unfortunate brother
forms no such good title to the high office of Chancellor as thy chivalrous and courageous denial es-
tablishes in thee to the truncheon of High Marshal.
10 Think of this, De Bracy, and begone to thy charge."

"Fickle tyrant!" muttered De Bracy, as he left
the presence of the Prince; "evil luck have they
who trust thee. Thy Chancellor, indeed! He who
hath the keeping of thy conscience shall have an
15 easy charge, I trow. But High Marshal of
England! that," he said, extending his arm, as if
to grasp the baton of office, and assuming a loftier
stride along the ante-chamber — "that is indeed a
prize worth playing for!"

20 De Bracy had no sooner left the apartment than
Prince John summoned an attendant.

"Bid Hugh Bardon, our scout-master, come
hither, as soon as he shall have spoken with Waldemar Fitzurse."

25 The scout-master arrived after a brief delay, during which John traversed the apartment with
unequal and disordered steps.

"Bardon," said he, "what did Waldemar desire
of thee?"

# Plot against the King

"Two resolute men, well acquainted with these northern wilds, and skilful in tracking the tread of man and horse."

"And thou hast fitted him?"

"Let your Grace never trust me else," answered the master of the spies.

"'Tis well," said the Prince. "Goes Waldemar forth with them?"

"Instantly," said Bardon.

"Bardon," said Prince John, "it imports our service that thou keep a strict watch on Maurice de Bracy, so that he shall not observe it, however. And let us know of his motions from time to time, with whom he converses, what he proposeth. Fail not in this, as thou wilt be answerable."

Hugh Bardon bowed, and retired.

"If Maurice betrays me," said Prince John — "if he betrays me, as his bearing leads me to fear, I will have his head, were Richard thundering at the gates of York."

# CHAPTER XXXV

## Isaac before the Grand Master

Our tale now returns to Isaac of York. Mounted upon a mule, the gift of the outlaw, with two tall yeomen to act as his guard and guides, the Jew had set out for the preceptory of Templestowe. The preceptory was but a day's journey from the demolished castle of Torquilstone, and the Jew had hoped to reach it before nightfall; accordingly, having dismissed his guides at the verge of the forest, and rewarded them with a piece of silver, he began to press on with such speed as his weariness permitted him to exert. But his strength failed him totally ere he had reached within four miles of the Temple court; racking pains shot along his back and through his limbs, and he was rendered altogether incapable of proceeding farther than a small market-town, where dwelt a Jewish rabbi of his tribe, eminent in the medical profession, and to whom Isaac was well known. Nathan Ben Israel received his suffering countryman with kindness. He insisted on his betaking himself to repose, and used remedies to check the progress of the fever which terror, fatigue, ill-usage, and sorrow had brought upon the poor old Jew.

# Isaac before the Grand Master

On the morrow, when Isaac proposed to arise and pursue his journey, Nathan remonstrated against his purpose. It might cost him, he said, his life. But Isaac replied that more than life and death depended upon his going that morning to Templestowe.

"To Templestowe!" said his host with surprise. "Wottest thou that Lucas de Beaumanoir, the chief of the order of Templars, and whom they term Grand Master, is now himself at Templestowe?"

"I know it not," said Isaac; "our last letters from our brethren at Paris advised us that he was at that city."

"He hath since come to England, unexpected by his brethren," said Ben Israel; "and he cometh among them with a strong and outstretched arm to correct and to punish. His countenance is kindled in anger against those who have departed from the vow which they have made."

"Nevertheless," said Isaac, "I must present myself at Templestowe, though he hath made his face like unto a fiery furnace seven times heated."

He then explained to Nathan the pressing cause of his journey.

"Thou seest," said Isaac, "how it stands with me, and that I may not tarry. Peradventure, the presence of this Lucas Beaumanoir, being the chief

---

LINE 8. Wottest: knowest.

man over them, may turn Brian de Bois-Guilbert
from the ill which he doth meditate, and that he
may deliver to me my beloved daughter Rebecca."

"Go thou," said Nathan Ben Israel, "and be
5 wise. If thou canst, keep thee from the presence
of the Grand Master, for to do foul scorn to our
people is his morning and evening delight. It may
be, if thou couldst speak with Bois-Guilbert in private, thou shalt the better prevail with him. But
10 do thou, brother, return to me as if it were to the
house of thy father, and bring me word how it has
sped with thee."

Isaac accordingly bade his friend farewell, and
about an hour's riding brought him before the
15 preceptory of Templestowe.

This establishment of the Templars, seated
amidst fair meadows and pastures, was strong and
well fortified. Two halberdiers, clad in black,
guarded the drawbridge, and others, in the same sad
20 livery, glided to and fro upon the walls with a fu-
nereal pace, resembling spectres more than soldiers.
A knight was now and then seen to cross the court
in his long white cloak, his head depressed on his
breast, and his arms folded. They passed each
25 other, if they chanced to meet, with a slow, solemn,
and mute greeting; for such was the rule of their

---

LINE **18. halberdiers**: soldiers armed with broad, sharp
blades on long handles. **20. livery**: distinctive clothes worn
by servants and retainers.

order, quoting thereupon the holy texts, " In many words thou shalt not avoid sin," and " Life and death are in the power of the tongue." In a word, the stern, ascetic rigor of the Temple discipline seemed at once to have revived at Templestowe 5 under the severe eye of Lucas Beaumanoir.

Isaac paused at the gate, to consider how he might seek entrance in the manner most likely to bespeak favor.

Meantime, Lucas Beaumanoir walked in a small 10 garden belonging to the preceptory, and held sad and confidential communication with a brother of his order, who had come in his company from Palestine.

The Grand Master was a man advanced in age, 15 as was testified by his long grey beard, and the shaggy grey eyebrows, overhanging eyes of which, however, years had been unable to quench the fire. A formidable warrior, his thin and severe features retained the soldier's fierceness of expression. His 20 stature was tall, and his gait, undepressed by age and toil, was erect and stately. His white mantle was shaped with severe regularity, being composed of what was then called burrel cloth, exactly fitted to the size of the wearer, and bearing on the left 25 shoulder the octangular cross peculiar to the order

---

LINE **1. holy texts** : Proverbs 10 : 19 and 18 : 21. **4. ascetic** : severely self-denying. **24. burrel cloth** : coarse russet cloth.

formed of red cloth. No vair or ermine decked this garment; but in respect of his age, the Grand Master, as permitted by the rules, wore his doublet lined and trimmed with the softest lambskin,
5 dressed with the wool outwards, which was the nearest approach he could regularly make to the use of fur, then the greatest luxury of dress. In his hand he bore that singular abacus, or staff of office, with which Templars are usually represented, hav-
10 ing at the upper end a round plate, on which was engraved the cross of the order, inscribed within a circle. His companion had nearly the same dress in all respects, but his extreme deference towards his superior showed that no other equality subsisted
15 between them. The preceptor, for such he was in rank, walked not in a line with the Grand Master, but just so far behind that Beaumanoir could speak to him without turning round his head.

"Conrade," said the Grand Master, "thou
20 knowest the life I have led, keeping each point of my order, striving with devils, striking down the roaring lion, who goeth about seeking whom he may devour, like a good knight and devout priest. But, by the Holy Temple I swear to thee, that save
25 thyself and some few that still retain the ancient severity of our order, I look upon no brethren whom I can bring my soul to embrace under that holy

---

LINE **1. vair**: squirrel fur.   **13. deference**: courteous regard.

name. What say our statutes, and how do our brethren observe them? They should wear no vain or worldly ornament, no crest upon their helmet, no gold upon stirrup or bridle-bit; yet who now go pranked out so proudly and so gaily as 5 the poor soldiers of the Temple? They are forbidden by our statutes to take one bird by means of another, to shoot beasts with bow, to halloo to a hunting-horn, or to spur the horse after game; but now, at hunting and hawking, and each idle sport of 10 wood and river, who so prompt as the Templars in all these fond vanities? Simpleness of diet was prescribed to them — roots, pottage, gruels, eating flesh but thrice a-week; and behold, their tables groan under delicate fare. Their drink was to be 15 water; and now, to drink like a Templar is the boast of each jolly boon companion. I shame to speak — I shame to think — of the corruptions which have rushed in upon us even like a flood. But I WILL purify the fabric of the Temple; and 20 the unclean stones in which the plague is, I will remove and cast out of the building."

"Yet, reverend father," said Mont-Fitchet, "let thy reformation be cautious, as it is just and wise."

"No, Mont-Fitchet," answered the stern old 25 man, "it must be sharp and sudden; the order is on the crisis of its fate. We must retrace our steps,

---

LINE 3. **crest**: plume on top of helmet.

and show ourselves the faithful champions of the Cross."

At this moment a squire, clothed in a threadbare vestment — for the aspirants after this holy order 5 wore during their novitiate the cast-off garments of the knights — entered the garden, and, bowing profoundly before the Grand Master, stood silent, awaiting his permission ere he presumed to tell his errand.

10 "Speak, Damian," said the Grand Master; "we permit thee. What is thine errand?"

"A Jew stands without the gate, noble and reverend father," said the squire, "who prays to speak with brother Brian de Bois-Guilbert."

15 "Thou wert right to give me knowledge of it," said the Grand Master. "Lead the Jew to our presence."

The squire departed with a profound reverence, and in a few minutes returned, marshalling in 20 Isaac of York. No naked slave, ushered into the presence of some mighty prince, could approach his judgment-seat with more profound reverence and terror than that with which the Jew drew near to the presence of the Grand Master. When he had ap-25proached within the distance of three yards, Beaumanoir made a sign with his staff that he should come no farther. The Jew kneeled down on the

---

LINE **5. novitiate :** time of trial or apprenticeship.

earth, which he kissed in token of reverence; then rising, stood before the Templars, his hands folded on his bosom, his head bowed on his breast.

"Damian," said the Grand Master, "retire, and have a guard ready to await our sudden call; and suffer no one to enter the garden until we shall leave it." The squire bowed and retreated. "Jew," continued the haughty old man, "mark me. Be brief in thy answers to what questions I shall ask thee, and let thy words be of truth; for if thy tongue doubles with me, I will have it torn from thy misbelieving jaws.".

The Jew was about to reply; but the Grand Master went on:

"Peace, unbeliever! not a word in our presence, save in answer to our questions. What is thy business with our brother Brian de Bois-Guilbert?"

Isaac gasped with terror and uncertainty. To tell his tale might be interpreted into scandalizing the order; yet, unless he told it, what hope could he have of achieving his daughter's deliverance?

"I am bearer of a letter," stammered out the Jew, "so please your reverend valor, to that good knight, from Prior Aymer of the Abbey of Jorvaulx."

"Give me the letter," said the Master. "A Templar cannot receive a letter, no, not from his father, without communicating the same to the Grand Master."

Beaumanoir then perused the letter in haste, with an expression of surprise and horror; read it over again more slowly; then holding it out to Conrade with one hand, and slightly striking it with the other, exclaimed: "Here is goodly stuff for one Christian man to write to another!"

Mont-Fitchet took the letter from his superior, and was about to peruse it. "Read it aloud, Conrade," said the Grand Master; "and do thou (to Isaac) attend to the purport of it, for we will question thee concerning it."

Conrade read the letter, which was in these words: "Aymer, by divine grace, prior of St. Mary's of Jorvaulx, to Sir Brian de Bois-Guilbert, a knight of the holy order of the Temple, wisheth health, with the bounties of King Bacchus and of my Lady Venus. Touching our present condition, dear brother, we are a captive in the hands of certain lawless and godless men, who have not feared to detain our person, and put us to ransom; whereby we have also learned of Front-de-Bœuf's misfortune, and that thou hast escaped with that fair Jewish sorceress whose black eyes have bewitched thee. We are heartily rejoiced of thy safety; nevertheless, we pray thee to be on thy guard in the matter of this second Witch of Endor; for we are privately assured that your Great Master, who

LINE 16. **Bacchus**: god of wine.   **17. Venus**: goddess of love.

466

careth not a bean for cherry cheeks and black eyes
comes from Normandy to diminish your mirth and
amend your misdoings. Wherefore we pray you
heartily to beware, and to be found watching.
And the wealthy Jew her father, Isaac of York, hav- 5
ing prayed of me letters in his behalf, I gave him
these, earnestly advising, and in a sort entreating,
that you do hold the damsel to ransom, seeing he
will pay you from his bags as much as may find
fifty damsels upon safer terms.                              10

"Given from this den of thieves, about the hour
of matins,

"AYMER PR. S. M. JORVOLCIENCIS."

"Den of thieves!" said the Grand Master,
"and a fit residence is a den of thieves for such a 15
prior." Then turning to Isaac, he said, "Thy
daughter, then, is prisoner with Brian de Bois-
Guilbert?"

"Ay, reverend valorous sir," stammered poor
Isaac, "and whatsoever ransom a poor man may 20
pay for her deliverance ——"

"Peace!" said the Grand Master. "This thy
daughter hath practised the art of healing, hath she
not?"

"Ay, gracious sir," answered the Jew with more 25
confidence; "and knight and yeoman, squire and

---

LINE 12. **matins**: midnight or morning prayers.

vassal, may bless the goodly gift which Heaven hath assigned to her. Many a one can testify that she hath recovered them by her art, when every other human aid hath proved vain; but the blessing of 5 the God of Jacob was upon her."

" Thy daughter worketh the cures, I doubt not," said the Grand Master, " by words and sigils, and periapts, and other mysteries."

" Nay, reverend and brave knight," answered 10 Isaac, " but in chief measure by a balsam of marvellous virtue."

" Where had she that secret? " said Beaumanoir.

" It was delivered to her," answered Isaac, reluctantly, " by Miriam, a sage matron of our tribe."

15 " Ah, false Jew! " said the Grand Master; " was it not from that same witch Miriam, the abomination of whose enchantments have been heard of throughout every Christian land? Her body was burnt at a stake, and her ashes were scattered to the 20 four winds; and so be it with me and mine order, if I do not as much to her pupil, and more also! I will teach her to throw spell and incantation over the soldiers of the blessed Temple! There, Damian, spurn this Jew from the gate; shoot him 25 dead if he oppose or turn again. With his daughter we will deal as the Christian law and our own high office warrant."

---

LINE **7. sigils**: signs. **8. periapts**: charms

# Isaac before the Grand Master

Poor Isaac was hurried off accordingly, and expelled from the preceptory, all his entreaties, and even his offers, unheard and disregarded. He could do no better than return to the house of the Rabbi, and endeavor, through his means, to learn 5 how his daughter was to be disposed of. He had hitherto feared for her honor; he was now to tremble for her life. Meanwhile, the Grand Master ordered to his presence the preceptor of Temple-stowe. 10

# CHAPTER XXXVI

## Preparation for the Trial

Albert Malvoisin, president, or, in the language of the order, preceptor of the establishment of Templestowe, was brother to that Philip Malvoisin who has been already occasionally mentioned in 5 this history, and was, like that baron, in close league with Brian de Bois-Guilbert.

Amongst dissolute and unprincipled men Albert of Templestowe might be distinguished; but with this difference from the audacious Bois-Guilbert, 10 that he knew how to throw over his vices and his ambition the veil of hypocrisy. Had not the arrival of the Grand Master been so unexpectedly sudden, he would have seen nothing at Templestowe which might have appeared to argue 15 any relaxation of discipline. And, even although surprised, and to a certain extent detected, Albert Malvoisin listened with such respect and apparent contrition to the rebuke of his superior, and made such haste to reform the particulars he censured 20 that Lucas Beaumanoir began to entertain a higher opinion of the preceptor's morals than the first

---

LINE **7**. dissolute: depraved; profligate.

appearance of the establishment had inclined him to adopt.

But these favorable sentiments on the part of the Grand Master were greatly shaken by the intelligence that Albert had received within a house of religion the Jewish captive; and when Albert appeared before him he was regarded with unwonted sternness.

"There is in this mansion, dedicated to the purposes of the holy order of the Temple," said the Grand Master, in a severe tone, "a Jewish woman, brought hither by a brother of religion, by your connivance, Sir Preceptor."

Albert Malvoisin was overwhelmed with confusion; for the unfortunate Rebecca had been confined in a remote and secret part of the building, and every precaution used to prevent her residence there from being known. He read in the looks of Beaumanoir ruin to Bois-Guilbert and to himself, unless he should be able to avert the impending storm.

"How comes it," continued the Grand Master, "I demand of thee once more, that thou hast suffered a brother to bring a Jewish sorceress into this holy place, to the stain and pollution thereof?"

"A Jewish sorceress!" echoed Albert Malvoisin, "good angels guard us!"

"Ay, brother, a Jewish sorceress," said the Grand Master, sternly. "I have said it. Darest thou deny that this Rebecca, the daughter of Isaac of York, and the pupil of the foul witch Miriam, is now lodged within this thy preceptory?"

"Your wisdom, reverend father," answered the preceptor, "hath rolled away the darkness from my understanding. Much did I wonder that so good a knight as Brian de Bois-Guilbert seemed so fondly besotted on the charms of this female, whom I received into this house merely to place a bar betwixt their growing intimacy, which else might have been cemented at the expense of the fall of our valiant and religious brother."

"It may be," said Beaumanoir, "that our brother Bois-Guilbert does in this matter deserve rather pity than severe chastisement, rather the support of the staff than the strokes of the rod; and that our admonitions and prayers may turn him from his folly, and restore him to his brethren."

"It were deep pity," said Conrade Mont-Fitchet, "to lose to the order one of its best lances, when the holy community most requires the aid of its sons. Three hundred Saracens hath this Brian de Bois-Guilbert slain with his own hand."

"The blood of these accursed dogs," said the Grand Master, "shall be a sweet and acceptable offering to the saints and angels whom they despise and blaspheme; and with their aid will we counteract the spells and charms with which our brother is entwined as in a net. But concerning this foul witch, who hath flung her enchantments over a brother of the Holy Temple, assuredly she shall die the death. Prepare the castle hall for the trial of the sorceress."

Albert Malvoisin bowed and retired, not to give directions for preparing the hall, but to seek out Brian de Bois-Guilbert. It was not long ere he found him, foaming with indignation at a repulse he had anew sustained from the fair Jewess. " The unthinking," he said — " the ungrateful, to scorn him who, amidst blood and flames, would have saved her life at the risk of his own! By Heaven, Malvoisin! I abode until roof and rafters crackled and crashed around me. I was the butt of a hundred arrows; they rattled on mine armor like hailstones against a latticed casement, and the only use I made of my shield was for her protection. This did I endure for her, and now the self-willed girl upbraids me that I did not leave her to perish. The devil, that possessed her race with obstinacy, has concentrated its full force in her single person!"

" The devil," said the preceptor, " possessed you both. I think old Lucas Beaumanoir guesses right, when he maintains she hath cast a spell over you."

" Lucas Beaumanoir?" said Bois-Guilbert, reproachfully. " Are these your precautions, Mal-

---

LINE **14.** butt: target.

voisin? Hast thou suffered the dotard to learn that Rebecca is in the preceptory?"

"How could I help it?" said the preceptor. "I neglected nothing that could keep secret your 5 mystery; but it is betrayed. But I have turned the matter as I could; you are safe if you renounce Rebecca. You are pitied — the victim of magical delusion. She is a sorceress, and must suffer as such."

10 "She shall not, by Heaven!" said Bois-Guilbert.

"By Heaven, she must and will!" said Malvoisin. "Neither you nor any one else can save her."

"I have it," said Bois-Guilbert. "Albert, thou art my friend. Thou must connive at her escape, 15 Malvoisin, and I will transport her to some place of greater security and secrecy."

"I cannot, if I would," replied the preceptor: "the mansion is filled with the attendants of the Grand Master. If you will be guided by my 20 counsel, you will give up this wild-goose chase, and fly your hawk at some other game. Think, Bois-Guilbert; thy present rank, thy future honors, all depend on thy place in the order. Shouldst thou adhere perversely to thy passion for this 25 Rebecca, thou wilt give Beaumanoir the power of expelling thee, and he will not neglect it. He is jealous of the truncheon which he holds in his

---

LINE 1. **dotard**: one whose mind is impaired by age.

trembling gripe, and he knows thou stretchest thy bold hand towards it. Doubt not he will ruin thee, if thou affordest him a pretext so fair as thy protection of a Jewish sorceress. Give him his scope in this matter, for thou canst not control him." 5

"Malvoisin," said Bois-Guilbert, "thou art a cold-blooded —— "

"Friend," said the preceptor, hastening to fill up the blank, in which Bois-Guilbert would probably have placed a worse word —— "a cold-blooded friend 10 I am, and therefore more fit to give thee advice. I tell thee once more, that thou canst not save Rebecca. I tell thee once more, thou canst but perish with her. Go hie thee to the Grand Master; throw thyself at his feet and tell him —— " 15

"Not at his feet, by Heaven! but to the dotard's very beard will I say —— "

"Say to him, then, to his beard," continued Malvoisin, coolly, "that you love this captive Jewess to distraction; and the more thou dost enlarge on thy 20 passion, the greater will be his haste to end it by the death of the fair enchantress."

"Thou speakest the truth, Malvoisin," said Brian de Bois-Guilbert, after a moment's reflection. "I will give the hoary bigot no advantage over me; 25 and for Rebecca, she hath not merited at my hand that I should expose rank and honor for her sake.

---

LINE 25. hoary: gray; aged. bigot: one blindly and stubbornly attached to a church, party, or belief.

I will cast her off; yes, I will leave her to her fate, unless —— "

" Qualify not thy wise and necessary resolution," said Malvoisin; " women are but the toys which amuse our lighter hours; ambition is the serious business of life. Perish a thousand such frail baubles as this Jewess, before thy manly step pause in the brilliant career that lies stretched before thee! For the present we part, nor must we be seen to hold close conversation; I must order the hall for his judgment seat."

" What! " said Bois-Guilbert, " so soon? "

" Ay," replied the preceptor, " trial moves rapidly on when the judge has determined the sentence beforehand."

" Rebecca," said Bois-Guilbert, when he was left alone, " thou art like to cost me dear. Why cannot I abandon thee to thy fate, as this calm hypocrite recommends? One effort will I make to save thee; but beware of ingratitude! for, if I am again repulsed, my vengeance shall equal my love. The life and honor of Bois-Guilbert must not be hazarded, where contempt and reproaches are his only reward."

The preceptor had hardly given the necessary orders, when he was joined by Conrade Mont-Fitchet, who acquainted him with the Grand Mas-

---

LINE **7.** baubles: trinkets; gewgaws.

ter's resolution to bring the Jewess to instant trial
for sorcery.

"It is surely a dream," said the preceptor; "we
have many Jewish physicians, and we call them not
wizards, though they work wonderful cures." 5

"The Grand Master thinks otherwise," said
Mont-Fitchet; "and, wizard or not, it were better
that this miserable damsel die than that Brian de
Bois-Guilbert should be lost to the order, or the
order divided by internal dissension." 10

"But are there grounds enough to condemn this
Rebecca for sorcery?" said Malvoisin. "Will not
the Grand Master change his mind when he sees
that the proofs are so weak?"

"They must be strengthened, Albert," replied 15
Mont-Fitchet — "they must be strengthened.
Dost thou understand me?"

"I do," said the preceptor, "nor do I scruple to
do aught for advancement of the order; but there
is little time to find engines fitting." 20

"Malvoisin, they *must* be found," said Conrade;
"well will it advantage both the order and thee.
This Templestowe is a poor preceptory; that of
Maison-Dieu is worth double its value. Thou
knowest my interest with our old chief; find those 25
who can carry this matter through, and thou art
preceptor of Maison-Dieu in the fertile Kent.
How sayst thou?"

"There is," replied Malvoisin, "among those

who came hither with Bois-Guilbert, two fellows whom I well know. It may be they know something of the witcheries of this woman."

"Away, seek them out instantly; and hark thee, if a byzant or two will sharpen their memory, let them not be wanting."

"They would swear the mother that bore them a sorceress for a zecchin," said the preceptor.

"Away, then," said Mont-Fitchet; "at noon the affair will proceed."

The ponderous castle-bell had tolled the point of noon, when Rebecca heard a trampling of feet upon the private stair which led to her place of confinement. The noise announced the arrival of several persons, and the circumstance rather gave her joy; for she was more afraid of the solitary visits of the fierce and passionate Bois-Guilbert than of any evil that could befall her besides. The door of the chamber was unlocked, and Conrade and the preceptor Malvoisin entered, attended by four warders clothed in black, and bearing halberds.

"Daughter of an accursed race!" said the preceptor, "arise and follow us."

"Whither," said Rebecca, "and for what purpose?"

"Damsel," answered Conrade, "it is not for thee to question, but to obey. Nevertheless, be it

LINE 5. **byzant**: gold coin of Constantinople, worth from three to five dollars.

known to thee, that thou art to be brought before the tribunal of the Grand Master of our holy order, there to answer for thine offences."

"May the God of Abraham be praised!" said Rebecca, folding her hands devoutly; "the name 5 of a judge, though an enemy to my people, is to me as the name of a protector. Most willingly do I follow thee; permit me only to wrap my veil around my head."

They descended the stair with slow and solemn 10 step, traversed a long gallery, and, by a pair of folding-doors placed at the end, entered the great hall in which the Grand Master had for the time established his court of justice.

The lower part of this ample apartment was filled 15 with squires and yeomen. As Rebecca passed through the crowd, her arms folded and her head depressed, a scrap of paper was thrust into her hand, which she received almost unconsciously, and continued to hold without examining its contents. 20 The assurance that she possessed some friend in this awful assembly gave her courage to look around, and to mark into whose presence she had been conducted.

# CHAPTER XXXVII

## Rebecca Tried for Sorcery

On an elevated seat, directly before the accused, sat the Grand Master of the Temple, in full and ample robes of flowing white, holding in his hand the mystic staff which bore the symbol of the
5 order. At his feet was placed a table, occupied by two scribes, chaplains of the order, whose duty it was to reduce to formal record the proceedings of the day. The black dresses, bare scalps, and demure looks of these churchmen formed a strong
10 contrast to the warlike appearance of the knights who attended. The preceptors, of whom there were four present, occupied seats lower in height and somewhat drawn back behind that of their superior; and the knights who enjoyed no such
15 rank in the order were placed on benches still lower, and preserving the same distance from the preceptors as these from the Grand Master. Behind them, but still upon the dais or elevated portion of the hall, stood the esquires of the order, in white
20 dresses of an inferior quality.

---

LINE 8. demure: sober.

The lower part of the hall was filled with guards, holding partizans, and with other attendants whom curiosity had drawn thither to see at once a Grand Master and a Jewish sorceress. By far the greater part of those inferior persons 5 were, in one rank or other, connected with the order, and were accordingly distinguished by their black dresses. But peasants from the neighboring country were not refused admittance; for it was the pride of Beaumanoir to render the edifying 10 spectacle of the justice which he administered as public as possible. A psalm commenced the proceedings of the day. The Grand Master then raised his voice and addressed the assembly.

" Reverend and valiant men, knights, preceptors, 15 and companions of this holy order, my brethren and my children! and you also, Christian brethren, of every degree! — be it known to you, that to us is committed, with this batoon, full power to judge and to try all that regards the weal of this 20 our holy order. But when the raging wolf hath made an inroad upon the flock, and carried off one member thereof, it is the duty of the kind shepherd to call his comrades together, that with bows and slings they may quell the invader. We have there- 25 fore summoned to our presence a Jewish woman, by name Rebecca, daughter of Isaac of York — a

---

LINE **19. batoon**: staff of office. **20. weal**: welfare.

woman infamous for sortileges and for witcheries; whereby she hath maddened the blood, and besotted the brain of a preceptor of our order, first in honor as in place. Our brother, Brian de Bois-Guil-
5 bert, is well known as a true and zealous champion of the Cross, by whose arm many deeds of valor have been wrought in the Holy Land. Neither have our brother's sagacity and prudence been less in repute among his brethren than his valor and
10 discipline; insomuch that knights, both in eastern and western lands, have named De Bois-Guilbert as one who may well be put in nomination as successor to this batoon, when it shall please Heaven to release us from the toil of bearing it. If we were
15 told that such a man, so honored, and so honorable, suddenly casting away regard for his character, his vows, his brethren, and his prospects, had associated to himself a Jewish damsel, defended her person in preference to his own, and, finally, was so
20 utterly blinded and besotted by his folly, as to bring her even to one of our own preceptories, what should we say but that the noble knight was possessed by some evil demon, or influenced by some wicked spell? If we could suppose it otherwise,
25 think not rank, valor, high repute, or any earthly consideration should prevent us from visiting him with punishment. For various and heinous are

---

LINE 1. sortileges: sorcery; magic.

the acts of transgression against the rule of our blessed order in this lamentable history.  1st, He hath walked according to his proper will.  2d, He hath held communication with an excommunicated person.  3d, He hath conversed with strange women.  4th, He hath not avoided, nay, he hath, it is to be feared, solicited, the kiss of woman.  For which heinous and multiplied guilt, Brian de Bois-Guilbert should be cut off and cast out from our congregation, were he the right hand and right eye thereof."

He paused.  A low murmur went through the assembly.  Some of the younger part, who had been inclined to smile, became now grave enough, and anxiously waited what the Grand Master was next to propose.

" Such," he said, " and so great should indeed be the punishment of a Knight Templar who wilfully offended against the rules of his order in such weighty points.  But if, by means of charms and of spells, Satan had obtained dominion over the knight, we are then rather to lament than chastise his backsliding ; and, imposing on him only such penance as may purify him from his iniquity, we are to turn the full edge of our indignation upon the accursed instrument, which had so well-nigh occasioned his utter falling away.  Stand forth, there-

---

LINE **4**. **excommunicated** : cut off from church-membership.

fore, and bear witness, ye who have witnessed these unhappy doings; and judge whether our justice may be satisfied with the punishment of this infidel woman, or if we must go on, with a bleeding heart, to the further proceeding against our brother."

Several witnesses were called upon to prove the risks to which Bois-Guilbert exposed himself in endeavoring to save Rebecca from the blazing castle, and his neglect of his personal defence in attending to her safety. The men gave these details with exaggerations, and their natural disposition to the marvellous was greatly increased by the satisfaction which their evidence seemed to afford.

"Were it not well, brethren," said the Grand Master, "that we examine something into the former life and conversation of this woman, specially that we may discover whether she be one likely to use magical charms and spells?"

Herman of Goodalricke was the fourth preceptor present; the other three were Conrade, Malvoisin, and Bois-Guilbert himself. Herman was an ancient warrior, whose face was marked with sabre scars, and had great rank and consideration among his brethren. He arose and bowed to the Grand Master, who instantly granted him license of speech. "I would crave to know, most reverend father, of our valiant brother, Brian de Bois-Guilbert, what he says to these wondrous accusations, and with what eye he himself now regards this Jewish maiden?"

"Brian de Bois-Guilbert," said the Grand Master, "thou hearest the question which our brother of Goodalricke desirest thou shouldst answer. I command thee to reply to him."

Bois-Guilbert turned his head towards the Grand Master when thus addressed, and remained silent.

"He is possessed by a dumb devil," said the Grand Master. "Speak, Brian de Bois-Guilbert, I conjure thee, by this symbol of our holy order."

Bois-Guilbert made an effort to suppress his rising scorn and indignation, the expression of which, he was well aware, would have little availed him. "Brian de Bois-Guilbert," he answered, "replies not, most reverend father, to such wild and vague charges. If his honor be impeached, he will defend it with his body, and with that sword which has often fought for Christendom."

"We forgive thee, brother Brian," said the Grand Master, "for boasting thy warlike achievements before us. Thou hast our pardon, judging thou speakest less of thine own suggestion than from the impulse of him whom, by Heaven's leave, we will quell and drive forth from our assembly." A glance of disdain flashed from the dark fierce eyes of Bois-Guilbert, but he made no reply. "And now," pursued the Grand Master, "we will search to the bottom this mystery of iniquity. Let

485

those who have aught to witness of the life and conversation of this Jewish woman stand forth before us."

There was a bustle in the lower part of the hall, and when the Grand Master inquired the reason, it was replied, there was in the crowd a bedridden man, whom the prisoner had restored to the perfect use of his limbs, by a miraculous balsam.

The poor peasant, a Saxon by birth, was dragged forward to the bar, terrified at the consequences which he might have incurred by the guilt of having been cured of the palsy by a Jewish damsel. Perfectly cured he certainly was not, for he supported himself forward on crutches to give evidence. Most unwilling was his testimony, and given with many tears; but he admitted that two years since, when residing at York, he was suddenly afflicted with a sore disease, while laboring for Isaac the rich Jew, in his vocation of a joiner; that he had been unable to stir from his bed until the remedies applied by Rebecca's directions, and especially a warming and spicy-smelling balsam, had in some degree restored him to the use of his limbs. Moreover, he said, she had given him a pot of that precious ointment, and furnished him with a piece of money withal, to return to the house of his father, near to Templestowe. "And may it please your

---

LINE **26. withal**: in addition.

gracious reverence," said the man, " I cannot think the damsel meant harm by me, though she hath the ill hap to be a Jewess."

" Peace, slave," said the Grand Master, " and begone! It well suits brutes like thee to be tamper-ing with hellish cures. Hast thou that unguent of which thou speakest? "

The peasant, fumbling in his bosom with a trembling hand, produced a small box, bearing some Hebrew characters on the lid, which was, with most of the audience, a sure proof that the devil had stood apothecary. Beaumanoir, after crossing himself, took the box into his hand, and said, " Is there no leech here who can tell us the ingredients of this mystic unguent? "

Two mediciners, as they called themselves, the one a monk, the other a barber, appeared, and avouched they knew nothing of the materials, excepting that they savored of myrrh and camphire, which they took to be Oriental herbs. But with the true professional hatred to a successful practitioner of their art, they insinuated that, since the medicine was beyond their own knowledge, it must necessarily have been compounded from an unlawful and magical pharmacopœia. When this medical research was ended, the Saxon peasant desired humbly to have back the medicine; but the

---

LINE 25. **pharmacopœia** : book containing directions for preparing medicines.

Grand Master frowned severely at the request. "What is thy name, fellow?" said he to the cripple.

"Higg, the son of Snell," answered the peasant.

5 "Then, Higg, son of Snell," said the Grand Master, "I tell thee, it is better to be bedridden than to accept the benefit of unbelievers' medicine that thou mayest arise and walk. Go thou."

Higg, the son of Snell, withdrew into the crowd, 10 but, interested in the fate of his benefactress, lingered until he should learn her doom.

At this period of the trial, the Grand Master commanded Rebecca to unveil herself. Opening her lips for the first time, she replied patiently, 15 but with dignity, that it was not the wont of the daughters of her people to uncover their faces when alone in an assembly of strangers. The sweet tones of her voice, and the softness of her reply, impressed on the audience a sentiment of pity and 20 sympathy. But Beaumanoir repeated his commands that his victim should be unveiled. The guards were about to remove her veil accordingly, when she stood up before the Grand Master, and said, " Nay, but for the love of your own daughters 25 — alas," she said, recollecting herself, " ye have no daughters! — yet for the remembrance of your mothers, for the love of your sisters, let me not be thus handled in your presence. I will obey you," she added, with an expression of patient sorrow

in her voice, which had almost melted the heart of
Beaumanoir himself; "ye are elders among your
people, and at your command I will show the
features of an ill-fated maiden."

She withdrew her veil, and looked on them with
a countenance in which bashfulness contended with
dignity. Her exceeding beauty excited a murmur
of surprise, and the younger knights told each other
with their eyes, in silent correspondence, that
Brian's best apology was in the power of her real
charms, rather than of her imaginary witchcraft.
But Higg, the son of Snell, felt most deeply the
effect produced by the sight of the countenance of
his benefactress. "Let me go forth," he said to
the warders at the door of the hall — "let me go
forth! To look at her again will kill me, for I have
had a share in murdering her."

"Peace, poor man," said Rebecca, when she
heard his exclamation; "thou hast done me no
harm by speaking the truth; thou canst not aid
me by thy complaints or lamentations. Peace, I
pray thee; go home and save thyself."

Higg was about to be thrust out by the compassion of the warders, but he promised to be silent,
and was permitted to remain. The two men-at-
arms, with whom Albert Malvoisin had not failed
to communicate upon the import of their testimony, were now called forward. They set forth
that Rebecca was heard to mutter to herself in an

unknown tongue; that the songs she sung by fits were of a strangely sweet sound, which made the ears of the hearer tingle and his heart throb; that she spoke at times to herself, and seemed to look 5 upward for a reply; that her garments were of a strange and mystic form, unlike those of women of good repute; that she had rings impressed with cabalistical devices, and that strange characters were broidered on her veil. All these circum-10 stances, so natural and so trivial, were gravely listened to as proofs, or at least as affording strong suspicions, that Rebecca had unlawful correspondence with mystical powers.

One of the soldiers had seen her work a cure upon 15 a wounded man brought with them to the castle of Torquilstone. " She did," he said, " make certain signs upon the wound, and repeated certain mysterious words, when the iron head of a square crossbow bolt disengaged itself from the wound, the 20 bleeding was stanched, the wound was closed, and the dying man was, within the quarter of an hour, walking upon the ramparts, and assisting the witness in managing a mangonel, or machine for hurling stones." This legend was probably founded 25 upon the fact that Rebecca had attended on the wounded Ivanhoe when in the castle of Torquilstone. But it was the more difficult to dispute the

LINE **8. cabalistical**: mystic. **20. stanched**: stopped flow of.

accuracy of the witness, as he drew from his pouch the very bolt-head which, according to his story, had been miraculously extracted from the wound; and as the iron weighed a full ounce, it completely confirmed the tale, however marvellous. 5

His comrade had been a witness from a neighboring battlement of the scene betwixt Rebecca and Bois-Guilbert, when she was upon the point of precipitating herself from the top of the tower. Not to be behind his companion, this fellow stated 10 that he had seen Rebecca perch herself upon the parapet of the turret, and there take the form of a milk-white swan, under which appearance she flitted three times round the castle of Torquilstone; then again settle on the turret, and once more 15 assume the female form.

Less than one-half of this weighty evidence would have been sufficient to convict any old woman, poor and ugly, even though she had not been a Jewess. United with that fatal circum- 20 stance, the body of proof was too weighty for Rebecca's youth, though combined with the most exquisite beauty.

The Grand Master had collected the suffrages and now in a solemn tone demanded of Rebecca 25 what she had to say against the sentence of condemnation which he was about to pronounce.

"To invoke your pity," said the lovely Jewess, with a voice somewhat tremulous with emotion,

" would, I am aware, be as useless as I should hold
it mean. To state, that to relieve the sick and
wounded of another religion cannot be displeasing
to the acknowledged Founder of both our faiths,
were also unavailing; to plead, that many things
which these men — whom may Heaven pardon! —
have spoken against me are impossible, would avail
me but little, since you believe in their possibility;
and still less would it advantage me to explain that
the peculiarities of my dress, language, and manners are those of my people — I had well-nigh said
of my country, but, alas! we have no country.
Nor will I even vindicate myself at the expense of
my oppressor, who stands there listening to the
fictions and surmises which seem to convert the
tyrant into the victim. God be judge between
him and me! but rather would I submit to ten such
deaths as your pleasure may denounce against me
than listen to the suit which that man has urged
upon me — friendless, defenceless, and his prisoner.
But he is of your own faith, and his lightest affirm-
ance would weigh down the most solemn protesta-
tions of the distressed Jewess. I will not therefore
return to himself the charge brought against me;
but to himself — yes, Brian de Bois-Guilbert, to
thyself I appeal, whether these accusations are not
false? "

There was a pause; all eyes turned to Brian de
Bois-Guilbert. He was silent.

# Rebecca Tried for Sorcery

"Speak," she said, "if thou art a man; if thou art a Christian, speak! I conjure thee, by the name thou dost inherit — by the knighthood thou dost vaunt — by the honor of thy mother — by the tomb and the bones of thy father — I conjure 5 thee to say, are these things true?"

"Answer her, brother," said the Grand Master, "if the Enemy with whom thou dost wrestle will give thee power."

In fact, Bois-Guilbert seemed agitated by con- 10 tending passions, and it was with a constrained voice that at last he replied, looking to Rebecca: "The scroll! — the scroll!"

"Ay," said Beaumanoir, "this is indeed testimony! The victim of her witcheries can only 15 name the fatal scroll, the spell inscribed on which is, doubtless, the cause of his silence."

But Rebecca put another interpretation on the words, and glancing her eye upon the slip of parchment which she continued to hold in her hand, she 20 read written thereupon in the Arabian character, *Demand a Champion!* The murmuring commentary which ran through the assembly at the strange reply of Bois-Guilbert gave Rebecca leisure to examine and instantly to destroy the scroll unob- 25 served. When the whisper had ceased, the Grand Master spoke.

---

LINE **4. vaunt**: boast.   **16. scroll**: roll of paper or parchment.   **22. commentary**: comment.

" Rebecca, thou canst derive no benefit from the evidence of this unhappy knight, for whom, as we well perceive, the Enemy is yet too powerful. Hast thou ought else to say? "

5 " There is yet one chance of life left to me," said Rebecca, " even by your own fierce laws. Life has been miserable — miserable, at least, of late — but I will not cast away the gift of God while He affords me the means of defending it. I 10 deny this charge; I maintain my innocence, and I declare the falsehood of this accusation. I challenge the privilege of trial by combat, and will appear by my champion."

" And who, Rebecca," replied the Grand Master, 15 " will lay lance in rest for a sorceress? who will be the champion of a Jewess? "

" God will raise me up a champion," said Rebecca. " It cannot be that in merry England, the hospitable, the generous, the free, where so many 20 are ready to peril their lives for honor, there will not be found one to fight for justice. But it is enough that I challenge the trial by combat: there lies my gage."

She took her embroidered glove from her hand, 25 and flung it down before the Grand Master, with an air of mingled simplicity and dignity which excited universal surprise and admiration.

# CHAPTER XXXVIII

## Rebecca Seeks a Champion

Even Lucas Beaumanoir himself was affected by the mien and appearance of Rebecca. His features relaxed in their usual severity as he gazed upon the beautiful creature before him, alone, unfriended, and defending herself with so much spirit and courage. At length he spoke.

"Damsel," he said, "if the pity I feel for thee arise from any practice thine evil arts have made on me, great is thy guilt. But I rather judge it the kinder feelings of nature, which grieves that so goodly a form should be a vessel of perdition. Repent, my daughter, confess thy witchcrafts, turn thee from thine evil faith, embrace this holy emblem, and all shall yet be well with thee here and hereafter. This do and live: what has the law of Moses done for thee that thou shouldst die for it?"

"It was the law of my fathers," said Rebecca; "it was delivered in thunders and in storms upon the mountain of Sinai, in cloud and in fire."

"Let our chaplain," said Beaumanoir, "stand forth, and tell this obstinate infidel ——"

---

LINE **11. perdition:** eternal death.

"Forgive the interruption," said Rebecca
meekly; "I am a maiden, unskilled to dispute for
my religion; but I can die for it, if it be God's will.
Let me pray your answer to my demand of a
5 champion."

"Give me her glove," said Beaumanoir. "Seest
thou, Rebecca, as this thin and light glove of thine
is to one of our heavy steel gauntlets, so is thy cause
to that of the Temple, for it is our order which thou
10 hast defied."

"Cast my innocence into the scale," answered
Rebecca, "and the glove of silk shall outweigh the
glove of iron."

"Then thou dost persist in thy refusal to con-
15 fess thy guilt, and in that bold challenge which thou
hast made?"

"I do persist, noble sir," answered Rebecca.

"So be it then, in the name of Heaven," said the
Grand Master; "and may God show the right!"

20 "Amen," replied the preceptors around him,
and the word was deeply echoed by the whole
assembly.

"Brethren," said Beaumanoir, "you are aware
that we might well have refused to this woman the
25 benefit of the trial by combat; but, though a Jewess
and an unbeliever, she is also a stranger and defenceless, and God forbid that she should ask the
benefit of our mild laws and that it should be refused
to her. Moreover, we are knights and soldiers as

well as men of religion, and shame it were to us, upon any pretence, to refuse proffered combat. Thus, therefore, stands the case. Rebecca, the daughter of Isaac of York, is defamed of sorcery practiced on the person of a noble knight of our holy order, and hath challenged the combat in proof of her innocence. To whom, reverend brethren, is it your opinion that we should deliver the gage of battle, naming him, at the same time, to be our champion on the field?"

"To Brian de Bois-Guilbert, whom it chiefly concerns," said the preceptor of Goodalricke.

"Albert Malvoisin," said the Grand Master, "give this gage of battle to Brian de Bois-Guilbert. It is our charge to thee, brother," he continued, addressing himself to Bois-Guilbert, "that thou do thy battle manfully, nothing doubting that the good cause shall triumph. And do thou, Rebecca, attend, that we assign thee the third day from the present to find a champion."

"That is but brief space," answered Rebecca, "for a stranger, who is also of another faith, to find one who will do battle, wagering life and honor for her cause, against a knight who is called an approved soldier."

"We may not extend it," answered the Grand Master; "the field must be foughten in our presence, and divers weighty causes call us on the fourth day from hence."

"God's will be done!" said Rebecca; "I put my trust in Him, to whom an instant is as effectual to save as a whole age."

"Thou hast spoken well, damsel," said the Grand
5 Master. "It remains but to name a fitting place of combat, and, if it so hap, also of execution. Where is the preceptor of this house?"

Albert Malvoisin, still holding Rebecca's glove in his hand, was speaking to Bois-Guilbert very
10 earnestly, but in a low voice.

"How!" said the Grand Master, "will he not receive the gage?"

"He will — he doth, most reverend father," said Malvoisin, slipping the glove under his own
15 mantle. "And for the place of combat, I hold the fittest to be the lists of St. George belonging to this preceptory."

"It is well," said the Grand Master. "Rebecca, in those lists shalt thou produce thy champion;
20 and if thou failest to do so, or if thy champion shall be discomfited by the judgment of God, thou shalt then die the death of a sorceress, according to doom. Let this our judgment be recorded."

Rebecca modestly reminded the Grand Master
25 that she ought to be permitted some opportunity of free communication with her friends, for the purpose of making her condition known to them,

---

LINE **21. discomfited:** defeated.

and procuring, if possible, some champion to fight in her behalf.

"It is just and lawful," said the Grand Master; "choose what messenger thou shalt trust, and he shall have free communication with thee in thy prison-chamber."

"Is there," said Rebecca, "any one here who, either for love of a good cause or for ample hire, will do the errand of a distressed being?"

All were silent; for none thought it safe, in the presence of the Grand Master, to avow any interest in the prisoner. Not even the prospect of reward, far less any feelings of compassion alone, could surmount this apprehension.

Rebecca stood for a few moments in indescribable anxiety, and then exclaimed, "Is it really thus? And in English land am I to be deprived of the poor chance of safety which remains to me, for want of an act of charity which would not be refused to the worst criminal?"

Higg, the son of Snell, at length replied, "I am but a maimed man, but that I can at all stir or move was owing to her charitable assistance. I will do thine errand," he added, addressing Rebecca, "as well as a crippled object can, and happy were my limbs fleet enough to repair the mischief done by my tongue. Alas! when I boasted of thy charity, I little thought I was leading thee into danger!"

"God," said Rebecca, "is the disposer of all.

To execute his message the snail is as sure a messenger as the falcon. Seek out Isaac of York — here is that will pay for horse and man — let him have this scroll. I know not if it be of Heaven the spirit which inspires me, but most truly do I judge that I am not to die this death, and that a champion will be raised up for me. Farewell! Life and death are in thy haste."

The peasant took the scroll, which contained only a few lines in Hebrew. Many of the crowd would have dissuaded him from touching a document so suspicious; but Higg was resolute in the service of his benefactress. She had saved his body, he said, and he was confident she did not mean to peril his soul.

"I will get me," he said, "my neighbor Buthan's good capul, and I will be at York within as brief space as man and beast may."

But, as it fortuned, he had no occasion to go so far, for within a quarter of a mile from the gate of the preceptory he met with two riders, whom, by their dress and their huge yellow caps, he knew to be Jews; and, on approaching more nearly, discovered that one of them was his ancient employer Isaac of York. The other was the Rabbi Ben Samuel; and both had approached as near to the preceptory as they dared, on hearing that the

LINE **17. capul**: work-horse.   **25. Rabbi Ben Samuel**: called Nathan Ben Israel in Chapter XXXV.

Grand Master had summoned a chapter for the trial of a sorceress.

"Friend," said the physician, addressing Higg, the son of Snell, "I refuse thee not the aid of mine art, but I relieve not with one asper those who beg 5 for alms upon the highway. Out upon thee! Hast thou the palsy in thy legs? then let thy hands work for thy livelihood; for, albeit thou be'st unfit for a speedy post, or for the warfare, or for the service of a hasty master, yet there be occupations 10 —— How now, brother?" said he, interrupting his harangue to look towards Isaac, who had but glanced at the scroll which Higg offered, when, uttering a deep groan, he fell from his mule like a dying man, and lay for a minute insensible. 15

The Rabbi now dismounted in great alarm, and hastily applied the remedies which his art suggested for the recovery of his companion. The object of his anxious solicitude suddenly revived; but it was to dash his cap from his head, and to throw dust on 20 his grey hairs. The physician was at first inclined to ascribe this sudden and violent emotion to the effects of insanity, but Isaac soon convinced him of his error.

"Child of my sorrow," he said, "why should thy 25 death bring down my grey hairs to the grave, till, in the bitterness of my heart, I curse God and die!"

---

LINE **5. asper:** Turkish coin worth less than a cent.

"Brother," said the Rabbi, in great surprise, "art thou a father in Israel, and dost thou utter words like unto these? I trust that the child of thy house yet liveth?"

5 "She liveth," answered Isaac; "but it is as Daniel even when within the den of the lions. Child of my love! — child of my old age! — oh, Rebecca, daughter of Rachel! the darkness of the shadow of death hath encompassed thee."

10 "Yet read the scroll," said the Rabbi; "peradventure it may be that we may yet find out a way of deliverance."

"Do thou read, brother," answered Isaac, "for mine eyes are as a fountain of water."

15 The physician read the following words:

"To Isaac of York, peace and the blessing of the promise be multiplied unto thee! My father, I am as one doomed to die for that which my soul knoweth not, even for the crime of witchcraft. My 20 father, if a strong man can be found to do battle for my cause with sword and spear, and that within the lists of Templestowe, on the third day from this time, peradventure our fathers' God will give him strength to defend the innocent, and her who hath 25 none to help her. Wherefore look now what thou doest, and whether there be any rescue. One Nazarene warrior might indeed bear arms in my behalf, even Wilfred of Ivanhoe. But he may not yet endure the weight of his armor. Nevertheless, send the tidings unto him, my father; for he hath favor among the strong men of his people, and he may find some one to do battle for my sake. And say unto Wilfred, the son of Cedric, that if Rebecca live, or if Rebecca die, she liveth or dieth 5 wholly free of the guilt she is charged withal."

Isaac listened with tolerable composure while Ben Samuel read the letter, and then again resumed the gestures and exclamations of Oriental sorrow, tearing his garments, besprinkling his head with 10 dust, and ejaculating, "My daughter! my daughter! flesh of my flesh, and bone of my bone!"

"Yet," said the Rabbi, "take courage, for this grief availeth nothing. Gird up thy loins, and seek out this Wilfred, the son of Cedric. It may 15 be he will help thee with counsel or with strength; for the youth hath favor in the eyes of Richard Cœur-de-Lion, and the tidings that he hath returned are constant in the land. It may be that he may obtain his letter, and his signet, command- 20 ing these men of blood that they proceed not in their purposed wickedness."

"I will seek him out," said Isaac, "for he is a good youth. But he cannot bear his armor, and what other Christian shall do battle for the op- 25 pressed of Zion?"

"Nay, but," said the Rabbi, "thou speakest as

---

LINE 6. **withal**: with.

one that knoweth not the Gentiles. With gold shalt thou buy their valor, even as with gold thou buyest thine own safety. Be of good courage, and do thou set forward to find out this Wilfred of Ivanhoe. I will also up and be doing. I will hie me to the city of York, where many warriors are assembled, and doubt not I will find among them some one who will do battle for thy daughter; for gold is their god, and for riches will they pawn their lives as well as their lands. Thou wilt fulfil, my brother, such promise as I may make unto them in thy name?"

"Assuredly, brother," said Isaac, "and Heaven be praised that raised me up a comforter in my misery! Howbeit, grant them not their full demand at once, for thou shalt find it the quality of this accursed people that they will ask pounds, and peradventure accept of ounces. Nevertheless, be it as thou willest, for I am distracted in this thing, and what would my gold avail me if the child of my love should perish!"

"Farewell," said the physician, "and may it be to thee as thy heart desireth."

They embraced accordingly, and departed on their several roads. The crippled peasant remained for some time looking after them.

"These dog Jews!" said he; "to take no more notice of a free guild-brother than if I were a bond slave or a Turk! They might have flung me a

# Rebecca Seeks a Champion

mancus or two, however. I was not obliged to bring their unhallowed scrawls, and run the risk of being bewitched, as more folks than one told me. I think I was bewitched in earnest when I was beside that girl! But it was always so with Jews or Gentile, whosoever came near her: none could stay when she had an errand to go; and still, whenever I think of her, I would give shop and tools to save her life."

---

LINE 1. mancus: Saxon coin worth about sixty cents.

# CHAPTER XXXIX

## Templar Interviews Rebecca

It was in the twilight of the day when her trial had taken place, that a low knock was heard at the door of Rebecca's prison-chamber. It disturbed not the inmate, who was then engaged in the even-
5 ing prayer recommended by her religion, and which concluded with the hymn:

> When Israel, of the Lord beloved,
>     Out of the land of bondage came,
> Her fathers' God before her moved,
> 10     An awful guide, in smoke and flame.
> By day, along the astonish'd lands
>     The cloudy pillar glided slow;
> By night, Arabia's crimson'd sands
>     Return'd the fiery column's glow.
>
> 15     There rose the choral hymn of praise,
>     And trump and timbrel answer'd keen
> And Zion's daughters pour'd their lays,
>     With priest's and warrior's voice between.

---

LINE 12. **cloudy pillar.** A cloud by day and a pillar of fire by night guided the Hebrews from Egypt, where they had been in captivity. **16. trump**: trumpet. **timbrel**: kind of drum.

# Templar Interviews Rebecca

No portents now our foes amaze,
    Forsaken Israel wanders lone;
Our fathers would not know THY ways,
    And THOU hast left them to their own.

Our harps we left by Babel's streams,     5
    The tyrant's jest, the Gentile's scorn;
No censer round our altar beams,
    And mute our timbrel, trump, and horn.
But THOU hast said, The blood of goat,
    The flesh of rams, I will not prize;     10
A contrite heart, an humble thought,
    Are Mine accepted sacrifice.

When the sounds of Rebecca's devotional hymn had died away in silence, the low knock at the door was again renewed. "Enter," she said, "if thou art a friend; and if a foe, I have not the means of refusing thy entrance."

"I am," said Brian de Bois-Guilbert, entering the apartment, "friend or foe, Rebecca, as the event of this interview shall make me."

Alarmed at the sight of this man, Rebecca drew backward with a cautious and alarmed, yet not a timorous, demeanor into the farthest corner of the apartment, as if determined to retreat as far as she could, but to stand her ground when retreat became no longer possible.

"You have no reason to fear me, Rebecca," said the Templar; "or, if I must so qualify my speech, you have at least *now* no reason to fear me."

---

LINE 7. **censer**: vessel for burning incense.

"I fear you not, Sir Knight," replied Rebecca, although her short-drawn breath seemed to belie the heroism of her accents; "my trust is strong, and I fear thee not."

5 "You have no cause," answered Bois-Guilbert, gravely. "Within your call are guards over whom I have no authority. They are designed to conduct you to death, Rebecca, yet would not suffer you to be insulted by any one, even by me."

10 "May heaven be praised!" said the Jewess; "death is the least of my apprehensions in this den of evil."

"Ay," replied the Templar, "the idea of death is easily received by the courageous mind, when the 15 road to it is sudden and open. A thrust with a lance, a stroke with a sword, were to me little; to you, a spring from a dizzy battlement, a stroke with a sharp poniard, has no terrors, compared with what either thinks disgrace. Thou art condemned to 20 die not a sudden and easy death, but a slow, wretched, protracted course of torture."

"And to whom — if such my fate — to whom do I owe this?" said Rebecca; "surely only to him who dragged me hither, and who now strives to 25 exaggerate the wretched fate to which he exposed me."

"Think not," said the Templar, "that I have so exposed thee; I would have bucklered thee against such danger with my own bosom, as freely as ever

I exposed it to the shafts which had otherwise reached thy life."

"Had thy purpose been the honorable protection of the innocent," said Rebecca, "I had thanked thee for thy care. But what is thy purpose, Sir Knight? Speak it briefly. If thou hast aught to do save to witness the misery thou hast caused, let me know it; and then, if so it please you, leave me to myself. The step between time and eternity is short but terrible, and I have few moments to prepare for it."

"I perceive, Rebecca," said Bois-Guilbert, "that thou dost continue to burden me with the charge of distresses which most fain would I have prevented."

"Sir Knight," said Rebecca, "I would avoid reproaches; but what is more certain than that I owe my death to thine unbridled passion?"

"You err — you err," said the Templar, hastily, "if you impute what I could neither foresee nor prevent to my purpose or agency. Could I guess the unexpected arrival of yon dotard, whom some flashes of frantic valor, and the praises yielded by fools have raised for the present above the hundreds of our order who think and feel as men free from such silly prejudices as are the grounds of his opinions and actions?"

"Yet," said Rebecca, "you sate a judge upon me; innocent — most innocent — as you knew me to be, you concurred in my condemnation; and if

I aright understood, are yourself to appear in arms to assert my guilt, and assure my punishment."

"That scroll which warned thee to demand a champion," said Bois-Guilbert, "from whom couldst thou think it came, if not from Bois-Guilbert? In whom else couldst thou have excited such interest?"

"A brief respite from instant death," said Rebecca, "which will little avail me. Was this all thou couldst do for one on whose head thou hast heaped sorrow, and whom thou hast brought near even to the verge of the tomb?"

"No, maiden," said Bois-Guilbert, "this was *not* all that I purposed. Had it not been for the accursed interference of the fool of Goodalricke, the office of the champion defender had devolved, not on a preceptor, but on a companion of the order. Then I myself — such was my purpose — had, on the sounding of the trumpet, appeared in the lists as thy champion, disguised indeed in the fashion of a roving knight; and then, let Beaumanoir have chosen not one but two or three of the brethren here assembled, I had not doubted to cast them out of the saddle with my single lance. Thus, Rebecca, should thine innocence have been avouched, and to thine own gratitude would I have trusted for the reward of my victory."

---

Line **25.** avouched: proclaimed; vouched for.

"This, Sir Knight," said Rebecca, "is but idle boasting — a brag of what you would have done had you not found it convenient to do otherwise. You received my glove, and my champion, if a creature so desolate can find one, must encounter 5 your lance in the lists; yet you would assume the air of my friend and protector!"

"Thy friend and protector," said the Templar, gravely, "I will yet be; but mark at what risk, or rather at what certainty, of dishonor; and then 10 blame me not if I make my stipulations before I offer up all that I have hitherto held dear, to save the life of a Jewish maiden."

"Speak," said Rebecca; "I understand thee not." 15

"Rebecca," said Bois-Guilbert, "if I appear not in these lists I lose fame and rank, and the hopes I have of succeeding to that mighty authority which is now wielded by the bigoted dotard Beaumanoir. Such is my certain doom, except I appear in arms 20 against thy cause. Accursed be he of Goodalricke, who baited this trap for me! and doubly accursed Albert de Malvoisin, who withheld me from the resolution I had formed of hurling back the glove at the face of the superstitious and superannuated 25 fool who listened to a charge so absurd, and against a creature so high in mind and so lovely in form as thou art!"

---

LINE **25. superannuated**: disqualified by age.

"And what now avails rant or flattery?" answered Rebecca. "Thou hast made thy choice between causing to be shed the blood of an innocent woman, or of endangering thine own earthly state 5 and earthly hopes. What avails it to reckon together; thy choice is made."

"No, Rebecca," said the knight, in a softer tone, and drawing nearer towards her, "my choice is NOT made; nay, mark, it is thine to make the elec-10 tion. If I appear in the lists, I must maintain my name in arms; and if I do so, championed or un-championed, thou diest by the stake and faggot, for there lives not the knight who hath coped with me in arms on equal issue or on terms of vantage, 15 save Richard Cœur-de-Lion and his minion of Ivanhoe. Ivanhoe, as thou well knowest, is unable to bear his corslet, and Richard is in a foreign prison. If I appear, then thou diest."

"And what avails repeating this so often?" 20 said Rebecca.

"Much," replied the Templar; "for thou must learn to look at thy fate on every side."

"Well, then, turn the tapestry," said the Jewess, "and let me see the other side."

25 "If I appear," said Bois-Guilbert, "in the fatal lists, thou diest by a slow and cruel death. But if I appear not, then am I a degraded and dishonored

---

LINE 1. rant: loud, extravagant speech.

knight, accused of witchcraft: the illustrious name which has grown yet more so under my wearing becomes a hissing and a reproach. I lose fame — I lose honor — I lose the prospect of such greatness as scarce emperors attain to; I sacrifice mighty 5 ambition; and yet, Rebecca," he added, throwing himself at her feet, " this greatness will I sacrifice — this fame will I renounce — this power will I forego, even now when it is half within my grasp, if thou wilt say, ' Bois-Guilbert, I receive thee for my 10 lover.' "

" Think not of such foolishness, Sir Knight," answered Rebecca, " but hasten to the Regent, the Queen Mother, and to Prince John; they cannot, in honor to the English crown, allow of the pro- 15 ceedings of your Grand Master. So shall you give me protection without sacrifice on your part, or the pretext of requiring any requital from me."

" With these I deal not," he continued; " it is thee only I address. Bethink thee, were I a fiend, 20 yet death is a worse, and it is death who is my rival."

" I weigh not these evils," said Rebecca, afraid to provoke the wild knight. " Be a man, be a Christian! If indeed thy faith recommends that 25 mercy which rather your tongues than your actions pretend, save me from this dreadful death, without

---

LINE 8. **forego**: go without.

seeking a requital which would change thy magnanimity into base barter."

"No, damsel!" said the proud Templar, springing up, "thou shalt not thus impose on me: if I renounce present fame and future ambition, I renounce it for thy sake, and we will escape in company. Listen to me, Rebecca," he said, again softening his tone; "England — Europe — is not the world. There are spheres in which we may act, ample enough even for my ambition. We will go to Palestine, where Conrade Marquis of Montserrat is my friend. I will form new paths to greatness," he continued, traversing the room with hasty strides; "Europe shall hear the loud step of him she has driven from her sons! Thou shalt be a queen, Rebecca: on Mount Carmel shall we pitch the throne which my valor will gain for you."

"A dream," said Rebecca — "an empty vision of the night, which, were it a waking reality, affects me not. Put not a price on my deliverance, Sir Knight — sell not a deed of generosity — protect the oppressed for the sake of charity, and not for a selfish advantage. Go to the throne of England; Richard will listen to my appeal from these cruel men."

"Never, Rebecca!" said the Templar, fiercely. "If I renounce my order, for thee alone will I

---

LINE **2. barter**: exchange of goods.

renounce it. Ambition shall remain mine, if thou refuse my love. Stoop my crest to Richard? — ask a boon of that heart of pride? Never, Rebecca, will I place the order of the Temple at his feet in my person. I may forsake the order; I never will degrade or betray it."

"Now God be gracious to me," said Rebecca, "for the succor of man is well nigh hopeless!"

"It is indeed," said the Templar; "for, proud as thou art, thou hast in me found thy match. If I enter the lists with my spear in rest, think not any human consideration shall prevent my putting forth my strength; and think then upon thine own fate — to die the dreadful death of the worst of criminals — to be consumed upon a blazing pile — dispersed to the elements of which our strange forms are so mystically composed — not a relic left of that graceful frame, from which we could say this lived and moved! Rebecca, it is not in woman to sustain this prospect — thou wilt yield to my suit."

"Bois-Guilbert," answered the Jewess, "thou knowest not the heart of woman. I tell thee, proud Templar, that not in thy fiercest battles hast thou displayed more of thy vaunted courage than has been shown by woman when called upon to suffer by affection or duty. I am myself a woman, tenderly nurtured, naturally fearful of danger, and impatient of pain; yet, when we enter those fatal lists, thou to fight and I to suffer, I feel the strong

assurance within me that my courage shall mount higher than thine. Farewell. I waste no more words on thee; the time that remains on earth to the daughter of Jacob must be otherwise spent : she must
5 seek the Comforter, who ever opens His ear to the cry of those who seek Him in sincerity and in truth."

"We part then thus?" said the Templar, after a short pause; "would to Heaven that we never met, or that thou hadst been noble in birth and
10 Christian in faith! There is a spell on me, by Heaven! I almost think yon besotted skeleton spoke the truth, and that the reluctance with which I part from thee hath something in it more than is natural. Fair creature!" he said, approaching
15 nearer, but with great respect, "so young, so beautiful, so fearless of death! and yet doomed to die. Who would not weep for thee? The tear, that has been a stranger to these eyelids for twenty years, moistens them as I gaze on thee. But it
20 must be — nothing may now save thy life. Thou and I are but the blind instruments of some irresistible fatality, that hurries us along, like goodly vessels driving before the storm, which are dashed against each other, and so perish. Forgive me,
25 then, and let us part at least as friends part. I have assailed thy resolution in vain, and mine own is fixed as the adamantine decrees of fate."

---

LINE **27. adamantine** : impenetrably hard.

"Thus," said Rebecca, "do men throw on fate the issue of their own wild passions. But I do forgive thee, Bois-Guilbert, though the author of my early death. There are noble things which cross over thy powerful mind; but it is the garden of the 5 sluggard, and the weeds have rushed up, and conspired to choke the fair and wholesome blossom."

"Yes," said the Templar, "I am, Rebecca, as thou hast spoken me, untaught, untamed. I have been a child of battle from my youth upward, high 10 in my views, steady and inflexible in pursuing them. Such must I remain — proud, inflexible, and unchanging; and of this the world shall have proof. But thou forgivest me, Rebecca?"

"As freely as ever victim forgave her executioner." 15

"Farewell, then," said the Templar, and left the apartment.

The preceptor Albert waited impatiently in an adjacent chamber the return of Bois-Guilbert. 20

"Thou hast tarried long," he said; "I have been as if stretched on red-hot iron with very impatience. What if the Grand Master, or his spy Conrade, had come hither? But what ails thee, brother? Thy step totters, thy brow is as black as night. Art 25 thou well, Bois-Guilbert?"

"Ay," answered the Templar, "as well as the

---

LINE 11. inflexible: unbending.

wretch who is doomed to die within an hour. Nay, by the rood, not half so well; for there be those in such state who can lay down life like a cast-off garment. By Heaven, Malvoisin, yonder girl hath 5 wellnigh unmanned me. I am half resolved to go to the Grand Master, abjure the order to his very teeth, and refuse to act the brutality which his tyranny has imposed on me."

" Thou art mad," answered Malvoisin; " thou 10 mayst thus indeed utterly ruin thyself, but canst not even find a chance thereby to save the life of this Jewess, which seems so precious in thine eyes. Beaumanoir will name another of the order to defend his judgment in thy place, and the accused 15 will as assuredly perish as if thou hadst taken the duty imposed on thee."

" 'Tis false; I will myself take arms in her behalf," answered the Templar, haughtily; " and should I do so, I think, Malvoisin, that thou 20 knowest not one of the order who will keep his saddle before the point of my lance."

" Ay, but thou forgettest," said the wily adviser, " thou wilt have neither leisure nor opportunity to execute this mad project. Go to Lucas Beau- 25 manoir, and say thou hast renounced thy vow of obedience, and see how long the despotic old man will leave thee in personal freedom. The words

---

LINE **6. abjure**: renounce under oath.

shall scarce have left thy lips, ere thou wilt either be an hundred feet under ground, in the dungeon of the preceptory, to abide trial as a recreant knight; or, if his opinion holds concerning thy possession, thou wilt be enjoying straw, darkness, and change 5 in some distant convent cell, stunned with exorcisms, to expel the foul fiend which hath obtained dominion over thee. Thou must to the lists, Brian, or thou art a lost and dishonored man."

"I will break forth and fly," said Bois-Guilbert 10 —"fly to some distant land to which folly and fanaticism have not yet found their way. No drop of the blood of this most excellent creature shall be spilled by my sanction."

"Thou canst not fly," said the preceptor: "thy 15 ravings have excited suspicion, and thou wilt not be permitted to leave the preceptory. Go and make the essay: present thyself before the gate, and command the bridge to be lowered, and mark what answer thou shalt receive. Thou art sur- 20 prised and offended; but is it not better for thee? Wert thou to fly, what would ensue but the reversal of thy arms, the dishonor of thine ancestry, the degradation of thy rank? Think on it. Where shall thine old companions in arms hide their heads 25

---

LINE **3. recreant**: unfaithful to a pledge. **4. possession**: possession of an evil spirit, the effect of Rebecca's witchcraft. **6. exorcisms**: ceremonies for driving out an evil spirit. **18. essay**: attempt.

when Brian de Bois-Guilbert, the best lance of the Templars, is proclaimed recreant, amid the hisses of the assembled people? What grief will be at the Court of France! With what joy will the haughty Richard hear the news, that the knight that set him hard in Palestine, and wellnigh darkened his renown, has lost fame and honor for a Jewish girl, whom he could not even save by so costly a sacrifice!"

"Malvoisin," said the Knight, "I thank thee — thou hast touched the strings at which my heart most readily thrills! Come of it what may, recreant shall never be added to the name of Bois-Guilbert. Would to God, Richard, or any of his vaunting minions of England, would appear in these lists! But they will be empty — no one will risk to break a lance for the innocent, the forlorn."

"The better for thee, if it prove so," said the preceptor; "if no champion appears, it is not by thy means that this unlucky damsel shall die, but by the doom of the Grand Master, with whom rests all the blame, and who will count that blame for praise and commendation."

"True," said Bois-Guilbert; "if no champion appears, I am but a part of the pageant, sitting indeed on horseback in the lists, but having no part in what is to follow."

"None whatever," said Malvoisin — "no more than the armed image of St. George when it makes part of a procession."

" Well, I will resume my resolution," replied the haughty Templar. " She has despised me — repulsed me — reviled me ; and wherefore should I offer up for her whatever of estimation I have in the opinion of others? Malvoisin, I will appear 5 in the lists."

He left the apartment hastily as he uttered these words, and the preceptor followed, to watch and confirm him in his resolution ; for in Bois-Guilbert's fame he had himself a strong interest, expecting 10 much advantage from his being one day at the head of the order, not to mention the preferment of which Mont-Fitchet had given him hopes, on condition he would forward the condemnation of the unfortunate Rebecca. Yet it required all Malvoisin's art to 15 keep Bois-Guilbert steady to the purpose he had prevailed on him to adopt. He was obliged to watch him closely to prevent his resuming his purpose of flight, to intercept his communication with the Grand Master, and to renew, from time to time, 20 the various arguments by which he endeavored to show that, in appearing as champion on this occasion, Bois-Guilbert, without either accelerating or ensuring the fate of Rebecca, would follow the only course by which he could save himself from degrada- 25 tion and disgrace.

---

LINE **23. accelerating** : hastening.

# CHAPTER XL

## Fitzurse Waylays King

When the Black Knight left the trysting-tree of the generous outlaw, he held his way straight to a neighboring religious house, called the priory of St. Botolph, to which the wounded Ivanhoe had 5 been removed when the castle was taken, under the guidance of the faithful Gurth and the magnanimous Wamba. On the succeeding morning the Black Knight was about to set forth on his journey, accompanied by the jester Wamba, who attended as 10 his guide.

"We will meet," he said to Ivanhoe, "at Coningsburgh, the castle of the deceased Athelstane, since there thy father Cedric holds the funeral feast for his noble relation. I would see your Saxon kin-15 dred together, Sir Wilfred, and become better acquainted with them than heretofore. Thou also wilt meet me; and it shall be my task to reconcile thee to thy father."

So saying, he took an affectionate farewell of 20 Ivanhoe, who expressed an anxious desire to attend

---

LINE 4. St. Botolph. His name survives in Boston (Botolph's-town).

upon his deliverer. But the Black Knight would not listen to the proposal.

"Rest this day; thou wilt have scarce strength enough to travel on the next. I will have no guide with me but honest Wamba, who can play priest or fool as I shall be most in the humor."

"And I," said Wamba, "will attend you with all my heart. I would fain see the feasting at the funeral of Athelstane; for, if it be not full and frequent, he will rise from the dead to rebuke cook, sewer, and cupbearer; and that were a sight worth seeing."

"Sir Knight of the Fetterlock, since it is your pleasure so to be distinguished," said Ivanhoe, "I fear me you have chosen a talkative and a troublesome fool to be your guide. But he knows every path and alley in the woods as well as e'er a hunter who frequents them; and the poor knave, as thou hast partly seen, is as faithful as steel."

"Nay," said the Knight, "an he have the gift of showing my road, I shall not grumble with him that he desires to make it pleasant. Fare thee well, kind Wilfred; I charge thee not to attempt to travel till to-morrow at earliest."

So saying, he extended his hand to Ivanhoe, who pressed it to his lips, took leave of the prior, mounted his horse, and departed, with Wamba for his companion. Ivanhoe followed them with his eyes until they were lost in the shades of the surrounding forest, and then returned into the convent.

But shortly after matin-song he requested to see the prior. The old man came in haste, and inquired anxiously after the state of his health.

"It is better," he said, "than my fondest hope could have anticipated; either my wound has been slighter than the effusion of blood led me to suppose, or this balsam hath wrought a wonderful cure upon it. I feel already as if I could bear my corslet; and so much the better, for thoughts pass in my mind which render me unwilling to remain here longer in inactivity."

"Now, the saints forbid," said the prior, "that the son of the Saxon Cedric should leave our convent ere his wounds were healed!"

"Nor would I desire to leave your hospitable roof, venerable father," said Ivanhoe, "did I not feel myself able to endure the journey, and compelled to undertake it."

"And what can have urged you to so sudden a departure?" said the prior.

"Have you never, holy father," answered the knight, "felt an apprehension of approaching evil, for which you in vain attempted to assign a cause? Have you never found your mind darkened, like the sunny landscape, by the sudden cloud, which augurs a coming tempest?"

"I may not deny," said the prior, crossing him-

self, " that such things have been, and have been of
Heaven. But thou, wounded as thou art, what
avails it thou shouldst follow the steps of him whom
thou couldst not aid, were he to be assaulted?"

" Prior," said Ivanhoe, " thou dost mistake — 5
I am stout enough to exchange buffets with any who
will challenge me to such a traffic. But were it
otherwise, may I not aid him, were he in danger, by
other means than by force of arms? It is but too
well known that the Saxons love not the Norman 10
race, and who knows what may be the issue if he
break in upon them when their hearts are irritated
by the death of Athelstane, and their heads heated by
the carousal in which they will indulge themselves?
I hold his entrance among them at such a moment 15
most perilous, and I am resolved to share or avert
the danger; which, that I may the better do, I
would crave of thee the use of some palfrey whose
pace may be softer than that of my *destrier*."

" Surely," said the worthy churchman; " you 20
shall have mine own ambling jennet. This will I
say for Malkin, for so I call her, that unless you were
to borrow a ride on the juggler's steed that paces a
hornpipe amongst the eggs, you could not go a
journey on a creature so gentle and smooth- 25
paced."

" I pray you, reverend father," said Ivanhoe,

---

LINE **19**. *destrier:* war-horse.   **21**. **ambling**: moving at
easy gait by lifting at once both legs on one side.

" let Malkin be got ready instantly, and bid Gurth
attend me with mine arms."

" Nay, but, fair sir," said the prior, " I pray you
to remember that Malkin hath as little skill in arms
5 as her master, and that I warrant not her enduring
the sight or weight of your full panoply."

" Trust me, holy father," said Ivanhoe, " I will
not distress her with too much weight; and if she
calls a combat with me, it is odds but she has the
10 worst."

This reply was made while Gurth was buckling
on the knight's heels a pair of large gilded spurs,
capable of convincing any restive horse that best
safety lay in being conformable to the will of his
15 rider.

The deep and sharp rowels with which Ivanhoe's
heels were now armed began to make the worthy
prior repent of his courtesy and ejaculate: " Nay,
but, fair sir, now I bethink me, my Malkin abideth
20 not the spur. Better it were that you tarry for the
mare of our manciple down at the grange, which
may be had in little more than an hour, and cannot
but be tractable, in respect that she draweth much
of our winter firewood, and eateth no corn."

25 " I thank you, reverend father, but will abide by

---

LINE **6. panoply**: suit of armor. **13. restive**: unruly.
**16. rowels**: spiked wheels on spurs. **21. manciple**: officer
who buys food; steward. **grange**: farm with its buildings.
**23. tractable**: easily handled.

your first offer, as I see Malkin is already led forth to the gate. Gurth shall carry mine armor; and for the rest, rely on it that, as I will not overload Malkin's back, she shall not overcome my patience. And now, farewell!" 5

Ivanhoe now descended the stairs more hastily and easily than his wound promised, and threw himself upon the jennet, eager to escape the importunity of the prior, who stuck as closely to his side as his age and fatness would permit, now sing- 10 ing the praises of Malkin, now recommending caution to the knight in managing her.

Ivanhoe lent but a deaf ear to the prior's grave advices and jests, and having leapt on his mare, and commanded his squire Gurth to keep close by his 15 side, he followed the track of the Black Knight into the forest, while the prior stood at the gate of the convent looking after him, and ejaculating: "St. Mary! how prompt and fiery be these men of war! I would I had not trusted Malkin to his keeping, for, 20 crippled as I am with the cold rheum, I am undone if aught but good befalls her. And yet," said he, recollecting himself, "as I would not spare my own old and disabled limbs in the good cause of Old England, so Malkin must e'en run her hazard on the 25 same venture."

In the meantime, the Black Champion, and his

---

LINE **21. rheum**: watery discharge from nose and eyes.

guide were pacing at their leisure through the
recesses of the forest. You are to imagine this
Knight, strong of person, tall, broad-shouldered,
and large of bone, mounted on his mighty black
5 charger, which seemed made on purpose to bear his
weight, so easily he paced forward under it, having
the visor of his helmet raised, in order to admit
freedom of breath, yet keeping the beaver, or under
part, closed, so that his features could be but im-
10 perfectly distinguished. But his ruddy embrowned
cheek-bones could be plainly seen, and the large and
bright blue eyes, that flashed from under the dark
shade of the raised visor; and the whole gesture
and look of the champion expressed careless gaiety
15 and fearless confidence.

The Jester wore his usual fantastic habit, but late
accidents had led him to adopt a good cutting falchion, instead of his wooden sword, with a targe to
match it; of both which weapons he had shown
20 himself a skilful master during the storming of
Torquilstone. On horseback he was perpetually
swinging himself backwards and forwards, now on
the horse's ears, then anon on the very rump of the
animal; now hanging both his legs on one side,
25 and now sitting with his face to the tail, moping,
mowing, and making a thousand apish gestures,
until his palfrey took his freaks so much to heart as

---

LINE **17. falchion** : broad-bladed, slightly curved sword.
**26. mowing** : making faces.

fairly to lay him at his length on the green grass —
an incident which greatly amused the Knight, but
compelled his companion to ride more steadily
thereafter.

At the point of their journey at which we take 5
them up, this joyous pair were engaged in singing.
And thus ran the ditty:

> Anna Marie, love, up is the sun,
> Anna Marie, love, morn is begun,
> Mists are dispersing, love, birds singing free,     10
> Up in the morning, love, Anna Marie.
> Anna Marie, love, up in the morn,
> The hunter is winding blithe sounds on his horn,
> The echo rings merry from rock and from tree,
> 'Tis time to arouse thee, love, Anna Marie.     15

### WAMBA

> O Tybalt, love, Tybalt, awake me not yet,
> Around my soft pillow while softer dreams flit,
> For what are the joys that in waking we prove,
> Compared with these visions, O Tybalt, my love?     20
> Let the birds to the rise of the mist carol shrill,
> Let the hunter blow out his loud horn on the hill,
> Softer sounds, softer pleasures, in slumber I prove, —
> But think not I dreamt of thee, Tybalt, my love.

"A dainty song," said Wamba, when they had 25
finished their carol. "I used to sing it with Gurth,
and we once came by the cudgel for being so entranced by the melody that we lay in bed two hours
after sunrise, singing the ditty betwixt sleeping and
waking."     30

# Ivanhoe

The Jester next struck into a sort of comic ditty, to which the Knight, catching up the tune, replied in the like manner.

### KNIGHT AND WAMBA

5 There came three merry men from south, west, and north
    Ever more sing the roundelay;
To win the Widow of Wycombe forth,
    And where was the widow might say them nay?

The first was a knight, and from Tynedale he came,
10    Ever more sing the roundelay;
And his fathers, God save us, were men of great fame,
    And where was the widow might say him nay?

Of his father the laird, of his uncle the squire,
    He boasted in rhyme and in roundelay;
15 She bade him go bask by his sea-coal fire,
    For she was the widow would say him nay.

### WAMBA

The next that came forth, swore by blood and by nails,
    Merrily sing the roundelay;
20 Hur's a gentleman, God wot, and hur's lineage was of Wales,
    And where was the widow might say him nay?

Sir David ap Morgan ap Griffith ap Hugh
    Ap Tudor ap Rhice, quoth his roundelay;
She said that one widow for so many was too few,
25    And she bade the Welshman wend his way.

---

LINE **6**. **roundelay**: song with refrain. **13**. **laird**: landholder. **20**. **Hur's**: he is. **hur's**: his. **22**. **ap**: son of.

But then next came a yeoman, a yeoman of Kent,
    Jollily singing his roundelay;
He spoke to the widow of living and rent,
    And where was the widow could say him nay?

BOTH        5

So the knight and the squire were both left in the mire,
    There for to sing their roundelay;
For a yeoman of Kent, with his yearly rent,
    There never was a widow could say him nay.

" I would, Wamba," said the Knight, " that our 10
host of the trysting-tree, or the jolly Friar, his
chaplain, heard this thy ditty in praise of our bluff
yeoman."

" So would not I," said Wamba, " but for the
horn that hangs at your baldric."      15

" Ay," said the Knight, " this is a pledge of
Locksley's good will, though I am not like to need
it. Three mots on this bugle will, I am assured,
bring round, at our need, a jolly band of yonder
honest yeomen."      20

" I would say, Heaven forefend," said the Jester,
" were it not that that fair gift is a pledge they
would let us pass peaceably."

" Why, what meanest thou? " said the Knight:
" thinkest thou that but for this pledge of fellowship 25
they would assault us? "

---

LINE **18.** mots: notes upon bugle. **21.** forefend: ward
off.

" Nay, for me I say nothing," said Wamba;
" for green trees have ears as well as stone walls.
But canst thou construe me this, Sir Knight?
When is thy purse better empty than full?"

5 " Why, never, I think," replied the Knight.

" Thou never deservest to have a full one, for so
simple an answer! Thou hadst best leave thy
money at home ere thou walk in the greenwood."

" You hold our friends for robbers, then? " said
10 the Knight of the Fetterlock.

" Ay, truly," answered Wamba. " And yet,"
added he, coming close up to the Knight's side,
" there be companions who are far more dangerous
for travellers to meet than yonder outlaws."

15 " And who may they be, for you have neither
bears nor wolves, I trow? " said the Knight.

" Marry, sir, but we have Malvoisin's men-at-
arms," said Wamba; " and let me tell you that, in
time of civil war, a half-score of these is worth a
20 band of wolves at any time. They are now expecting their harvest, and are reinforced with the
soldiers that escaped from Torquilstone; so that,
should we meet with a band of them, we are like to
pay for our feats of arms. Now, I pray you, Sir
25 Knight, what would you do if we met two of
them? "

" Pin the villains to the earth with my lance,
Wamba, if they offered us any impediment."

" But what if there were four of them? "

" They should drink of the same cup," answered the Knight.

" What if six," continued Wamba, " and we as we now are, barely two; would you not remember Locksley's horn? " 5

" What! sound for aid," exclaimed the Knight, " against a score of such *rascaille* as these, whom one good knight could drive before him, as the wind drives the withered leaves? "

" Nay, then," said Wamba, " I will pray you for 10 a close sight of that same horn that hath so powerful a breath."

The Knight undid the clasp of the baldric, and indulged his fellow-traveller, who immediately hung the bugle round his own neck. 15

" Tra-lira-la," said he, whistling the notes; " nay, I know my gamut as well as another."

" How mean you, knave? " said the Knight; " restore me the bugle."

" Content you, Sir Knight, it is in safe keeping. 20 When Valor and Folly travel, Folly should bear the horn, because she can blow the best."

" Nay, but, rogue," said the Black Knight, " this exceedeth thy license. Beware ye tamper not with my patience." 25

" Urge me not with violence, Sir Knight," said the Jester, keeping at a distance from the impatient

---

LINE **7.** *rascaille:* rabble. **17. gamut:** musical scale.

champion, " or Folly will show a clean pair of heels, and leave Valor to find out his way through the wood as best he may."

" Nay, thou hast hit me there," said the Knight, 5 " and sooth to say, I have little time to jangle with thee. Keep the horn an thou wilt, but let us proceed on our journey."

" You will not harm me, then? " said Wamba.

" I tell thee no, thou knave ! "

10 " Ay, but pledge me your knightly word for it," continued Wamba, as he approached with great caution.

" My knightly word I pledge ; only come on with thy foolish self."

15 " Nay, then, Valor and Folly are once more boon companions," said the Jester, coming up frankly to the Knight's side ; " but, in truth, I love not such buffets as that you bestowed on the burly Friar, when his holiness rolled on the green like a 20 king of the nine-pins. And now that Folly wears the horn, let Valor rouse himself and shake his mane ; for, if I mistake not, there are company in yonder brake that are on the lookout for us."

" What makes thee judge so? " said the Knight.

25 " Because I have twice or thrice noticed the glance of a morrion from amongst the green leaves. Had they been honest men, they had kept the path."

---

LINE **26. morrion** : kind of helmet without visor.

"By my faith," said the Knight, closing his visor, "I think thou be'st in the right on't."

And in good time did he close it, for three arrows flew at the same instant from the suspected spot against his head and breast, one of which would 5 have penetrated to the brain, had it not been turned aside by the steel visor. The other two were averted by the gorget, and by the shield which hung around his neck.

"Thanks, trusty armorer," said the Knight. 10 "Wamba, let us close with them," and he rode straight to the thicket. He was met by six or seven men-at-arms, who ran against him with their lances at full career. Three of the weapons struck against him, and splintered with as little effect as if 15 they had been driven against a tower of steel. The Black Knight's eyes seemed to flash fire even through the aperture of his visor. He raised himself in his stirrups with an air of inexpressible dignity, and exclaimed, "What means this, my 20 masters!" The men made no other reply than by drawing their swords and attacking him on every side, crying, "Die, tyrant!"

"Ha! St. Edward! Ha! St. George!" said the Black Knight, striking down a man at every 25 invocation; "have we traitors here?"

His opponents, desperate as they were, bore back

---

LINE **8. gorget**: armor for throat and upper chest.
**26. invocation**: call for aid or protection.

from an arm which carried death in every blow, and it seemed as if the terror of his single strength was about to gain the battle against such odds, when a knight, in blue armor, who had hitherto kept 5 himself behind the other assailants, spurred forward with his lance, and taking aim, not at the rider but at the steed, wounded the noble animal mortally.

"That was a felon stroke!" exclaimed the 10 Black Knight, as the steed fell to the earth, bearing his rider along with him.

And at this moment Wamba winded the bugle, for the whole had passed so speedily that he had not time to do so sooner. The sudden sound made 15 the murderers bear back once more, and Wamba, though so imperfectly weaponed, did not hesitate to rush in and assist the Black Knight to rise.

"Shame on ye, false cowards!" exclaimed he in the blue harness, who seemed to lead the assail- 20 ants, "do ye fly from the empty blast of a horn blown by a jester?"

Animated by his words, they attacked the Black Knight anew, whose best refuge was now to place his back against an oak, and defend himself with his 25 sword. The felon knight, who had taken another spear, watching the moment when his formidable antagonist was most closely pressed, galloped against him in hopes to nail him with his lance against the tree, when his purpose was again inter-

cepted by Wamba. The Jester, making up by
agility the want of strength, and little noticed by
the men-at-arms, who were busied in their more
important object, hovered on the skirts of the fight,
and effectually checked the fatal career of the Blue 5
Knight, by hamstringing his horse with a stroke of
his sword. Horse and man went to the ground;
yet the situation of the Knight of the Fetterlock
continued very precarious, as he was pressed close
by several men completely armed, and began to 10
be fatigued, when a grey-goose shaft suddenly
stretched on the earth one of the most formidable
of his assailants, and a band of yeomen broke forth
from the glade, headed by Locksley and the jovial
Friar, who soon disposed of the ruffians, all of whom 15
lay on the spot dead or mortally wounded. The
Black Knight thanked his deliverers with a dignity
they had not observed in his former bearing, which
hitherto had seemed rather that of a blunt, bold
soldier than of a person of exalted rank. 20

"It concerns me much," he said, "even before
I express my full gratitude to my ready friends, to
discover, if I may, who have been my unprovoked
enemies. Open the visor of that Blue Knight,
Wamba, who seems the chief of these villains." 25

The Jester instantly made up to the leader of the
assassins, who, bruised by his fall, and entangled

---

LINE **6. hamstringing**: cutting great tendon at back of
knee.

under the wounded steed, lay incapable either of flight or resistance.

"Come, valiant sir," said Wamba, "I have dismounted you, and now I will unhelm you."

So saying, with no very gentle hand he undid the helmet of the Blue Knight, which, rolling to a distance on the grass, displayed to the Knight of the Fetterlock grizzled locks, and a countenance he did not expect to have seen under such circumstances.

"Waldemar Fitzurse!" he said in astonishment; "what could urge one of thy rank and seeming worth to so foul an undertaking?"

"Richard," said the captive knight, looking up to him, "thou knowest little of mankind, if thou knowest not to what ambition and revenge can lead every child of Adam."

"Revenge!" answered the Black Knight; "I never wronged thee. On me thou hast nought to revenge."

"My daughter, Richard, whose alliance thou didst scorn — was that no injury to a Norman, whose blood is noble as thine own?"

"Thy daughter!" replied the Black Knight. "A proper cause of enmity, and followed up to a bloody issue! Stand back, my masters, I would speak to him alone. And now, Waldemar Fitzurse, say me the truth: confess who set thee on this traitorous deed."

"Thy father's son," answered Waldemar, "who,

in so doing, did but avenge on thee thy disobedience to thy father."

Richard's eyes sparkled with indignation, but his better nature overcame it.

"Thou dost not ask thy life, Waldemar?" said the King.

"He that is in the lion's clutch," answered Fitzurse, "knows it were needless."

"Take it, then, unasked," said Richard; "the lion preys not on prostrate carcasses. Take thy life, but with this condition, that in three days thou shalt leave England, and go to hide thine infamy in thy Norman castle, and that thou wilt never mention the name of John of Anjou as connected with thy felony. If thou art found on English ground after the space I have allotted thee, thou diest; or if thou breathest aught that can attaint the honor of my house, by St. George! I will hang thee out to feed the ravens from the very pinnacle of thine own castle. Let this knight have a steed, Locksley, and let him depart unharmed."

"But that I judge I listen to a voice whose behests must not be disputed," answered the yeoman, "I would send a shaft after the skulking villain that should spare him the labor of a long journey."

"Thou bearest an English heart, Locksley,"

---

Line 17. attaint: stain.

said the Black Knight, " and well dost judge thou art the more bound to obey my behest : I am Richard of England ! "

At these words the yeomen at once kneeled down before him, and at the same time tendered their allegiance, and implored pardon for their offences.

" Rise, my friends," said Richard, in a gracious tone, looking on them with a countenance in which his habitual good-humor had already conquered the blaze of hasty resentment. " Your misdemeanors, whether in forest or field, have been atoned by the loyal services you rendered my distressed subjects before the walls of Torquilstone, and the rescue you have this day afforded to your sovereign. Arise, my liegemen, and be good subjects in future. And thou, brave Locksley —— "

" Call me no longer Locksley, my Liege, but know me under the name which, I fear, fame hath blown too widely not to have reached even your royal ears : I am Robin Hood of Sherwood Forest."

" King of outlaws, and Prince of good fellows ! " said the King, " who hath not heard a name that has been borne as far as Palestine ? But be assured, brave outlaw, that no deed done in our absence, and in the turbulent times to which it hath given rise, shall be remembered to thy disadvantage."

" True says the proverb," said Wamba,

> " ' When the cat is away,
> The mice will play.' "

"What, Wamba, art thou there?" said Richard; "I have been so long of hearing thy voice, I thought thou hadst taken flight."

"I take flight!" said Wamba; "when do you ever find Folly separated from Valor? There lies 5 the trophy of my sword, that good grey gelding, whom I heartily wish upon his legs again, conditioning his master lay there houghed in his place. It is true, I gave a little ground at first, for a motley jacket does not brook lance-heads as a steel doublet 10 will. But if I fought not at sword's point, you will grant me that I sounded the onset."

"And to good purpose, honest Wamba," replied the King. "Thy good service shall not be forgotten." 15

"I confess my deadly treason!" exclaimed, in a submissive tone, a voice near the King's side, "and pray leave to have absolution before I am led to execution!"

Richard looked around, and beheld the jovial 20 Friar on his knees. His countenance was gathered so as he thought might best express the most profound contrition, his eyes being turned up, and the corners of his mouth drawn down.

"For what art thou cast down, mad priest?" 25 said Richard.

"Most gracious sovereign," answered Friar

---

LINE **7. conditioning**: on condition that. **8. houghed**: hamstrung. **10. brook**: endure; withstand.

Tuck, "alas! that my sacrilegious fist should ever have been applied to the ear of the Lord's anointed!"

"Ha! ha!" said Richard, "sits the wind there?
5 In truth, I had forgotten the buffet, though mine ear sung after it for a whole day. But if the cuff was fairly given, I will be judged by the good men around, if it was not as well repaid; or, if thou thinkest I still owe thee aught, and will stand forth
10 for another counterbuff —— "

"By no means," replied Friar Tuck, "I had mine own returned, and with usury: may your Majesty ever pay your debts as fully!"

"If I could do so with cuffs," said the King,
15 "my creditors should have little reason to complain of an empty exchequer."

"And yet," said the Friar, resuming his demure, hypocritical countenance, "I know not what penance I ought to perform for that most sacrilegious
20 blow!"

"Speak no more of it, brother," said the King,
"after having stood so many cuffs from Paynims and misbelievers, I were void of reason to quarrel with the buffet of a clerk so holy as he of Copman-
25 hurst. Yet, mine honest Friar, I think it would be best both for the church and thyself that I should

---

LINE **16**. **exchequer**: treasury. **19**. **sacrilegious**: violating sacred things. **22**. **Paynims**: non-Christians, especially Mohammedans.

procure a license to unfrock thee, and retain thee
as a yeoman of our guard, serving in care of our
person."

"I pray you to leave me as you found me," said
the Friar; "or, if in aught you desire to extend 5
your benevolence to me, that I may be considered
as the poor clerk of St. Dunstan's cell in Copmanhurst, to whom any small donation will be most
thankfully acceptable."

"I understand thee," said the King, "and the 10
holy clerk shall have a grant of vert and venison in
my woods of Wharncliffe. Mark, however, I will
but assign thee three bucks every season; but if
that do not prove an apology for thy slaying thirty,
I am no Christian knight nor true king." 15

"Your Grace may be well assured," said the
Friar, "that I shall find the way of multiplying
your most bounteous gift."

"I nothing doubt it, good brother," said the
King. 20

The Friar, afraid perhaps of giving offence by continuing the conversation in too jocose a style — a
false step to be particularly guarded against by
those who converse with monarchs — bowed profoundly, and fell into the rear. 25

At the same time, two additional personages
appeared on the scene.

---

Line **11. vert and venison**: right to cut growing trees
and kill deer. **22. jocose**: joking.

# CHAPTER XLI

## From Outlaw Feast to Saxon Funeral

The new-comers were Wilfred of Ivanhoe, on the
prior of Botolph's palfrey, and Gurth, who attended
him, on the knight's own war-horse. The astonishment of Ivanhoe was beyond bounds when he
5 saw his master besprinkled with blood, and six or
seven dead bodies lying around in the little glade
in which the battle had taken place. Nor was he
less surprised to see Richard surrounded by so
many outlaws of the forest, a perilous retinue for a
10 prince. He hesitated whether to address the King
as the Black Knight-errant, or in what other manner
to demean himself towards him. Richard saw his
embarrassment.

" Fear not, Wilfred," he said, " to address Rich-
15 ard Plantagenet as himself, since thou seest him in
the company of true English hearts, although it
may be they have been urged a few steps aside by
warm English blood."

" Sir Wilfred of Ivanhoe," said the gallant out-
20 law, stepping forward, " my assurances can add
nothing to those of our sovereign; yet, let me say
somewhat proudly, that of men who have suffered

544

much, he hath no truer subjects than those who now stand around him."

"I cannot doubt it, brave man," said Wilfred, "since thou art of the number. But what mean these marks of death and danger — these slain men, and the bloody armor of my Prince?"

"Treason hath been with us, Ivanhoe," said the King, "but, thanks to these brave men, treason hath met its meed. But, now I bethink me, thou too art a traitor," said Richard, smiling — "a most disobedient traitor; for were not our orders positive that thou shouldst repose thyself at St. Botolph's until thy wound was healed?"

"It is healed," said Ivanhoe — "it is not of more consequence than the scratch of a bodkin. But why — oh why, noble Prince, will you thus vex the hearts of your faithful servants, and expose your life by lonely journeys and rash adventures, as if it were of no more value than that of a mere knight-errant, who has no interest but what lance and sword may procure him?"

"And Richard Plantagenet," said the King, "desires no more fame than his good lance and sword may acquire him; and Richard Plantagenet is prouder of achieving an adventure, with only his good sword and his good arm to speed, than if he led to battle an host of an hundred thousand armed men."

---

LINE **9. meed:** reward. **15. bodkin:** pointed instrument for piercing holes in cloth.

"But your kingdom, my Liege," said Ivanhoe — "your kingdom is threatened with dissolution and civil war; your subjects menaced with every species of evil, if deprived of their sovereign."

5 "Ho! ho! my kingdom and my subjects!" answered Richard, impatiently; "I tell thee, Sir Wilfred, the best of them are most willing to repay my follies in kind. For example, my very faithful servant, Wilfred of Ivanhoe, will not obey my posi-10tive commands, and yet reads his king a homily, because he does not walk exactly by his advice. Which of us has most reason to upbraid the other? Yet forgive me, my faithful Wilfred. The time I have spent, and am yet to spend, in concealment is, 15as I explained to thee at St. Botolph's, necessary to give my friends and faithful nobles time to assemble their forces, that, when Richard's return is announced, he should be at the head of such a force as enemies shall tremble to face, and thus 20subdue the meditated treason, without even unsheathing a sword. Too sudden an appearance would subject me to dangers other than my lance and sword, though backed by the bow of bold Robin, or the quarter-staff of Friar Tuck, and the 25horn of the sage Wamba, may be able to rescue me from."

Wilfred bowed in submission, well knowing how

LINE 10. **homily**: sermon.

vain it was to contend with the wild spirit of chivalry which so often impelled his master upon dangers which he might easily have avoided. The young knight sighed, therefore, and held his peace; while Richard went on in conversation with Robin Hood. "King of outlaws," he said, "have you no refreshment to offer to your brother sovereign?"

"In troth," replied the outlaw, "for I scorn to lie to your Grace, our larder is chiefly supplied with — " He stopped, and was somewhat embarrassed.

"With venison, I suppose?" said Richard, gaily; "better food at need there can be none; and truly, if a king will not remain at home and slay his own game, methinks he should not brawl too loud if he finds it killed to his hand."

"If your Grace, then," said Robin, "will again honor with your presence one of Robin Hood's places of rendezvous, the venison shall not be lacking; and a stoup of ale, and it may be a cup of reasonably good wine, to relish it withal."

The outlaw accordingly led the way, followed by the buxom monarch, more happy, probably, in this chance meeting with Robin Hood and his foresters than he would have been in again assuming his royal state, and presiding over a splendid circle of peers and nobles. Novelty in society and adventure were the zest of life to Richard Cœur-de-Lion. In the lion-hearted king, the brilliant, but

useless, character of a knight of romance was in
great measure realized and revived. His feats of
chivalry furnished themes for bards and minstrels,
but afforded none of those solid benefits to his
5 country on which history loves to pause, and hold
up as an example to posterity. But in his present
company Richard showed to the greatest imaginable advantage. He was gay, good-humored, and
fond of manhood in every rank of life.

10 Beneath a huge oak-tree the silvan repast was
hastily prepared for the King of England, surrounded by men outlaws to his government, but
who now formed his court and his guard. As the
flagon went round, the rough foresters soon lost
15 their awe for the presence of Majesty. The song
and the jest were exchanged, the stories of former
deeds were told with advantage; and at length,
and while boasting of their successful infraction of
the laws, no one recollected they were speaking in
20 presence of their natural guardian. The merry
King, nothing heeding his dignity any more than
his company, laughed, quaffed, and jested among
the jolly band. The natural and rough sense of
Robin Hood led him to be desirous that the scene
25 should be closed ere anything should occur to disturb its harmony, the more especially that he
observed Ivanhoe's brow clouded with anxiety.
"We are honored," he said to Ivanhoe, apart,
"by the presence of our gallant sovereign; yet

I would not that he dallied with time which the circumstances of his kingdom may render precious."

"It is well and wisely spoken, brave Robin Hood," said Wilfred, apart; "and know, moreover, that they who jest with Majesty, even in its gayest mood, are but toying with the lion's whelp, which, on slight provocation, uses both fangs and claws."

"You have touched the very cause of my fear," said the outlaw. "My men are rough by practice and nature; the King is hasty as well as goodhumored; nor know I how soon cause of offence may arise, or how warmly it may be received; it is time this revel were broken off."

"It must be by your management, then, gallant yeoman," said Ivanhoe; "for each hint I have assayed to give him serves only to induce him to prolong it."

"Must I so soon risk the pardon and favor of my sovereign?" said Robin Hood, pausing for an instant; "but, by St. Christopher, it shall be so. I were undeserving his grace did I not peril it for his good. Here, Scathlock, get thee behind yonder thicket, and wind me a Norman blast on thy bugle, and without an instant's delay, on peril of your life."

---

LINE **1. dallied**: trifled.  **7. whelp**: cub.  **18. assayed**: attempted.

Scathlock obeyed his captain, and in less than five minutes the revellers were startled by the sound of his horn.

"It is the bugle of Malvoisin," said the Miller, starting to his feet, and seizing his bow. The Friar dropped the flagon, and grasped his quarter-staff. Wamba stopt short in the midst of a jest, and betook himself to sword and target. All the others stood to their weapons. Richard called for his helmet and the most cumbrous parts of his armor, which he had laid aside; and while Gurth was putting them on, he laid his strict injunctions on Wilfred, under pain of his highest displeasure, not to engage in the skirmish which he supposed was approaching.

"Thou hast fought for me an hundred times, Wilfred, and I have seen it. Thou shalt this day look on, and see how Richard will fight for his friend and liegeman."

In the meantime, Robin Hood had sent off several of his followers in different directions, as if to reconnoitre the enemy; and when he saw the company effectually broken up, he approached Richard, who was now completely armed, and, kneeling down on one knee, craved pardon of his sovereign.

"For what, good yeoman?" said Richard, somewhat impatiently. "Have we not already granted thee a full pardon for all transgressions?

Thou canst not have time to commit any new offence since that time?"

"Ay, but I have though," answered the yeoman, "if it be an offence to deceive my prince for his own advantage. The bugle you have heard was none of Malvoisin's, but blown by my direction, to break off the banquet."

He then rose from his knee, folded his arms on his bosom, and, in a manner rather respectful than submissive, awaited the answer of the King. The blood rushed in anger to the countenance of Richard; but it was the first transient emotion, and his sense of justice instantly subdued it.

"The King of Sherwood," he said, "grudges his venison and his wine-flask to the King of England! It is well, bold Robin! but when you come to see me in merry London, I trust to be a less niggard host. Thou art right, however, good fellow. Let us therefore to horse and away. Wilfred has been impatient this hour. Tell me, bold Robin, hast thou never a friend in thy band, who, not content with advising, will needs direct thy motions and look miserable when thou dost presume to act for thyself?"

"Such a one," said Robin, "is my lieutenant, Little John, and I will own to your Majesty that I am sometimes displeased by the freedom of his

LINE **26. Little John.** See page 617.

counsels; but, when I think twice, I cannot be
long angry with one who can have no motive for
his anxiety save zeal for his master's service."

"Thou art right, good yeoman," answered
Richard; "and if I had Ivanhoe, on the one hand,
to give grave advice, and recommend it by the sad
gravity of his brow, and thee, on the other, to trick
me into what thou thinkest my own good, I should
have as little the freedom of mine own will as any
king in Christendom. But come, sirs, let us merrily
on to Coningsburgh, and think no more on't."

Robin Hood assured them that he had detached
a party in the direction of the road they were to
pass, and that he had little doubt they would find
the ways secure, or, if otherwise, would receive such
timely notice of the danger as would enable them to
fall back on a strong troop of archers, with which
he himself proposed to follow on the same route.

The wise and attentive precautions adopted for
his safety touched Richard's feelings, and removed
any slight grudge which he might retain on account
of the deception the outlaw captain had practiced
upon him. He once more extended his hand to
Robin Hood, assured him of his full pardon and
future favor, as well as his firm resolution to re-
strain the tyrannical exercise of the forest rights
and other oppressive laws, by which so many English yeomen were driven into a state of rebellion.

The outlaw's opinion proved true; and the King,

attended by Ivanhoe, Gurth, and Wamba, arrived without any interruption within view of the Castle of Coningsburgh, while the sun was yet in the 5 horizon.

There are few more beautiful or striking scenes in England than are presented by the vicinity of this ancient Saxon fortress. The soft and 10 gentle river Don sweeps through an amphitheatre, in which cultivation is richly blended with woodland, and on a mount ascending from the river, well

553

defended by walls and ditches, rises this ancient edifice, which was, previous to the Conquest, a royal residence of the kings of England. The keep is situated on a mount at one angle of the
5 inner court, and forms a complete circle of perhaps twenty-five feet in diameter. The wall is of immense thickness, and is propped or defended by six huge external buttresses, which project from the circle, and rise up against the sides of the tower as
10 if to strengthen or to support it. These massive buttresses are solid when they arise from the foundation, and a good way higher up; but are hollowed out towards the top, and terminate in a sort of turrets communicating with the interior of
15 the keep itself.

A huge black banner, which floated from the top of the tower, announced that the obsequies of the late owner were still in the act of being solemnized. Above the gate was another banner, on which the
20 figure of a white horse, rudely painted, indicated the nation and rank of the deceased by the well-known symbol of Hengist and his Saxon warriors.

All around the castle was a scene of busy commo-
25 tion; for such funeral banquets were times of general and profuse hospitality, which not only

---

LINE **4. keep**: tower or stronghold of a castle. **8. buttresses**: supports built against a wall. **17. obsequies**: funeral rites. **20. white horse**: emblem of ancient Saxons.

every one who could claim the most distant con-
nexion with the deceased, but all passengers whatsoever, were invited to partake. The wealth and
consequence of the deceased Athelstane occasioned
this custom to be observed in the fullest extent.          5

Numerous parties, therefore, were seen ascending
and descending the hill on which the castle was
situated; and when the King and his attendants
entered the open and unguarded gates of the external barrier, the space within presented a scene 10
not easily reconciled with the cause of the assem-
blage. In one place cooks were toiling to roast huge
oxen and fat sheep; in another, hogsheads of ale
were set abroach, to be drained at the freedom of
all comers. Groups of every description were to 15
be seen devouring the food and swallowing the
liquor thus abandoned to their discretion. Nor
did the assistants scorn to avail themselves of those
means of consolation, although, every now and
then, as if suddenly recollecting the cause which 20
had brought them together, the men groaned in
unison, while the females, of whom many were
present, raised up their voices and shrieked for very
woe.

Mendicants were, of course, assembled by the 25
score, together with strolling soldiers returned from
Palestine; pedlars were displaying their wares;
travelling mechanics were inquiring after employ-

---

LINE **14. abroach**: on tap.

ment; and wandering palmers, hedge-priests, Saxon minstrels, and Welsh bards were muttering prayers, and extracted mistuned dirges from their harps, crowds, and rotes. Jesters and jugglers 5 were not awanting, nor was the occasion of the assembly supposed to render the exercise of their profession improper.

Such was the scene in the castle-yard at Coningsburgh when it was entered by Richard and his fol- 10 lowers. The seneschal or steward deigned not to take notice of the groups of inferior guests who were perpetually entering and withdrawing; nevertheless, he was struck by the good mien of the Monarch and Ivanhoe, more especially as he imagined 15 the features of the latter were familiar to him. Besides, the approach of two knights was a rare event at a Saxon solemnity, and could not but be regarded as a sort of honor to the deceased and his family. And in his sable dress, and holding in 20 his hand his white wand of office, this important personage conducted Richard and Ivanhoe to the entrance of the tower. Gurth and Wamba speedily found acquaintances in the courtyard, nor presumed to intrude themselves any farther until 25 their presence should be required.

---

LINE **1. hedge-priests**: poor, ignorant priests. **4. crowds**: kind of violin. **rotes**: sort of hurdy-gurdy.

# CHAPTER XLII

## Funeral Rites Stopped

The mode of entering the great tower of Coningsburgh Castle is very peculiar, and partakes of the
rude simplicity of the early times in which it was
erected. A flight of steps, deep and narrow, leads
up to a low portal in the south side of the tower, by 5
which one may gain access to a small stair within
the thickness of the main wall of the tower, which
leads up to the third story of the building — the
two lower being dungeons or vaults, which neither
receive air nor light, save by a square hole in the 10
third story, with which they seem to have communicated by a ladder.

By this difficult and complicated entrance, the
good King Richard, followed by his faithful Ivanhoe, was ushered into the round apartment which 15
occupies the whole of the third story from the
ground. Wilfred, by the difficulties of the ascent,
gained time to muffle his face in his mantle, as it
had been held expedient that he should not present
himself to his father until the King should give 20
him the signal.

---

LINE 19. **expedient**: advisable.

There were assembled in this apartment, around
a large oaken table, about a dozen of the most
distinguished representatives of the Saxon families
in the adjacent counties.  These were all old, or at
least elderly, men.  The downcast and sorrowful
looks of these venerable men, their silence and their
mournful posture, formed a strong contrast to the
levity of the revellers on the outside of the castle.
Their grey locks and long full beards, together with
their antique tunics and loose black mantles, suited
well with the singular and rude apartment in which
they were seated.

Cedric, seated in equal rank among his countrymen, seemed yet, by common consent, to act as
chief of the assembly.  Upon the entrance of
Richard (only known to him as the valorous Knight
of the Fetterlock) he arose gravely, and gave him
welcome by the ordinary salutation, *Waes hael*,
raising at the same time a goblet to his head.  The
King, no stranger to the customs of his English
subjects, returned the greeting with the appropriate words, *Drinc hael*, and partook of a cup
which was handed to him.  The same courtesy
was offered to Ivanhoe, who pledged his father in
silence.

When this introductory ceremony was performed,
Cedric arose, and, extending his hand to Richard,
conducted him into a small and very rude chapel,
excavated out of one of the external buttresses.

# Funeral Rites Stopped

As there was no opening, saving a very narrow loophole, the place would have been nearly quite dark but for two flambeaux or torches, which showed, by a red and smoky light, the arched roof and naked walls, the rude altar of stone, and the 5 crucifix of the same material.

Richard and Wilfred followed the Saxon Cedric into this apartment of death, where, as their guide pointed with solemn air to the untimely bier of Athelstane, they followed his example in devoutly 10 crossing themselves, and muttering a brief prayer for the weal of the departed soul.

This act of pious charity performed, Cedric again motioned them to follow him, gliding over the stone floor with a noiseless tread; and, after ascend- 15 ing a few steps, opened with great caution the door of a small oratory, which adjoined to the chapel. A beam of the setting sun found its way into its dark recess, and showed a female of a dignified mien, whose long mourning robes, and flowing 20 wimple of black cypress enhanced the whiteness of her skin, and the beauty of her light-colored and flowing tresses.

" Noble Edith," said Cedric, after having stood a moment silent, as if to give Richard and Wilfred 25 time to look upon the lady of the mansion, " these are worthy strangers come to take a part in thy

---

LINE **17. oratory** : room for prayer.   **21. wimple** : covering for neck, chin, and sides of face.   **cypress** : crape-like fabric.

sorrows. And this, in especial, is the valiant knight who fought so bravely for the deliverance of him for whom we this day mourn."

"His bravery has my thanks," returned the
5 lady; "although it be the will of Heaven that it should be displayed in vain. I thank, too, his courtesy, and that of his companion, which hath brought them hither to behold the mother of Athelstane, in her deep hour of sorrow and lamentation.
10 To your care, kind kinsman, I entrust them, satisfied that they will want no hospitality which these sad walls can yet afford."

The guests bowed deeply to the mourning parent, and withdrew with their hospitable guide.

15 Another winding stair conducted them to an apartment of the same size with that which they had first entered, occupying indeed the story immediately above. From this room, ere yet the door was opened, proceeded a low and melancholy strain
20 of vocal music. When they entered, they found themselves in the presence of about twenty matrons and maidens of distinguished Saxon lineage. Four maidens, Rowena leading the choir, raised a hymn for the soul of the deceased. The others were
25 divided into two bands, of which one was engaged in bedecking, with such embroidery as their skill and taste could compass, a large silken pall, des-

---

LINE 27. **pall**: cloth, generally black or purple, over coffin, hearse, or tomb.

tined to cover the bier of Athelstane, while the others busied themselves in selecting, from baskets of flowers placed before them, garlands, which they intended for the same mournful purpose. The behavior of the maidens was decorous, if not marked with deep affliction; but now and then a whisper or a smile called forth the rebuke of the severer matrons.

Rowena paid her greeting to her deliverer with a graceful courtesy. Her demeanor was serious, but not dejected; and it may be doubted whether thoughts of Ivanhoe, and the uncertainty of his fate, did not claim as great a share in her gravity as the death of her kinsman.

To Cedric, who was not remarkably clear-sighted on such occasions, the sorrow of his ward seemed so much deeper than any of the other maidens that he deemed it proper to whisper the explanation, " She was the affianced bride of the noble Athelstane." It may be doubted whether this communication went a far way to increase Wilfred's disposition to sympathize with the mourners of Coningsburgh.

Having thus formally introduced the guests to the different chambers in which the obsequies of Athelstane were celebrated, Cedric conducted them into a small room for the exclusive accommodation of honorable guests slightly connected with the deceased. He assured them of every accommodation, and was about to withdraw when the Black Knight took his hand.

"I crave to remind you, noble thane," he said; "that when we last parted you promised, for the service I had the fortune to render you, to grant me a boon."

"It is granted ere named, noble Knight," said Cedric; "yet, at this sad moment —— "

"Of that also," said the King, "I have bethought me; but my time is brief; neither does it seem to me unfit that, when closing the grave on the noble Athelstane, we should deposit therein certain prejudices and hasty opinions."

"Sir Knight of the Fetterlock," said Cedric, coloring, and interrupting the King in his turn, "I trust your boon regards yourself and no other; for in that which concerns the honor of my house, it is scarce fitting that a stranger should mingle."

"Nor do I wish to mingle," said the King, mildly, "unless in so far as you will admit me to have an interest. As yet you have known me but as the Black Knight of the Fetterlock. Know me now as Richard Plantagenet."

"Richard of Anjou!" exclaimed Cedric, stepping backward with the utmost astonishment.

"No, noble Cedric — Richard of England! whose deepest interest — whose deepest wish, is to see her sons united with each other. And, how now, worthy thane! hast thou no knee for thy prince?"

" To Norman blood," said Cedric, " it hath never bended."

" Reserve thine homage then," said the Monarch, " until I shall prove my right to it by my equal protection of Normans and English." 5

" Prince," answered Cedric, " I have ever done justice to thy bravery and thy worth."

" And now to my boon," said the King. " I require of thee, as a man of thy word, to forgive and receive to thy paternal affection the good knight, 10 Wilfred of Ivanhoe. In this reconciliation thou wilt own I have an interest — the happiness of my friend, and the quelling of dissension among my faithful people."

" And this is Wilfred ! " said Cedric, pointing 15 to his son.

" My father ! — my father ! " said Ivanhoe, prostrating himself at Cedric's feet, " grant me thy forgiveness ! "

" Thou hast it, my son," said Cedric, raising 20 him up. " The son of Hereward knows how to keep his word, even when it has been passed to a Norman. But let me see thee use the dress and costume of thy English ancestry : no short cloaks, no gay bonnets, no fantastic plumage in my decent 25 household. He that would be the son of Cedric must show himself of English ancestry. Thou art about to speak," he added, sternly, " and I guess the topic. The Lady Rowena must complete two years' mourning, as for a betrothed husband: all our Saxon ancestors would disown us were we to treat of a new union for her ere the grave of him she should have wedded is yet closed. The ghost of Athelstane himself would stand before us to forbid such dishonor to his memory."

It seemed as if Cedric's words had raised a spectre; for scarce had he uttered them ere the door flew open, and Athelstane, arrayed in the garments of the grave, stood before them, pale, haggard, and like something arisen from the dead!

The effect of this apparition on the persons present was utterly appalling. Cedric started back as far as the wall of the apartment would permit, and, leaning against it, gazed on the figure of his friend with eyes that seemed fixed, and a mouth which he appeared incapable of shutting. Ivanhoe crossed himself, repeating prayers in Saxon, Latin, or Norman-French, as they occurred to his memory.

In the meantime a horrible noise was heard below stairs, some crying, "Secure the treacherous monks!" — others, "Down with them into the dungeon!" — others, "Pitch them from the highest battlements!"

"In the name of God!" said Cedric, addressing what seemed the spectre of his departed friend, "if thou art mortal, speak! — if a departed spirit, say for what cause thou dost revisit us, or if I can do aught that can set thy spirit at repose. Living or dead, noble Athelstane, speak to Cedric!"

"I will," said the spectre, very composedly, "when I have collected breath, and when you give me time. Alive, saidst thou? I am as much alive as he can be who has fed on bread and water for three days, which seem three ages. Yes, bread and water, father Cedric!"

"Why, noble Athelstane," said the Black Knight, "I myself saw you struck down by the fierce Templar towards the end of the storm at Torquilstone, and, as I thought, and Wamba reported, your skull was cloven through the teeth."

"You thought amiss, Sir Knight," said Athelstane, "and Wamba lied. My teeth are in good order, and that my supper shall presently find. No thanks to the Templar though, whose sword turned in his hand, so that the blade struck me flatlings, being averted by the handle of the good mace with which I warded the blow. But as it was, down I went, stunned, indeed, but unwounded. Others, of both sides, were beaten down and slaughtered above me, so that I never recovered my senses until I found myself in a coffin — an open one, by good luck! — placed before the altar of the church of St. Edmund's. I sneezed repeatedly — groaned — awakened, and would have

---

LINE **19.** **flatlings:** with flat side.

arisen, when the sacristan and abbot, full of terror, came running at the noise, surprised, doubtless, and no way pleased, to find the man alive whose heirs they had proposed themselves to be. I asked
5 for wine; they gave me some, but it must have been highly medicated, for I slept yet more deeply than before, and wakened not for many hours. I found my arms swathed down, my feet tied so fast that mine ankles ache at the very remembrance;
10 the place was utterly dark. I had strange thoughts of what had befallen me, when the door of my dungeon creaked, and two villain monks entered."

"Have patience, noble Athelstane," said the King, "take breath — tell your story at leisure."
15 "A barley loaf and a pitcher of water — that *they* gave me," said Athelstane, "the niggardly traitors, whom my father, and I myself, had enriched. The nest of foul, ungrateful vipers — barley bread and ditch water to such a patron as I
20 had been! I will smoke them out of their nest, though I be excommunicated!"

"But, noble Athelstane," said Cedric, grasping the hand of his friend, "how didst thou escape this imminent danger? did their hearts relent?"
25 "Did their hearts relent!" echoed Athelstane. "Do rocks melt with the sun? I should have been there still, had not some stir in the convent, which

---

LINE **1. sacristan**: sexton.

I find was their procession hitherward to eat my funeral feast, summoned the swarm out of their hive. At length down came the gouty sacristan, with an unstable step and a strong flavor of wine about his person. Good cheer had opened his heart, for he left me a nook of pasty and a flask of wine instead of my former fare. I ate, drank, and was invigorated; when, to add to my good luck, the sacristan locked the door beside the staple, so that it fell ajar. The light, the food, the wine set my invention to work. The staple to which my chains were fixed was more rusted than I or the villain abbot had supposed. Even iron could not remain without consuming in the damps of that infernal dungeon."

" Take breath, noble Athelstane," said Richard, " and partake of some refreshment, ere you proceed with a tale so dreadful."

" Partake!" quoth Athelstane. " I have been partaking five times to-day; and yet a morsel of that savory ham were not altogether foreign to the matter: and I pray you, fair sir, to do me reason in a cup of wine."

The guests, though still agape with astonishment, pledged their resuscitated landlord, who thus proceeded in his story. He had indeed now many more auditors than those to whom it was commenced.

---

LINE 22. **do me reason**: pledge me.

"Finding myself freed from the staple, I dragged myself upstairs, and was at length directed, by the sound of a jolly roundelay, to the apartment where were the worthy sacristan and a huge beetle-browed, 5 broad-shouldered brother of the grey-frock and cowl, who looked much more like a thief than a clergyman. I burst in upon them, and the fashion of my grave-clothes, as well as the clanking of my chains, made me more resemble an inhabitant of 10 the other world than of this. Both stood aghast; but when I knocked down the sacristan with my fist, the other fellow fetched a blow at me with a huge quarter-staff."

"This must be our Friar Tuck, for a count's 15 ransom," said Richard, looking at Ivanhoe.

"He may be the devil, an he will," said Athelstane. "Fortunately, he missed the aim; and on my approaching to grapple with him, took to his heels and ran for it. I failed not to set my own 20 heels at liberty by means of the fetter-key, which hung amongst others at the sexton's belt, and then I went to the stable and found in a private stall mine own best palfrey. Hither I came with all the speed the beast could compass — man and 25 mother's son flying before me wherever I came, taking me for a spectre, the more especially as, to prevent my being recognized, I drew the corpse-hood over my face. I had not gained admittance into my own castle, had I not been supposed to be the attendant of a juggler who is making the people in the castle-yard very merry, considering they are assembled to celebrate their lord's funeral. So I got admission, and I did but disclose myself to my mother, and eat a hasty morsel, ere I came in quest of you, my noble friend."

"And you have found me," said Cedric, " ready to resume our brave projects of honor and liberty. I tell thee, never will dawn a morrow so auspicious as the next for the deliverance of the noble Saxon race."

" Talk not to me of delivering any one," said Athelstane; " it is well I am delivered myself. I am more intent on punishing that villain abbot. He shall hang on the top of this Castle of Conings-burgh, in his cope and stole; and if the stairs be too strait to admit his fat carcass, I will have him craned up from without."

" For shame, noble Athelstane," said Cedric; " forget such wretches in the career of glory which lies open before thee. Tell this Norman prince, Richard of Anjou, that, lion-hearted as he is, he shall not hold undisputed the throne of Alfred."

" How ! " said Athelstane, " is this the noble King Richard ? "

" It is Richard Plantagenet himself," said Cedric; " yet I need not remind thee that, coming hither a

---

LINE 16. **stole** : strip of silk or other material hanging from back of neck over shoulders and down to knees.

guest of free-will, he may neither be injured nor detained prisoner: thou well knowest thy duty to him as his host."

"Ay, by my faith!" said Athelstane; "and my duty as a subject besides, for I here tender him my allegiance, heart and hand."

"My son," said Edith, "think on thy royal rights!"

"Think on the freedom of England, degenerate prince!" said Cedric.

"Mother and friend," said Athelstane, "a truce to your upbraidings! Bread and water and a dungeon are marvellous mortifiers of ambition, and I rise from the tomb a wiser man than I descended into it. Since these plots were set in agitation, I have had nothing but hurried journeys, indigestions, blows and bruises, imprisonments, and starvation; besides that they can only end in the murder of some thousands of quiet folk. I tell you, I will be king in my own domains, and nowhere else; and my first act of dominion shall be to hang the abbot."

"And my ward Rowena," said Cedric — "I trust you intend not to desert her?"

"Father Cedric," said Athelstane, "be reasonable. The Lady Rowena cares not for me; she loves the little finger of my kinsman Wilfred's

---

LINE **13. mortifiers**: deadeners; subduers.

glove better than my whole person. There she stands to avouch it. Nay, blush not, kinswoman; there is no shame in loving a courtly knight better than a country franklin; and do not laugh neither, Rowena, for grave-clothes and a thin visage are, 5 God knows, no matter of merriment. Nay, an thou wilt needs laugh, I will find thee a better jest. Give me thy hand, or rather lend it me, for I but ask it in the way of friendship. Here, cousin Wilfred of Ivanhoe, in thy favor I renounce and 10 abjure —— Hey, by St. Dunstan, our cousin Wilfred hath vanished! Yet, unless my eyes are still dazzled with the fasting I have undergone, I saw him stand there but even now."

All now looked around and inquired for Ivanhoe; 15 but he had vanished. It was at length discovered that a Jew had been to seek him; and that, after very brief conference, he had called for Gurth and his armor, and had left the castle.

"Fair cousin," said Athelstane to Rowena, 20 "could I think that this sudden disappearance of Ivanhoe was occasioned by other than the weightiest reason, I would myself resume —— "

But he had no sooner let go her hand, on first observing that Ivanhoe had disappeared, than 25 Rowena, who had found her situation extremely embarrassing, had taken the first opportunity to escape from the apartment.

"Certainly," quoth Athelstane, "women are

the least to be trusted of all animals, monks and abbots excepted. I am an infidel, if I expected not thanks from her, and perhaps a kiss to boot. These cursed grave-clothes have surely a spell on them, every one flies from me. To you I turn, noble King Richard, with the vows of allegiance, which, as a liege subject —— "

But King Richard was gone also, and no one knew whither. At length it was learned that he had hastened to the courtyard, summoned to his presence the Jew who had spoken with Ivanhoe, and, after a moment's speech with him, had called vehemently to horse, thrown himself upon a steed, compelled the Jew to mount another, and set off at a rate which, according to Wamba, rendered the old Jew's neck not worth a penny's purchase.

"Every one I speak to vanishes as soon as they hear my voice," said Athelstane. "Come, my friends, such of you as are left, follow me to the banquet-hall, lest any more of us disappear."

# CHAPTER XLIII

## A Champion

Our scene now returns to the exterior of the castle, or preceptory, of Templestowe, about the hour when the bloody die was to be cast for the life or death of Rebecca. It was a scene of bustle and life, as if the whole vicinity had poured forth its 5 inhabitants to a rural feast.

The eyes of a very considerable multitude were bent on the gate of the preceptory of Templestowe, with the purpose of witnessing the procession; while still greater numbers had already surrounded 10 the tiltyard belonging to that establishment. This inclosure was formed on a piece of level ground adjoining to the preceptory, which had been levelled with care, for the exercise of military and chivalrous sports. It occupied the brow of a soft and gentle 15 eminence, was carefully palisaded around, and was amply supplied with galleries and benches for the use of the spectators.

On the present occasion a throne was erected for the Grand Master at the east end, surrounded with 20

LINE **11. tiltyard:** place for tournament.

573

seats of distinction for the preceptors and knights of the order. Over these floated the sacred standard, called *Le Beau-seant*, which was the ensign, as its name was the battle-cry, of the Templars.

5 At the opposite end of the lists was a pile of faggots, so arranged around a stake as to leave a space for the victim to be chained to the stake by the fetters which hung ready for that purpose. Beside this deadly apparatus stood four black 10 slaves, whose color and African features, then so little known in England, appalled the multitude, who gazed on them as on demons employed about their own diabolical exercises. These men stirred not, excepting now and then, under the direction 15 of one who seemed their chief, to shift and replace the ready fuel. They looked not on the multitude. In fact, they seemed insensible of their presence, and of everything save the discharge of their own horrible duty.

20 One by one the sullen sounds of the heavy bell of the church of St. Michael of Templestowe fell successively on the ear, leaving but sufficient space for each to die away in distant echo, ere the air was again filled by repetition of the iron knell. These 25 sounds, the signal of the approaching ceremony, chilled with awe the hearts of the assembled multitude, whose eyes were now turned to the preceptory, expecting the approach of the Grand Master, the champion, and the criminal.

# A Champion

At length the drawbridge fell, the gates opened, and a knight, bearing the great standard of the order, sallied from the castle, preceded by six trumpets, and followed by the knights, preceptors, two and two, the Grand Master coming last, mounted 5 on a stately horse. Behind him came Brian de Bois-Guilbert, armed cap-à-pie in bright armor, but without his lance, shield, and sword, which were borne by his two esquires behind him. His face, though partly hidden by a long plume which 10 floated down from his barret-cap, bore a strong and mingled expression of passion, in which pride seemed to contend with irresolution. He looked ghastly pale, as if he had not slept for several nights, yet reined his pawing war-horse with the 15 habitual ease and grace proper to the best lance of the order of the Temple.

On either side rode Conrade of Mont-Fitchet and Albert de Malvoisin, who acted as godfathers to the champion. They were in their robes of 20 peace, the white dress of the order. Behind them followed other companions of the Temple, with a long train of esquires and pages clad in black, aspirants to the honor of being one day knights of the order. After these neophytes came a guard 25 of warders on foot, in the same sable livery, amidst

---

LINE **7. cap-à-pie**: from head to foot. **11. barret-cap**: small flat cap. **13. irresolution**: indecision. **25. neophytes**: beginners; persons newly admitted. **26. warders**: keepers; watchmen.

whose partizans might be seen the pale form of the accused, moving with a slow but undismayed step towards the scene of her fate. She was stript of all her ornaments. A coarse white dress, of the simplest form, had been substituted for her Oriental garments; yet there was such an exquisite mixture of courage and resignation in her look that even in this garb, and with no other ornament than her long black tresses, each eye wept that looked upon her, and the most hardened bigot regretted the fate that had converted a creature so goodly into a vessel of wrath.

A crowd of inferior personages belonging to the preceptory followed the victim, all moving with the utmost order, with arms folded and looks bent upon the ground.

This slow procession moved up the gentle eminence, on the summit of which was the tiltyard, and, entering the lists, marched once around them from right to left, and when they had completed the circle, made a halt. There was then a momentary bustle, while the Grand Master and all his attendants, excepting the champion and his godfathers, dismounted from their horses, which were immediately removed out of the lists.

The unfortunate Rebecca was conducted to the black chair placed near the pile. On her first glance at the terrible spot where preparations were making for a death alike dismaying to the mind and painful to the body, she was observed to shudder and shut her eyes, praying internally, doubtless, for her lips moved, though no speech was heard. In the space of a minute she opened her eyes, looked fixedly on the pile as if to familiarize her mind with 5 the object, and then slowly and naturally turned away her head.

Meanwhile, the Grand Master had assumed his seat; and when the chivalry of his order was placed around and behind him, each in his due rank, a 10 loud and long flourish of the trumpets announced that the court were seated for judgment.

The Grand Master commanded the herald to stand forth and do his devoir. The trumpets then again flourished, and a herald, stepping forward, 15 proclaimed aloud: "Oyez, oyez, oyez. Here standeth the good knight, Sir Brian de Bois-Guilbert, ready to do battle with any knight of free blood who will sustain the quarrel allowed and allotted to the Jewess Rebecca; and to such cham- 20 pion the reverend and valorous Grand Master here present allows a fair field, and equal partition of sun and wind, and whatever else appertains to a fair combat." The trumpets again sounded, and there was a dead pause of many minutes. 25

"No champion appears for the appellant," said the Grand Master. "Go, herald, and ask her

---

LINE **14**. devoir: duty. **16**. Oyez: hear ye.

whether she expects any one to do battle for her in this her cause."

The herald went to the chair in which Rebecca was seated; and Bois-Guilbert, suddenly turning his horse's head towards that end of the lists, in spite of hints on either side from Malvoisin and Mont-Fitchet, was by the side of Rebecca's chair as soon as the herald.

"Is this regular, and according to the law of combat?" said Malvoisin, looking to the Grand Master.

"Albert de Malvoisin, it is," answered Beaumanoir; "for in this appeal to the judgment of God we may not prohibit parties from having that communication with each other which may best tend to bring forth the truth of the quarrel."

In the meantime, the herald spoke to Rebecca in these terms: "Damsel, the honorable and reverend the Grand Master demands of thee, if thou art prepared with a champion to do battle this day in thy behalf, or if thou dost yield thee as one justly condemned to a deserved doom?"

"Say to the Grand Master," replied Rebecca, "that I maintain my innocence, and do not yield me as justly condemned lest I become guilty of mine own blood. Say to him that I challenge such delay as his forms will permit, to see if God, whose opportunity is in man's extremity, will raise me up a deliverer; and when such uttermost space is passed, may His holy will be done!"

The herald retired to carry this answer to the Grand Master.

"God forbid," said Lucas Beaumanoir, "that Jew or Pagan should impeach us of injustice! Until the shadows be cast from the west to the eastward, will we wait to see if a champion shall appear for this unfortunate woman. When the day is so far passed, let her prepare for death."

The herald communicated the words of the Grand Master to Rebecca, who bowed her head submissively, folded her arms, and, looking up towards heaven, seemed to expect that aid from above which she could scarce promise herself from man. During this awful pause, the voice of Bois-Guilbert broke upon her ear; it was but a whisper, yet it startled her more than the summons of the herald had appeared to do.

"Rebecca," said the Templar, "dost thou hear me?"

"I have no portion in thee, cruel, hard-hearted man," said the unfortunate maiden.

"Ay, but dost thou understand my words?" said the Templar; "for the sound of my voice is frightful in mine own ears. I scarce know on what ground we stand, or for what purpose they have

---

LINE **6. impeach**: accuse.

brought us hither. This listed space — that chair — these faggots — I know their purpose, and yet it appears to me like something unreal."

"My mind and senses," answered Rebecca, "tell me alike that these faggots are destined to consume my earthly body, and open a painful but a brief passage to a better world."

"Dreams, Rebecca — dreams," answered the Templar — "idle visions. Hear me, Rebecca," he said, proceeding with animation; "a better chance hast thou for life and liberty than yonder knaves and dotard dream of. Mount thee behind me on my steed — on Zamor, the gallant horse that never failed his rider. Mount, I say, behind me; in one short hour is pursuit and inquiry far behind — a new world of pleasure opens to thee — to me a new career of fame. Let them speak the doom which I despise, and erase the name of Bois-Guilbert from their list of monastic slaves! I will wash out with blood whatever blot they may dare to cast on my scutcheon."

"Tempter," said Rebecca, "begone! Not in this last extremity canst thou move me one hair's-breadth from my resting-place. Surrounded as I am by foes, I hold thee as my worst and most deadly enemy; avoid thee, in the name of God!"

Albert Malvoisin, alarmed and impatient at the

---

LINE **21. scutcheon**: shield bearing coat of arms.
**26. avoid thee**: depart.

REBECCA AND THE TEMPLAR

"Mount thee behind me on my steed — on Zamor, the gallant
horse that never failed his rider."

duration of their conference, now advanced to interrupt it.

"Hath the maiden acknowledged her guilt?" he demanded of Bois-Guilbert; "or is she resolute in her denial?"

"She is indeed *resolute*," said Bois-Guilbert.

"Then," said Malvoisin, "must thou, noble brother, resume thy place to attend the issue. The shades are changing on the circle of the dial. Come, brave Bois-Guilbert — come, thou hope of our holy order, and soon to be its head."

As he spoke in this soothing tone, he laid his hand on the knight's bridle, as if to lead him back to his station.

"False villain! what meanest thou by thy hand on my rein?" said Sir Brian, angrily. And shaking off his companion's grasp, he rode back to the upper end of the lists.

The judges had now been two hours in the lists, awaiting in vain the appearance of a champion.

It was the general belief that no one could or would appear for a Jewess accused of sorcery; and the knights, instigated by Malvoisin, whispered to each other that it was time to declare the pledge of Rebecca forfeited. At this instant a knight, urging his horse to speed, appeared on the plain advancing towards the lists. A hundred voices exclaimed, "A champion! — a champion!" And, despite the prejudices of the multitude, they shouted unanimously as the knight rode into the tiltyard. The second glance, however, served to destroy the hope that his timely arrival had excited. His horse, urged for many miles to its utmost 5 speed, appeared to reel from fatigue, and the rider, however undauntedly he presented himself in the lists, either from weakness, weariness, or both, seemed scarce able to support himself in the saddle.

To the summons of the herald, who demanded 10 his rank, his name, and purpose, the stranger knight answered readily and boldly: " I am a good knight and noble, come hither to sustain with lance and sword the just and lawful quarrel of this damsel, Rebecca, daughter of Isaac of York; to uphold the 15 doom pronounced against her to be false and truthless, and to defy Sir Brian de Bois-Guilbert, as a traitor, murderer, and liar; as I will prove in this field with my body against his, by the aid of God."

20 " The stranger must first show," said Malvoisin, " that he is good knight, and of honorable lineage. The Temple sendeth not forth her champions against nameless men."

" My name," said the knight, raising his helmet, 25 " is better known, my lineage more pure, Malvoisin, than thine own. I am Wilfred of Ivanhoe."

" I will not fight with thee at present," said the

---

Line **6. undauntedly**: fearlessly.

Templar, in a changed and hollow voice. "Get thy wounds healed, purvey thee a better horse, and it may be I will hold it worth my while to scourge out of thee this boyish spirit of bravado."

"Ha! proud Templar," said Ivanhoe, "hast thou forgotten that twice didst thou fall before this lance? Remember the lists at Acre; remember the passage of arms at Ashby; remember thy proud vaunt in the halls of Rotherwood, and the gage of your gold chain against my reliquary, that thou wouldst do battle with Wilfred of Ivanhoe, and recover the honor thou hadst lost! By that reliquary, and the holy relic it contains, I will proclaim thee, Templar, a coward in every court in Europe — in every preceptory of thine order — unless thou do battle without farther delay."

Bois-Guilbert turned his countenance irresolutely towards Rebecca, and then exclaimed, looking fiercely at Ivanhoe: "Dog of a Saxon! take thy lance, and prepare for the death thou hast drawn upon thee!"

"Does the Grand Master allow me the combat?" said Ivanhoe.

"I may not deny what thou hast challenged," said the Grand Master, "provided the maiden accepts thee as her champion. Yet I would thou wert in better plight to do battle. An enemy of

---

LINE **2. purvey**: provide.   **10. reliquary**: casket for sacred relics.

our order hast thou ever been, yet would I have thee honorably met with."

"Thus — thus as I am, and not otherwise," said Ivanhoe; "it is the judgment of God — to His keeping I commend myself. Rebecca," said he, riding up to the fatal chair, "dost thou accept of me for thy champion?"

"I do," she said — "I do," fluttered by an emotion which the fear of death had been unable to produce — "I do accept thee as the champion whom Heaven hath sent me. Yet no — no — thy wounds are uncured. Meet not that proud man; why shouldst thou perish also?"

But Ivanhoe was already at his post, and had closed his visor, and assumed his lance. Bois-Guilbert did the same; and his esquire remarked, as he clasped his visor, that his face, which had, notwithstanding the variety of emotions by which he had been agitated, continued during the whole morning of an ashy paleness, was now become suddenly very much flushed.

The trumpets sounded, and the knights charged each other in full career. The wearied horse of Ivanhoe, and its no less exhausted rider, went down, as all had expected, before the well-aimed lance and vigorous steed of the Templar. This issue of the combat all had foreseen; but although the spear of Ivanhoe did but, in comparison, touch the shield of Bois-Guilbert, that champion, to the astonishment of all who beheld it, reeled in his saddle, lost his stirrups, and fell in the lists.

Ivanhoe, extricating himself from his fallen horse, was soon on foot, hastening to mend his fortune with his sword; but his antagonist arose 5

YIELD OR DIE

not. Wilfred, placing his foot on his breast, and the sword's point to his throat, commanded him to yield him, or die on the spot. Bois-Guilbert returned no answer.

"Slay him not, Sir Knight," cried the Grand 10

Master, "unshriven and unabsolved; kill not body and soul! We allow him vanquished."

He descended into the lists, and commanded them to unhelm the conquered champion. His eyes were closed; the dark red flush was still on his brow. As they looked on him in astonishment, the eyes opened; but they were fixed and glazed. The flush passed from his brow, and gave way to the pallid hue of death. Unscathed by the lance of his enemy, he had died a victim to the violence of his own contending passions.

"This is indeed the judgment of God," said the Grand Master.

---

LINE **1. unshriven**: without having confessed. **unabsolved**: unforgiven.

# CHAPTER XLIV

## Farewell All

When the first moments of surprise were over, Wilfred of Ivanhoe demanded of the Grand Master if he had manfully and rightfully done his duty in the combat.

"Manfully and rightfully hath it been done," said the Grand Master; "I pronounce the maiden free and guiltless. The arms and the body of the deceased knight are at the will of the victor."

"I will not despoil him of his weapons," said the Knight of Ivanhoe, "nor condemn his corpse to shame: he hath fought for Christendom. God's arm, no human hand, hath this day struck him down. But let his obsequies be private, as becomes those of a man who died in an unjust quarrel. And for the maiden —— "

He was interrupted by a clattering of horses' feet, advancing in such numbers, and so rapidly, as to shake the ground before them; and the Black Knight galloped into the lists. He was followed by a numerous band of men-at-arms, and several knights in complete armor.

"I am too late," he said, looking around him. "I had doomed Bois-Guilbert for mine own property. Ivanhoe, was this well, to take on thee such a venture, and thou scarce able to keep thy saddle?"

"Heaven, my Liege," answered Ivanhoe, "hath taken this proud man for its victim."

5  "Peace be with him," said Richard, looking steadfastly on the corpse, "if it may be so; he was a gallant knight, and has died in his steel harness full knightly. But we must waste no time. Bohun, do thine office!"

10  A knight stepped forward from the King's attendants, and, laying his hand on the shoulder of Albert de Malvoisin, said, "I arrest thee of high treason."

The Grand Master had hitherto stood astonished 15 at the appearance of so many warriors. He now spoke.

"Who dares to arrest a knight of the Temple of Zion, within the girth of his own preceptory, and in the presence of the Grand Master? and by whose 20 authority is this bold outrage offered?"

"I make the arrest," replied the knight — "I, Henry Bohun, Earl of Essex, Lord High Constable of England."

"And he arrests Malvoisin," said the King, 25 raising his visor, "by the order of Richard Plantagenet, here present. Conrade Mont-Fitchet, it is well for thee thou art born no subject of mine. But for thee, Malvoisin, thou diest with thy brother Philip ere the world be a week older."

"I will resist thy doom," said the Grand Master.

"Proud Templar," said the King, "thou canst not: look up, and behold the royal standard of England floats over thy towers instead of thy Temple banner! Dissolve thy chapter, and depart 5 with thy followers to thy next preceptory, if thou canst find one which has not been made the scene of treasonable conspiracy against the King of England. Or, if thou wilt, remain, to share our hospitality, and behold our justice." 10

"To be a guest in the house where I should command?" said the Templar; "never! Knights, squires, and followers of the Holy Temple, prepare to follow the banner of *Beau-seant!*"

The Grand Master spoke with a dignity which 15 confronted even that of England's king himself, and inspired courage into his surprised and dismayed followers. They drew together in a dark line of spears, from which the white cloaks of the knights were visible among the dusky garments of 20 their retainers, like the lighter-colored edges of a sable cloud. The multitude, who had raised a clamorous shout of reprobation, paused and gazed in silence on the formidable and experienced body to which they had unwarily bade defiance, and 25 shrunk back from their front.

---

LINE **1. doom**: judgment; sentence. **23. reprobation**: strong disapproval. **25. unwarily**: without precautions against accident or danger.

The Earl of Essex, when he beheld them pause in their assembled force, dashed the rowels into his charger's sides, and galloped backwards and forwards to array his followers, in opposition to a band so formidable. Richard alone, as if he loved the danger his presence had provoked, rode slowly along the front of the Templars, calling aloud: "What, sirs! Among so many gallant knights, will none dare to splinter a spear with Richard?"

"The brethren of the Temple," said the Grand Master, riding forwards in advance of their body, "fight not on such idle and profane quarrel; and not with thee, Richard of England, shall a Templar cross lance in my presence."

With these words the Grand Master gave the signal of departure. Their trumpets sounded a wild march, of an Oriental character, which formed the usual signal for the Templars to advance. They changed their array from a line to a column of march, and moved off as slowly as their horses could step, as if to show it was only the will of their Grand Master, and no fear of the opposing and superior force, which compelled them to withdraw.

"By the splendor of Our Lady's brow!" said King Richard, "it is pity that these Templars are not so trusty as they are disciplined and valiant."

The multitude, like a timid cur which waits to bark till the object of its challenge has turned his

THE DEPARTURE OF THE TEMPLARS

back, raised a feeble shout as the rear of the squadron left the ground.

During the tumult which attended the retreat of the Templars, Rebecca saw and heard nothing : she was locked in the arms of her aged father, giddy, and almost senseless, with the rapid change of circumstances around her. But one word from Isaac at length recalled her scattered feelings.

"Let us go," he said, "my dear daughter, my recovered treasure — let us go to throw ourselves at the feet of the good youth."

"Not so," said Rebecca. "Oh no — no — no ! I must not at this moment dare to speak to him. Alas ! I should say more than —— No, my father, let us instantly leave this evil place."

"But, my daughter," said Isaac, "to leave him who hath come forth like a strong man with his spear and shield, holding his life as nothing, so he might redeem thy captivity; and thou, too, the daughter of a people strange unto him and his — this is service to be thankfully acknowledged."

"It is — it is — most thankfully — most devoutly acknowledged," said Rebecca; "it shall be still more so — but not now — for the sake of thy beloved Rachel, father, grant my request — not now ! "

"Nay, but," said Isaac, insisting, "they will deem us more thankless than mere dogs ! "

"But thou seest, my dear father, that King Richard is in presence, and that —— "

"True, my best — my wisest Rebecca. Let us hence — let us hence! Money he will lack, for he has just returned from Palestine, and, as they say, from prison; and pretext for exacting it, should he need any, may arise out of my simple traffic with his brother John. Away — away, let us hence!"

And hurrying his daughter in his turn, he conducted her from the lists, and by means of conveyance which he had provided, transported her safely to the house of the Rabbi Nathan.

The Jewess having now retired unobserved, the attention of the populace was transferred to the Black Knight. They now filled the air with "Long life to Richard with the Lion's Heart, and down with the usurping Templars!"

"Notwithstanding all this lip-loyalty," said Ivanhoe to the Earl of Essex, "it was well the King took the precaution to bring thee with him, noble Earl, and so many of thy trusty followers."

The Earl smiled and shook his head.

"Gallant Ivanhoe," said Essex, "dost thou know our master so well, and yet suspect him of taking so wise a precaution! I was drawing towards York, having heard that Prince John was making head there, when I met King Richard, like a true knight-errant, galloping hither to achieve in his own person this adventure of the Templar and the

Jewess, with his own single arm. I accompanied
him with my band, almost maugre his consent."

"And what news from York, brave Earl?" said
Ivanhoe; "will the rebels bide us there?"

"No more than December's snow will bide 5
July's sun," said the Earl; "they are dispersing;
and who should come posting to bring us the news,
but John himself!"

"The traitor! — the ungrateful, insolent
traitor!" said Ivanhoe; "did not Richard order 10
him into confinement?"

"Oh! he received him," answered the Earl, " as
if they had met after a hunting party; and, pointing to me and our men-at-arms, said, ' Thou seest,
brother, I have some angry men with me; thou 15
wert best go to our mother, carry her my duteous
affection, and abide with her until men's minds
are pacified.' "

"And this was all he said?" inquired Ivanhoe;
"would not any one say that this prince invites 20
men to treason by his clemency?"

"Just," replied the Earl, "as the man may be
said to invite death who undertakes to fight a combat, having a dangerous wound unhealed."

"I forgive thee the jest, Lord Earl," said Ivan- 25
hoe; "but, remember, I hazarded but my own
life — Richard, the welfare of his kingdom."

---

LINE **2. maugre**: in spite of; without.

"Those," replied Essex, "who are specially careless of their own welfare are seldom remarkably attentive to that of others. But let us haste to the castle, for Richard meditates punishing some of the subordinate members of the conspiracy, though he has pardoned their principal."

From the judicial investigations which followed on this occasion, it appears that Maurice de Bracy escaped beyond seas, and went into the service of Philip of France, while Philip de Malvoisin and his brother Albert, the preceptor of Templestowe, were executed, although Waldemar Fitzurse, the soul of the conspiracy, escaped with banishment, and Prince John, for whose behoof it was undertaken, was not even censured by his good-natured brother. No one, however, pitied the fate of the two Malvoisins, who only suffered the death which they had both well deserved, by many acts of falsehood, cruelty, and oppression.

Briefly after the judicial combat, Cedric the Saxon, summoned to the court of Richard, tushed and pshawed more than once at the message, but refused not obedience. In fact, the return of Richard had quenched every hope that he had entertained of restoring a Saxon dynasty in England.

Moreover, it could not escape even Cedric's reluctant observation that his project for an absolute union among the Saxons, by the marriage of Rowena and Athelstane, was now completely at an end, by the mutual dissent of both parties concerned. Rowena had always expressed her repugnance to Athelstane, and now Athelstane was no less plain and positive in proclaiming his resolution never to pursue his addresses to the Lady 5 Rowena. Even the natural obstinacy of Cedric sunk beneath these obstacles, where he, remaining on the point of junction, had the task of dragging a reluctant pair up to it, one with each hand.

There remained betwixt Cedric and the deter- 10 mination which the lovers desired to come to only two obstacles — his own obstinacy, and his dislike of the Norman dynasty. The former feeling gradually gave way before the endearments of his ward and the pride which he could not help nour- 15 ishing in the fame of his son. Cedric's aversion to the Norman race of kings was also much undermined — first, by consideration of the impossibility of ridding England of the new dynasty; and, secondly, by the personal attention of King Richard, 20 who delighted in the blunt humor of Cedric, and so dealt with the noble Saxon that, ere he had been a guest at court for seven days, he had given his consent to the marriage of his ward and his son Wilfred of Ivanhoe. 25

The nuptials of our hero, thus formally approved by his father, were celebrated in the most august of

---

LINE 1. dissent: disagreement.

temples, the noble minster of York. The King himself attended, and the church gave her full solemnities.

Gurth, gallantly apparelled, attended as esquire upon his young master, whom he had served so 5 faithfully, and the magnanimous Wamba, decorated with a new cap and a most gorgeous set of silver bells. Sharers of Wilfred's dangers and adversity, they remained the partakers of his more prosperous career.

10 But, besides this domestic retinue, these distinguished nuptials were celebrated by the attendance of the high-born Normans, as well as Saxons, joined with the universal jubilee of the lower orders, that marked the marriage of two individuals as a 15 pledge of the future peace and harmony betwixt two races, which, since that period, have been so completely mingled that the distinction has become wholly invisible. Cedric lived to see this union approximate towards its completion; for, as the 20 two nations mixed in society and formed intermarriages with each other, the Normans abated their scorn, and the Saxons were refined from their rusticity. But it was not until the reign of Edward the Third that the mixed language, now termed 25 English, was spoken at the court of London, and that the hostile distinction of Norman and Saxon seems entirely to have disappeared.

---

LINE 1. **minster**: monastery church; cathedral.

# Farewell All

It was upon the second morning after this happy bridal that the Lady Rowena was made acquainted by her handmaid Elgitha, that a damsel desired admission to her presence, and solicited that their parley might be without witness. Rowena wondered, hesitated, became curious, and ended by commanding the damsel to be admitted, and her attendants to withdraw.

She entered — a noble and commanding figure, the long white veil, in which she was shrouded, overshadowing rather than concealing the elegance and majesty of her shape. Rowena arose, and would have conducted her lovely visitor to a seat; but the stranger looked at Elgitha, and again intimated a wish to discourse with the Lady Rowena alone. Elgitha had no sooner retired with unwilling steps than, to the surprise of the Lady of Ivanhoe, her fair visitant kneeled on one knee, pressed her hands to her forehead, and bending her head to the ground, in spite of Rowena's resistance, kissed the embroidered hem of her tunic.

"What means this, lady?" said the surprised bride; "or why do you offer to me a deference so unusual?"

"Because to you, Lady of Ivanhoe," said Rebecca, rising up and resuming the usual quiet dignity of her manner, "I may lawfully, and without rebuke, pay the debt of gratitude which I owe to Wilfred of Ivanhoe. I am — forgive the bold-

ness which has offered to you the homage of my
country — I am the unhappy Jewess for whom
your husband hazarded his life against such fearful
odds in the tiltyard of Templestowe."

5   "Damsel," said Rowena, "Wilfred of Ivanhoe
on that day rendered back but in slight measure
your unceasing charity towards him in his wounds
and misfortunes. Speak, is there aught remains
in which he or I can serve thee?"

10   "Nothing," said Rebecca, calmly, "unless you
will transmit to him my grateful farewell."

"You leave England, then?" said Rowena,
scarce recovering the surprise of this extraordinary
visit.

15   "I leave it, lady, ere this moon again changes.
My father hath a brother high in favor with
Mohammed Boabdil, King of Granada: thither
we go, secure of peace and protection, for the payment of such ransom as the Moslem exact from
20 our people."

"And are you not then as well protected in England?" said Rowena. "My husband has favor
with the King; the King himself is just and generous."

25   "Lady," said Rebecca, "I doubt it not; but the
people of England are a fierce race, quarrelling ever
with their neighbors or among themselves, and
ready to plunge the sword into the bowels of each
other. Such is no safe abode for the children of

my people. Farewell; yet, ere I go, indulge me one request. The bridal veil hangs over thy face; deign to raise it, and let me see the features of which fame speaks so highly."

" They are scarce worthy of being looked upon," said Rowena; " but, expecting the same from my visitant, I remove the veil."

She took it off accordingly; and, partly from the consciousness of beauty, partly from bashfulness, she blushed so intensely that cheek, brow, neck, and bosom were suffused with crimson. Rebecca blushed also; but it was a momentary feeling, and, mastered by higher emotions, past slowly from her features like the crimson cloud which changes color when the sun sinks beneath the horizon.

" Lady," she said, " the countenance you have deigned to show me will long dwell in my remembrance. There reigns in it gentleness and goodness; and if a tinge of the world's pride or vanities may mix with an expression so lovely, how should we chide that which is of earth for bearing some color of its original? Long, long will I remember your features, and bless God that I leave my noble deliverer united with —— "

She stopped short — her eyes filled with tears. She hastily wiped them, and answered to the anxious inquiries of Rowena: " I am well, lady — well. But my heart swells when I think of Tor-

quilstone and the lists of Templestowe. Farewell.
One, the most trifling, part of my duty remains
undischarged. Accept this casket; startle not at
its contents."

5 Rowena opened the small silver-chased casket,
and perceived a carcanet, or necklace, with ear-
jewels, of diamonds, which were obviously of immense value.

"It is impossible," she said, tendering back the
10 casket. "I dare not accept a gift of such consequence."

"Yet keep it, lady," returned Rebecca. "Think
ye that I prize these sparkling fragments of stone
above my liberty? or that my father values them
15 in comparison to the honor of his only child?
Accept them, lady — to me they are valueless. I
will never wear jewels more."

"You are then unhappy!" said Rowena, struck
with the manner in which Rebecca uttered the last
20 words: "Oh, remain with us, and I will be a sister
to you."

"No, lady," answered Rebecca, the same calm
melancholy reigning in her soft voice and beautiful
features; "that may not be. And unhappy,
25 lady, I will not be. He to whom I dedicate my
future life will be my comforter, if I do His
will."

"Have you then convents, to one of which you
mean to retire?" asked Rowena.

" No, lady," said the Jewess; " but among our
people, since the time of Abraham downwards,
have been women who have devoted their thoughts
to Heaven, and their actions to works of kindness
to men — tending the sick, feeding the hungry,
and relieving the distressed. Among these will
Rebecca be numbered. Say this to thy lord, should
he chance to inquire after the fate of her whose life
he saved."

There was an involuntary tremor in Rebecca's
voice, and a tenderness of accent, which perhaps
betrayed more than she would willingly have expressed. She hastened to bid Rowena adieu.

" Farewell," she said. " May He who made
both Jew and Christian shower down on you His
choicest blessings! The bark that wafts us
hence will be under weigh ere we can reach the
port."

She glided from the apartment, leaving Rowena
surprised as if a vision had passed before her. The
fair Saxon related the singular conference to her
husband, on whose mind it made a deep impression.
He lived long and happily with Rowena, for they
were attached to each other by the bonds of early
affection, and they loved each other the more from
the recollection of the obstacles which had impeded
their union. Yet it would be inquiring too curiously to ask whether the recollection of Rebecca's
beauty and magnanimity did not recur to his mind

more frequently than the fair descendant of Alfred
might altogether have approved.

Ivanhoe distinguished himself in the service of
Richard, and was graced with farther marks of the
5 royal favor. He might have risen still higher but
for the premature death of the heroic Cœur-de-
Lion, before the Castle of Chaluz, near Limoges.
With the life of a generous, but rash and romantic,
monarch perished all the projects which his ambi-
10 tion and his generosity had formed; to whom may
be applied, with a slight alteration, the lines composed by Johnson for Charles of Sweden —

> His fate was destined to a foreign strand,
> A petty fortress and an "humble" hand;
> 15 He left the name at which the world grew pale,
> To point a moral, or adorn a TALE.

---

LINE **2. approved**. Thackeray in *Rebecca and Rowena*,
an amusing sequel to *Ivanhoe*, has given one answer to this
question.

*Sir H. Raeburn*

Sir Walter Scott

# APPENDIX

## SIR WALTER SCOTT

**Ancestry.** In Scott's home at Abbotsford hangs a picture of William Scott, who, caught during a raid on Sir Gideon Murray's lands, was given his choice between being hanged and marrying Meiklemouthed Meg, Sir Gideon's ugliest daughter. The picture shows this ancestor of Sir Walter Scott deciding to go to the gallows. Three days later, however, he married the large-mouthed daughter, and he never regretted his choice. Meg handed down to all her descendants, Sir Walter included, a trace of her large mouth.

Sir Walter's father, the first of his fighting and riding clan to live in a city, was an honest, hard-working, methodical Edinburgh lawyer. His kind-hearted mother, who was the daughter of a professor in Edinburgh University, had a good memory and could paint striking word pictures of the past.

**Childhood.** Walter was born in Edinburgh, August 15, 1771, four years before the beginning of the American Revolution. He was the ninth of twelve children. When eighteen months old, he suffered an attack of teething-fever, which left him lame for life. Because his parents thought country air would strengthen him, he was sent to live with his grandfather at Sandy-Knowe near some fine crags and a ruined tower. On

603

bright days a shepherd took him out to the fields and, while the sheep were grazing, let him roll on the grass.

Despite his illness Walter was "a sweet-tempered bairn, a darling with all about the house." He learned to climb with great nimbleness and to ride at a gallop his tiny Shetland pony, about the size of a Newfoundland dog. Although he became a healthy, strong boy, because of his lameness he seldom played games. Instead he would gather a group of children about him and tell them stories.

From his grandmother he heard thrilling tales of attacks and escapes on the Scottish Border. His Aunt Janet read to him history, stories, and ballads until he could repeat long passages by heart. These he recited with so much spirit that the clergyman, while visiting the family, complained, "One may as well speak in the mouth of a cannon as where that child is."

A relative tells of his reading aloud at the age of six. "He was reading a poem to his mother when I went in. I made him read on: it was the description of a shipwreck. His passion rose with the storm. 'There's the mast gone,' says he; 'crash it goes; they will all perish.' After his agitation he turns to me; 'That is too melancholy,' says he; 'I had better read you something more amusing.'"

**Schooldays.** Scott studied under private teachers, in the Edinburgh High School, and in Edinburgh University. Of his class standing he says, "I glanced like a meteor from one end of the class to the other." Under Dr. Adam he became a first-rate Latin student because his instructor expected him to do well and he felt it a matter of honor to prove that the good opinion was justified. But in a Greek class the professor called him a dunce, and his classmates nicknamed him the *Greek Blockhead*.

In one of his classes Walter was eager to stand above another boy but unable to pass him. At last he noticed that, whenever the teacher asked a question, the lad grasped a button on his waistcoat and thought out the answer. Walter figured that without the button to seize the lad would become confused and wouldn't be able to think. When he had a chance, he cut off the button and during the next recitation passed his rival.

Of his schooling Scott says, " So, on the whole, I made a brighter figure in the yards than in the class." In spite of his lameness he was a bold climber and was always in the thickest of the fights between the town boys and the schoolboys. He was liked because of his good nature, readiness to help his friends, and endless supply of entertaining stories. Some of these he made up; others he knew because of his wide and random reading of the books in public and private libraries.

When he was thirteen years old, he came upon Percy's *Reliques*, a collection of stirring ballads. One summer afternoon under a great plane tree he began to read these ballads. " The summer day sped onward so fast," he said years afterwards, " that notwithstanding the sharp appetite of thirteen, I forgot the dinner hour, was sought for with anxiety, and was still found entranced in my intellectual banquet." When he could " scrape five shillings together," he bought the books and read them again and again.

Of his failure to master some of his school subjects, Scott said, " It is with the deepest regret that I recollect in my manhood the opportunities of learning which I neglected in my youth. Through every part of my literary career I have felt pinched and hampered by my ignorance."

**Profession.** At the suggestion of his father Scott studied law. After being admitted to the bar in 1792, he practiced for fourteen years and was a sound lawyer, though not a great one. Because he preferred trudging over the country in search of beautiful scenery and places where battles or sieges had taken place to poring over law books, his father said that Walter was better fitted to be a peddler than a lawyer. On these excursions he sometimes walked thirty miles in a day, a good tramp for a lame youth.

In 1799 he was appointed sheriff of Selkirkshire at a salary of about $1500 a year for life. In 1806 he became Clerk of Sessions of the Court of Edinburgh. For five years he served without pay, while an invalid enjoyed the salary but did none of the work of the office. After this time he received a salary of almost $6500 a year.

**Marriage.** Coming out of church one Sunday evening during a shower, Scott offered his umbrella to an attractive young lady in a green mantle. The offer was accepted, and Scott fell in love with the borrower, Margaret Stuart Belches. For six years he hoped to marry this lady, but the objection of parents or a misunderstanding prevented the marriage.

On Christmas eve, 1797, he married Charlotte Carpenter (Charpentier), a beautiful, lively French girl, who had come to England after the death of her father during the French Revolution. Because Mrs. Scott was kind, true-hearted, and brave in adversity, their home was happy.

**Home Life.** As Scott was an out-of-door man, a few months after his marriage he rented a cottage at Lasswade on the Esk. Six years later when he became

*Wide World Photo*

ABBOTSFORD

sheriff of Selkirkshire, he moved to a larger house at Ashestiel on the Tweed.

He has been called " the hardest worker and the heartiest player in the kingdom." At Lasswade he did his writing at night, but headaches made him at Ashestiel change his daily routine. He rose at five and at six was at his desk hard at work with his books about him and with at least one favorite dog looking on. By the time of the family breakfast, between nine and

ten, he had "broken the neck of the day's work."
On rainy days he frequently worked at his desk all day.
When the weather was fair, he usually wrote two or
three hours after breakfast, and by one o'clock was out
and on horseback, often with his greyhounds about

*Burton Holmes, from Ewing Galloway*

THE ARMORY AT ABBOTSFORD

him, or was in a boat on the Tweed with a salmon spear
in his hand.

When Scott's income was increased by the salary of
the Clerkship of Session, he bought a large estate at
Abbotsford five miles lower down the Tweed than
Ashestiel and thirty miles from Edinburgh. With his
swords, bows, targets, lances, turkeys, cows, calves,
dogs, pigs, ponies, and chickens he moved to his new
home. The neighbors found his moving day as amus-

THE LIBRARY AT ABBOTSFORD

ing as a circus parade. In later years he added hundreds of acres to the estate, planted trees, and tore down the cottage and built a castle.

Abbotsford has been called a museum because in its halls, library, armory, and other rooms are many rare

*Burton Holmes, from Ewing Galloway*

MELROSE ABBEY NEAR ABBOTSFORD

objects given to Scott or collected by him. Among these are the purse of Rob Roy, the pistols taken from Napoleon's carriage at Waterloo, the cross carried by Mary, Queen of Scots, when she went to the scaffold, rare pictures and books, antlers of stags, and old Scottish armor and weapons.

When Scott became famous, countless guests and tourists journeyed to his home. Because the castle was filled with guests most of the time, Lady Scott used to say that Abbotsford was a hotel in all but name.

**Writings.** While Scott was practicing law, he began to write poetry. Before the age of forty he was the author of three great poems, *The Lay of the Last Minstrel*, *Marmion*, and *The Lady of the Lake*, which made him the best-known writer in Great Britain. But when Lord Byron's poems became widely popular, Scott left the field of poetry to his rival and began to write novels.

Coming across one of his partly written stories while he was searching for fishing-tackle, he went to work on it, completed it in five weeks, and published it without his name as *Waverley*. Other novels followed at the rate of two a year. Everybody wondered who the author, " The Great Unknown," was. At last the secret leaked out. Some of his novels are *Guy Mannering*, *The Antiquary*, *Old Mortality*, *Rob Roy*, *The Heart of Midlothian*, *The Bride of Lammermoor*, *Ivanhoe*, *Kenilworth*, *Quentin Durward*, *The Talisman*, *The Monastery*, and *The Abbot*.

**Financial Troubles.** Although Scott earned during his lifetime about $700,000, he was not a good business man and had the bad habit of spending his money before he earned it. In 1826 Constable, his publisher, and Ballantyne and Company, his printer, failed. As he was a silent partner in both concerns, a debt of nearly $600,000 was left on his shoulders. By taking advantage of the bankruptcy law, he might have escaped the payment of most of this sum and have had for his own use all his future earnings. Instead he set to work to pay every penny, and in the six years before his death paid more than half of the amount. Fifteen years after his death, through the value of the copyrights of his books the payment of the debt was completed.

**The Man.** Washington Irving, who visited Scott in 1817, gives us a good picture of his host at the age of forty-six. " He was tall and of a large and powerful frame. His dress was simple and almost rustic. An old green shooting coat with a dog-whistle at the buttonhole, brown linen pantaloons, stout shoes that tied at the ankles, and a white hat that had seen service. He came limping up the gravel-walk, aiding himself by a stout walking-staff, but moving rapidly and with vigor. By his side jogged along a large, iron-gray stag-hound of most grave demeanor, who took no part in the clamor of the canine rabble, but seemed to consider himself bound for the dignity of the house to give me a courteous reception."

Scott was a hero made out of the same stuff as the heroes he put into his books. He not only assumed a debt most of which he might have legally escaped, but drove away at his work to pay it when he was so sick that it was torture for him to sit up and hold a pen or dictate to his secretary. While writing *Ivanhoe*, a romance which has entertained and cheered millions, he was suffering acute pain. Of his sufferings he said, " I have no idea of these things preventing a man from doing what he has a mind."

**Last Days.** After three or four strokes of apoplexy, in the hope of regaining strength he sailed for Italy in a frigate provided by the British government. It was too late. He soon grew homesick for the hills and streams he loved. When he returned to Abbotsford, his friends, family, and dogs welcomed him heartily.

A few days later he thought that he could write again. When his chair was wheeled to his desk, he found that his fingers would not clasp the pen. With tears rolling

*Wide World Photo*

DRYBURGH ABBEY, WHERE SCOTT IS BURIED

down his cheeks he gave up the attempt and sank back into his chair. He died on September 21, 1832, at the age of sixty-one.

His last words were spoken to his son-in-law. "Lockhart," he said, "I may have but a minute to speak to you. My dear, be a good man — be virtuous — be religious — be a good man. Nothing else will give you any comfort when you come to lie here."

MONUMENT TO SIR WALTER SCOTT IN EDINBURGH

# Supplementary Reading

## SUGGESTED SUPPLEMENTARY READING

*The Life of Scott*, J. G. Lockhart
*Sir Walter Scott*, R. H. Hutton
*Abbotsford*, Washington Irving
The novels of Scott mentioned in the account of his life,
    especially *Quentin Durward* and *The Talisman*,
    which is about Richard Cœur-de-Lion
*Harold*, Bulwer-Lytton
*Hereward the Wake*, Charles Kingsley
*Black Arrow*, Robert Louis Stevenson
*Rebecca and Rowena*, William Makepeace Thackeray
*The Scottish Chiefs*, Jane Porter
*The Merry Adventures of Robin Hood*, Howard Pyle
*Robin Hood*, George C. Harvey
*Bold Robin Hood and His Outlaw Band*, Louis Rhead
*Robin Hood, His Book*, Eva March Tappan
*The Oxford Book of Ballads*, Book V
*Heroes of Chivalry and Romance*, A. J. Church
*Men of Iron*, Howard Pyle
*With Spurs of Gold*, F. N. Greene and D. W. Kirk
*Boy's Book of Chivalry*, H. Hall
*Story of King Arthur and His Knights*, Howard Pyle
*Knights and Their Days*, Doran
*When Knights Were Bold*, Eva March Tappan
*The Age of Chivalry*, Thomas Bulfinch
*The Book of Romance*, Andrew Lang
*The Story of the Crusades*, E. M. Wilmot-Buxton
*Heroes Every Child Should Know*, H. W. Mabie
*A History of England*, C. R. L. Fletcher and Rudyard
    Kipling
*Story of the English*, H. A. Guerber

# Appendix

*Stories of English History*, A. J. Church
*England's Story*, Eva March Tappan
*A History of Everyday Things in England*, Marjorie and C. H. B. Quennell
*The Rainbow Song Book*, Adèle Marie Shaw, Elizabeth Alden, and C. Irving Valentine

## WILLIAM THE CONQUEROR

One purpose of Scott in writing *Ivanhoe* was to show how the Anglo-Saxons, who inhabited England, were treated by their conquerors, the Normans.

In 1066, Harold, the last of the Saxon kings, defeated his rebel brother Tostig and the Norwegians in the Battle of Stamford Bridge. He then marched against William the Conqueror, who, claiming the throne of England, had crossed the English Channel. With his Norman cavalry and archers William defeated Harold and his English foot-soldiers and axe-men in the Battle of Hastings, one of the decisive battles of history. After the battle had lasted from nine in the morning till late afternoon, William's cavalry pretended flight. When the Saxons rushed after them in a disorderly mob, it was easy for the Normans to turn and cut to pieces their pursuers. After the battle William became king of England; and the clever, educated, adventurous Normans governed, and for a while bullied, the great, slow, dogged Saxons.

The rulers spoke French; the farmers and laborers, Anglo-Saxon. Because the nobles had to converse with the workers, a mixed language came gradually into use. From this union of Anglo-Saxon and French arose our present English language, which has been enriched by words from Latin, Greek, and other languages.

## RICHARD I

Richard I or Richard the Lion-Hearted was more than six feet tall, fair-haired, and blue-eyed. As most of his life was spent in France, he never learned to speak

RICHARD AND SALADIN

the English language. During his reign from 1189 to 1199 he spent only seven weeks in England. In spite of many admirable qualities he was really a royal adventurer, who found his chief joy in the battle and the tournament.

Soon after his coronation Richard collected a vast sum of money and a mighty army, and with his rival, King Philip of France, set out on the Third Crusade.

# Appendix

The crusades were called holy wars because the purpose of the warriors was to capture from the Turks the sepulcher of Christ. Each soldier wore a cross, and the nations had crosses of different colors — England white, France red, Italy blue. A Knight Templar wore a red cross on a white background.

Although Richard was a gallant soldier and born leader and won some brilliant victories, he quarreled with his allies and failed to regain Jerusalem. All that he secured was a truce for three years with Saladin, the Sultan of Egypt and Syria, and security for the pilgrims who wished to visit the holy places.

On his way back to England, Richard was shipwrecked. While making his way across Europe in the disguise of a merchant, he was captured near Vienna by the Duke of Austria and handed over to the Emperor of Germany. There is a story that Richard's minstrel Blondel, wandering about Europe in search of his master, sang under the windows of every prison he came upon. When one day he had sung a stanza under the window of a gloomy tower, he was overjoyed to hear Richard sing the second stanza. After a year in prison, Richard was released on the payment of a ransom so huge that every Englishman had to contribute one-fourth of his personal property and priests were forced to strip the churches. The events of *Ivanhoe* took place in 1194, just after Richard had reached England.

After a few weeks in England, Richard crossed the English Channel and spent the remaining six years of his life in war with Philip of France. While besieging an obscure castle, he was struck down by an arrow from the walls.

# Robin Hood

## JOHN

John, who became king after the death of Richard, is commonly considered the worst king in English history. He was a bad son, a bad brother, a bad king, and a bad man. His conspiracy against his brother Richard while Richard was in the Holy Land and in a German prison is described in *Ivanhoe*.

## ROBIN HOOD

Whether Robin Hood was a real person is not definitely known. One story is that Robin was the son of a nobleman and fled to the forest because he couldn't pay his debts; another, that he shot one of the king's deer; and a third, that he slew a forester who had threatened his life. In Sherwood Forest he became the prince of outlaws. He stopped travelers in the woods, robbing the fat abbots, monks, and merchants, and giving to the poor and needy. He shed no blood if he could help it and was kind to women and children. Because he hid his spoils in the forest, the woods were called Robin Hood's barn.

Little John, Friar Tuck, Maid Marian, and Allan-a-Dale were four members of his band. Little John, who was seven feet tall, was second in skill and strength only to Robin Hood, the most skillful archer who ever shot an arrow from a long-bow. Friar Tuck or the Clerk of Copmanhurst, the priest of the band, had been a monk in a great abbey. Allan-a-Dale was the famous minstrel. Maid Marian, a young lady of rank, ran away from home to wed Robin Hood.

# Appendix

## KNIGHTHOOD

The business of the knight was war. In the tournament, a dangerous kind of sham battle, he learned the arts and tricks of war.

At the age of seven or eight the aspirant to knighthood was taken from the care of his mother and sent to act as a page in the household of a knight. He was the constant attendant of his master and mistress, waited on them in the hall and at table, and went out hunting with them. He was taught to honor women, sing, play the lute, hunt, hawk, ride a horse, cast a spear, and carry a shield.

At fourteen or fifteen the boy became a squire and began seven years of severer training. In a heavy suit of chain armor he practiced running, leaping to the saddle, turning somersaults, throwing the lance, and wielding the sword and battle-axe. He also cared for the knight's horses and saw to it that his arms and armor were polished until they shone. When a knight mounted his horse, a squire stood at each stirrup, and others carried his armor and buckled it on him. In tournament or battle the squire raised the knight from the ground if unhorsed, carried him to a place of safety if wounded, and buried him if killed.

The ceremony of becoming a knight varied. Commonly, after the bath of purification, the candidate fasted and prayed for twenty-four hours, and, alone in the church, knelt all night before the altar, on which lay his armor. The next day in a solemn religious ceremony he promised to be loyal to God and the king, to be true, to be pure, to prefer honor to gain, and to honor and protect women. After he had taken his vows, he was clothed in armor, a sword was girded on him, and spurs were fastened to his heels. Then he knelt to receive the accolade. A knight struck him on the shoulder with the flat of his sword and said, " In the name of God, Saint Michael, and Saint George, I dub thee knight. Be brave, ready, and loyal." Lastly, he was given a war-horse, shield, and lance; then he leaped into the saddle, and galloped up and down to show his skill in horsemanship.

If a knight proved unfaithful to his vows, his shield was reversed, his spurs taken from him, and his armor broken. In a sermon in the church he was declared dead to the order.

### FEUDALISM

Under the feudal system all the land belonged to the king. When he parceled it out to his nobles, they became his vassals and the lands received were called fiefs. The nobles in turn gave smaller tracts of land to their followers. This dividing up of the land might be carried through any number of stages.

When a vassal received a fief, he knelt before the lord, placed his clasped hands within those of the lord, and swore to be his " man " and to serve him in all ways that a free man should. This service included supplying the lord with knights for his wars, paying ransom when he was taken captive, and contributing money when his eldest son was knighted and when his eldest daughter was married. If a vassal proved unfaithful, his land was taken from him and given to some one else.

The lord in turn protected his vassal. And in a time

when fighting was an every-day occurrence and the government had no navy, standing army, or police, this was by no means a small return for the services rendered. In times of danger the vassals fled to the castles of their lords.

The lowest landholders under the feudal system were the peasants, who did the work. Some were freemen, others serfs. The serf farmed about forty acres of land. These fields he did not own, but they could not be taken from him if he worked for the lord a part of the time and gave him food and money. The serf might, for example, be required to supply two oxen for his lord's use in winter and one in summer, to work three days a week for him, to pay him a hen, sixteen eggs, and a little money every year, and to follow him to war.

## RELIGIOUS ORDERS

Long ago some religious men decided that to lead a holy life one must get away from the wicked world. Having wandered into the desert or another lonely place, these men lived in caves or rude huts and gave themselves up to fasting, prayer, and thought. They were called hermits or anchorites. When the hermits began to band themselves together in communities, monasteries and monastic orders sprang up.

In 529 St. Benedict founded the Benedictines, the largest order of monks and the one that did most for the advancement of education. To the three vows of obedience, poverty, and chastity, he added that of manual labor for seven hours a day. As a result, the monks were healthy and happy.

# The Jester

Early in the thirteenth century, St. Francis of Assisi and his friars or brothers, instead of retiring from the wicked world, went out to help by preaching, teaching, and caring for the sick. These Franciscans, known as Gray Friars from the color of their gowns, vowed to remain poor and beg for a living. The Dominicans or Black Friars, Carmelites or White Friars, and Augustinians were three other orders of wandering friars.

Two orders of military monks, half monk and half soldier, are mentioned in *Ivanhoe*, the Knights Templars and the Knights Hospitallers. The Knights Templars, founded in Jerusalem, had six establishments or preceptories in England. They escorted pilgrims from the coast up to Jerusalem and also waged war against the Mohammedans. At first the Knights Hospitallers cared for the sick and wounded crusaders, but later the order became military.

The Knights Templars wore a Maltese (eight-pointed) cross of red on a white field. *Beau-seant* was both their war cry and the name of their banner, which was black above to indicate that they were fierce to their foes and white below to denote that they were kind to their friends.

## THE JESTER

The jester or court fool was not an idiot or numskull but a person who, because he was witty, clever, and original, was retained by a wealthy man or noble to while away the time and amuse his family and friends. In jest he often said to his master and others what from the lips of some one else would have been considered an insult. He wore a fool's cap with ass's ears and a cock's comb, tight-fitting clothes of various colors, bells on his cap and sometimes on other parts of his dress, and a large collar. In his hand he carried a bauble or stick with an ass-eared head carved on it.

## NORMAN CASTLE

On the top of a rugged hill a Norman baron built a square or round tower with walls eight or ten feet thick and narrow windows. This keep or donjon was the stronghold of his castle. The main floor, reached by a removable wooden staircase, was small, cold, dark, and damp. Under it was the dungeon for traitors and captured enemies. Around the keep was a courtyard, in which were commonly a storehouse, stables, a kitchen, and a chapel.

Surrounding the courtyard was a wall five or six feet thick and fifteen to twenty-five feet high with towers and a gateway, closed by a gate and the portcullis, a heavy plank grating which could be raised and dropped. Usually outside of the wall was a moat or wide ditch filled with water. At the gateway a drawbridge, which could be raised or lowered at will, crossed the moat. Frequently at the end of the drawbridge was a barbican or outwork. Beyond this sometimes was a high fence made of strong stakes pointed at the top.

To capture such a castle, the attackers had to tear down the palisade, seize the outwork, and cross the moat. Then they must break through the gate and portcullis or batter down or scale the wall. Finally they had to capture the keep or starve out the inhabitants.

The defenders shot arrows at the attackers, thrust with spears, hacked with swords and battle-axes, threw down stones and weapons, or poured down melted lead or burning pitch.

### ARMS AND ARMOR

The warrior of the time of *Ivanhoe* wore on his head a helmet or steel hat with a visor or iron grating, which could be raised or drawn down over the face. A coat

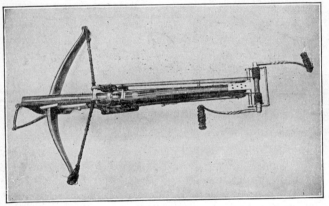

CROSSBOW

of mail made of steel links woven together or a coat of plate armor made of overlapping steel plates covered his body. Steel gauntlets or gloves, leggings, and shoes completed his dress. In his left hand he carried a shield, sometimes three or four feet long; in his right, a huge spear with a pennant or tiny flag on it. At his side hung a sword. To carry such heavy arms and armor was

623

work, and to handle the weapons while riding a fiery, galloping war-horse required practice and skill.

The most deadly weapon of the foot-soldier, the long-bow, was much like the bow used so skillfully by the

BOAR SPEAR

American Indians. Made of a piece of tough yew about six feet long and carefully strung with a strong cord, it could drive a steel-pointed arrow through an oak beam four inches thick. The crossbow, shown in

HALBERD

the picture, had to be reversed and wound up after each discharge, but the firing of the long-bow was more rapid than that of the musket of later date. With no smoke to obscure his vision the archer could shoot accurately at a distance of two hundred yards or more.

# Arms and Armor

When archers battled against mailclad knights mounted on powerful horses, they either found joints and weak spots in the armor or shot down the horses. An unhorsed knight burdened with fifty pounds of iron

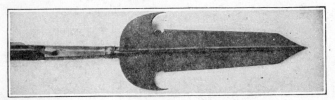

PARTIZAN

armor and arms couldn't move fast enough to accomplish much on the battle field.

The arrow of the long-bow was called a shaft; of the crossbow, a bolt. In *Ivanhoe* the long-bow arrow

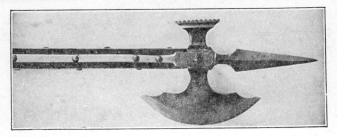

BATTLE AXE

is occasionally called "the cloth-yard shaft" or "the grey-goose shaft."

In the pictures the long handles of the halberd, partizan, and boar spear are not shown.

# STUDY QUESTIONS

# Appendix

## STUDY QUESTIONS

### Chapter I

1. When did the events of *Ivanhoe* take place? Find on the map the places mentioned.

2. Why did the Saxons dislike the Normans?

3. Describe the dress of Gurth and Wamba. What sort of person was each?

4. Why was Fangs " unfit for his trade "?

5. How did the Normans become the rulers of England?

### Chapter II

1. Contrast as to appearance, dress, and conduct the Prior and the Templar.

2. Why did Wamba misdirect Bois-Guilbert and the Prior?

3. Why didn't Bois-Guilbert and the Prior follow Wamba's directions?

4. Why did the Prior advise Bois-Guilbert to be more courteous in speech?

5. How was the castle of Rotherwood defended?

6. What was a palmer? a Knight Templar?

### Chapter III

1. Compare Cedric's dining hall with the great hall of Penhurst Castle.

2. What sort of person was Cedric?

3. Why was Cedric in a bad humor?

4. Why did Cedric entertain the unwelcome guests?

5. What did Cedric say about his son?

6. Why was Rowena eager to hear the news from Palestine?

# Study Questions

### Chapter IV

1. Compare Cedric's supper with a supper or dinner that you have enjoyed.
2. Describe Rowena.
3. Was Cedric a good host? Give reasons.
4. How did Wamba defend Gurth when Cedric angrily threatened to throw the swineherd into the prison-house?
5. Why did Rowena draw her veil around her face?
6. Why did the Templar say to the Prior, " I shall wear no collar of gold of yours at the tournament "?

### Chapter V

1. In a play based on *Ivanhoe*, what part of this chapter would be most exciting?
2. In this play how should the actor taking the part of Isaac make up, dress, and act?
3. Why was Bois-Guilbert eager to fight with Ivanhoe?
4. By whom and in what way was Ivanhoe defended?
5. Why did the Prior retire very early?

### Chapter VI

1. After saying that visitors were not permitted to steal away from the castle so early in the morning, why did Gurth obey the Palmer so briskly?
2. Why was the Palmer given an uncomfortable cell next to Isaac's?
3. Which would you prefer, Rowena's apartment or your own room? Why?
4. Why did the Pilgrim save the Jew?

# Appendix

5. How did Isaac repay the Palmer?

6. What hints are there that the Palmer was not a palmer?

### Chapter VII

1. Draw a diagram of the lists.

2. Compare the appearance of Rebecca and Rowena.

3. What kind of man was Athelstane?

4. Why did Prince John order the families of Cedric and Athelstane to make room for Isaac?

5. In what respects was Isaac different at the tournament from what he was at Cedric's home? Why?

### Chapter VIII

1. What was the difference between a courtesy contest and a combat to the death? Which did the lower order of spectators prefer? Why?

2. Why did the Disinherited Knight challenge Bois-Guilbert by striking the Templar's shield with the sharp end of his lance?

3. How did the Disinherited Knight overthrow Bois-Guilbert?

4. How did the Disinherited Knight show that he was a good sportsman?

5. Describe the arms and armor of a knight.

### Chapter IX

1. Why did Prince John suggest to the Disinherited Knight that he select Alicia as the Queen of Love and Beauty?

2. How did the Disinherited Knight select the Queen of Love and Beauty?

# Study Questions

3. Why did Prince John turn pale as death when he heard the whisper, " It might be the King "?

4. Did the choice of the Queen of Love and Beauty please or displease Prince John? Fitzurse? Cedric? the spectators? Why?

5. Who were especially interested in the success of the Disinherited Knight? Why was each interested?

### Chapter X

1. Why did the Disinherited Knight refuse to accept either arms or ransom from Bois-Guilbert?

2. When did Isaac's love of gold struggle with his desire to be generous to Gurth and the Disinherited Knight?

3. Why did Gurth call Rebecca " an angel from heaven "?

4. How did Gurth happen to be serving as the Disinherited Knight's squire?

5. How did Gurth outwit the Jew?

6. Why didn't Gurth want to go to the Jew's house?

### Chapter XI

1. How did Gurth show his loyalty to the Disinherited Knight?

2. How did Gurth escape the payment of a ransom?

3. Compare a quarter-staff bout with a fencing match or a boxing match.

4. What is the meaning of the robber's reply to Gurth: " Three quarts of double ale had rendered thee as free as thy master "?

5. Why didn't the thieves take the Disinherited Knight's money?

# Appendix

### Chapter XII

1. Why was the general tournament more dangerous than single encounters?

2. Imagine that you were a spectator at the second day's tournament. Picture what you saw.

3. Compare a general tournament with a football game.

4. Why did Athelstane join Bois-Guilbert's side?

5. What were the laws of the general tournament?

6. What were the two most exciting moments of the tournament?

### Chapter XIII

1. Why did Prince John turn pale as death when he received the message: " Take heed to yourself, for the Devil is unchained "?

2. How did Locksley win the archery prize?

3. Which in your opinion is the better sport, archery or rifle shooting? Why?

4. Why did Prince John have a grudge against Locksley?

5. As a spectator would you have enjoyed the first day's tournament, the general tournament, or the archery contest most? Why?

6. Why did Prince John change the date of the archery contest?

### Chapter XIV

1. What kind of man was Prince John?

2. Compare Prince John as a host with another host you know or have read about, Cedric, for example.

# Study Questions

3. Why did Prince John fail in his attempt to gain the support of the Saxons?

4. What is the most dramatic moment in this chapter?

5. How did the Normans' clothes and manners differ from the Saxons'?

6. Why did Cedric leave the banquet?

### Chapter XV

1. Why did Fitzurse take pains to reunite and combine the scattered members of Prince John's party?

2. What was Fitzurse's opinion of Prince John? of De Bracy?

3. What was De Bracy's plan to win a fair bride? Why did Fitzurse object to it?

4. When news came that Richard had been released from prison, how did Fitzurse persuade Prince John's followers to continue their support of the Prince?

### Chapter XVI

1. What humor is there in this chapter?

2. How did the Black Knight show that he liked his horse?

3. What is the most dramatic moment in the chapter?

4. What did the Black Knight see when the Clerk of Copmanhurst opened his door?

5. How did the knight get the hermit to share the pasty and to bring out some wine?

# Appendix

### Chapter XVII

1. Which do you like the better, the knight's song or the hermit's song? Why?
2. Compare the knight's song with a popular song you know.
3. What stopped the merrymaking?

### Chapter XVIII

1. Is this one of the most entertaining chapters of *Ivanhoe?* Why?
2. Why was Cedric eager to have Rowena marry Athelstane?
3. Why was Cedric angry at Gurth?
4. What reasons had Gurth for saying that he would never forgive Cedric?
5. Why didn't Rowena attend the banquet?
6. When Ivanhoe was injured, why didn't Cedric have him cared for?

### Chapter XIX

1. Why did the Saxons permit Isaac and Rebecca to travel with their party?
2. How did Gurth escape?
3. Imagine yourself Wamba and give an account of the attack, your escape, and your meeting Gurth and Locksley.
4. Why was Gurth, soon after renouncing his master, eager to help him?

### Chapter XX

1. Why was Locksley ready to aid? Have you found out Locksley's other name?

# Study Questions

2. Why did Locksley go to Friar Tuck's hut?

3. What happened when Locksley knocked on Friar Tuck's door?

4. What is the meaning of, " Get thine iron pot on thy head "?

### Chapter XXI

1. What humor is there in this chapter?

2. Who was Harold? What did Cedric tell Athelstane about him?

3. What in this chapter arouses the reader's curiosity?

4. Why did De Bracy change his plans? What change did he make?

### Chapter XXII

1. Why did Front-de-Bœuf claim Isaac as his prisoner?

2. Why was Isaac placed in the dungeon-vault of the castle?

3. How did Isaac show his courage?

4. How did Isaac show that he had not forgotten those who had been kind to him?

5. What is the most dramatic moment in this chapter?

### Chapter XXIII

1. Compare in appearance De Bracy the outlaw and De Bracy the wooer.

2. How did De Bracy try to persuade Rowena to marry him?

# Appendix

3. What broke down Rowena's courage and made her weep?

4. Why didn't De Bracy kill Ivanhoe when the wounded knight was in his power?

### Chapter XXIV

1. Compare Rebecca and Rowena. Which do you admire more? Why?

2. What is the most dramatic moment in this chapter?

3. How did Rebecca find out that the tall man dressed like a bandit was not an outlaw?

4. How has Scott made it clear that the events of Chapters XXII, XXIII, and XXIV happened at the same time?

### Chapter XXV

1. In the chapter what information is there about the education of Front-de-Bœuf? De Bracy? Bois-Guilbert? Friar Tuck? Wamba? Gurth? Locksley? the Black Knight?

2. How did Locksley, Gurth, Wamba, and the Black Knight sign the challenge?

3. Why did Front-de-Bœuf think the challenge no laughing matter?

4. What is the meaning of the sentence: " Sting-less! " replied Front-de-Bœuf; " fork-headed shafts of a cloth-yard in length, and these shot within the breadth of a French crown, are sting enough "?

5. Why was Wamba chosen to play the part of a priest?

# Study Questions

## Chapter XXVI

1. What humor is there in this chapter?
2. Why did Cedric say, " I am somewhat deaf "?
3. What is the meaning of the sentence: " I trust — no disparagement to your birth — that the son of Witless may hang in a chain with as much gravity as the chain hung upon his ancestor the alderman "?
4. How did Wamba show his heroism? his common sense?
5. What did Athelstane do or say to increase our respect for him?
6. Why did Rebecca wish to speak with the pretended friar?

## Chapter XXVII

1. How did Athelstane show that he was not a coward?
2. Who was Ulrica? Why was she planning to help the Saxons to capture the castle?
3. Why did Front-de-Bœuf order his archers to send an arrow through the monk's frock? Why did he recall the order?
4. Why didn't Front-de-Bœuf send to Prior Aymer money or men?
5. What jesting reply did Wamba make when Front-de-Bœuf threatened to hang the captives up by the feet? to tear the scalp from his head and pitch him from the battlements?
6. In what ways did Cedric almost lose his chance to escape?

# Appendix

## Chapter XXVIII

1. How did Rebecca persuade Isaac not to abandon Ivanhoe?

2. How had Rebecca become such a skillful doctor and nurse?

3. When did Ivanhoe's manner toward Rebecca change? Why?

4. Why did Isaac's hired party desert him in the hour of need?

5. Show that De Bracy in his treatment of Ivanhoe pursued a middle course between good and evil.

## Chapter XXIX

1. Draw a diagram of Torquilstone, showing the keep, wall, turrets, postern gate, moat, drawbridge, outwork, and palisades.

2. Compare Torquilstone with a modern fort. Compare the attack and defense of the castle with twentieth-century warfare.

3. How did the besiegers capture the outwork?

4. How did the Black Knight prove himself a wise and brave leader?

5. What was the most exciting part of the fight?

6. Was the glory won by the knights of Ivanhoe's time worth the price paid by themselves and others? Give reasons.

7. In the twentieth century what takes the place of chivalry?

## Chapter XXX

1. How did Ulrica secure revenge?

2. After Front-de-Bœuf fell, why did Bois-Guilbert

oppose De Bracy's suggestion that they deliver up the prisoners?

3. Was De Bracy a coward? Give reasons.

4. Why did the loss of the outwork make it more difficult for Bois-Guilbert and De Bracy to defend the castle?

5. What did De Bracy say about Locksley's skill as an archer?

### Chapter XXXI

1. How did Locksley and Ulrica save Cedric and the Black Knight?

2. How did the Black Knight overthrow De Bracy and take him prisoner?

3. Tell of Bois-Guilbert's carrying off Rebecca and fighting with Athelstane.

4. How did Ulrica die?

5. What deed told about in the chapter required the greatest courage?

6. What happened to the principal characters in the story when Torquilstone was captured?

7. What event earlier in the story did the Black Knight's whispering to De Bracy remind you of?

### Chapter XXXII

1. How were the spoils divided?

2. Why and how was Gurth made free?

3. Tell of the interchange of cuffs.

4. Why was the jolly Friar late in joining the band at the trysting-tree?

# Appendix

### Chapter XXXIII

1. What sentence in the chapter is worth memorizing?
2. How were the ransoms fixed?
3. How did Locksley show kindness to Isaac? Why?
4. Was Isaac a miser? Give reasons.
5. What kind of pen did Locksley provide Prior Aymer with?

### Chapter XXXIV

1. Show that De Bracy again pursued a middle course between good and evil.
2. What is the meaning of the statement: " I say the best prison is that made by the sexton "?
3. Prove that Prince John trusted neither Fitzurse nor De Bracy.
4. What plan was formed to get rid of King Richard?

### Chapter XXXV

1. Why did the Grand Master decide to purify the Knights Templars? How did he proceed?
2. How did the Grand Master treat Isaac?
3. How did Isaac's attempt to rescue his daughter injure her?
4. Why did the Grand Master consider Rebecca a sorceress?

### Chapter XXXVI

1. Prove that Albert Malvoisin was a hypocrite.
2. What is the meaning of Mont-Fitchet's statement

about the proofs: "They must be strengthened, Albert"?

3. What advice did Albert Malvoisin give Bois-Guilbert?

4. Why were Malvoisin and Mont-Fitchet so willing to aid the Grand Master in bringing Rebecca to instant trial for sorcery.

5. How did Malvoisin explain the presence of Rebecca in the preceptory?

### Chapter XXXVII

1. Compare Rebecca's trial with the trial at present of an accused person.

2. Imagine yourself present at the trial, and paint a word picture of the trial hall and the spectators.

3. What did the witnesses say about Rebecca? Which of their statements were false?

4. How did Rebecca escape the sentence of condemnation?

5. What part in the trial of Rebecca was played by Higg, the son of Snell?

6. What do you think of Beaumanoir as a judge? Why?

### Chapter XXXVIII

1. What did Rebecca say in her letter to her father?

2. How did she secure a messenger?

3. What is the meaning of Isaac's statement: "They will ask pounds, and peradventure accept of ounces"?

4. What dangers did Higg run when he became Rebecca's messenger?

5. Why did the Grand Master tell Malvoisin to give Rebecca's glove to Bois-Guilbert? Why was Bois-Guilbert unwilling to take the glove?

## Chapter XXXIX

1. What plan of escape did Bois-Guilbert propose to Rebecca?

2. How had Bois-Guilbert planned to save Rebecca when he told her to demand a champion?

3. How did Malvoisin persuade Bois-Guilbert not to try to fly to a distant land or refuse to fight against Rebecca's champion?

4. Do you admire Rebecca? Why?

5. If Bois-Guilbert had been an honorable man, what would he have done?

## Chapter XL

1. What humor is there in the chapter?

2. What is the most exciting moment in the chapter?

3. How was King Richard saved?

4. How did Wamba ride?

5. Why did Ivanhoe follow King Richard?

6. Would King Richard have blown the bugle? Give reasons.

## Chapter XLI

1. Compare King Richard with the present king of England or president of the United States.

2. Why did Robin Hood hesitate to give King Richard refreshments?

# Study Questions

3. How did Robin Hood break off the banquet? Why?

4. What Saxon funeral customs are mentioned?

## Chapter XLII

1. How did Athelstane escape from his imprisonment?

2. What humor is there in the chapter?

3. How is Ivanhoe's reconciliation with his father brought about?

4. Why did Athelstane say, " Every one I speak to vanishes as soon as they hear my voice "?

5. Why did Richard follow Ivanhoe?

6. Why was Athelstane willing to give up his claim to the throne of England? to the hand of Rowena?

## Chapter XLIII

1. Imagine that you were a spectator in the gallery of the tiltyard. Describe what you saw.

2. What final attempt to save Rebecca did Bois-Guilbert make?

3. How was Rebecca saved?

4. Why did the spectators expect Ivanhoe to be killed?

## Chapter XLIV

1. Picture the departure of the Templars.

2. Why did Rebecca desire to speak with Rowena?

3. Why did Rebecca and Isaac leave England?

4. How does the story end for each important character?

5. Why did Cedric consent to the marriage of Rowena and Ivanhoe?

# Appendix

## SPEECHES AND THEMES

1. On a diagram like this but large enough to fill a sheet of paper, trace Isaac of York, the Black Sluggard,

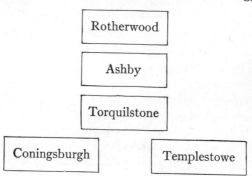

Friar Tuck, Bois-Guilbert, Ivanhoe, and the other important characters through the story. Show on the diagram which characters traveled together to Rotherwood, which went together from Rotherwood to Ashby, etc.

2. Imagine yourself one of the following. Then tell of your experience.

> *a.* As Friar Tuck tell of entertaining the king or exchanging blows with him.
>
> *b.* As Cedric tell of the appearance and victory of the Disinherited Knight, Prince John's banquet, the capture of your party, or your escape from Torquilstone.
>
> *c.* As Isaac tell of the Palmer's kindness, your experiences in Torquilstone, your escape from Torquilstone, your ransom, or your interview with the Grand Master.

642

# Speeches and Themes

*d.* As Rebecca tell of your escape from Torquilstone or your trial.

*e.* As Gurth tell about your experience with the outlaws.

*f.* As King Richard tell how a fool saved your life.

*g.* As Locksley tell about the archery contest.

*h.* As Athelstane tell of the second day's tournament.

*i.* As Wamba tell about one of your adventures.

*j.* As Rebecca, Rowena, or Ivanhoe tell about the first day's tournament.

*k.* As Rowena tell a close friend about your two suitors.

*l.* As Rebecca write from Torquilstone a letter to a friend.

*m.* As Rowena write a letter to a friend after the second day's tournament.

*n.* As a captive in Torquilstone write to Robin Hood or the Black Knight for assistance.

3. Make up another adventure of Richard, Robin Hood, Wamba, or Bois-Guilbert; for example, an adventure of Bois-Guilbert in Palestine or of Richard while returning from Palestine to England.

4. Have Ivanhoe come to life this year in your city or town and let him tell in his own way about what he sees.

5. Write to a boy or girl friend who has not read *Ivanhoe* a letter telling what character impressed you most and why. Also narrate enough of an exciting or amusing part of the story to arouse interest in the book.

6. Write for the Ashby *Journal* an account of the archery contest.

7. Did you like the ending of the story? Give reasons. If you were not satisfied with the ending, rewrite the last chapter.

8. In a moving picture of *Ivanhoe* what parts should be omitted?

9. Compare Ivanhoe with a living American hero.

10. Compare Rotherwood with a modern home.

11. What information about life in England during the Middle Ages is given in *Ivanhoe?* Use these topics in planning your answer: government, language, dress, homes, occupations, amusements, modes of travel, outlaws, superstitions, drinking, food, cruelty, classes of society, arms and armor.

12. Was Richard a good king? Give reasons.

13. Which character in the book would you rather be if you had to be one of them? Why?

14. Why were Robin Hood and his companions outlaws?

15. How did it happen that Athelstane attended his own funeral?

16. Would you like *Ivanhoe* better if Athelstane had not been brought back to life? Give reasons.

17. Do you admire Ivanhoe or King Richard more? Why?

18. What is the best chapter in *Ivanhoe?* Give reasons for choice.

19. Why do you like or dislike *Ivanhoe?*

20. Compare *Ivanhoe* with the best story by another author that you have read.

21. What are the most dramatic moments in *Ivanhoe?*

# TEXT QUESTIONS

# Test Questions

Write no answers in this book. Place in a column on a sheet of paper the numbers 1, 2, 3, 4, etc. Opposite each number write the word or words which correctly fill the blank in the sentence, or answer the question in one word or a few words.

1. An Anglo-Saxon who placed himself under the protection of a baron had to fight for the baron and lost his . . . .

2. A person whose business it was to entertain a household with his jokes and witty remarks was called a . . . .

3. What language did farmers, laborers, and serfs speak?

4. Prior Aymer wagered . . . . . that Bois-Guilbert would consider Rowena more beautiful than any woman he had seen in a year.

5. Who was said to have banished his son because the son was in love with Rowena?

6. To what military order did Bois-Guilbert belong?

7. At the upper table in Cedric's hall sat the principal members of the family and . . . .

8. What was the color of Cedric's hair?

9. From what country was Rowena eager to hear news?

10. What was Bois-Guilbert's complexion?

11. In Cedric's dining hall where did the Palmer sit down?

12. What was attached to the upper end of the Palmer's long staff?

13. In Cedric's dining hall who offered Isaac his seat?

14. Who thought it wise to separate Cedric and Bois-Guilbert early in the evening?

15. Prior Aymer said that the best language in which to talk about the woods and hunting was the . . . .

# Appendix

16. Ivanhoe's cell was between Isaac's and . . . .

17. In what language did Bois-Guilbert tell his slaves to seize Isaac when at a distance from Cedric's mansion?

18. Why did Bois-Guilbert plan to have Isaac seized and taken to the castle of Front-de-Bœuf or Malvoisin?

19. Who kept Richard a prisoner for a year?

20. Where was the tournament held?

21. Who was the chief and leader of the challengers?

22. What was the prize of the first day's tournament?

23. On the first day of the tournament, after the Norman challengers had defeated their opponents, Cedric said to . . . . . , "Are you not tempted to take the lance?"

24. When the Disinherited Knight entered the lists, with what part of his lance did he touch Bois-Guilbert's shield?

25. Alicia was the daughter of . . . .

Select the expression which makes a true statement:

26. When Prince John grew pale at the thought that the Disinherited Knight might be King Richard, Fitzurse told him that Richard (was in Palestine, was a captive in Austria, was taller and had broader shoulders than the disguised knight, never entered tournaments in disguise).

27. Prince John was (cunning, straightforward, patriotic, honest).

28. Gurth, while the squire of the Disinherited Knight, feared discovery from none save (Cedric, Rowena, Wamba, Isaac).

29. After the first day's tournament squires and pages in abundance offered to serve the Disinherited Knight because they wished to (hear the story of the tournament, congratulate him, inspect his horse and armor, find out who he was).

30. After the first day's tournament the Disinherited Knight accepted from the squires of the challengers (money

equal in value to four hundred fifty dollars, four horses, four suits of armor, four horses and four suits of armor).

31. In the quarter-staff bout Gurth gained an advantage over the Miller when (the Miller became tired, the Miller became angry, Gurth lost his temper, the leader of the thieves coached Gurth).

32. Gurth knew that his captors were robbers when (they asked him the name of his master, the Miller began to deal blows with his quarter-staff, they doubted his story, he saw their masks).

33. The Captain of the thieves believed Gurth's answer about Isaac when (he saw the money, Gurth repeated his story, he saw Hebrew characters on the purse, Gurth defeated the Miller).

34. In the second day's tournament Ivanhoe was saved from defeat by (the Black Sluggard, Prince John, Athelstane, the heralds).

35. The Black Sluggard bore on his shield (the picture of a sluggard, *Desdichado*, the picture of a black horse, no device at all).

36. After the second day's tournament Prince John awarded the victor's wreath to Ivanhoe because (the Black Sluggard could not be found, Ivanhoe was a Saxon, Ivanhoe had been seriously wounded, Rowena selected Ivanhoe).

37. Prince John knew that the letter which said, "The Devil is unchained," was not forged, because (it had been delivered by a Frenchman, it was the handwriting and seal of the King of France, it was tied with floss-silk, Ivanhoe had returned to England in disguise).

38. Although Prince John needed every minute to prepare his party for a contest with King Richard, he did not cancel the archery contest because (he enjoyed watching Locksley shooting at a willow wand, a Saxon had won both

tournaments, he wished to gain the support of the common people, he hoped that Locksley would win).

39. Cedric refused to drink to the health of Ivanhoe because (Ivanhoe had been disobedient, Ivanhoe had returned in disguise, Ivanhoe had been severely wounded, Ivanhoe and Athelstane had been on opposite sides in the general tournament).

40. At the banquet Prince John was amused at the garb of the Saxons, which was (a long loose garment covered by a small cloak, a short cloak covered with fur and embroidery, a long undergarment so loose as to resemble a shirt, a short tight-fitting garment covered by a long sleeveless cloak).

41. Fitzurse objected to De Bracy's plan to wed an heiress because (he had not been consulted, Prince John needed De Bracy and his Free Companions, Fitzurse was in love with Rowena, he feared that Bois-Guilbert would steal Rowena from De Bracy).

42. After the crowning of Prince John, (De Bracy, Bois-Guilbert, Fitzurse, Front-de-Bœuf) expected to be his chief minister).

43. The Clerk of Copmanhurst opened his door to the Black Knight because (he feared the Black Knight would beat down the door, he wished to show the Black Knight the road, he wanted to find out who this disguised knight was, the Black Knight was hungry and tired).

44. The Clerk of Copmanhurst began to eat venison pie when the Black Knight (said that it was good, put some on the Clerk's plate, cut it with his dagger, told him that in the East a host always eats with his guest).

45. While the Black Knight was singing *The Crusader's Return*, the hermit once or twice (fell asleep, went to the door, joined in the singing, applauded).

46. The knight and the hermit spent the evening in

(serious conversation, making merry, prayer for their country, discussion of the tournament).

47. Gurth was bound because he had (stolen a pig, run away, deserted Ivanhoe, helped the Normans).

48. When the Saxons saw a lean dog howling, they thought some evil near. This shows that they were (superstitious, thoughtful, cowardly, opposed to the Normans).

49. One reason Cedric thought the outlaws would not molest him while he was going back to Rotherwood was that (he had no money, Gurth and Wamba were with him, the outlaws were chiefly Saxons, the laws against theft were severe).

50. When Cedric's party was attacked in the forest, Wamba showed his (wit, disloyalty, cowardice, courage).

Some of the following are true statements about the story and some are false. If, for example, number 51 is true, write *True* opposite 51 on your paper; if it is false, write *False*.

51. After an evening of song and wine with the Black Knight, Friar Tuck was so drunk that he could not help Locksley.

52. The outlaws showed their love of liberty by disobeying Locksley's orders.

53. Around the outer wall of the castle of Torquilstone was a deep moat.

54. By telling of the brave deeds of the early Saxons, Cedric stirred Athelstane up to fight for the reëstablishment of the Saxon rule of England.

55. Isaac loved his money more than he loved his daughter.

56. Isaac was able to pay the huge sum demanded by Front-de-Bœuf.

# Appendix

57. Front-de-Bœuf and Bois-Guilbert regretted the interruption of the horn more than De Bracy.

58. De Bracy showed himself a gentleman when he tried to persuade Rowena to marry him.

59. Rebecca began to admire Bois-Guilbert when he spoke of hanging her neck and arms with pearls and diamonds and sharing a throne with her.

60. Bois-Guilbert was dressed like a bandit when he went to the turret to talk with Rebecca.

61. Wamba, Gurth, the Black Knight, and Locksley signed their names in full at the end of the challenge.

62. When the Normans asked that a man of religion be sent to receive the confession of the captives, Friar Tuck was sent.

63. Wamba was better fitted to act the part of the friar than Cedric.

64. Cedric considered Athelstane's life more valuable than his own.

65. In the presence of the brutal Front-de-Bœuf, Wamba showed himself a coward.

66. The elder Front-de-Bœuf secured possession of Torquilstone by murdering Ulrica's father and brothers.

67. Ivanhoe showed race prejudice.

68. Ivanhoe said that he brought good fortune to all who were kind to him.

69. Rebecca spoke against war and chivalry because she was a coward.

70. To capture the outwork, the attackers had to tear down, climb over, or break through the palisade.

71. Reginald Front-de-Bœuf murdered his father.

72. The moat was between the outwork and the castle.

73. Cedric rescued Ivanhoe from the burning castle.

74. When Bois-Guilbert was carrying off Rebecca from

**the** burning castle, Athelstane tried to rescue her because **he was** in love with her.

75. The outlaws were among themselves justly governed.

76. Friar Tuck was disliked by the outlaws.

77. When Isaac showed his gratitude by falling at the feet of the outlaw chief and trying to kiss the hem of his green coat, Locksley was pleased.

78. Because of Prior Aymer's high position the outlaws treated him respectfully.

79. Fitzurse supported Prince John because he considered King Richard a tyrant.

80. Fitzurse believed that it was wiser to kill King Richard than to imprison him.

81. The Grand Master discovered that the Knights Templars were breaking the laws of the order.

82. The Grand Master showed in conversation with Isaac that he was superstitious.

83. Malvoisin planned to bribe witnesses to testify against Rebecca.

84. Bois-Guilbert was ambitious to become Grand Master of the Knights Templars.

85. The Grand Master believed that Bois-Guilbert was guilty and Rebecca innocent.

86. Because the physicians had no knowledge of the ointment which Higg used, it must have been prepared by a sorceress.

87. Isaac received calmly the news that Rebecca was to be put to death as a witch.

88. Rebecca was willing to change her religion to escape death.

89. Bois-Guilbert wished to save Rebecca from death without seeking repayment.

90. When Bois-Guilbert rapped at the door of Rebecca's room in the preceptory, she was praying.

91. Ivanhoe, when he followed King Richard through the forest, rode a war-horse.

92. Wamba hamstrung Fitzurse's horse.

93. Robin Hood grudged Richard his venison and wine.

94. Richard always followed Ivanhoe's advice.

95. After his return to life Athelstane was eager to win Rowena and the throne of England.

96. Athelstane quickly forgave the monks and abbots who had kept him in a dungeon.

97. Rebecca preferred death to flight with Bois-Guilbert.

98. Although Ivanhoe's wounds were not healed, he was able to defeat Bois-Guilbert because of his superior skill.

99. When departing from the preceptory of Templestowe, the Templars showed discipline.

100. Rebecca's failure to thank Ivanhoe before leaving the tiltyard showed that she was ungrateful.

## VOCABULARY TEST

Write no answers in this book. In each sentence look at the italicized word. Then find in the next line or lines a word or expression which means the same or almost the same as the italicized word. On a sheet of paper write, opposite the numbers 1, 2, 3, 4, etc., the words selected.

### Chapter I

1. They were united by *mutual* interests.

   common, slight, wide, family, business

2. Anglo-Saxon was abandoned to the use of *rustics*.

   city people, country people, slaves, swineherds and jesters, laborers

# Vocabulary Test

3. The sun was setting upon a rich glassy *glade.*

   hill, valley, open space, wooded space, farm

## Chapter II

4. He was a handsome though somewhat *corpulent* person.

   proud, red-blooded, sickly, dishonest, fat

5. They wore bracelets upon their *swarthy* legs.

   skinny, powerful, sweaty, dark, nimble

6. The Abbot thanked his *sage* adviser.

   cautious, honest, wise, kind, conscientious

## Chapter III

7. Prior Aymer was a *jovial* priest.

   religious, jolly, charitable, self-denying, worldly

8. The Saxon churl has shown his poverty and his *avarice.*

   greed, industry, courtesy, bad manners, dishonesty

9. The *adjacent* forest abounded with outlaws.

   trackless, oak, endless, dense, neighboring

## Chapter IV

10. The small wild-fowls were brought in upon *spits.*

    pointed rods, wooden platters, trays, dishes, servers

11. Rowena was Cedric's *ward.*

    daughter, person having royal Saxon blood, **daughter-in-law,** person having guardian, niece

# Appendix

### Chapter V

12. Decaying brands lay scattered on the *ample* hearth.

    narrow, large, spic and span, fiery, attractive

13. Our *bards* are no more.

    childhood friends, sorrows, poets, victories, happy days

14. He *gulls* women and boys with gauds and toys.

    interests, delights, amuses, attracts, deceives

### Chapter VI

15. The Palmer was grateful for the *boon*.

    compliment, horse, gift, armor, seat by the fire

16. With *alacrity* Gurth obeyed.

    briskness, sullenness, courtesy, caution, a heavy heart

17. Thou art *pious* on this summer morning.

    disagreeable, religious, hungry, cheerful, keen

### Chapter VII

18. His astonishment was *ludicrous*.

    marvelous, genuine, pretended, justified, laughable

19. Prince John bore upon his hand a *falcon*.

    ring, gold chain, bracelet, hawk, glove

20. The people resented his *presumption*.

    stinginess, extravagance, forwardness, dishonesty, boasting

# Vocabulary Test

### Chapter VIII

**21.** The challengers showed superior *dexterity*.

skill, intelligence, preparation, courage, endurance

**22.** The shock was *irresistible*.

feeble, overpowering, loudly applauded, unexpected, ineffective

**23.** Bois-Guilbert *foiled* a third knight.

challenged, killed, injured, applauded, beat off

### Chapter IX

**24.** He remained *incognito* for a certain space.

at court, in distress, in disguise, in hiding, silent

**25.** Fitzurse did not remove the Prince's *apprehensions*.

cunning, ambition, pride, fear, carelessness

**26.** The voices of *menials* were heard.

heralds, servants, town criers, rascals, landowners

### Chapter X

**27.** He lifted his *visor*.

front piece of helmet, staff of authority, broadsword, battle-axe, right hand

**28.** I will *requite* the risk you run.

report, remember, be grateful for, profit by, repay

**29.** He paced the apartment with a dejected *mien*.

eye, spirit, bearing, step, countenance

# Appendix

## Chapter XI

30. They arrived on the open *heath.*

    road, waste land, farm land, meadow, field

31. He tried to *parry* the thrust.

    dodge, flee from, prevent, ward off, return

32. He dealt blows with either end of his weapon *alternately.*

    in turn, skillfully, in haste, powerfully, gleefully

## Chapter XII

33. These laws *abated* the dangers.

    lessened, increased, removed, pointed out, multiplied

34. The knight threw aside his *apathy.*

    lance, battle-axe, enemy, courtesy, lack of interest

35. The marshals removed his *casque.*

    armor, throat armor, helmet, cloak, tent

## Chapter XIII

36. Can the yeoman *cleave* that rod?

    hit, split, cut, break, wield

37. He won a smile from a *bonny* lass.

    bony, coquettish, serious, good-looking, shy

38. Prince John threatened to expel Locksley as a *craven.*

    base coward, disloyal subject, boaster, thief, outlaw

# Vocabulary Test

## Chapter XIV

39. He was not *acute* of perception.

    slow, dull, keen, careful, afraid

40. Prince John's *petulance* got the start.

    cunning, disloyalty, fickleness, sense of humor, ill humor

## Chapter XV

41. Fitzurse *doffed* his bonnet.

    put on, took off, put a feather on, soiled, pulled down

42. To the *covetous* he promised wealth.

    grasping, poor, unhappy, downtrodden, cowardly

## Chapter XVI

43. The path leads to a *morass*.

    precipice, rock, cleared space in woods, hill, swamp

44. His *clutches* were instantly in the pasty.

    forks, spoons, hands, knives, daggers

## Chapter XVII

45. He threw into the notes a *plaintive* enthusiasm.

    noisy, spirited, sincere, mournful, happy

46. The *pasty* is made hot.

    meat pie, soup, venison, iron, pudding

# Appendix

## Chapter XVIII

47. His plan was *practicable*.

   original, workable, useless, unusual, expensive

48. His *paternal* affection gained the victory.

   warm, sincere, rugged, brotherly, fatherly

## Chapter XIX

49. He made an *ineffectual* attempt to rescue his master.

   unexpected, brave, fruitless, feeble, successful

50. The mules may transport the *litter*.

   baggage, rubbish, carriage, wounded man, covered couch

## Chapter XX

51. They promised *implicit* obedience.

   unwilling, unquestioning, joyful, constant, daily

52. His *nocturnal* drinks prevented his recognizing the voice.

   night, intoxicating, mixed, numerous, imported

## Chapter XXI

53. His better nature is *torpid*.

   energetic, alert, weary, sleeping, dead

54. Harold returned a *magnanimous* answer.

   prompt, definite, vague, noble, spiteful

# Vocabulary Test

## Chapter XXII

55. His hair and beard were *disheveled*.

gray, of the same color, long, thin, disordered

56. I have not the means of satisfying your *exorbitant* demand.

unusual, insulting, foolish, excessive, heartless

## Chapter XXIII

57. De Bracy held council with his *confederates*.

associates, assistants, enemies, generals, soldiers

58. Rowena spoke in a tone of *indifference*.

uncertainty, lack of interest, great enthusiasm, anxiety, independence

## Chapter XXIV

59. He admired her *fortitude*.

beauty, sportsmanship, courage, honesty, enthusiasm

60. Her cheek *blanched* not.

quivered, burned, turned red, grew pale, changed color

## Chapter XXV

61. He seemed impatient of their *jocularity*.

slowness, sleepiness, stinginess, soberness, joking

62. He imitated the *deportment* of a friar.

appearance, dress, voice, speech, behavior

# Appendix

### Chapter XXVI

63. *Fidelity* has honor upon earth.

    affection, courage, wisdom, faithfulness, generosity

64. Wamba recommended that spell as *omnipotent*.

    magical, unusual, all-powerful, without power, safe

### Chapter XXVII

65. Ulrica uttered *impotent* curses.

    profane, powerless, powerful, loud, deep

66. He thrust into Cedric's *reluctant* hand a gold byzant.

    unwilling, grasping, muscular, horny, clumsy

### Chapter XXVIII

67. Fever was *averted*.

    cured, prevented, feared, quarantined, awaited

68. Rebecca had *lustrous* eyes.

    twinkling, piercing, dreamy, bewitching, shining

### Chapter XXIX

69. Ivanhoe had an *ardent* desire to mingle in the affray.

    intense, foolish, uncontrollable, short-lived, natural

70. She fortified her mind against the *impending* evils.

    unbearable, unending, threatening, unknown, numerous

# Vocabulary Test

### Chapter XXX

71. He shook his hand with a gesture of *menace*.

    explanation, impatience, despair, threatening, emphasis

72. The devil is said to be *omniscient*.

    all-knowing, sinful, sly, treacherous, like a lion

### Chapter XXXI

73. The Templar's weapon was *trenchant*.

    trembling, raised, deadly, heavy, sharp

74. The raft formed a *precarious* passage for two men.

    slippery, narrow, safe, perilous, protected

### Chapter XXXII

75. The *dauntless* outlaws secured vast spoils.

    lawless, fearless, conscienceless, pitiless, disciplined

76. The spoils were divided with *laudable* impartiality.

    painstaking, laughable, praiseworthy, strict, wise

### Chapter XXXIII

77. He exhibited a *whimsical* mixture of pride and terror.

    wise, unwise, odd, commonplace, interesting

78. Thy plan *transcends*.

    is foolish, is surpassing, is workable, is dangerous, is accepted

# Appendix

### Chapter XXXIV

79. The *sagacity* of the Templar was needed.

    courage, experience in war, recklessness, cunning, shrewdness

80. Fitzurse asked for two *resolute* men.

    brutal, experienced, war-loving, determined, honest

### Chapter XXXV

81. The Grand Master was a *formidable* warrior.

    worthy of fear, cowardly, foreign, brave, loyal

82. His mantle bore on the left shoulder an *octangular* cross.

    four-angled, five-angled, six-angled, seven-angled, eight-angled

### Chapter XXXVI

83. He threw over his vices the veil of *hypocrisy*.

    hypnotism, pretense, courage, frankness, religion

84. He listened with apparent *contrition*.

    attention, interest, penitence, joy, fear

### Chapter XXXVII

85. At his feet were two *scribes*.

    peasants, knights, guards, secretaries, dogs

86. They *insinuated* that the medicine was magical.

    said, hinted, proved, swore, believed

# Vocabulary Test

## Chapter XXXVIII

87. *Peradventure* we shall find a way of deliverance.

    perhaps, soon, probably, certainly, by trying

88. He may obtain Richard's *signet*.

    signature, staff of office, permission, seal, blessing

## Chapter XXXIX

89. Ivanhoe was Richard's *minion*.

    rival, supporter, knight, favorite, companion

90. Display thy *vaunted* courage.

    praised, feared, lofty, lion, boasted

## Chapter XL

91. Wamba made up by *agility* the want of strength.

    courage, nimbleness, intelligence, wit, ability

92. The Friar resumed his *demure* countenance.

    mournful, jovial, sober, tanned, laughable

## Chapter XLI

93. Richard was a *buxom* monarch.

    plump, reckless, brave, jolly, disguised

94. It was a *transient* emotion.

    permanent, deep, traitorous, brief, uncontrollable

663

# Appendix

### Chapter XLII

95. The danger was *imminent*.

    imaginary, terrifying, exaggerated, far away, close at hand

96. The behavior of the maidens was *decorous*.

    silly, disagreeable, proper, inconsiderate, rebuked

### Chapter XLIII

97. Next came the warders in *sable* livery.

    white, black, shining, fur, showy

98. On Bois-Guilbert's brow was the *pallid* hue of death.

    flushed, tanned, pale, dark, awe-inspiring

### Chapter XLIV

99. Rowena expressed her *repugnance* to Athelstane.

    disappointment, regret, gratitude, antagonism, loyalty

100. Wait until men's minds are *pacified*.

    calmed, developed, aroused, enlightened, wearied

## NAMING THE SPEAKER

Name the speaker of each of the following. Write the answers on a sheet of paper, not in the book.

1. The son who has disobeyed me is no longer mine.
2. Second to NONE.
3. For he that does good, having the unlimited power to do evil, deserves praise not only for the good which he performs, but for the evil which he forbears. Fare thee well, gallant outlaw!

4. I tell thee, proud Templar, that not in thy fiercest battles hast thou displayed more of thy vaunted courage than has been shown by woman when called upon to suffer by affection or duty.

5. Yet, brother, take my advice, and file your tongue to a little more courtesy.

6. I did but make a mistake between my right hand and my left; and he might have pardoned a greater who took a fool for his counsellor and guide.

7. If, as a stranger in our land, you should require the aid of other judgment to guide your own, we can only say that Alicia, the daughter of our gallant knight Waldemar Fitzurse, has at our court been long held the first in beauty as in place.

8. Seventy-eight — thou art a good fellow — seventy-nine — and deservest something for thyself — eighty completes the tale, and I trust thy master will reward thee handsomely.

9. I have a tough hide, that will bear knife or scourge as well as any boar's hide in my herd.

10. A man can but do his best, but my grandsire drew a good long bow at Hastings, and I trust not to dishonor his memory.

11. Good brother, I have no provisions here which even a dog would share with me, and a horse of any tenderness of nurture would despise my couch; pass therefore on thy way, and God speed thee.

12. I have heard men talk of the blessings of freedom, but I wish any wise man would teach me what use to make of it now that I have it.

13. Seven feet of English ground, or, as the King of Norway is said to be a giant, perhaps we may allow him twelve inches more.

14. I will pay thee nothing — not one silver penny will I

pay thee — unless my daughter is delivered to me in safety and honor!

15. Besides, I have late experience that arrant thieves are not the worst men in the world to have to deal with.

16. God will raise me up a champion.

17. No man shall aid me, but the ears of all men shall tingle to hear of the deed which I shall do! All is possible for those who dare to die!

18. Hasty hand catches frog for fish; by my bauble, yonder is none of my Lady Rowena, see but her long dark locks!

19. Cast my innocence into the scale, and the glove of silk shall outweigh the glove of iron.

20. I will abide by you in aught that becomes a knight, whether in the lists or in the camp; but this highway practice comes not within my vow.

21. Bread and water and a dungeon are marvellous mortifiers of ambition, and I rise from the tomb a wiser man than I descended into it.

22. I am a maiden, unskilled to dispute for my religion; but I can die for it, if it be God's will.

23. When Valor and Folly travel, Folly should bear the horn, because she can blow the best.

24. This damsel hath wept enough to extinguish a beacon light.

25. Well, we shall see what good they will make by exchanging a fool for a wise man. Truly, I fear they will lose in valor what they may gain in discretion.

## NAMING THE PERSON, ROOM, OR BUILDING DESCRIBED

In each of the following what person, room, or building is described?

1. Her profuse hair, of a color betwixt brown and flaxen, was arranged in a fanciful and graceful manner in

numerous ringlets, to form which art had probably aided nature.

2. He wore a high square yellow cap of a peculiar fashion, assigned to his nation to distinguish them from Christians, and which he doffed with great humility at the door of the hall.

3. His garment was of the simplest form imaginable, being a close jacket with sleeves, composed of the tanned skin of some animal, on which the hair had been originally left, but which had been worn off in so many places that it would have been difficult to distinguish, from the patches that remained, to what creature the fur had belonged.

4. His face was broad, with large blue eyes, open and frank features, fine teeth, and a well-formed head, altogether expressive of that sort of good humor which often lodges with a sudden and hasty temper.

5. Besides the massive golden signet ring which marked his ecclesiastical dignity, his fingers were loaded with precious gems; his sandals were of the finest leather which was imported from Spain; his beard trimmed to as small dimensions as his order would possibly permit, and his shaven crown concealed by a scarlet cap richly embroidered.

6. He was provided also with a cap, having around it more than one bell, about the size of those attached to hawks, which jingled as he turned his head to one side or other; and as he seldom remained a minute in the same posture, the sound might be considered as incessant.

7. Coarse sandals, bound with thongs, on his bare feet; a broad and shadowy hat, with cockle-shells stitched on its brim, and a long staff shod with iron, to the upper end of which was attached a branch of palm, completed his attire.

8. The companion of the church dignitary was a man past forty, thin, strong, tall, and muscular; an athletic figure, which long fatigue and constant exercise seemed to

have left none of the softer part of the human form, having reduced the whole to brawn, bones, and sinews, which had sustained a thousand toils, and were ready to dare a thousand more.

9. For about one quarter of the length of the apartment the floor was raised by a step, and this space, which was called the dais, was occupied only by the principal members of the family and visitors of distinction.

10. The walls of the apartment were so ill-finished and so full of crevices, that the rich hangings shook to the night blast, and the flame of the torches streamed sideways into the air, like the unfurled pennon of a chieftain.

11. With his garments collected beneath him to keep his limbs from the wet pavement, he sat in a corner of his dungeon, where his folded hands, his disheveled hair and beard, his furred cloak and high cap, seen by the wiry and broken light, would have afforded a study for Rembrandt, had that celebrated painter existed at the period.

12. A beam of the setting sun found its way into its dark recess, and showed a female of a dignified mien, whose long mourning robes, and flowing wimple of black cypress, enhanced the whiteness of her skin, and the beauty of her light-colored and flowing tresses.

13. He had no weapon, excepting a poniard at his belt, which served to counterbalance the weight of the bunch of rusty keys that hung at his right side.

14. The wall is of immense thickness, and is propped or defended by six huge external buttresses, which project from the circle, and rise up against the sides of the tower as if to strengthen or to support it.

15. His green cassock and vizard were now flung aside. His long luxuriant hair was trained to flow in quaint tresses down his richly furred cloak.

16. On horseback he was perpetually swinging himself

backwards and forwards, now on the horse's ears, then anon on the very rump of the animal; now hanging both his legs on one side, and now sitting with his face to the tail, moping, mowing, and making a thousand apish gestures, until his palfrey took his freaks so much to heart as fairly to lay him at his length on the green grass.

17. Her long disheveled gray hair flew back from her uncovered head; the delight of gratified vengeance contended in her eyes with the fire of insanity; and she brandished the distaff which she held in her hand.

18. You are to imagine this Knight, strong of person, tall, broad-shouldered, and large of bone, mounted on his mighty black charger, which seemed made on purpose to bear his weight, so easily he paced forward under it, having the visor of his helmet raised, in order to admit freedom of breath, yet keeping the beaver, or under part, closed, so that his features could be but imperfectly distinguished.

19. His white mantle was shaped with severe regularity, being composed of what was then called burrel cloth, exactly fitted to the size of the wearer, and bearing on the left shoulder the octangular cross peculiar to the order, formed of red cloth.

20. It was a bold bluff countenance, with broad black eyebrows, a well-turned forehead, and cheeks as round and vermilion as those of a trumpeter, from which descended a long and curly black beard.